DEATH OF THE PLANET OF THE APES™

MORE *PLANET OF THE APES* FROM TITAN BOOKS

Planet of the Apes: Tales from the Forbidden Zone
edited by Rich Handley and Jim Beard
Planet of the Apes Omnibus 1 by Michael Avallone and Jerry Pournelle
Planet of the Apes Omnibus 2
by John Jakes, David Gerrold, and William T. Quick
Planet of the Apes Omnibus 3 by George Alec Effinger
Planet of the Apes Omnibus 4 by William Arrow

Dawn of the Planet of the Apes: Firestorm by Greg Keyes
Dawn of the Planet of the Apes—the Official Movie Novelization
by Alex Irvine
Planet of the Apes: The Evolution of the Legend
by Joe Fordham and Jeff Bond
Rise of the Planet of the Apes and Dawn of the Planet of the Apes: The Art of the Films by Matt Hurwitz, Sharon Gosling, and Adam Newell

War for the Planet of the Apes: Revelations by Greg Keyes
War for the Planet of the Apes—The Official Movie Novelization
by Greg Cox

DEATH OF THE PLANET OF THE APES™

AN ORIGINAL NOVEL BY
ANDREW E.C. GASKA

TITAN BOOKS

DEATH OF THE PLANET OF THE APES™
Print edition ISBN: 9781785653582
E-book edition ISBN: 9781785653599

Published by Titan Books
A division of Titan Publishing Group Ltd
144 Southwark Street, London SE1 0UP

First edition: November 2018
1 3 5 7 9 10 8 6 4 2

A CIP catalogue record for this title is available from the British Library.

Printed and bound in the United States.

DEDICATION

For Roddy, who proved an ape can fly,
For Adrien,
And for the rest of you…
You blew it up!
…Damn you.
Damn you all to hell.

DEATH OF THE PLANET OF THE APES

CHARACTER KEY

HUMAN ASTRONAUTS

George Taylor, Colonel
Donovan Maddox, Colonel
Eddie Rowark, Major
John Brent, Major
Alan Virdon, Major
Robert Marx, Commander
William Hudson, Commander
Maryann Stewart, Lieutenant
Thomas Dodge, Lieutenant
John Landon, Lieutenant
Judy Franklin, Lieutenant
Jeff Allen, Lieutenant

MUTANTS

Albina
Ongaro
Caspay
Adiposo
Mendez XXVI
Ygli VII
Verger
Be-One
Be-Three
Be-Six
Be-Eight

HALF-BREEDS

Mungwortt
Messias
Dinge
Abomination, the

CHIMPANZEES

Zira, Doctor
Cornelius, Doctor
Milo, Doctor
Seraph, Doctor
Lykos, Doctor
Pinchus, Doctor
Galen, Doctor
Lucius

Liet
Jaila
Tian
Consus
Liberus
Quirinus
Jerry

ORANGUTANS

Zaius, Doctor
Sabian, Elder
Zao, Elder
Gaius, President
Maximus, Doctor
Arlus, Doctor
Honorius, Doctor
Reverend, the
Hestia
Senia
Vitus
Celia
Camilla

GORILLAS

Ursus, General
Marcus, Chief
Dangral, Major
Aurelios, Lieutenant
Cerek, Chief
Xirinius, Sub-Chief
Duignan, Sergeant
Jaffe, Private
Kananaios, Preacher
Julius
Malia

HUMAN MILITARY

Theodore Lazenbe, General
Eugene Taylor, Admiral

HUMAN SCIENTISTS

Otto Hasslein, Doctor
Stanton, Doctor
Kriegstein, Doctor

HUMAN CIVILIANS

Gillian Taylor
Jo Taylor
Tammy Taylor

TABLE OF CONTENTS

ACT III: INTO THE LABYRINTH

ACT IV: ANNIHILATION AND HOPE

PROLOGUE
ORBITAL DECAY

In one of the countless galaxies in the universe lies a medium-sized star. One of its satellites—a blue and insignificant planet—has satellites of its own.

Artificial satellites.

Man-made.

Far above that blue and green marble, one of those orbiters was losing a two-thousand-year-long battle with gravity. A dirty panel on its ventral side displayed her name, *USA-33*. It wasn't a fancy name, but it was the name by which man had known her. No record remained of what "USA" had stood for. Hefted into space perched on top of a massive Titan IV rocket, "Oosa" was what used to be called a "keyhole satellite." Her mission was referred to as reconnaissance, but in fact she was a spy, designed to keep watch over a totalitarian government distrustful of its own citizens.

Her solar panels malformed from the many collisions she had suffered, the errant satellite careened around the planet at fantastic speeds, clattering through the haze of an immature ring, all the time drifting closer and closer to the atmosphere.

Closer to fiery death.

While her computer still functioned, her booster fuel had

depleted long ago. She had no way of stopping her spindly descent.

Oosa had put up the good fight for two millennia. Some fifteen hundred years earlier she had received her last modification—a finite AI package. The upgrade was designed to allow her to make limited decisions of her own while remaining subservient to her human masters' whims.

She had been masterless for a long time. Her primary camera eye still functioned, and Oosa had continued broadcasting everything she witnessed on a signal that had long since ceased being received. She had seen the brilliant cherry blossoms of nuclear exchange that had blanketed the planet, the lights from a thousand cities flickering, and then finally blinking out. She had even survived the destruction of the planet's moon some nine centuries past.

Even the moon had been a victim of mankind's foolish wars.

Oosa-33 danced at the edge of the upper atmosphere, feeling its heat as she drew toward its inevitable embrace. The friction wouldn't claim her quickly, though. She would linger. She would burn. In all likelihood, the bulk of her would survive the agony long enough to smash into the Earth's surface.

As she hurtled over the continents, the planet edged into the sunrise. Oosa-33 focused on a region of the east coast of what used to be her homeland. There, the first light of morning began to lick the planet's ruddy surface.

Dawn was approaching. An army gathered at the ragged cliffs on the edge of a barren wasteland—an organized military force preparing to raid the enemy encampment. Gorilla Lieutenant Dangral gazed at the stars disappearing in the growing light. One was brighter than the rest, moving across the sky at speed while the rest crawled lazily. It held his attention for a moment.

Trepidation seized him. For generations his family had passed along the tale of the destruction that came from the sky and laid waste to most of the world. As a child, he had feared it would come again. As he watched the arcing light, irrational distress gave way to uncertainty, and finally a conclusion.

A meteor, he assured himself. *Nothing more.* Dangral composed himself, wiping the sweat from his pronounced brow. His childhood preacher would consider it an omen of some kind, but things like that were for the superstitious.

Dangral was considered a handsome gorilla—well-groomed, tall, and distinguished. His snout was nicely shaped, his skin oiled, and his mane always kempt. A soldier, he wore a smart dark leather vest and gloves, mauve pants and shirt, a bandolier across his left shoulder with a brown suede field pack.

For many years ape culture had been divided into a caste system, largely along racial lines—political and academician orangutans, medical and scientific chimpanzees, and soldier and service-minded gorillas. The system had been flawed, of course. If a gorilla was so inclined, why shouldn't he be allowed the opportunity to become a politician? A doctor?

Indeed, after centuries of restrictions that was finally possible. Yet stereotypes still ran rampant. While the orangutans were philosophical and the chimpanzees intellectual, the gorillas were considered dimwitted. Dangral, however, was far from stupid, and he wasn't alone. They were quick to anger, and the stigma of ignorance still clung to their necks, thanks to the allegedly superior orangutans.

He gritted his teeth, angry at all of it.

Whether they liked it or not, gorillas were on the rise.

That's where General Ursus came in. A gifted speaker, Ursus could convince you to walk naked into the Forbidden Zone without a wineskin or a gun. He was the epitome of what all gorillas could accomplish. He led the army, and his mission was the protection of all apes. Even the sniveling, cowardly chimpanzees.

Such deep thoughts. Dangral smiled grimly. *You'd think I was an orangutan in a gorilla's suit*. Shaking his head, the lieutenant returned his attention to the here and now.

For the past few weeks the general had led his gorillas on a sweep through the provinces. Their goal was nothing short of extermination. Those who weren't slaughtered had been rounded up in cages, to be used for scientific research. Nearly every enclave had been wiped off the face of Simia, leaving only the bluff he and the army now stood upon. The cliff face was riddled with holes—a fire ant colony gone awry—and like such a colony, these caves and tunnels were rife with pests.

Vermin.

Humans.

This was their last stronghold.

These bluffs lay in the outer territories of Simia, on the eastern border of the Forbidden Zone. High atop those same cliffs stood an array of massive crosses covered with animal pelts designed to simulate massive apes of lore, like the indomitable Kigor. Apparently, scarecrows weren't enough to frighten the creatures away anymore, however, for directly beneath them the humans had taken lair. What perplexed Dangral most was that the mouths of the caves were built into a sheer cliff face, with the ones closest to the ground still a good 200 feet above it. There seemed no way for the humans to reach them, much less leave them to raid the apes' crops.

Yet Ursus's forces had found a solution. While the army positioned cannons on the canyon floor, ready to collapse the openings, a platoon of crack gorilla commandos approached the cliffs from the Simia side, using rope and tackle to set themselves up for the assault. They would drop down on their unsuspecting quarry.

The searing sun poked its head over the crescent mountain range. Orange fingers of light reached past the eastern peaks to caress them. From his mount between two of the massive scarecrows, the imposing General Ursus adjusted his bulbous helm. He nodded and gave the order.

"Bugler, sound the attack."

Dawn had arrived, and with it came war.

The horn blared three times. Nearly fifty gorillas leapt backward off the edge of the cliff, rifles slung over their shoulders. The platoon's field leader, Dangral, descended with them. As he plummeted, invigoration embraced him.

This is what it means to be alive!

Action, honor, and combat!

A gorilla's code by which to live. The cord attached to his harness snapped tight as he reached the end of the rope. The lieutenant deftly unslung his automatic rifle and laid down suppressing fire into the mouth of the cave. His fellow troops did the same. As machine-gun rounds lit up the still-dark openings, Dangral saw that he had hit a target. A single elderly human male had slept near the entrance—likely an inept watch guard—and was immediately riddled with as many holes as the cliff face itself.

"I don't know how they got this high," he said, and he sneered, "but they thought they were safe here."

They are not.

Swiftly the gorillas swung themselves to the lip of the cave. As soon as their boots found purchase, they pulled the knotted cords and let their harnesses slip. Dropping to the ledge, they let their rappelling cables loose and sent them swaying in the early morning breeze. Then they charged forward, a cacophony of machine-gun fire echoing throughout the caves and across the canyon.

It was over quickly. The all-clear signal given, Ursus himself rappelled to the caves below.

Lieutenant Dangral saluted him.

"Sir. Inside, I..." He trailed off. Ursus wasn't listening. Something about the cave's walls had distracted the ape general. Removing his glove, he inspected them, touching the smoothed entrance. It felt wrong to him. Something about it was... artificial.

Dangral's confusion was palpable. He swallowed, appearing eager to give his report as soon as possible.

"Sir?"

Ursus turned. "Go on, Lieutenant. Show me what you've got."

The junior officer nodded, leading Ursus deep into the tunnel. As they passed one branch in particular, the general felt a rush of air caress his fur. Ursus immediately deciphered one of the secrets.

"There is a way out on the Simia side," he growled. His scouts had looked hard for such an entrance. It must have been hidden well.

"Yes, sir," Dangral replied. "The few humans that escaped fled into our territory. We are tracking them now."

"Good work, soldier."

The lieutenant half smiled, but hesitated.

There was something else, and Ursus knew what it was. Army

intel had been collecting reports of strange manifestations, out in the Forbidden Zone. Twelve of his best had ventured into that territory. Only one, Private Cormac, had returned, driven insane by whatever horror he had witnessed there.

Ursus imagined an enemy force of some kind that was responsible, lurking in the zone and preparing to invade the ape nation. Army cartographers had triangulated the last known positions of his scouts, and determined that the outer territories of southeast Simia would be the most likely place for such a border crossing.

His hands had been tied by the council, however. His orders were explicit. He was not to enter the Forbidden Zone.

Dangral led him further into the honeycombed cliff, to a chamber dimly lit by a smoldering fire. Human bodies littered the floor. Animal hides were piled in the corners, obviously where the beasts slept.

In the center of the room was a conundrum.

There stood a hearth, midden, and posts. Wooden pillars were lashed together as well as any ape would make them. Ursus circled the hearth. It was clearly the work of some sort of artisan—be it ape or human.

Rage welled up inside of him. Before he could express it, however, there was a clanking sound. Almost imperceptible. His boot skipped across a small hide pouch underfoot. He and Dangral promptly looked down. Dangral was uneasy. Ursus himself bent down to examine the contents of the purse. Bone. Wood. Carved sticks, essentially—to an untrained eye. Yet Ursus knew what they were.

Tools.

"Tools?" the gorilla general muttered. "Tools?" His voice rose.

That was what he had seen at the cave entrance.

Tool marks!

Some misguided "humanitarian" chimpanzees were building habitats for these creatures, out here on the edge of everything the apes knew. Ursus was sure of it—it was the only rational explanation.

These caves were ape-made, certainly, he thought. *Except...* There had been no sanctioned expeditions for nearly a year—ever since Zaius had used the army to recall that overzealous team of chimp archeologists sent into the Forbidden Zone. Since then, the chimpanzees had been kept in check. *As they should be.*

Ursus inhaled, puffed out his chest, and said it aloud. "Man-made?" The very notion was ludicrous—but the evidence suggested otherwise. Ursus was an orphan. When he was young, his guardian had warned him that not all humans were stupid—that some were more dangerous than others. He had thought it impossible.

"Lieutenant!" Ursus shouted. "Touch nothing. Get everyone out of these caves." He was caught up in a fervor now. "Withdraw!"

As the troops scrambled to follow their commander's orders, Ursus clenched the tools in his massive fist. One of the bone slivers snapped under the pressure, piercing his palm. His hand grew wet within its glove. Ursus didn't flinch. He cherished the pain. It reminded him what was real.

Humans with tools! he roared in his head.

Then a half-smile crept across his muzzle. Nearly two decades ago his predecessor, General Aleron, had faced a similar situation. A human had wrestled a rifle from a gorilla soldier and used it to kill the ape. That had happened in a tunnel not unlike this one. Aleron had collapsed the cave and buried all evidence, to prevent the ape community from finding out that humans could—under pressure—use a firearm.

This was worse.

Here were signs of *thought*. Intelligence.

Civilization.

There was no way the savage humans had come up with this on their own. They were too stupid. Good at mimicry, of course. But he had always subscribed to the concept of "human see, human do." No, someone else was teaching them, and it wasn't the damn chimpanzee pacifists. It was someone out there, beyond the edge of the Forbidden Zone. As terrible as the implications were, they might also provide what he needed to wrest control from the orangutans. The Forbidden Zone had been unclaimed for far too long—and any threat coming from there would be Simia's biggest challenge.

Pocketing the tools, he quickly formulated a plan. He would begin by emulating his predecessor. He would go one further, though.

"Lieutenant, have the artillery ready." The general's eyes darted to and fro. "As soon as we clear out, I want all of these caves demolished under heavy fire." Nothing would be left. He would fire on the cliff face until it collapsed in on itself.

His mind raced. His plan would be glorious.

"Cartographer!"

The soldier rushed forward, carrying rolled maps in a pouch slung over his shoulder.

"Simia," Ursus demanded. The soldier nodded and produced the map Ursus sought—the map of the entire ape nation. Moving to a pile of human bodies, he spread out the dyed parchment and plotted his next move. "Get me four couriers. Each one will take a cardinal direction. I want messages sent to every division, including the Security Police. I'm recalling the army.

"There," he stabbed at the map. "We make camp just outside of Ape City."

"The entire army, sir?"

"That's what I said, soldier." He turned to Dangral. "I also think it's time for a battlefield promotion, *Major* Dangral."

Dangral was flabbergasted. "General, sir, I, thank you—"

Ursus slapped him on the back. "I need apes I can trust at my side." The words were for his subordinate, but his thoughts were on the horizon. "We're going to war." Dangral nodded quickly, eager to carry out his general's orders. Before he could run off, however, Ursus seized the gorilla's arm.

"To make that happen, Dangral, you…" Ursus's eyes fired steel beams deep into the morning mist. "…you and I—we have a date with the council."

ACT I
REPERCUSSIONS

CHAPTER 1
TOMORROW IS THE FUTURE'S PAST

A few days earlier

"Oh my God, I'm back! I'm home."

The astronaut wept.

"All the time, it was..."

On a windswept shoreline of craggy rocks, Colonel George Taylor and his companion, the human woman known as Nova, found the Statue of Liberty. Half rising out of the surf, Lady Liberty's jagged spiked head stabbed the sky, rust causing it to look like a skull.

Nova could not speak. She was aware, but primitive. She would not—could *not—understand what the statue meant.*

Taylor didn't care. To him, everything was abundantly clear. He was on Earth. This planet of apes was his planet's future, and that meant...

"We finally, really did it," he whispered to ghosts.

Nuclear annihilation. His world was dead.

The irony did not escape him. He had been disgusted with mankind, had despised what they had grown to be. So, he became an astronaut, and insisted on being among the first to travel to the stars. Scientists had sent him and his crew at near light speed toward another world. Time dilated, and while less than two years had passed for them, two thousand *had passed for the Earth. If Taylor couldn't find a new race that was better than man, he'd hoped that humanity would have evolved so much by the time they arrived in the future that he would find only peace.*

Mankind's evolution had been interrupted.

He and his crew had crashed on what he had thought was an alien world—a world ruled by apes. Anthropoids hunted humans here. They became his enemy. They killed and maimed his crew.

Not all of them were butchers, however. Some of them had proven to be kind—Zira, her fiancé Cornelius, and her nephew Lucius. The majority of them, however—the gorillas, orangutans, and their zealot leader Dr. Zaius—were trouble. Zaius had tried to mutilate him. Taylor had barely escaped.

With Nova in tow, he had fled into this Forbidden Zone.

So here he was, standing before a symbol of oblivion. But he wasn't here, really. His body was, but his thoughts raced backward. Demanding safe passage, Taylor's mind became anchored to a conversation he'd had with his fellow astronaut, Landon, upon their crash landing in this godforsaken place.

"Time's wiped out everything you ever knew," he'd said, speaking of a world he'd thought was light years away. "It's all dust."

Except it wasn't time that had destroyed everything.

It was man.

"You maniacs." Taylor fell to his knees. "You blew it up!" Man had finished it, done themselves in. Set the clock back to zero. "Goddamn you." He spat out the words and slammed his fist into the spongy beach. Water swept in to cover his indiscretion, eliminating all trace of the muddy imprint.

"Goddamn you all to hell."

Then his limbs were jelly. Falling forward, he crashed face-first into the rushing surf. Salt stung his eyes and liquid filled his nose and ears. The orangutan Zaius had been determined to rid the planet of the pestilence of man. He had feared that one day an intelligent human would rise and destroy everything ape society had struggled to build.

The thing was, Zaius had been right.

Man does destroy, *Taylor acknowledged. The mute testament of the Forbidden Zone and the broken remains of the statue were proof enough. Taylor had known it in his heart—known the truth about his kind. He had known as far back as the Second World War. What he first felt in the Pacific became cemented in his mind now.*

Brine burned his throat. He did not want to stand.

Let the sea finish this.

Yet Nova would have none of it. The beautiful savage pulled Taylor from the surf, her eyes transfixed on the green-and-brown giantess that towered before them. A primitive, she had no gauge for what she was looking at. It had crippled her mate, and that would be enough for her. Taylor was virile, potent—but the idol before them was more so. To her, it was a black god of death.

Liberty 2 curved around a bend in time. Inside, her cabin was thick with silence. Her crew were asleep in cryogenic glass cases—stuffed trophies on display. She had approached the speed of light and raced ahead in time. Her mission: rescue the crew of the American National Space Administration's lost lamb, *Liberty 1*. Specifically, as per Admiral Eugene Taylor's orders, to rescue her skipper.

Colonel George Taylor.

His son.

Liberty 1 wasn't supposed to need rescuing. She'd been aimed at Alpha Centauri and hurled into the future—all in the name of science. To prove Dr. Otto Hasslein's hypothesis: that as one approached the speed of light, time slowed, becoming ponderous. *Liberty 1* was tasked to establish a colony on an alien world, or return to Earth centuries later—her crew having aged less than a year. The men who sent her to the stars would never hear back from her.

Then, inexplicably, a signal made its way back to Earth.

An SOS from the future.

It was inconceivable.

Except there it was, and its existence fit with Hasslein's theories. He postulated that near light speed, acceleration could warp the very fabric of space itself, creating a bend that he had humbly called a Hasslein Curve. Hypothetically, that bend could allow travel to and *from* the future, but only between the vessel's point of origin and its final destination.

Hasslein insisted that the hypothesis be tested—that a follow-up ship be sent to find Taylor and his crew. The doctor found support in the form of Admiral Taylor, and the project was green-lighted. *Liberty 2* shared the same configuration, or nearly so. Her components were modular, with subtle changes that would make her fit for a rescue. X-comm buoys were added, as well. Automatically ejected from the ship at regular intervals, they provided data that would give Hasslein his answers.

Thus she cruised through space like a slumbering shark—sleek, barely conscious, and at speed. Her crew at rest, she barreled beyond the space-time continuum and toward the origin of the SOS transmission.

Then, there was life.

A computer terminal blinked as *Liberty 2* released another

buoy, birthing it into the time stream behind her. As she prepared to cycle down again, the vessel checked her surroundings. Analysis of incoming data indicated that she was ghosting an unidentified object—starship, asteroid, comet, or something else entirely. A motive projectile.

Liberty 1?

The ship's computer attempted to calculate the enigma's destination, or determine if it really existed at all. Regardless, *Liberty 2* increased her speed to keep pace less than a light year behind it.

Suddenly, a change.

Proximity alarms clanged, and *Liberty 2* picked up *two* transponder signals—one from the UFO she had been ghosting, another from an approaching vessel that came barreling through the Hasslein Curve. That second projectile collided with the unidentified object, and didn't stop.

Magnetic tapes hummed and whirled, until sensor analysis was complete. Both objects registered as *Liberty 1*. Assessing the irrationality of the data, the ship dumped it and began running a self-diagnostic. It was a conundrum too difficult for her to work out on her own. She needed guidance.

Liberty 2's recyclers kicked in, flooding the cabin with precious air. As the newcomer barreled toward her, the ship began to thaw her crew.

Cryosleep drained Brent. It drained them all.

Inside the glass coffins, colors faded. Ruddy flesh tones melted away to ensanguined purples and muted blues. The chamber was flooded with the necessary mix of gases. Each person's temperature needed to be lowered to a state of near suspended animation, and it had to be accomplished in a way that didn't damage the flesh or nerve cells. A precise cocktail of intravenous drugs coupled with the desaturating light and a chamber filled with inert vapors made this so.

ANSA astronaut Major John Christopher Brent was waking up. The first thing he felt was a fuzzy glow in his chest, not unlike being drunk. The sensation flowed outward in waves, leaving his extremities the last to defrost. He hated it. The bright azure sea had overwhelmed him. Now, its waves receded.

For Brent, hypersleep was no respite—he experienced strange and vivid dreams of violence, and remembered them upon awakening. He knew he couldn't talk about that—ANSA's psych boys would pull him from the program. They would claim it was liable to be the early telltales of something much worse. There had been three recorded cases of it since ANSA developed their suspension chambers, and one had led to deaths.

"Hibernation psychosis," they called it.

This time waking was different. In addition to the heat, he felt a vibration deep in his chest. Alarms blared loudly enough that he could hear them from inside of the pod. As the fever grew, so did the reverb. Brent realized they weren't coming from inside of him, but from the ship itself. *Liberty 2* rumbled with the sound of a passing subway train. Semiconscious, he was tossed around in his crystal casket.

Adrenaline effectuated the waking process, posthaste.

Is this another of the dreams?

As suddenly as it was upon them, it passed. The ship's proximity klaxons died down, and a deafening silence replaced them. The first one up, Brent stumbled to the sensor terminal, and swiped sleep's crumbs from his eyes. He was greeted with a simple message.

RECOGNITION ERROR
SELF-DIAGNOSIS IN PROGRESS

Whatever danger there had been—if there was any at all—he had missed it. When life support and hull integrity checked out fine, he shuffled back to the slumber chambers. Of the six crystal pods in the cabin, only one other was occupied. While a Liberty-class ship normally only carried four, *Liberty 2* had been hastily upgraded to carry two additional passengers. So modified, she could complete her mission and bring Colonel Taylor and his entire crew home.

The other case slid open and Brent's skipper, Colonel Donovan Andrew Maddox, sat up.

"You missed the fireworks, Skipper." When Maddox simply raised an eyebrow, Brent continued. "Looks like we had a near collision of some kind. Ship woke us up early to take care of it, but it was over before it even started. Computer's running a self-diagnostic on the sensors now—we should know what's what within the hour."

Maddox nodded. The older man had looked better, his eyes bloodshot and his face puffy. His facial hair hadn't come in as more than stubble—hypersleep had apparently slowed his metabolism, more so than Brent's.

Brent examined his own face in the mirror. However long they'd been in hypersleep, he had grown a full beard. Dark blond, the same color as his hair. Liking the new look, he used a razor to clean it up—neat and trim. Then he headed for the cockpit.

Once there he noticed that Maddox hadn't bothered with his own appearance. The colonel sat in the port-side command chair. Through the viewport beyond, Brent saw that they were approaching a planet.

Fast.

"Skipper." Maddox only nodded as his navigator sat down at his station. Brent began pre-checks for orbital insertion, scanning a series of dark instrumentation along the cockpit's starboard controls. He flipped a few switches and the boards dimly came to life before fading into conservation mode and disappearing again.

"Skipper, banks two through eight are out. Must have blown a fuse."

"It's not important now," Maddox waved him off. "We don't need them to do this job. Let's see if we can pick up a broadcast signal."

And if not, get the hell back to Earth, Brent thought. The signal from *Liberty 1* had brought them this far. If Taylor was still down there, he might have set up a short-range TX-9. From orbit, they'd be able to pick it up and follow it in.

Brent stared at the ship's chronometer. General Lazenbe had assured them that *Liberty 2* would be able to return to Earth with barely any passage of time. The proof—according to the science guys—was that the SOS from Taylor's ship had made it back to ANSA in the first place. Still, the question pulled at Brent's sleeve. *How much time has passed?* Connected to Bank 7, the clock's indicator finally jumped back to life, but it was blinking. The number was always the same.

0000:00:00

The chronometer would need to be reset to get an accurate Earth-time reading. However far they had traveled, Brent would have to wait to find out how much time had passed. So he turned his attention to the planet that lay before them, dimly visible through a haze.

A brave new world, he thought.

This planet's ring system—if you could call it that—was young, maybe a millennium old or less, and in the early stages of coalescence. Pebbly reflective debris surrounded the sphere in a sort of spiraling haze, reflecting diffused light on the planet's night side. Once the diagnostics were done they would be able to figure out what system they were in, but wherever it was, it was far from home.

Ruby light stabbed his eyes, demanding his attention. "Skipper," Brent said, "transponder signal coming from surface side!"

"Okay," Maddox acknowledged. "In we go." He retracted *Liberty 2*'s fusion ring, bringing it neatly flush to her cylindrical hull. As they wove gently through the field of particles, Brent was reminded of an old movie he'd seen as a kid. A seagoing ship pierced a dense fog bank to reveal a hidden treasure on the other side. Beyond the mist lay an island that time had forgotten, guarded by a ferocious primal beast.

Gravel clattered across the hull and echoed through the cabin. As they parted the curtain of haze, the planet stood revealed. Settling into high orbit, *Liberty 2* was a tapered rod spinning around a murky crystal ball. A brown and blue sphere accented with a smattering of green splashes, the planet appeared capable of supporting life of some kind. The vegetation—assuming that was what the green was—appeared to be sparse. There was no way to tell if the atmosphere would be breathable.

Unless the trees down there are brown and tan, it's not going to be a fun place to visit.

"Skipper," Brent said, "maneuver to separation attitude ready at three plus oh five plus oh three."

Punching his own numbers into the terminal in front of him, Maddox replied, "I read completion of maneuver at three-twenty-oh-niner…" He paused. "…and separation three plus fifteen hundred."

"Aye, Skipper," Brent acknowledged. Metallic clamps released. Resounding echoes penetrated the cabin. Brent began priming the secondary thrusters. Like its predecessor, *Liberty* 2 was modular, allowing for a variety of mission configurations without requiring the crew to leave the cockpit. The command capsule had a lander component attached in the rear. With the flick of a switch the shuttle, the command capsule, and the lander would disengage, leaving the bulk of *Liberty* 2 behind to await their return. "All booster functions are proceeding normally," he continued. "The sequencing is in good shape. Standing by for the burn."

Maddox stopped him. "Hold burn. Confirm the pitch gimbal motor number four is disabled. I read a questionable indication on the ECS on pitch one."

Brent looked over the Environmental Control Subsystem display. All indicators looked good to him. For whatever reason, Maddox was stalling.

"ECS in the green, Skipper."

With a heavy breath, Maddox finally gave the order.

"Go."

Brent fired the shuttle thrusters. She slid deftly from her

berth. The arrow-headed bird glided into low orbit and toward atmospheric entry.

Yet Brent couldn't get his mind off the chronometer. While the skipper was content to let it blink zeroes forever, he wasn't. As they approached the atmosphere, Brent quietly disconnected the main transfer circuit and rerouted power from the secondary line. Instantly the numbers on its face leapt to life, climbing at an incredible rate.

No…

It can't be.

It just can't.

Outside, the belly of the ship took on the pale orange glow of re-entry.

Lazenbe lied.

"Skipper," he said. "You should have a look at th—"

BOOM!

Metal twisted as ceramic tiles danced into view. Something had slammed into *Liberty 2*, fast and hard.

That something was Oosa—*USA-33*. The errant satellite had met her end head-on. With the collision, *Liberty 2*'s chronometer stopped climbing—but the crew had bigger issues to address. The strike had sheared off the shuttle's right wing.

Nearby, *Liberty 2* dove into the planet's atmosphere, spiraling toward oblivion.

CHAPTER 2
TRAPPED IN THE FORBIDDEN ZONE

Ape shall not kill ape.

It was the Lawgiver's first testament.

However…

Ape could—and had, on occasion—make ape disappear in the night.

That addendum weighed heavily on Security Chief Cerek's shoulders. It wasn't the words of the Lawgiver. It was an unwritten rule among the ape establishment. True, there were executions, but they were few and far between and any citizen found guilty of so severe a crime was ceremonially stripped of his "ape" status by the clergy. The last words spoken to the damned were delivered by a minister.

"May the Lawgiver judge you kindly, for you are no ape."

The newly appointed head of the Secret Security Police, Cerek was a godly gorilla. He attended all weekly ceremonies and said his prayers every night. The teachings of the Lawgiver had prompted him toward a life in law enforcement.

The enforcement of God's will.

When he had achieved his goal, he had learned that some laws were meant to be bent. Much to his chagrin.

In truth, Ape City was supported by a relatively small constabulary. The much more substantial Secret Police were in fact no secret, and that was intentional. Hushed whispers and well-placed rumors ensured that the majority of apes remained law-abiding. No one wanted Cerek's apes rapping on the door during dinner.

Fear kept the populace in line.

When Security Chief Marcus had been killed at the hands of a dirty human animal, Cerek had been tasked to take up the mantle. His first duty had been to close out any outstanding cases left by the previous administration. Clear out the jailhouses. Wipe the slate clean. For most offenders it had been a simple matter of letting them go with a slap on the wrist. For some it meant transfer to the Reef—Ape City's island prison for thieves, apostates, adulterers, and assailants.

Then there were the prisoners in the wagon below him—the gorilla-chimp crossbreed called Mungwortt, and the orangutan elder Zao. These two were different. Their cases required special consideration. Both had seen a human speak and—for different reasons—neither was likely to keep quiet about it. They couldn't just be thrown into prison. They could tell their story there just as easily as they could in the town square.

Nor could they be publicly tried. Given the chance to speak out. No, with either of these ways, word would spread. In Mungwortt's case he was too stupid to keep his snaggle-toothed mouth shut. In Zao's, he was too defiant. The elder also knew… other things. Dangerous things that those in power wished to suppress, lest Ape City and all of Simia be turned on its head.

Cerek didn't know what those things were. He didn't want to.

There are some things best left buried in the dark. A preacher had said that, long ago. It had left an impression on his young mind, and now, that was exactly what he intended to do. Bury his problems.

It was the pitch of night, and he and four of his officers rode the two prisoners to the outskirts of ape territory. They had passed over the border of the Forbidden Zone and were just beyond its boundaries. There were no stars. Instead, the only light came from torches affixed to the wagon, and the ever-constant soft luminousness of the horizon. Light that came from a place where there should be none.

The wagon stopped and the chief regarded the two apes as they were pulled down, then forced to stand straight. Burlap sacks obscured their features. Behind them yawned the blackness of a great pit. They were a strange duo—the retired orangutan a former council member of great stature, the half-breed a lowly sanitation worker. Unlikely ever to have come into more than fleeting contact, they were now condemned to a shared fate.

High atop the cliff face, mute scarecrows stood as shadows and mocked them, hardly visible in the flickering torchlight. Cerek nodded and the sacks were ripped away.

Zao winced, his eyes adjusting to the torches.

"So is that it, Cerek?" he asked, showing no fear. "Is this what happens to dissidents who disappear in the middle of the night?" His voice rising, Zao shook with fury. "You take them to the Forbidden Zone and leave them to the mercy of the desert?"

Cerek was stone-faced, cold. "Not exactly." He pulled out a scroll and unrolled it, moving closer to a torch.

"Zao and Mungwortt," he said in his official voice. "You have been found guilty of treason and blasphemy. Your crimes are speaking out against *The Sacred Scrolls*, and causing malicious mischief against the betterment of apekind. You have been sentenced to exile from Ape City."

A dimwit to the end, Mungwortt simply tilted his head.

"Exile?" Zao queried. "Is that all?"

Cerek rolled up the parchment, raised his hand, and nodded to the guards who flanked the prisoners.

"May God and the Lawgiver both have mercy on your souls."

The guards shoved.

The exiles fell. One of them let loose a grunt.

Most likely the idiot.

They were quickly gobbled up by the pitch. Cerek listened and heard the sound of bodies bouncing along the sides of the pit on the way down. To their credit, neither screamed. Finally, a wet crunch echoed in his ears, followed by silence. Still he listened.

Then, another sound.

Steady, rhythmic, and it didn't come from the pit. It was behind them. An ape on horseback entered the circle of light cast by the torches. Young, he was a gorilla messenger.

Army, Cerek mused, *from the looks of him.*

"I have ridden since morning," the newcomer said. "I carry a message for Security Chief Cerek. The message comes from General Ursus himself." He held out a scroll.

Cerek took it. The writing upon it seemed alive with licking torchlight. That light danced in Cerek's eyes as well. When he finished he rolled the scroll and tucked it into his leather tunic. Facing the messenger, he nodded.

"Message received and understood."

The courier reciprocated, spun his horse, and started back toward the north. Cerek addressed his men.

"We ride back at once." He unhitched a horse from the wagon. "General Ursus has returned from the highlands." He threw a saddle over the horse, pausing to regard the gaping hole into which the two exiles had been dumped. Only for a moment.

"There is much work to be done."

* * *

A few days earlier

"How will you survive?" Lucius asked the talking human called Taylor.

"He won't survive," Dr. Zaius assured them. He decided to appeal to the mutant human one last time. "Do you know what kind of life awaits you out there, Taylor?" When the astronaut offered no response, the doctor continued. "That of an animal. If you aren't eventually hunted down and killed by apes, some jungle beast will devour you."

At that Taylor's eyes lit up. "Then there is another jungle."

The orangutan shrugged. He suspected there was, but had no proof one way or another. He decided to bait Taylor and see if the human would bite.

"Of course, you could return with us." He dangled the hook. "Our society might find a place for you and your mate."

"Sure," Taylor scoffed. "In a cage."

Zaius smirked. Any false softness that had been there was gone. His stare was penetrating.

"Where else but in a cage does man belong?"

Zaius let them go.

The gorilla soldiers descended and were ready to overtake the human and his mate, but with a wave of his hand he stopped them. That no longer concerned him. Whether killed here or in the Forbidden Zone, today or within a week's time, Taylor could do no more damage. There was another matter, however, with which he had to deal. Swiftly.

Zaius addressed the squad leader, Aurelios.

"Lieutenant, fetch your explosives. We're going to seal up the cave."

"Yes, sir!" Aurelios and his apes rushed back to their cart. As he did so, the chimpanzee Cornelius scrambled to Zaius's side.

"Seal the cave?"

Zaius was adamant. "That is correct," he declared, turning back and forth to address both Cornelius and Zira. "And you will both stand trial for heresy."

Without responding Cornelius turned back to peer at the cave, while Zira interjected. All of her fiancé's work was about to be destroyed. The most important discovery in all of ape history. As an archeologist, he had to be devastated.

"But the proof!" she argued. "The doll!"

"In a few minutes there will be no doll." Zaius shook his head. "There can't be. I'm sorry."

"Dr. Zaius!" Cornelius said urgently. "Dr. Zaius, you mustn't! You promised!"

Zaius stared silently at the young chimp scientist. So full of vigor over his discovery. Full of conviction. As was I, he thought. So many years ago. Zaius sympathized, yet there were greater issues at stake. Finally, he replied.

"What I do, I do with no pleasure." Lieutenant Aurelios approached Cornelius from behind, and Zaius gave the order. "Silence him!"

"Doctor—?" Cornelius said, only to be cut off as the gorillas dragged him away. Zira tried to rush to her fiancé's side. Zaius stopped her, and she watched helplessly as the soldiers covered the archeologist's mouth with a leather muzzle meant for humans. The doctor held her fast, peering into the distance where Taylor and Nova sat astride their horse, diminishing in size as they rode along the beach.

Then Lucius spoke.

"Dr. Zaius, this is inexcusable!" the young chimp protested. "Why must knowledge stand still?"

Zaius looked the lad over. Youth. *He sighed. The chimp was too young to understand. Perhaps Lucius's generation would find a new way to deal with that which had burned in the hearts of Zaius and his forefathers.*

Perhaps. For now, however—under Zaius's watch—the old ways would stand firm.

The young ape waved his hands.

"What about the future?" he pressed.

Zaius looked again toward the indistinct shape of man, woman, and horse. Waves lapped at their footprints, dissolving them in the surf. Soon there would be no trace they had ever even existed.

What about it, indeed, *he mused. Zaius was certain he had done the right thing. "I may just have saved it for you."*

Zira was watching the retreating humans, too. "What will he find out there, Doctor?" she asked.

Having travelled that way decades ago, Zaius knew what lay ahead for Taylor.

If he truly is a man out of his time…

Zaius frowned. "His destiny."

The present

Lucius sat alone, scribbling his thoughts. The young chimp was perched high upon Carrion Hill, grease pencil laboriously marking the parchment.

> This is the truth eternal.
> Whatever thinks, can speak.
> And whatever speaks… can murder.

With dusk falling, the expedition team had stopped to raise camp at the foot of a sharp incline, the top of which was crowned by a trio of tall curved boulders. Carrion Hill was so named because those rocks looked almost like the ribcage of some ancient gigantic beast, sun-dried and turned to stone. It was a known marker within the Forbidden Zone, and coming across the hill had given the party a sense of relief.

The Zone itself had a way of turning an ape around, and it wasn't uncommon for the curious and the foolish to find themselves wandering its wastes for weeks on end. Now, at least, they knew they were about half a day's journey from Ape City.

At the base of the hill, four gorillas hastily assembled the one tent they had brought with them—the one in which Zaius himself would sleep. Others tended to the horses, while two more built a fire near a petrified tree that had died upright centuries ago, its arms forever raised in surrender to the harsh cruelty of the land. The earth here was dried and cracked and thirsty for water.

The camp lay in the creeping shadow of the three stone ribs. The setting sun cast a dazzling array of light between the massive monoliths.

Cornelius had been bound and gagged ever since the morning's fiasco at the pit, but the orangutan Minister of Science hadn't considered Zira or her nephew Lucius as a threat. He had allowed them to travel with the group on word of honor that they would not try to escape.

Footsteps crunched in the gravel and sand. Zaius climbed the hill, determined to make peace with the young chimpanzee at its zenith. Still preoccupied with his writings, Lucius almost didn't notice the minister's approach. As Zaius crested the hill, however, the chimp dropped the pencil and tucked the parchment into his sleeve.

"Doctor," Lucius said without looking up. Zaius simply nodded and sat down on the rock next to the boy. He scanned the horizon. The desert floor had turned orange and purple as the sun fell beyond the mountains.

"Even out here, amongst all this death, there is beauty," Zaius reflected.

Lucius looked to the same sky and nodded.

"I first found out about man when I was much younger than you," Zaius continued. "My father took me out to the shoreline, not too far from the cave." Zaius remembered the cracked ruins of that gargantuan statue. "He showed me what they had done to their own civilization, and told me then why we must never let the secret be told. Apekind would be thrown into chaos, and life as we know it would be irreparably changed."

Lucius crossed his arms and turned away. The sun finally gave up its gaudy display and sulked away below the horizon. Realizing his cause was hopeless, Zaius prepared to do the same.

"Very well," the doctor said. He leaned forward, putting his weight on his cane before rising. At his feet lay the grease pencil.

"What is this?" Zaius demanded. Looking up, he noticed the hastily hidden scroll that jutted from Lucius's sleeve. The orangutan grabbed the startled boy's arm and snatched the parchment. Before the chimp could protest, Zaius was reading it. His eyes widened.

When the astronaut, Taylor, first came amongst us

from a voyage in outermost space, he perceived that his ship had passed through a fold in the fourth dimension...

That dimension is time, and Taylor knew he had aged beyond the elapsed time of his voyage by two thousand years.

Taylor did not know the name of the strange planet on which he had set foot, where apes—risen to great estate—had acquired the power of tongues, while man—fallen from his zenith to become a beast of the earth—had lost the means of speech and was... ignorant.

"He may have once dominated this planet," Zaius said, and he trembled, "but man has always been ignorant!" He lifted the parchment and waved it in accusation. "Taylor was nothing more than a mutant, do you understand?"

"This is for my personal journal," Lucius insisted. "You have no right—"

Zaius crumpled the paper in his hands. "This is science fiction, not science fact!" Pointing at the chimpanzee, the doctor dropped his voice menacingly. "You'd best keep these mad ramblings to yourself, Lucius, or—"

"Or what?" Lucius spat, defiant. He motioned toward the cart below, where Cornelius was bound. "You'll gag me, too?"

Zaius didn't reply.

Gathering himself, the doctor sighed the boy's name. "Lucius. I can forgive the vagaries of youth, but only so much. You are old enough to be tried as an adult, remember that. I'd hate to see you working in a labor force with your aunt and her fiancé." He paused for effect. "Or hanging beside them." Stuffing the scrunched parchment in his pocket, he turned and moved back toward the camp, speaking over his shoulder.

"Let this be your last warning."

As Zaius neared the base of the hill, Zira descended upon him.

"Doctor, I demand that you either free my fiancé at once," she insisted, "or put me in shackles beside him."

Dr. Zaius blinked. Twice.

Is there no end to this?

The chimpanzee psychiatrist thrust her arms out in front of her, closed her eyes, turned her head, and lifted her snout. Defiant.

Zaius scoffed.

Impetuous chimp. He thought of Lucius. *Make that "chimps." All of them.*

"Very well, then." Zaius looked to his guards, and nodded toward Lieutenant Aurelios. Immediately the security officer moved forward, shackles at the ready. As he approached, however, Zaius raised a hand.

"Lieutenant, your key, please." The confused gorilla returned the cuffs to his belt, reached into the pocket on his bandolier, and produced a master key. Zaius took it, and examined it. Zira still stood with arms outstretched, but then opened one eye, tilting her head ever so slightly. When Zaius looked up at her, Zira immediately turned her head away and slammed her eye shut. The minister sighed deeply, and slipped the key into the palm of her right hand.

I do not enjoy my role in this, he mused. Even his old mentor, Zao, had needed to be silenced before he could expose the truth—that man had once ruled the planet, and that ape had risen from the ashes of man's society. The secret had to be kept, lest ape society collapse under its weight.

It must!

Zira looked at Zaius and smiled.

"Go," he said simply, gesturing with his snout. *Before I change my mind.*

Without another word, Zira swept up a blanket and pillow and scrambled toward the wagon.

"But you are still under arrest," he added. "All three of you." She turned and bowed, then continued on her way. As he watched her go, Aurelios addressed him.

"Orders, Doctor?"

"Collect the boy and bed down for the night." Zaius waved at the hill. "We could all use some sleep."

Cornelius napped lightly, his mouth still covered in leather, his hands shackled by chains to a rung in the wagon's floorboards. Zira swung open the cage door and sprang to her lover. She untied the mask and quickly unlocked his shackles.

Then Cornelius was awake. "Zira!" he said in alarm. "We are in enough trouble—"

"No, no, it's alright." She peppered his face with kisses. "The good doctor himself gave me the key."

"The good… I see," Cornelius rubbed his strained wrists. "And the charge of heresy?"

Zira cast her eyes down and shook her head, then sat next to him, her back to the wagon's wall. Settling in, she rested her head on his shoulder and drew a deep breath.

"It's alright, Zira. They can't put us away for—"

"It's not that," she interjected. "Cornelius, it's…" Zira grew silent. Patient as ever, Cornelius waited for her to continue. "I'm worried about Taylor."

"Taylor?" Cornelius scoffed. She frowned, and her eyes were knives. Instantly he knew his error. Taylor *had* tried to save them from Zaius's accusations of heresy.

"Zira, I… understand." Unable to meet her gaze, he looked straight ahead and slowly nodded. "I'm… concerned as well." Taylor had tried to strike a deal with Zaius, urging him to grant Zira and Cornelius clemency. The human had shown his gratitude for their help, and tried to help them in kind.

Gratitude, from a human.

"He is quite insufferable, there's no doubt about that," Cornelius said. "But he is unique, and not only because he talks." He could hardly believe the words coming out of his own mouth. "But because of his mind."

A thinking human.

"Oh, Cornelius!" Zira exclaimed, "Y-you…" She stammered. "You love him too, don't you?"

Cornelius sighed. *Does she have to use the word… "love"? It's so… dramatic.* Still, he knew better than to argue with his fiancée. He thought of his childhood pet, a simple raccoon. *One can love an animal,* he said to himself, *and Taylor is indeed much more than any animal.*

"I suppose so." He nodded and squeezed Zira's hand. "Whatever becomes of us, I hope he finds what he's looking for."

"They have to survive, Cornelius. They just have to," she said vehemently. "This could be the start of a new species."

As Zira curled around him and drifted off to sleep, Cornelius thought about it.

It's a good thing Dr. Zaius was unaware of Nova's... condition. A good thing indeed.

CHAPTER 3
DIAGNOSES

Roughly one week earlier

Taylor and Nova had escaped, thanks to Zira. Her nephew Lucius had tricked the guard and they were free. Now Cornelius, Zira, and Lucius joined them on a trek to the Forbidden Zone. Their destination was the archeological site where Cornelius and his team had dug the previous year. The apes' goal was to find proof that intelligent humans were the missing link in ape evolution. Taylor's goal was, as he put it, to "get the hell outta Dodge," find a jungle beyond Zaius's reach, and start anew.

They stopped at the head of a gorge. Ahead of them, the terrain fell away abruptly to a vast, irregular river of deep blue-green water. The wagon would only slow them down. Taylor and the apes unloaded the wagon and repacked their provisions and equipment on the backs of horses.

He and Lucius moved toward the precipice of the cliff as Nova wandered off. Suddenly, she dropped to her knees. The apes noticed something was amiss, and it was Lucius who mentioned it.

"Something's wrong with your mate," the young chimp declared. Taylor peered in her direction. Nova was retching. He and the others moved quickly to her.

"Nova?" he asked gently, placing a hand on her shoulder.

Zira squatted down beside them. "Let me handle this." When Taylor hesitated, she grew defiant. "You may be smarter than I am," she said, "but I'm the veterinary here."

He saw there was no arguing with the lady chimp. She was strong, and he admired her for it. So he acquiesced.

Zira led Nova back toward the wagon. Taylor watched the females leave and promptly decided he should occupy his thoughts with other things. He looked down at the twisting river as Cornelius fetched the horses.

"Cornelius," Taylor echoed through the canyon, "where does this river lead to?"

"It flows into a sea some miles from here," the chimpanzee replied. "That's where we'll find the diggings." From where they stood, they could see massive sandstone cliffs that rose from either riverbank. Taylor's curiosity was piqued.

"And beyond that?"

"I don't know," Cornelius admitted. "You can't ride along the shore at high tide, and we had no boats on our last expedition."

Taylor thought about that. "You've never told me," he said. "Why do you call this the Forbidden Zone?"

"No one knows," the chimp said. "It's an ancient taboo, set forth in The Sacred Scrolls.*" He swept his arm across the horizon. "The Lawgiver pronounced this whole area deadly."*

Lucius was more than a little spooked.

"Shouldn't we be moving on?" he queried.

"I'm for that." Taylor squeezed the words out the side of his mouth. He scanned for Nova. She stood in the shade of the wagon, leaning against it as Zira looked after her. The young woman's sickness seemed to have passed. As the males approached, she rushed to Taylor, smiling all the way.

"What's the diagnosis, Doctor?" he asked as Nova threw her arms around him. "A touch of the sun?"

"She's not sick at all," Zira declared. She could tell he didn't understand. "She's pregnant."

Instantly the look on Taylor's face was one of confusion. Slowly, consternation gave way to wonder. Finally, a broken jagged smile claimed his face.

"So," Taylor said, and he beamed, "I'm not an altogether different breed after all." He turned to an astonished Cornelius. "You see?"

As the gaping scientist nodded, Zira turned and shook her head. It had been a simple thing to diagnose Nova. The nausea, sudden weakness, the desire to nest—even the way the human female looked at her mate.

Zira knew it because she felt all the same symptoms. Looked at Cornelius the same way. The human female wasn't the only one who was pregnant.

Zira, too, was with child.

Now

Zira could not sleep. She and Cornelius lay beneath an ancient desiccated tree, not too far from Lucius and equidistant from both the wagon and Zaius's tent. The makeshift camp formed a triangle with the tent at its apex. Aurelios and his security team slept in the center around the fire, with two gorillas walking the perimeter, one guard awake at the tent, and another pretending to be awake, stationed near the three chimpanzees.

Staring at her slumbering lover, Zira cupped his hand and brought it to her abdomen, giving flight to the fancy that Cornelius might dream he felt the baby move.

The baby he doesn't know about yet.

Her belly had swollen. She was certain he had noticed that she had put on some weight, but he was much too proper to say anything, or even care. She was his fiancée, and that was all he would care about.

He will make a good husband. She smiled. That smile quickly faded with doubt. *But should he be a father?*

If they were going to be imprisoned for heresy, then at the least they would be marked for their entire lives. There would be no careers for either of them. In all likelihood they would have their degrees revoked, and they would be demoted to the rank of second-class citizen. The burden of shame would fall not just on them, but on their offspring, as well. A child of heretics would not have an easy life. There would be no enrollment in the academy. They might wind up a clerk, a farrier, or worse.

Zira harrumphed. She pushed Cornelius's hand away, flopped around and turned her back on him. Any child of hers deserved a better life than that. Her expression darkened.

If my child can't have a better life, she thought, *should I have a child at all?*

She had colleagues who took care of such things, and quietly. They were veterinarians, of course—not proper medical doctors—but with their knowledge of comparative anatomy, it wasn't much of a stretch for them to apply their skills to apes, as well. Dr. Galen had operated a back-alley office himself, disguising it as a private practice.

Zira squeezed her eyes almost shut.

Cornelius cannot know.

Turning flat on her back, she looked to the heavens and sighed. The soft glow of the cloud-shrouded starless night was framed by the tree's petrified limbs. She imagined that its arthritic branches were reaching out to the sky for a taste of rain that would never come.

Then it did.

She was sure she had imagined the first drop. The second not so much—it splashed right across her brow.

Those drips weren't alone.

The sky fluttered, and a torrent crashed to earth.

They were drowning in the desert.

The northern tip of the Forbidden Zone received its first rain in seasons. Water plummeted from above like a waterfall. Cornelius and Zira took refuge against the tree, clutching each other close as the ground at their feet turned to mush, threatening to hold them fast. Rivulets glided over his fur and down his nose. Then the stiff breeze transmogrified into a gale and the torrential downpour went sideways.

Confused, Aurelios and his apes attempted to secure the horses, lest they run. Eager to help his compatriots, the guard assigned to watch over the apostates stuck his ruddy finger in Cornelius's face.

"You!" He reached behind his belt. "Give me your hands."

As the soaked gorilla brought his handcuffs around to bind the chimpanzees, he suddenly arched his back and collapsed in a heap. A short figure stood behind the fallen ape, wielding the guard's purloined club.

"Lucius!" Cornelius said breathlessly. *What has the boy done now?*

"Come on!" the rebellious youth said, crouching low and sloshing through mud and rain, moving for the horses. Cornelius realized what he had in mind. With the gorillas distracted and Zaius still in his tent, now was the time.

"Lucius?" Zira looked up. Cornelius grabbed her hand and yanked her away from the tree. "No, Cornelius," she protested, "tell him to stop! We mustn't… I can't—" Nevertheless he pulled her along the slick ground. The desert floor was so much sludge.

Worse than that, the ooze beneath them began bubbling. As he struggled to keep Zira and himself upright, the nearest of those mud bubbles burst.

Within it sat a monster.

The size of a melon, it was black, fat, and slick. Its dual knobby tongues were horned and its two bulbous eyes bulged. Similar creatures emerged all around them. One of them licked its eyes as it sprung, and its freakish brethren did the same. Toad-things bounced and whizzed, to and fro.

Cornelius had heard of such things, but he had never seen one in person. Feral toads hibernated beneath the cracked desert floor, awaiting a rain that never came—until now. They had been awakened by the first drops of wet and shed their muddy shells, eager to find both food and mates. As he and Zira batted the things away, Lucius plowed right through them. He gestured toward a pair of horses tied to a bush just past the tent.

The creatures crisscrossed the camp like cannon fire. The chimpanzees were all but forgotten as the gorillas fought against the downpour and the hellish amphibian assault. And there was the croaking.

So much croaking.

"Can you stand?" Cornelius shouted over the rain and cries of alarm.

"Yes, but we can't go." Zira stopped and peered at him, as if making a decision. "Cornelius, I'm—"

"Stop there!"

It was Lieutenant Aurelios, pistol drawn. Rain poured down the gorilla's glossy features. The lieutenant nodded at his fallen guard—the gorilla Lucius had clubbed. "So, we add assault to the charges." Aurelios's eyes became slits. "Or is it murder?"

Zira was quiet.

"What, *him*?" Cornelius said. "No, no, you've got it wrong." With a hand raised in supplication, he reached down to the prone gorilla and tapped the guard's carotid artery. A steady pulse greeted him.

"No, he is very much alive—you see?" he said. "He, ah, slipped in the mud, yes? Hit his head on a toad, I'm afraid." As if on cue, one of the wild amphibians hopped past Aurelios. Another flew at the tree and smashed into it.

Aurelios looked over the two prisoners.

Two.

"Where is the other one?" he demanded.

Lucius had been lucky. Zaius had remained in his tent, and the gorillas hadn't noticed him. Aurelios's and Zaius's steeds in tow, he sloshed through the muddy field. Fleshy projectiles zigged and zagged. Water poured from the sky. A choir of the grotesque throbbed, and beneath it, he felt a rumble rising from the ground. Pausing at the tent he looked up. On the hill above them, the rib-bone boulders were moving. Swaying.

They're sliding.

The tent flap flew open, revealing an enraged Zaius. Peering through the rain, the orangutan squinted at the figure leading the two horses. A moment later it dawned on the minister what he was seeing.

"Guards!" he bellowed over the din. "The apostates are escaping! Arrest—"

He didn't get to finish his words. Lucius dropped the reins and charged headfirst. The minister braced himself for an impact.

Rain and toads continued their assault.

Near the tree, as Cornelius was preoccupied with Aurelios, Zira watched the drama at the tent. The hillside dissolved into a cascade of mud, and the craggy boulders that had rested there for millennia were loosened. The nearest one slammed onto its side and slid down the incline.

"Lucius!" Zira shouted.

Cornelius and Aurelios turned.

The purloined horses galloped away in panic. The young chimpanzee body-slammed Zaius, throwing him past his tent. The doctor slid away in the mud, but Lucius wasn't so lucky. The boy's foot became tangled in the tent line, and he went down.

The boulder slammed into the tent.

Mud and toads splattered.

Zira screamed again.

"Lucius!"

CHAPTER 4
A PORTENT OF INTREPIDITY

Morning chased away the storm. The clouds receded rapidly with the sun, vaporizing as if they had never been, the destruction they had wrought the only evidence of their passing.

The camp was buried in a foot of mud and a ton of fallen stone. It was littered with toad-things, living and dead. The apes had lost the two horses and much of their supplies. The wagon, at least, was intact.

Lucius, however, was dead.

The gorillas buried him in the firmest ground they could locate, nervously watching for more of the melon-sized monsters. Zaius oversaw the ceremony, and as he finished reading from the funerary scroll the gorillas all raised their rifles and fired into the sky. Clutching the scroll in his hand, he approached the two grieving chimpanzees, offering genuine condolences.

"He was—" The doctor lowered his voice and leaned in closer. "He saved my life. I caught him stealing the horses and called for the guard. He could have run, but instead—"

"Just let us go," Zira said. She buried her head in her fiancé's chest and wept.

"You know I cannot." He stopped and thought for a moment. Opening his satchel, he replaced the scroll and his hand brushed against the crumpled parchment he had snatched from Lucius—the beginnings of Taylor's tale.

A wave of compassion seized him.

"Is there anything I can do—within the limits of my authority—to ease your sorrow, child?" he asked.

After a beat, it was Cornelius who spoke.

"Marry us," he said. "Here." He stood tall. "Now."

Zira raised her head. "Cornelius?"

The chimpanzee's gaze was unflinching. "Lucius gave his life, first trying to save Zira and me from prosecution, and then to save you from certain death. He believed in truth and freedom. He loved Zira and wanted her to be happy. He wanted the two of us to be together." He stopped to weigh his words. "If you refuse to drop these charges we will face them with dignity, grace, and conviction. But if we must face a tribunal"—Cornelius sighed—"let us do so as ape and wife."

Both Zira and Zaius gawked at him. The orangutan turned to Zira.

"And is this what you want?"

She blinked her tear-swollen eyes, then smiled.

"Yes, Doctor."

Zaius shook his head. "Very well." Rummaging through his bag for the wedding scroll, he called to the gorillas who stood a short distance away.

"Lieutenant! Assemble your men. We have another ceremony to perform."

Their trek seemed endless. The small patches of mostly dead shrubs that had marked the landscape for days had given way to sterile stone. Taylor could only hope that their provisions would hold out.

Then the rolling landscape of rock and sand morphed into something familiar. Taylor's gaze darted across the horizon.

"I know this place."

He was certain of it. Not like he knew the Statue of Liberty, yet this was a place he had been through, and not long ago. On his trek through the Forbidden Zone, with Dodge and…

With Dodge and Landon.

Landon was an excellent navigator out in space, but on the ground he couldn't find his way out of a paper bag. The *Liberty 1* had crashed into a dead lake deep within the Forbidden Zone, and they had crossed the desert for more than a day—yet it had seemed like forever. He'd been forced to endure Landon's constant sniveling about home, and about the member of their crew who *hadn't* survived—Maryann Stewart.

Now they were all gone. Dodge was dead, Stewart was dead, and Landon might as well be, after what the apes had done to him. Taylor looked for the jagged rock—the one where Landon had hung their dog tags. It didn't take him long to find it. The tags were dirty, and Dodge's short chain tag had broken away, but the other set was intact.

Taylor's tags were still complete.

He ran his fingers across the bumps and grooves—the only surviving testament to his existence. Landon's tags weren't there—the distressed man had pulled them from the sands and pocketed them like a coveted prize. For all the good it had done him. Dr. Zaius had lobotomized Landon, leaving him little more than a zombie.

"A sort of living death," Zaius had called it. Taylor was to have been next.

Without uttering a word he went to work, scavenging the petrified branches of dead foliage and fashioning them into crosses. One for Dodge, one for Stewart, and one for Landon. Then he stood back and inspected his crude handiwork.

"There," he said to no one—as if his companion wasn't even there. Back home, he hadn't given a damn about ceremony. Here, it was something to hold tight. They hadn't been his friends—he had been their commander, and he had been a jackass. He'd thought the graveyard would put his regrets to rest.

He was wrong.

Landon was right. I should have cut him some slack. Taylor shook himself back to reality, stuffing his own tags into the waistline of his ragged loincloth. *Some things are worth keeping.* An animal grunt brought him back to the present. It came from behind him.

Must be Nova with the horse.

"Sorry about that," he said without turning. A buzzing droned in his ear, indistinct but definitely there. He waved away any insect that might be the culprit. There were none. Taylor turned. "I had some unfinished business that needed to be—"

There was no Nova.

No horse, either.

Three short yards away stood a nightmare.

The gargantuan pig-like beast grunted, spewing hot air from its fist-sized nostrils. Its acrid breath was palpable—he could taste it even from this distance. The desert air smelled of vomit, and… and something else.

Rotten meat.

The creature was six feet long and four feet high at the shoulder. Its long snout curled past broken, weathered tusks that tapered into a face that seemed to writhe. While it was massive, it was also lean—too lean for its size. It looked emaciated. *Hungry.* Ribs showed through scar-crossed flesh.

No food in a long time, Taylor guessed. *Lucky for him I just happened to be passing through.* He wished fervently to have the gun that was holstered on their horse's saddle, and wondered where Nova had gone.

Then he realized why the face seemed to be moving.

Maggots.

The pig-thing was being eaten alive.

The beast coiled, ready to attack. The buzzing intensified. Taylor crouched, reaching for a nearby rock.

The monster sprung.

The horizon whirled.

Trapped in the impromptu centrifuge, John Christopher Brent feared he would paint the cockpit with bile. He and his skipper shouted command sequences at each other, desperate to regain control. Maddox's orders were erratic—rife with indecision. Brent knew they had to move while they still had some working control boards. Their one chance was to disengage the lander command module from the shuttle and ditch the bird before it blew.

Finally, Maddox agreed, but Brent hadn't waited for his skipper to give the "go" sign. By the time the colonel nodded, the sequence was ready. Once again clamps disengaged. Explosive bolts fired, freeing the lander from the dead albatross of the shuttle. Brent cranked full power into the lander's thrusters, and she shot out of the shuttle as if she had been fired from a cannon.

It still wasn't fast enough.

As the shuttle spiraled downward toward its inevitable doom, its one good wing slammed into the side of the lander. The lander—with the command capsule attached to it—corkscrewed through the atmosphere. Even so, Maddox and Brent finally gained some semblance of control.

The skipper smiled. Brent nodded in return. The sound of the ship's thrusters drowned out nearly everything. Maddox struggled to be heard over the din.

"Find a clearing to land in," he bellowed.

"Skipper!" Brent responded. "We are still miles from the source of the transponder signal."

"Forget the damn TX-9—we need to put down now!"

The commander was right. If they didn't save themselves, the crew of *Liberty 2* wouldn't be saving anyone else. So the younger astronaut nodded and began scanning the terrain. It wasn't the most hospitable place, but there was level enough ground for the lander to rest while they made repairs.

He found a likely spot. The lander rotated so that its nose was facing upward and her engines were blasting toward the desert floor below. Vertical, she was suspended in the sky. Soon her thrusters would taper off, lowering her slowly to the ground. They were going to make it. Despite everything, they were going to touch down in one piece.

Retro thrusters activated, and so did the warning signals on Brent's dashboard.

"Extending landing struts," Maddox ordered. "Touchdown in T-minus—"

"We've got a problem in fuel pod two." Brent tried to deactivate the pod, rerouting fuel consumption to draw from the other two tanks. He couldn't do it. The connection had been severed—it would have to be done manually.

"Keep us on descent," Maddox said. "I've got it!" The skipper unbuckled his belt and rolled from his chair, falling to the downward-facing rear of the cabin. His landing was awkward, but he didn't seem to break anything in the maneuver. He worked his way past the sleep capsules and down to the engine access port. He unshackled the airlock door between the cabin and the lander's thruster array.

Then the fuel pod erupted.

A searing light blasted the cabin, catching Maddox in the face. *Liberty 2*'s engines exploded. The lander portion destroyed, the command capsule fell from its vertical descent, belly-flopped, and slammed hard into the desert floor.

Maddox was as good as dead.

The sea was dead. Few living apes knew what catastrophe had befallen the area surrounding it, deep in the Forbidden Zone—only that it had been this way for centuries.

On its shore, a metal monster gleamed in the afternoon sun. Its nose was conical and sharp, its fused silica eyes set wide. Its shell was hard and battle-worn, and behind what appeared to be wings it tapered to a crumpled, slender, tubular tail. It was gigantic and intimidating.

Worse than that, it was alien.

A name was stamped brazenly on the side of the tail.

LIBERTY 1

It had been waterlogged, seemingly stuck to the bottom of the inland sea for all time, but nature had another idea. Air pockets trapped within its shell had conspired with a raging storm to dislodge the object from its watery grave. The apes at the site had taken advantage of that, lassoed several lines to the behemoth, and guided it to shore. It beached hard on the rocky crags, irreparably damaging the long cylindrical tube which formed its tail. Once it was partially out of the water, the apes had labored to build a dam around it and drain that small section of lake.

They removed the vessel's sole occupant, the desiccated corpse of a strangely garbed human female, and buried her beneath a rocky pile some thirty yards from the waterline.

Poring over sun-dried manuals found in the behemoth's belly, the apes had located the ship's power source, and discovered how to reactivate it. They had removed circuit boards and let them dry out in the sun before replacing them in their designated slots. Most of the apes on the team couldn't comprehend what they were looking at, let alone make repairs to such a monstrosity.

The chimpanzee in charge, however, was no common ape. Dr. Milo was a genius among his own kind—the most preeminent engineer and physicist of the ape community. Standing on one of the craft's side fins, Milo hovered at the behemoth's yawning side maw, peering inside.

Its belly smelled musty, but there was little to be done about that. From his vantage point he could see the extent of the damage. As much progress as had been made, there was still so much to be done.

Too much, he mused. *This is impossible.*

As he stepped out of the blazing desert sun and into the damp shade of the forward chamber, Milo sighed. His assistant—a scholarly female named Seraph—was there already, busy removing delicate components. He took one of those components from her hand, its burnt surface obscuring whatever its purpose might have been. He fiddled with the small device, turning it this way and that, in vain.

Seraph rested her hand on his shoulder. He moved away immediately—intimate touch, no matter what the sentiment behind it, made Milo uneasy. His assistant for more than a year now, Seraph should have known better. He decided to let this one indiscretion go unanswered, though, and focus on the task at hand.

"It's too far gone," he said, and he stopped playing with the broken mechanism. Too many irreplaceable parts had been damaged. He simply didn't have the resources he needed to bring this metallic creature back to life. If he could replace the irreplaceable, there would be a chance—no, he was certain he could fix it. But nothing of this sort existed in ape society.

Seraph opened her mouth as if to say something, as if anything anyone could say would make this better.

Abruptly there was a thunderous boom.

Milo blinked. It had come from outside—something big, rolling across the heavens. A storm? Racing to the egress he looked up and witnessed the tail end of a midair explosion. A trail of fire streaked across the sky.

A daytime comet.

Abruptly it broke in two, with one part spiraling downward at an alarming rate. The other half, however, did something astonishing.

Did it just change course? Instantly Milo was ecstatic. His prayers had been answered. The second part of the object arced across the horizon, only to melt into the canyon walls. As the first part slammed into the desert floor, another explosion rang out. It was soon followed by a third that rolled across the desert terrain.

He knew exactly what to do. Where to look.

"Dr. Seraph." Milo smiled. "Assemble two teams. Leave Doctors Pinchus and Lykos with me." He tossed the charred and useless component over his shoulder. "Take the rest. Go see what's out there."

Taylor might as well have been a rag doll.

The beast charged low, scooping the astronaut up with its tusks and throwing him over its head. He rolled off the pig-thing's desiccated back, slammed into the desert floor, and narrowly escaped its trampling hooves. Somehow he still held the rock he had grabbed. As he rolled into a crouch, Taylor felt the sting of burning on his arm. There, glowing wriggling things inched their way toward his armpit. Some of the worms infesting the pig's face had come loose on him.

Hot to the touch, he thought. *Radioactive!*

Quickly he flicked them from his skin, and then scanned the terrain for the boar. Somehow, it had gotten behind him. As he turned, it pounced, knocking him on his back. The wind *whooshed* out of his lungs.

The hum in his ear grew louder.

The creature's rancid jaws yawned wide.

BOOM!

The sky let loose a massive explosion. The beast recoiled and looked upward, confused. That was all Taylor needed. He swung the rock, landing a solid blow on the creature's skull. Glowing maggots flew from its face. Taylor scrambled.

The beast howled.

Its weight fell on him, and the howl became a screech. He was coated in glowing grubs and hot wet ichor. The screech rattled in its throat, and it issued one last putrid breath.

What in hell?

A beautiful savage peeked over the top of the husky corpse, fearful eyes begging for his.

"Nova!" he exclaimed.

She had impaled the thing. A petrified stick, modified into a cross, protruded from its back. One of the grave markers he had made for his dead friends, it was sunk in deep. Taylor pulled himself out from under the dead monster and pulled her close. His eyes squeezed shut, the astronaut held her against him.

"Nova, I—" There was a clattering behind them. Something… *changed.*

The makeshift cross fell to the ground.

The pig-thing was gone.

The animal's blood evaporated. The burns on his arm disappeared, as did the glowing maggots. He bore no wounds, no bruises.

They were alone.

Taylor looked to Nova for any indication of what had happened, but her worried features and grasping embrace didn't offer any answers. Her lips were chapped. His throat was dry.

Hallucinations… He licked his finger and ran it across her ragged lip. *It had to be the dehydration.* Despite it all, Taylor realized how happy he was to have her. Of all the horrors he had endured—the Pacific, Japan, Korea, even Ape City—the one thing he couldn't face was isolation. Not now. Nothing would be worse than being alone.

Irony for the man who hates everyone.

Then Nova's eyes sparked. She pointed to a nearby crest. He pushed aside his fears, and together they mounted the horse.

"Alright," Taylor said. "Let's see what you found."

CHAPTER 5
THE WORLD WE'D MADE

Pacific Theater of War
1944

Three angry shark-faced planes pierced the clouds above the dark and briny sea.

The sky was moonless, the clouds dense and milky. Part of the 45th Fighter Squadron, the Curtiss P-40 Warhawks flew in staggered formation. In the lead was First Lieutenant Edward Rowark. A Bronx boy on the short side, "Eddie" was a former street brawler. When he had a shot at flying for the Air Force, he gave up the gang life for the military.

Eddie was followed by his wingman, Flight Officer Joseph Tagliante. "Joey" was a braggart from the lower east side of Manhattan. Whether because he was brave or just stupid, Tagliante was fearless. He didn't talk about home, and the rest of the squadron suspected he had signed up to get away from it.

Bringing up the rear was Second Lieutenant George Taylor. In his early twenties, Taylor was already an ace pilot. With twenty-eight confirmed kills in only two years, he was cocky, arrogant, and insufferable. Despite this, or because of it, he and Rowark got along.

Having engaged the Japanese and taken heavy losses, the three pilots were on their way home. Their ammo depleted and their fuel low, they were running silent—no radio contact. Taylor wasn't sure where the rest of the 45th had gotten to—or even if any of them had survived.

All he knew was that he wanted a cold beer.

Lost in the thought of frothy hops, he almost didn't notice the dim light that crept into the darkness. As the glow increased, he scanned the sky for a source. Straining his neck behind him, he found it.

"What the hell?"

It was a burning sphere. Its size and distance were indeterminate—the wall of cloud cover saw to that—and it seemed to hang in the sky, like a far-off celestial body. It was no moon, however, and it certainly wasn't a star. The phosphorescent orb burned white through the fog, always keeping pace. Taylor decided to test it, yet it always matched any course correction.

Becoming concerned, Taylor reached for his radio. Running silent or not, Rowark and Tagliante needed to know about this. Before he could speak, the radio squawked.

"George, Joe, you seeing this?" Rowark said. "I've got a bogey off the starboard wing. Looks like a goddamn foo fighter, over."

Taylor looked around in the haze. What Eddie was seeing wasn't his ball of fire—there were at least three others around them, all matching speed and course. He depressed the call button.

"Looks like we're surrounded, boys. Over."

"Copy that, over," Tagliante replied.

The closest ball of light seemed to pulse from white to a dull orange and back.

"Well," Taylor said to himself, "what the hell are you?"

He never got his answer. The fireballs came alive, burning red and zigging around in wild arcs. Coming right for them.

"Holy shit!"

The closest one barreled toward Taylor's Warhawk. He threw up his arm to shield himself, a futile gesture at best. It made no difference.

Just as quickly as they had appeared, they were gone.

Rowark came over the radio again. "Son of a—"

The sky ruptured with light. Explosions rocked the shivering fighter craft. Bursts of fire ballooned as shells detonated around them.

They were under attack.

"Can't get clear," Tagliante said. Zigging when he should have zagged, he just wasn't fast enough. A cannon shell sheared off his port wing. As the crippled P-40 began to spin, another shell crashed through its cockpit.

Rowark was next as an exploding shell clipped his rudder.

"I'm out, Taylor!" the radio blared. "See you downside!"

Then there was static.

Unable to see anything in the soup of clouds, Taylor could only guess that Rowark had gone into the drink. At that moment he had his own problems. Something slammed into his P-40, throwing him into a spin. Taylor squinted and gritted his teeth, ready for the blast.

It didn't come. Instead, his engine began to sputter. Pressing his face against the canopy, he couldn't see what had happened, but he could guess—he had taken an engine hit. Somehow, the 20mm shell had been a dud. Lodged in the turbocharger, it had failed to detonate.

"Lucky, lucky…" Taylor muttered.

The shock had taken its toll on the motor, however—she sputtered and stalled.

Killed the turbine, *he realized. Amid a rapid array of explosions, Taylor spiraled downward. If he could get her to a lower altitude, though, he knew he could restart his P-40's engine* without *the wrecked turbocharger. The question was, at that speed could he restart her and pull up before he smashed into the ocean?*

"Let's find out," he mumbled aloud. He cranked the electric starter, but it wasn't having any of it.

Dead, *he reckoned.*

So was he, if he didn't move fast. Running out of airspace, Taylor threw the P-40 into an even steeper dive. Increasing rotation speed, he spun her around, windmilling the propeller. In the infernal fog, he couldn't gauge how much altitude he still had as the ocean rushed up to greet him.

"Come on, sweetheart," he begged the plane, "don't let a guy down."

With that, she sprung to life.

Taylor yanked hard. Muscles strained and metal ground. Angry painted eyes glared and white triangle teeth gnashed. Flaps deployed and the air itself defied them.

Timid, begrudgingly, the plane pulled up. No longer careening headfirst into the ocean, she skimmed it instead. One of her landing gear doors popped open and snapped loose, a victim of friction. He pulled up a bit, lest the aircraft caught the waves again and somersaulted into oblivion.

High above, muffled explosions and murky flashes of light peppered the clouds. Down below, the sea air was thick with salt and brine. Taylor flew his fighter through the foggy gloom. Mimicking his P-40's painted shark face, he cracked a toothy grin—he'd made it. All he had to do was get close to an Allied ship or base, and ditch. One way or another, though, he was out of the fight.

He sighed in relief.

Up ahead, dark shapes threw strange shadows across the sky.

There was something in the water.

"Oh, shi—"

The Warhawk barreled through a wall of machine-gun fire. Burning metal jackets tore through the fuselage. Shrapnel chewed the spent engine. Unable to see anything clearly in the relentless haze, Taylor pulled up and over a massive shape—a Japanese destroyer. Her gun crews had been blanketing the sky with shells, and they had just punched his ticket.

Finally giving up, the engine sighed and burst into flames.

Smoke filled the cockpit. Groping through it, the coughing pilot grabbed his survival pack. Hitting the flaps and banking hard, he stalled, threw open the canopy, and tumbled out. Flak found the undetonated shell lodged in his engine casing. The P-40 Warhawk blossomed into an expanding plume of orange-red, muted by the gray haze that hugged the sea.

Fiery debris danced across the waves.

Taylor broke the surface, gasping for air. His right arm was limp, pain sizzled through his shoulder—he had dislocated it when he hit the water. Squirming, starting to go under again, he twisted and pulled. With a pop, *the arm went back into its socket. He screamed beneath the waves, and brine filled his lungs.*

Stubbornly he pushed himself to the surface again. Wet salt stung his eyes, seared his throat, and burned his nostrils. Sputtering and treading water, he watched as the waves extinguished the last flaming bits of his aircraft. Aside from a floating wing here and a propeller blade there, the remnants of the P-40 Warhawk were swallowed by the swell.

With one eye open, he waited.

Voices barked in Japanese. Piercing the fog, they echoed over the rolling waves.

Blood burned in his temples.

His labored breath rang in his ears.

The voices moved off, getting further away. As the ocean calmed, Taylor inflated his emergency raft. Pulling himself into it, he scanned the sky for a break in the mist. Wet as they were, he still had his pocket maps. All he needed was a star to figure out where the hell he was, and which direction was land.

All he wanted now was to go home.

Favoring his sore shoulder, Taylor reached for his paddle. He never noticed the drifting Japanese patrol boat that had been deployed to look for him. Never saw the rifle butt that smashed into the side of his head.

He did get to see stars.

It was the screaming that roused him.

George Taylor awoke with a start. He sat up in haste, pushing through a thick wall of humidity. Immediately he regretted it. His head throbbing, a torrent of nausea overtook him. As he bit back bile, a foul stench of feces and rotting meat invaded his nostrils. Insistent, the bile returned, and this time he let it.

When he was done his sore lips and dry throat told him that he was dehydrated. His head wound was tender, the blood caked in his scalp. The Japanese soldier who had struck him had hit hard. Taylor had no idea how long he had been out.

In a small dirty hut with six other men, the young pilot had been stripped to his skivvies. His arms were tied behind his back and his legs bound together. The other prisoners of war were in the same condition or worse. The pungent smell of rot that filled the hut came from a man sitting in the far corner—from the necrotic remains of his arm, to be exact. Catatonic, the rotting man stared into the void.

Although Taylor couldn't see well enough to be sure, he believed all the men were American. Then he recognized one of them.

"Eddie," he whispered.

The other pilot was bruised and battered, with one eye swollen shut. He was unconscious.

Outside, the screams continued. There was a small gap at the base of the wall, between the hut's posts—just enough to let a bit of light into the murk of the stifling sweatbox. Lowering himself awkwardly to the floor, he pressed his face against the opening and squinted as his eyes adjusted to daylight.

A pair of legs greeted him.

A soldier stood guard with his back to the hut, his attention fixed on the commotion. Judging from the buildings, beach, and trees, the POWs were being held in a village on a Pacific island. Outside, a troop of Japanese soldiers had rounded up the local women and children. They were all of Asian descent.

Chinese? *Taylor considered briefly.*

The soldiers were upon them. As some of the local men rushed to the families' aid, they were shot dead. Taylor shut his eyes, but the sounds remained. Tortured pleas mixed with sick laughter, screams of pain met with a gurgling of blood or the report of a rifle.

He struggled against the ropes that held him.

The Japanese sentry noticed.

A boot to the face, and Taylor was out again.

Taylor and Rowark were marched outside. It had been days—he had lost track of how many. Weeks, maybe.

The POWs had been given little food, and what they had received was usually fouled. Most of them had died from their wounds, until only the two pilots and the still-catatonic rotting man remained in the hut.

A pit had been dug on the beach, and eight men Taylor didn't know had been lowered into it before it was filled with wet sand. Buried to their chests, the men were immobilized. The two pilots were led to the edge of the pit, spaced about three feet apart, and made to stand there. Leaning toward Rowark, Taylor spoke out the side of his mouth.

"Any idea—"

"No," Rowark breathed. Neither knew who the other prisoners were. Taylor only knew that they were important somehow—and that they weren't American. He and Rowark were forced to kneel. Guards came from behind, dragging the rotting man up beside them. Still in a stupor, he wavered on his knees but kept his balance.

The officer in charge approached them, leaning down to meet Rowark's gaze. Like the rest of the captors, he wore khaki shorts and a cap. On one side of his belt was a holstered Type 94 Nambu pistol. On the other was a Type 94 shin guntõ—a Japanese officer's sword—in a metal scabbard suspended from two brass mounts. Stabbing his finger toward the buried men, the officer shouted at the three Americans in Japanese.

Neither pilot had any idea what was going on.

When Rowark failed to reply, the officer turned his attention to the buried men and gave an order. As the soldiers spit on them, the men pleaded in some Asian dialect. The officer called his troops to attention, their rifles unslung and their bayonets at the ready.

On his order, they charged. As the trapped men were butchered, Rowark shut his eyes. This time, Taylor couldn't.

When the screaming became muffled whimpers, the officer produced a submachine gun, spraying the pit with bullets and ending the carnage. After a moment's pause, he leaned in again—focused on Taylor.

This time, he whispered instead of yelling.

Taylor struggled to grasp the words. It was a threat, that much he knew.

"I…" he started, "I don't understand—"

"Don't say anything," Rowark warned.

The officer drew his blade. The soldiers pushed the rotting man forward. There were flies coming off of his diseased arm—the insects buzzed all around.

One swift stroke, and the rotting man's head rolled across the sand.

"You son of a—" Rowark tried to stand. The soldiers were on him, kicking him back down.

Taylor stared at the sands as they soaked up the blood, leaving only a damp red stain.

The swordsman approached.

Taylor was next.

The officer shouted at Eddie again. He had recognized Rowark as the most senior Allied officer they had captured. They had gotten whatever it was they wanted from the buried men and then used them to threaten the second lieutenant. Whatever else they were after, they thought Rowark had it. Taylor and the rotting man were just fodder to get him to break.

The soldiers pushed Taylor forward. He straightened his shoulders. Raised his chin.

"Taylor, George," he said. "Second Lieutenant, United States Army Air Force. Service number 0109047818—"

The officer raised his sword, but Taylor refused to close his eyes. The shin guntõ blade gleamed.

From the village, there was a shout, also in Japanese. Another officer and his entourage stormed up the beach toward them. The new arrival tore into the embarrassed swordsman. The other soldiers saluted and quickly got in line with the commander. Shamed, the officer surrendered his sidearm, but kept the shin guntõ.

Rowark and Taylor were hauled back to the hut. Just before they reached it, Taylor saw the disgraced officer fall on his own sword. He didn't know what it meant, and he didn't care.

They were alive.

It was night, and the new commander had fed them. Their arms had been untied and the food had been clean. Their dog tags had been returned, and they had even been given a smoke each. For prisoners of war, they were being treated well.

"What d' you suppose, Eddie?" Taylor exhaled.

"I don't know what to think." Rowark took a last drag on his cigarette. "Prisoner exchange?"

That crooked grin stole across George's face again. "You mean they're releasing us."

"I didn't say that," Eddie snapped. "I was just thinking out loud." Angry, he flicked the spent cigarette against the wall. "They also give you a last meal and a cigarette before they shoot you," he suggested. "Remember that!"

The door to the hut swung wide, revealing four soldiers. While they were armed, their weapons weren't drawn.

A good sign, *Taylor thought. They gestured outside. Suspicious, Rowark and Taylor followed. The moon was full. The two Americans were led down a torchlit path and into the village. All was quiet.*

Listening to the waves gently crash against the shore, George savored the night breeze. The pilots were taken to two small huts. Side by side with their doors open wide, they could see that each held a large tub of water. The soldiers motioned each of them inside.

They're letting us bathe?

Glancing at each other, the two grimy men shrugged and entered their respective huts, each with two soldiers following behind. Inside Taylor's hut, one of the Japanese pointed to a pipe. Taylor stretched out his arm, allowing the soldier to shackle him to it.

Insurance, *Taylor rationalized.* So I don't skip out on the bath.

As the door closed, one of the Japanese men spoke for the first time, surprising Taylor with broken English.

"Water cure," he said.

"Wha—"

Sucker-punched, he doubled over. One man grabbed him from behind, pushing him down to the floor. Grasping at Taylor's hair, the soldier yanked the pilot's head back. The other pulled a soaked towel from the tub and smothered their prisoner with it. He heard the clank of a bucket, and the soldiers drenched the towel again and again.

Pinned with the material pulled tight over his face, Taylor felt his chest seize up. He couldn't breathe. The towel was suffocating. His ears ringing, he could hear Eddie fighting his guards in the next hut.

Red crept over his eyes, and he knew he was passing out. As he started to go limp, the soldiers tore the towel away and released him. Taylor heaved and gasped. Tried to get up, leaning against the water-filled tub.

He managed to get one deep draw of air.

Before he could manage a second breath, Taylor's head was shoved underwater. The nightmare was far from over.

CHAPTER 6
HOME BITTER HOME

"Water!" Taylor exclaimed. *And not a mirage.*

While he had been fighting the pig-thing, Nova had been foraging for something they could eat. What she had found was more watering hole than oasis, but it gave him what he needed most.

Hope.

As he scrambled off the horse, however, Taylor was cautious. He, Dodge, and Landon had camped nearby on their Forbidden Zone trek. He himself had scouted the surrounding foothills and found nothing. How could they have been this close to water and passed it by?

"The trees…" He let the words trail off. Taylor studied the landscape with intent. While there were more dried tufts of stale green here, the foliage closest to the hole was dead.

Poisoned?

Regardless, they had no choice. He knelt over the murky pool, cupping the water to his mouth and taking a tentative sip.

Fresh. He smiled. *Must be fed from an underground spring.*

He nodded. Nova and the horse joined him for a drink.

* * *

Tokyo, Japan
1946

"I'll drink to that!" Rowark cheered.

Taylor and Rowark clinked glasses and tossed back another round of bourbon—neat. It was 1946, and the two pilots had been liberated. The Solomon Islands were taken by Allied forces, and the two pilots had been among the survivors. The Hiroshima bomb had been dropped, and Japan was occupied. The war was over.

The two men sat in a small bar in the Õmori district, tying one on for the last time before they shipped back home. Nearly two years together in hell had created a bond between them that was greater than brotherhood. They were going back to their respective homes in different parts of the country, but neither of them could fathom the idea of life without the other at his side.

So, they got shit-faced.

It was late, nearly midnight. The bar was open past curfew only because the two pilots refused to leave. The Japanese staff did little to discourage them. No one wanted to anger Americans, especially drunk ones.

Rowark looked dissatisfied with their latest drink.

"Garbage," he spouted, knocking over the empty snifter in disgust. "Barkeep!" he growled. "You're holding out on us. I asked for Crow, not this watered-down crap." Uncomfortable with where this looked to be going, the bartender backed away slowly, but Rowark grabbed the man by the collar and snapped him back. "Where's the good stuff?"

The bartender turned and looked to Taylor.

"Want no trouble," he murmured.

"Eddie," Taylor interjected, "leave the man alone. We're in Japan, remember? They don't have it here."

Rowark sobered for a second and seemed to realize for the first time exactly where he was. Letting the bartender go, he dusted him off and adjusted the man's apron. As he did, trucks could be heard arriving outside.

"Sorry, pal," he mumbled. "Forgot myself for a second." Reaching into his pocket, he pulled out a wad of yen and tucked it in the Japanese man's shirt pocket. Then he turned toward the bar's front window.

"Uh-oh," he said. "Looks like closing time after all."

Three U.S. Army trucks had pulled up outside. Taylor's first thought was that Rowark was right—the MPs were here to close the bar, and probably take them to the dry tank for the night. Only the GIs who poured off the truck weren't MPs, and weren't headed for the bar. Instead, they lined up across the street. Outside Nakamura Hospital.

"Something's up," Taylor surmised.

An officer appeared, addressing the men. With a blow of a whistle they charged the hospital, leaving only a lonely private to stand watch outside.

"No shit," Rowark replied. Grabbing an unopened bottle of whiskey from behind the bar, he took it and headed toward the trucks. A hasty Taylor paid for the drinks and the bottle and took off after him.

"Hey, soldier," Rowark called out in the street. "What's buzzin', cousin?"

"Halt!" the nervous young sentry shouted back. "Who goes there?"

"At ease, Private." Rowark flashed his silver bars. "I'm Lieutenant Rowark and"—he turned to indicate Taylor coming up behind him—"this fine fellow is Lieutenant Taylor, both courtesy of the Army Air Force."

"Sirs!" The private noticed the bottle in Eddie's hand, and seemed to relax a bit. "Y'all late for the party, sirs?"

Rowark narrowed his eyes. "What party would that be, soldier?"

When doubt crossed the private's face, Taylor jumped in.

"Don't yank the man's chain, Eddie. Of course *that's why we're*

here." Patting the boy on the back, he shrugged at his companion. "Might as well go on in have a look-see."

Taking a dissatisfied swig from the bottle, Rowark agreed.

Inside, the lobby was vacant. They were met with distant sounds of chaos. Elsewhere in the building, men were hooting, women were screaming, and glass was breaking. Rowark and Taylor entered cautiously, finding cover as they went. Taylor picked up a broken chair leg to use as a club, while Rowark was content with his bottle as a weapon. When they heard gunfire, they hastened their approach.

A Japanese doctor stumbled out into the corridor and slumped against the wall. As blood pooled around him, two army buddies within the room held down the dead man's screaming patient while a third had his way with her.

Taylor boiled over. This *was the party. Some jackass army officer had got it in his head to have his men let off a little steam—and there were nearly fifty men who got off those trucks. The entire hospital, including its female staff and patients, was their playground.*

He thought about the Japanese officers who had assaulted the village in the Solomons. About the atrocities that had been committed there. Some might say this was tit for tat.

For Taylor, however, it wasn't payback.

Payback didn't exist.

Like the people on that island, these patients were innocents. The fact that they were Japanese didn't make it alright. They were people.

We stop them from committing atrocities, *he fumed,* and then do the same to them? *Without further thought he moved toward the pinned woman. Twirling his purloined chair leg in a wide arc, he clipped the two restrainers in the head before mashing it into her assailant's face. As he pounded on the overeager GI, Rowark gently set down his bottle and tackled the other two, fists flying.*

Taylor tried to help the frightened woman, but she kicked and clawed at him. Her eyes were tightly shut.

"Look at me!" he demanded.

Slowly she opened her eyes.

"Okay?" he whispered.

Shaking, she nodded. Taylor took off his jacket and put it around her shoulders, then opened the closet and gestured for her to hide. Tears streaming down her face, she nodded and complied.

Down the corridor, the two men could hear more of the same. A lot more. They had their work cut out for them. Rowark picked up his bottle and took one last gulp. Holding it by the neck, he rapped it against the wall, shattering it and sending up a spray. The broken glass made for a menacing weapon.

"You ready?" he asked.

Taylor wished Rowark had offered him a swig before he broke that bottle. He licked his dry lips and nodded once. With his friend a step behind him, Taylor rushed toward the melee.

Brent had dragged Maddox a safe distance from the downed craft, fearful of additional explosions that never came. The engine had managed to snuff itself out in the crash, causing an explosion of shrapnel but no fireball. After some time had passed, Brent ventured back into the ship to find water and supplies.

His skipper was in shock. Blinded and tossed around, Maddox likely had broken ribs and internal bleeding. Still, the ship had suffered worse than its commander. While many of her control components were intact, the exploding engine had shorted out all main power systems. For all intents and purposes, she was dead on arrival and beyond repair.

Liberty 2 wouldn't be rescuing anyone.

Still, it could have been worse. Strapped into his control couch, Brent had weathered the accident. He was shaken and dizzy, but not broken. The ship's de facto medical officer, at least he was fit to administer first aid. For what it was worth.

Water in hand, he approached the prone Maddox. The colonel awoke with a start.

"No. No, no, Skipper, it's me again," Brent assured him. "Just me."

"Brent…?" After a moment, Maddox seemed to realize where he was. What had happened. He licked his lips. "Did you contact Earth?"

"I tried to, sir." Brent grimaced. "Not a crackle." He had to tell Maddox what he had discovered in orbit.

Had to.

"Skipper, I took an Earth time reading just before re-entry."

Maddox fought his pain and concentrated on the conversation. "What'd you get?"

"Three-niner-five-five," Brent replied.

Maddox stared at him. "Three thousand, nine hundred and fifty-five—"

"AD," Brent clarified. *At least,* he reminded himself. The counter had slowed down as it approached its final date, but had frozen at 3955 when the power went out. There was no way of knowing how far it would have gone.

"Almighty God," Maddox whispered. The man was slipping, and Brent knew it. Switching gears, he worked to focus his skipper's attention on the positives.

"Well, we were following Taylor's trajectory," he said, scanning the horizon. "So whatever happened to us must have happened to him."

"What about us?" Maddox said. "Where… where are we?"

Brent fumbled with the medical kit. "Well, in my opinion, skipper," he said, trying to remember everything the scientists had told them, "we've passed through a Hasslein Curve, a bend in time."

Focus on the positive, he reminded himself.

"I don't know what planet we're on, but the fact is, we're both of us here, we're breathing, we're conscious, we got plenty of oxygen, water." Brent paused and placed a rebreather over Maddox's face. "Here."

Maddox inhaled. He was slipping away, and Brent knew what he was thinking. Brent was here because of orders, but Maddox was here for another reason. He was here because of the Korean War. Taylor was his friend.

"Yeah, we're gonna be alright, Skipper. We're gonna be alright." He needed to keep the man's mind busy. Keep him from drifting off into despair. "As soon as you feel better, we'll run a navigational estimate."

"God," Maddox muttered, "if I could only see the sun."

Brent tilted his head. "It's up there, alright. You can feel it."

"Yes, but which sun?"

"I don't know," Brent admitted. "I don't know." Despite his intentions, frustration was beginning to grip him. "Our computer's shot. We're lucky to be alive."

"Lucky?" Maddox mocked. "No. If it's 3955 AD, I…" He trailed off. "Oh my God. My wife. My two daughters." His eyes went wide. "Dead. Everyone I ever knew."

His voice became a whisper.

"Everyone."

Korea
1953

Shrapnel flew and tracers lit the sky.

Nineteen-year-old airman Donovan Maddox was in trouble, and Lieutenant George Taylor was the only one close enough to do something about it.

The acceleration of his F-86 Sabre's jet engine threw Taylor back into his seat. Blood squeezed from his torso into his legs—he was seconds from passing out. Taylor launched a missile that the MiG tried to evade, but her Russian pilot jinked when he should have janked. The projectile disintegrated the enemy aircraft's tail, sending it into a spin before it burst into a ball of flames.

"Taylor!" Maddox exclaimed. "I—"

"You're good to go, Donny. Let's take the rest of them."

Maddox affirmed. As Taylor maneuvered his plane into formation, he noticed a sparkle out in his periphery. An instant later they were peppered with machine-gun fire. As shrapnel danced around his cockpit, Taylor looked for the source.

Three MiGs came at them from the sun. His canopy compromised, Taylor was completely reliant on his breathing apparatus to keep him from passing out. As one MiG took after Maddox, Taylor lined up another in his sights. His ammo was low, his guns nearly depleted. Weighing his options, he decided to use his last missile.

He pressed the firing stud; the rocket shot from his underbelly and went right up the MiG's tail pipe. It continued through the engine, plowing through the fuselage and out the plane's nose before igniting the entire craft. Pieces of the pilot ejected with the cockpit canopy as the plume scattered debris to the winds above contested soil.

The Cold War, *Taylor thought mockingly.* There's nothing cold about jacketed metal tearing through a person. Nothing cold about a fiery death. *He scanned the skyline, caught a flash in the distance, and checked his radar. It was Maddox taking out his assailant. Donny was back in the game.*

"Good boy."

On his instruments, a blip moved up behind him.

The MiGs, *Taylor concluded.* There were three. *He and Donovan had only snagged two of them. The warning indicator lit up a second later.*

Taylor pushed the stick low and hard, narrowly avoiding the incoming missile. As it skimmed over his canopy, he let loose with his machine gun, punching it and taking it out of the game with a flash and a thud. Then he dropped his Sabrejet down low and continued his maneuver through and around, completing the arc and looping back to confront his enemy.

While still more than a mile away, the MiG was on a collision course. Taylor lined up the Russian pilot for the kill and depressed his firing stud.

Nothing.

Guns are dry.

Even so, Taylor piloted his F-86 directly at his opponent, full thrust. He still had a chance to take the bastard with him.

The heavens opened.

Washed him with light.

Taylor saved his retinas by flipping his helmet visor down. Looking up, he located the source—something big, something glowing, and something aimed right at him. The light seared his cockpit. The fireball devoured the MiG. It claimed other planes, too. On both sides. Swooping jet fighters were incinerated, leaving only flaming shrapnel. The remaining planes scattered. Squinting, Taylor realized he was hurtling straight for oblivion.

He banked hard.

The comet sizzled.

Heat slammed him.

Taylor blacked out.

A nova filled the sky.

"Nova," Taylor said.

He was trying to teach her to speak. They sat at the watering hole, washing up and replenishing their supplies. The horse welcomed the rest.

Again and again he said her name, then his. He showed her his rediscovered dog tags, pointing out the letters. While often met with a confused stare, Taylor did note that she pointed to him when he said his name. There was some semblance of recognition.

Gotta start somewhere, he mused. *Might as well be at the bottom.*

"Here." He placed the dog tags around her neck. "There's a prize." He smiled. "You go to the head of the class." Nova regarded the metal tag with fascination.

"Why don't we just settle down and found a colony?" Taylor said mockingly. "All the kids'll learn to talk. Sure they will." He decided they had stayed long enough. The absurd was taking hold.

"Now, where in hell do we go from here?" Taylor looked to the heavens for hope.

"Well," he said, "we might make it yet."

Mounting up, they ventured anew.

Scant hours later, they reached a sharp incline. The horse gingerly made its way up the rocky climb, finally mounting its crest. Before them lay a desiccated riverbed.

Beyond that, a city buried in eons of sand. A place he had visited often. Where there had been lots of lovemaking, but no love. New York City. Specifically, Manhattan.

Back again, he reflected.

Ursus had returned.

A pious ape, he bowed as he entered the chapel. After every sojourn or campaign, he made his way here to give thanks to the Lawgiver. Later he would speak with Gaius and the council. He would see his Act passed. He would have his invasion, but first he would seek guidance.

First he would pray.

Helmet under arm, Ursus approached the altar to find that all was not as it should be. An orangutan doctor was there, putting his medical tools back into his sewn purse. Two gorillas were lifting a stretcher with a body on it—one covered in a holy purple cloth. Nearby, a group of female chimpanzees wept.

"Forgive me, Doctor," Ursus said. "Who—?"

The doctor replied. "The reverend, General. The High Patriarch has passed. It was his time."

The reverend had lived a long life—longer than most apes. Everyone had known his day would come soon. No one had expected it to be today, and there would be no expedient replacement. The clergy would deliberate for weeks. There would be political maneuvering and grandstanding, before ceremony itself would dictate who the new head of the Church would be.

"Has Dr. Zaius been informed?" he asked. As Chief Defender of the Faith, it would be Zaius's duty to pull them through this difficult time.

"It's my understanding that Dr. Zaius has gone on an expedition—" Ursus knew where, even before the doctor finished his sentence. "—into the Forbidden Zone."

As the reverend's body was carried past him, Ursus bowed his head in respect.

This might be apekind's darkest hour.

The High Patriarch was dead.

The Defender of the Faith was absent.

They would have no spiritual guidance.

CHAPTER 7
WHAT LIES BENEATH

The Chrysler Building. The Empire State. He might as well have been staring at the pyramids. Taylor wanted to be stunned. Wanted to feel the same rage he had at seeing the twisted remnants of the Statue of Liberty. Yet he couldn't.

He had nothing left.

Only the tallest sand-swept skyscrapers jutted from the earth, silent testament to man's folly.

They might as well be tombstones.

From his vantage point, he guessed that they must be in what was left of Brooklyn. *Greenpoint, maybe?* The dried-up bed was the East River and beyond it, of course, Manhattan.

"Home sweet home."

Taylor was talking to himself more and more now—not that Nova seemed to mind. In fact, she seemed enchanted by his voice. The one thing that made him different was the fact that he could talk. If he didn't exercise that little gift, he might as well climb up a tree.

"Just look at this graveyard." He made a sweeping motion with his arm. "The grand climax of fifty thousand years of human culture." He turned to Nova, waiting for an acknowledgment of his joke. Of course, there would be none.

She goggled at the petrified skyscrapers, her whole body shaking, occasionally darting her eyes to and from Taylor.

She's afraid, he realized. *I'm being an ass. Again?*

No. Still.

Thinking of the child she carried, Taylor realized there were more important things to worry about.

The child. *His* child.

After a pause, he reached back and put his arm on her thigh, comforting her.

"I wonder who lives here now…" He thought of the mutant boar and its maggot-riddled face. "Besides the radioactive worms."

Why were these trespassers allowed to get so close to the city?

The beautiful woman wearing a blue stole stood at the rail above tracks 19–11. The vast concourse below was man-made, its smooth tiles accentuated at the far end by an incongruous splash of craggy lava stone. This was her people's amphitheater, their senate chamber, and here their council held court to decide the course of an entire race. Once that council had consisted of seven members—now there were but five. As a lineage went extinct, it was irreplaceable.

Their bodies and minds forever altered by the long-term effects of radiation and natural selection, those who lived here were no longer human. Isolationists, these mutants were a patient, peace-loving people whose very flesh was sensitive to the light of the sun. They were robed in whites and tans accentuated with colored stoles to denote their guilds. Their skin was smooth and flawless, their hands were gloved, and their heads covered in wrappings that only exposed the flesh of their faces.

For millennia they had prevailed beneath this desolate Forbidden Zone. They waited here below the planet's crust for the day the surface itself would once again be habitable. Until then they were content to wait and watch over their charge—the God almighty responsible for turning them into the beautiful beings they were.

They were its children. The epitome of their race.

The balustrade was normally reserved for His Holiness—Mendez XXVI. Their violet-stoled monarch was absent, however, sequestered away in the Corridor of Busts. That left only the four to confer. There was the yellow-adorned Ongaro, Albina with her blue shawl, the fat man in red called Adiposo, and the green-garbed and bespectacled Caspay. Their colored vestments were adorned with precious metals that had been forged in the fires of radiation.

While Mendez was in self-imposed isolation, Albina often lingered here. Mostly, the others deferred to her. All save for Caspay.

Years ago, before she had ascended to guildmaster, a youthful Albina had spurned him. The glasses-wearing mutant had sought an unnatural relationship that was taboo, and her adherence to scripture had finally forced him to withdraw. Ever since, vying for dominance, the elder statesman had been swift to reassert himself.

He approached her now, his expression dour. Albina turned, ready to be challenged. Instead, Caspay nodded his head once, relaying the details of the invader threat directly to her mind. Focusing on the upper world, she closed her eyes.

Savages. Albina's eyebrow twitched. She saw a man and a woman on horseback—but the man was no savage, he was intelligent, and she recognized his mind. *One of the three so-called "astronauts"—Mr. Taylor—has returned.*

Mr. Taylor, Mr. Dodge, and Mr. Landon had passed through

the Forbidden Zone months ago. The most susceptible to their influence, Mr. Landon had been tagged and made their unwitting spy. They had followed his thoughts to Ape City, but there he had been butchered. The savagery done to Mr. Landon's mind had severed the connection, violently, and a feedback loop had lashed out at them. That cost them the mind of their conduit, the General of the Defense.

The general had been rendered vegetative.

If Mr. Taylor was indeed a scout sent back here by his ape masters, then an invasion might be imminent. The concept was…

Terrifying.

Mr. Taylor and the woman are on the periphery of our range, Caspay communicated. *We attempted traumatic hypnosis. It was brief and… unsuccessful.* This was cause for concern. Without the mind of the General of the Defense to augment them, their illusions grew harder and harder to maintain.

There was the sound of robes. Ongaro and Adiposo joined them. Together they descended the stairs toward the sealed doors of the Corridor of Busts. All four knew what had to be done—one of them had to break the Holy Reverie. The Holy of Holies had to be informed. Only one of them was bold enough to do it.

I will go, Albina asserted.

The Corridor of Busts was far more than ornamental. Each likeness was cast in ceramics and coated with a different hue of metallic plating in order to add permanence to its form. Each was a representation of a Mendez long gone. Together, they told a story.

The bust of Mendez I appeared healthy and virile. The next two generations bore evidence of decay, clearly showing the results of long-time exposure to radiation. After that, the busts changed. The faces resembled Mendez I yet again, but clean, with no trace of contamination. Even more telling, all the busts onward were identical in facial structure. They all looked exactly like Mendez XXVI.

The combined history of the mutant race resided within them. Each was a receptacle of thoughts and experiences of those former holies, sealed in a psionic phylactery. They weren't technological in the traditional sense, but instead contained quartz and other energy resonators. On those crystals the Mendez lineage had imprinted the entirety of their psyches—the accumulated memories and knowledge of all the previous twenty-five rulers of the mutant society, accessible through mental communion and physical contact.

One day the current Mendez would reside there with them.

For the past fortnight, however, He had sought the advice of His progenitors. Petitioned them for guidance in staving off an invasion by the apes—particularly now that the General of the Defense had been rendered vegetative. His Holiness had started with His immediate predecessor—Mendez XXV—and worked His way down the line. With each successive contact the message was the same: it appeared as if there was no hope.

Then He had connected with the mind of Mendez XIV. Under the reign of the former Holiness their society had unearthed a tunnel wherein they had discovered the remnants of New Manhattan—and an entirely different tribe of mutant survivors. Ones brought about not by the blessed kiss of God, but by man's science. These mutants were heathens, the result of cross-gene manipulation and mechanical intervention. They were the Inheritors and the Makers, and they made things that were unnatural.

Therein lies your answer, Mendez XIV whispered in His skull.

Abruptly another person's thoughts interjected.

Holiness…

The cogitation was invasive, yet polite. It held both a sense of trepidation and of haste. It was enough to break the reverie. His contact with XIV severed, Mendez XXVI assessed this newcomer.

Albina, He sent. She knew better than to interfere—for her to have done so had to be taken very seriously. He nodded inwardly, and a quick burst from her told Him everything He needed.

For the first time in weeks, His Holiness spoke aloud.

"Alert the Overseers," He said, and His voice echoed in the absolute silence. "The heterogeneous experiment must be activated."

When she didn't reply immediately, He didn't need to read her thoughts to know what she was thinking. Long ago, the experiment had been deemed heretical. As much as it might affect their enemies, its power—unbridled and unchecked—could spell doom for the Fellowship of the Holy Fallout, as well.

Desperate times call for desperate measures, He sent.

Albina acknowledged as much, and beamed the Overseers their orders. When she was done, He spoke aloud again.

"If successful, it will be the key to keeping the apes at bay." Yet He knew the value of caution. "First, we will test it…" He paused. "…on astronaut Mr. Taylor."

"Talking humans." Ursus clenched the scroll in his vice-like hands. "Why am I not surprised."

"Yes, sir," Dangral responded. The newly minted major had no idea why Ursus wouldn't be surprised. To him, the idea of a talking human was both ludicrous and blasphemous. *Better to agree now and sort it out later,* he reflected.

Before Ursus even made it back to his command center, he had demanded the paperwork of every major division of the city. The general didn't want to be blindsided. He wanted to know everything that had occurred in his absence. This time, however, his cause was specific. Ursus needed irrefutable proof of the human threat. Something even the gutless president would be unable to deny.

Poring over the reports, he found the most valuable ammunition in those from Zaius and newly appointed Security Police Chief Cerek—in particular the scrolls concerning the human called "Bright Eyes."

"A mutation," Zaius had called the man.

It all fit. The hearth and midden. The tools.

Mutant humans.

There had long been rumors of something unknown living in a fabled jungle that lay beyond the Forbidden Zone. Scouts had been sent. They had either disappeared or returned insane.

This "Bright Eyes" had been held within their grasp, but had escaped with the help of some sniveling chimpanzees. This had prompted Zaius to enlist Lieutenant Aurelios and his honor guard. Together they had set off in pursuit.

Maybe the Zone will swallow them whole.

Ignoring Dangral as if he wasn't there, Ursus continued reviewing the reports, and discovered some business about a second human, as well—one that had been lobotomized. Later in the documents the beast was given a name.

"Landon."

The beast had killed Simia's Security Police chief. In doing so, it had removed the only gorilla who might have stood in Ursus's way. Marcus was dead.

A stick by itself is easily snapped, he reflected. *Many bundled together are nearly unbreakable. Second scroll, third verse.* One of the Lawgiver's earliest proverbs.

Ursus had worked hard to unite the gorillas under his banner. He knew that they were stronger together. Unlike the insufferable chimpanzees, who actually *celebrated* their differences. Or the stuffy orangutans, who reveled in pointless debate.

Marcus had been the last holdout—the one gorilla who opposed Ursus's point of view, and the only one strong enough to draw others to his side. Marcus and his police force had operated outside the purview of the army, but now he was gone. His replacement—Cerek—was already sympathetic to Ursus's politics. It wouldn't be long before the Security Police were absorbed and placed under the general's command.

Returning to the report, he found that there was no official record "Landon" had spoken. Most likely Zaius had attempted to deal with it quietly—an attempt at protecting the citizenry from the awful truth. But that kind of protection wasn't what the apes needed. Not now. The truth could be *exactly* what was needed. What Ursus needed.

"Practice drills," he muttered to himself.

He would draft an order. Humans would be taken from the cages and used as live targets with which his army would train. It had been a long time since they'd faced a serious threat. His soldiers weren't as hard as they used to be—the attack on the cliffs had shown him as much. No humans should have escaped.

His troops needed more blood on their hands.

But what else could he implement?

A clamor arose outside in the courtyard.

"You hear that, Major?" Ursus gestured toward the window. "That's what you get with a democracy, and for what?" he growled. "All to stop the vivisections, and protect a bunch of stupid animals." He shook his head. "Idiots."

"Yes, sir," Dangral replied. "Should I—"

"No," Ursus said. "For now we must be patient. The *last* thing we need is an inquiry." His head throbbed, though. *We also don't need any damned distractions.*

Someone knocked on his door.

"Come!" Ursus said, and the door opened.

It was his aide. "I'm sorry, sir, but he insisted that he speak with you—" A cloaked figure brushed past the young ape.

"Thank you, Private," the newcomer said curtly. "That will be enough." With a nod from Ursus, the private withdrew. The general gestured to Dangral as well, and the major followed.

The visiting ape was gnarled, his back hunched. His likeness shrouded by cloth, nonetheless Ursus knew him well. It was retired elder Sabian. An informant for the military and the High Council, Sabian had been tasked with watching over high-ranking officials who might develop loose tongues as they entered their senior years. His latest activities were covered in the reports.

When Minister of Science Zao had threatened to reveal mankind's dark and turbulent past, sharing the information with the general population, Sabian had turned him in. As a result Zao had been exiled to the Forbidden Zone, thus condemned by his former student, Dr. Zaius himself.

Ursus arched his brow.

Zao is dead, he realized. *It meant that much to Zaius.*

"Elder Sabian," Ursus said, rising. "What can I do for you?"

"General," Sabian responded, taking a seat across from him. "It's more what we can do for each other. This is a sad time for Ape City—for all of Simia, in fact. We have no High Patriarch to guide us through our current trials and tribulations. It's *most* distressing."

Frowning, the gorilla sat again and leaned back in his chair. When Ursus was young, Sabian had been Chief Defender of the Faith, and therefore a confidant of the preacher Kananaios—the general's evangelistic guardian. Sabian had visited their home many times, and Ursus was well aware of the theatrics he favored.

The elder continued. "I am well aware of your intentions," he said, "and your need to pass a security declaration." He paused and steepled his fingers. "If you had the backing of the Church, you would gain popular support amongst the citizenry. With the support of the Citizens' Council, the assembly would have no choice but to act as you wish them to."

"Yes, yes," Ursus said with a wave, "but without a High Patriarch, the Church is powerless." Frowning, he added, "We both know it will take time for a new minister to be picked."

"All true," Sabian acknowledged. "However—" The orangutan raised a shriveled finger. "—a Chief Defender of the Faith can hasten that."

Ursus was confused.

Dr. Zaius was Chief Defender of the Faith.

"The doctor isn't here," he said, "and even if he was, he wouldn't support—" Without warning Sabian had produced a small legal scroll, pulling it from his vest. Cutting Ursus off, he read from it.

"In the absence of the current Chief Defender of the Faith, a *former* Defender may come out of retirement and assume the duties of the office." Then Ursus saw where Sabian was going.

He liked it.

The elder replaced the scroll in his pocket. "Once in office, that Defender can be sworn in as the interim patriarch." He glared long and hard at the gorilla general. "All it takes is for a senior government official to propose as much, during council session. Surely someone would second the motion."

Ursus had friends in the assembly. Though timid, at least one or two of them could be relied upon to do as much. It was exactly what he had been looking for. With this, he could call an emergency session.

Today.

Sabian would become High Patriarch, and Ursus would receive the backing of the Church.

Both apes smiled.

Zaius stared. As his expedition returned from the Forbidden Zone and neared the city limits, the wagon and horses slowed. Lieutenant Aurelios dismounted first, approaching the soldiers stationed outside the city gates. After a moment's discussion, the lieutenant turned back.

Cornelius grimaced.

It didn't take a behavioral specialist to read the confusion on the gorilla's face. Soon Zaius stepped from the wagon and moved up to join them, leaning on his cane as he went.

"Cornelius."

Zira spoke, but Cornelius wasn't listening. His attention was on Zaius and the gorillas at the gate.

"Cornelius," she said again. "*Cornelius!*"

"What—" He shook his head. "Yes, dear?"

"I'm pregnant."

"What?" Confusion held court in his skull. "When? How?"

Zira harrumphed, crossing her arms. "I would think you'd know that much, at least."

Mouth agape, Cornelius struggled to reply. "Yes, of course, dear," he said. "I mean, this is fantastic news, I just..." His words trailed off. Zira began to suspect he wasn't even listening to her.

If he wants to keep his handsome head, he'd better not be looking at another chimp, she thought. Anger frothing over, she finally followed his gaze.

Why is the army at the city gates? she wondered. *Where are the Security Police?*

Zira's eyes went wide as saucers.

Are we under martial law?

They narrowed to slits.

Ursus.

Zaius walked back to the wagon now, coming around to the rear. Quietly he unlocked the door.

"Now, you two..." Zaius eyed the nearby gorilla soldiers. "Listen to me. I am offering you a reprieve."

Zira squeezed Cornelius's hand. Zaius, however, looked far from happy.

"If you be true apes of your word, you will do as I ask of you now." His eyes were all but shuttered. "Ape City needs your help."

CHAPTER 8
FALLING TOO CLOSE TO THE SUN

The night was near pitch—with a clear sky, there was nothing to reflect any ambient light. Outside the city, the humans in the cages had settled in, and the gorillas guarding them were dozing, as well.

The time to strike was now.

Six chimpanzees dressed in black rose from Lake Ape. Few if any could have expected it. Apes despised water, and the stealthy simians knew as much. It would be the least likely place for the guards to be watching.

Their leader, Liet, shook water from her ear. The swim hadn't been as bad as she had feared, although from the look of them, Liberus and Consus had not fared as well. They seemed intent on wringing every last drop from their fur. Quirinus, on the other hand, appeared to feel no ill effects whatsoever. One of the few chimpanzee athletes, he had won awards in both archery and freestyle swimming.

Liet produced the keys she had taken from her late husband's lab. Dr. Galen had been a surgeon assigned to the academy, and as such had been allowed access to the human cages. Each of her group carried a copy, so each made for a different cage.

To no avail. Galen had been killed nearly a month earlier, and the keys were now outdated—the locks had been changed.

"Abort?" Jaila asked. Before Liet could respond, the youngest ape, Tian, held a finger up to indicate that they should wait. No more than sixteen years old, the rebellious youth crouched and slipped into the night.

Huddled around a fire near the wagons were the only two guards who were awake. The nearest one had his back to the boy, sitting on a rotting log and holding a pear over the fire on a stick. On the guard's belt, jangling against the log when he moved, was a set of keys.

Tian crouched behind the gorilla, then froze as the guard raised his head to sniff the air.

"You smell that?"

The other guard's nostrils flared. "It's nothing. Dead animal on the lake bed."

The first guard inhaled again. "Smells like wet chimp."

"How do you know what a wet chimp smells like?"

"I could tell you stories..."

The two guards laughed heartily, shaking with amusement. That was all he needed. Moments later Tian made his way back to the cages, keys in hand.

Liet smiled at him.

Examining the purloined keys, Liberus shook his head.

"This isn't all of them," he said. "Worse, only two are for cages." He motioned toward the ones nearest the forest. Liet weighed his words. While dozens of humans would still be left behind, thirty would be saved. A small victory was still a victory.

"Do it," she commanded.

Liberus opened the first cage wide, bracing himself for the humans to run.

Nothing happened. He moved closer to peer inside. The creatures merely stared back at him.

"Here." Liberus hefted the keys. "Get the other cage." As he turned around to hand them to Tian, he added, "Why don't they—"

He never finished. Two humans leapt and kicked him to the ground. That was all the signal the others needed. As the panicked beasts trampled Liberus, Tian rushed to the other cage and fumbled with the lock. While Jaila and Consus tried to herd the freed animals toward the trees, Liet and Quirinus waded through the human stampede, pulling Liberus out of harm's way.

"Are you—?" Liet started.

"I think I broke a rib," he wheezed.

"Hey!" It was a guard, the one with the candied fruit. Liet pulled Liberus to his feet.

"Go!" he hissed. "I'll distract them!" Before either of them could stop him, Liberus rushed toward the gorillas, getting just close enough for them to see him in their torchlight.

"You, stop!" the guard bellowed.

Liberus turned and limped off after the humans. The gorilla gave chase, glancing in disgust over his shoulder at his fellow guard.

"I told you I smelled wet chimp!"

With the guards properly distracted, Liet and the others rushed to the other cage. Tian had done his job yet again. As the humans trapped in the adjacent cages rattled their bars, they made a dash for the safety of the trees.

All but one.

Liet knew her group had a few scant seconds before they were seen. Regardless, she entered the cage.

"Come on." She beckoned to the lone human as he stumbled around in a stupor.

"Be careful," Jaila warned.

There was something wrong with this male. More than that, there was something familiar about him. As she approached, Liet could see he had a large scar on his forehead, the result of invasive surgery.

Suddenly she recognized him—as did Jaila.

"Liet," Tian warned. "We have to go. The guards—"

She pulled the boy to her.

"This one." She indicated the dazed human. "This one comes with us."

"But how—" Tian stopped himself. "Done," he nodded. Tian called Quirinus over, and together they led the dimwitted human into the night.

Mungwortt and Zao lived. Barely conscious, they lay in an uneven pile at the bottom of the exile pit past the edge of Simia. It had been a drop of some fifty feet, ending with a grisly crunch. Trapped beneath the Forbidden Zone, they needed help.

Zao looked as if something had broken. Mungwortt had fared somewhat better, landing on his shoulder, his arm loosened in its socket. Despite the pain, he made use of that dislocated limb to free himself from his bonds, the ropes spiraling off.

He peered around, and his eyes acclimated to the darkness. It wasn't absolute. Above them there grew a glowing moss. Its pale luminescence carried down the walls of the pit and helped to define their shape. There were other tunnels down here—he could make out the silhouettes of their entrances against the crude stone walls. Taking a step forward he fumbled, tripping over something hard and round.

It was a skull, and it was an ape's.

The floor around them was littered with bones, the bleached remains of those who had stood against the simian way and were silenced before a public trial became necessary. Worse, those bones looked to have been chewed.

Zao groaned, still barely conscious.

"Wake up," Mungwortt said urgently. "Wake up!" He grabbed hold of the orangutan and sat him up. Zao roared with pain, and clutched at his hip. As the tortured cry reverberated through the caverns, cerise stars twinkled into existence. But they weren't stars, Mungwortt realized. They were eyes—red eyes reflecting light. There was something alive in here.

"Who goes there?" Mungwortt called out. "Man or ape?"

Zao gritted a retort. "Neither, I suspect."

The creatures in the shadowed tunnels crept closer, until they were visible. Their skins glowed faintly, not unlike the fungus-smattered walls. Their shoulders were slumped like apes, but their bodies were relatively hairless, like a human's, with only a mane of white fur around their faces. Each beast had a strange shining spot on one ear.

There were a lot of them.

Desperate for a weapon, Mungwortt scavenged a piece of barbed wire and wrapped it around his fist. As he did, the creatures surged.

The white ones were upon them.

The first creature to reach them received an uppercut as

Mungwortt's barb-wired fist smashed its face. There was a crunch of bone and the spatter of something dark and wet. The beast fumbled and fell back with a shriek that ended abruptly—the white thing had landed on a pile of sharp splintered bones.

Enthralled, its brethren watched, murmuring to one another. As the beast writhed, they did nothing. White flesh was stained darkly. A damp gurgle was followed by an echoing sigh—then silence.

Zao dragged himself to the bled-out beast. His examination was brief.

"You broke its jaw," he told Mungwortt, "and impaled it on this skeleton."

"Is that good?"

"I think so," Zao panted. "They'll respect you now. They—"

Two white ones grabbed Mungwortt from behind and pinned him.

Zao yelped.

A wall of bodies rushed forward.

As Taylor and Nova approached the dead riverbed, a wall of fire erupted in front of them, shooting ten feet into the air. Taylor gripped the reins tightly as the panicked horse tried to dance away.

What the hell is feeding the flames? Taylor wondered. Perhaps it was a dry brush fire of some kind, though there was no foliage even close to the burning zone. He could feel the heat coming from it, and it was getting hotter.

Taylor let the horse have her way as she galloped down a hill and back the way they had come. A concerned Nova pawed at his back as they made their way toward the desert. After a time he halted the beast and pointed her to the south. This way would be rougher, but he was pretty sure they could handle it. He was determined to enter the ruins of the city.

"Let's try another way," he said.

The quiet wind picked up and ruffled through Taylor's dirty hair. He was certain he had gone the right way, and scanned ahead for familiar landmarks. Only there were none.

It's all wrong, he mused. *Where the hell are we?*

As if his thoughts angered the sky, it grumbled and shrank as sound itself drained from the air. With it went the light. There were no clouds, yet it was overcast. An invisible storm seemed to brew above them. Then…

Silence.

Taylor felt the hair on his arms tingle.

Suddenly there was lightning.

Electricity leapt from hidden clouds. It slammed the ground around them, forcing Taylor to kick the horse to speed as the lightning bolts gave chase. Then the violence faded. He glanced over his shoulder twice to see the lightning retreat. The sky brightened.

Spinning the horse, he brought her to a full stop. There was nothing behind them but dry desert and clear skies. Far beyond were the cliffs and hills that had rimmed the East River, suddenly miles away.

What the hell? he demanded silently. This time the earth replied, growling deep within its bowels. A vibration ran up the horse's legs, reaching her human riders. He looked down, and not a moment too soon. In panic he pulled the reins hard.

With a twist of rending stone, the earth split asunder. The horse reared, narrowly evading the yawning chasm that appeared in front of them. Spinning again, Taylor turned the horse to face…

…rock.

The earth stopped moving, and with it came silence. They were against the cliffs again, the ones bordering the river. Behind them, the newly formed gorge remained. Up ahead, a wall of stone blocked their way.

"That wasn't here," he insisted. "A minute ago, that wasn't here."

Nova gawked at the cliff face, fear and confusion written across her features. It was all Taylor needed.

"I'm not the only one," he growled. "She sees it, too." The boar-thing, the flames, the earthquake and the lightning—whatever they were encountering, it was no delusion. It was a shared experience.

Slowly Taylor dismounted. Weighing his options, he turned to Nova, taking her hand.

"Listen," he said. "Listen, now. If you lose me"—he pointed to her, and then his own chest—"If you lose me, try to find Zira. Remember? Zira." He emphasized the syllables. "Go find Zee-rah."

He patted her hand. "Zira."

Then Taylor pulled his rifle from the saddle holster and cautiously approached the cliff wall. Afraid to touch it, he brought his rifle up over his head and smashed it down on the rock.

Except there was no rock. There was nothing at all.

Taylor fell through the wall that wasn't there.

Korea
1953

Lieutenant Taylor was falling up. A tinny voice buzzed in his ear.

"Taylor!" It took him a moment to figure out who it was.

Airman First Class Donovan Maddox. The new kid. Donny.

It took another minute to figure out where he was.

I'm alive.

In my cockpit.

Flying.

Up.

Judging from the pressure, he was sure he was climbing fast. If he wasn't careful he'd exceed the Sabrejet's ceiling and then come crashing back down to earth. His labored breathing echoed in his flight mask. Behind it, there was a desperate cry on his radio.

"George, level off, goddamn it!"

Taylor cleared his throat. "I hear you, Donny."

Maddox sounded relieved. "You alright?"

I should be dead, *Taylor knew. That meteor had been on a collision course. No matter how good a pilot he was, there was no way he would have gotten out of its way in time. Unless…*

"We lost Roy and Frankie," Maddox said. "Then the meteor… it changed course."

As crazy as that sounded, Taylor knew it to be true. If it hadn't altered its trajectory, he would have been incinerated, as well.

What the hell was that thing? A goddamn UFO?

"Where is it now?"

"Damn thing went down a few miles north. Lit up a nice path across the hillside."

Taylor banked right. He could see it now—the destruction the meteor had wrought. Trees were ablaze in its wake.

"Good to see you're still with us, Lieutenant." That was Captain Lazenbe. "MiGs have broken off and we've got new orders." The captain continued as if nothing unusual had occurred. "They want us on the ground." Lazenbe rattled off the coordinates. Shaken, Taylor changed course for the new airstrip.

Whether by design or the luck of the draw, death had passed him by.

* * *

"The reverend has passed away," Maximus told Zaius. They stood within the halls of the Zaius museum. The doctor had been on his way to his office when the orangutan had stopped him. "In your absence, the assembly requested an elder to come out of retirement and enforce the Articles of Faith. Someone to guide us… spiritually… in this time of crisis."

"Who?" Zaius asked.

"Elder Sabian."

It was as he feared. Once Chief Defender of the Faith, the ancient orangutan was in favor of the quota system and even stricter separation across racial lines. His policies were severe and military-minded. Sabian had always been a political rival—to both Zaius and Zao before him—and it was he who had been assigned by the Secret Police to watch over Zao. Sabian had ultimately betrayed him.

Before I sent Zao into exile, Zaius lamented. Yet he couldn't dwell on that. There was damage to undo.

"The time of crisis is past" he assured Maximus. "The incumbent Chief Defender of the Faith has returned, and Elder Sabian need not carry the burden any longer. He can return to his retirement, secure in the knowledge that he served all of Simia when he was needed most."

"Once he was sworn in," Maximus said, "a motion was passed to name him the interim reverend." As they entered the reception area of his office, Zaius paused and frowned.

Sabian is now the High Patriarch?

"Dr. Zaius!" his secretary exclaimed. "Good day, sir, I—we weren't expecting you."

That's strange. "You may inform the council that I have returned from the Forbidden Zone. I carry important news, and require an emergency session immediately."

Hestia hesitated and looked to Maximus. When he nodded, she ran off to complete her assigned task. Zaius did not like the implications. He removed his key from his inner coat pocket. Maximus tapped him on the shoulder before he tried the door.

"You understand," Maximus said, "space is at a premium right now, and with you away…"

The door swung open of its own accord. Sabian shuffled out into the reception room, dressed in priestly purple vestments—vestments he hadn't worn for twenty years. Somehow it looked as if he had never stopped wearing them. Sabian seemed to revel in his own appearance.

"Someone had to defend the faith," the elder said, "while you were away."

The trial was a private affair. The High Council itself would act as judge and jury with the fate of the heretical chimpanzee scientists, Cornelius and Zira, on the docket. The orangutan Dr. Zaius reported the findings of his sojourn into the Forbidden Zone.

"We tracked the human beast—'Bright Eyes'—to learn if he was indeed part of a tribe of speaking humans," he said to the court. "When we discovered he was not, he was left to die. The state's original supposition, that the creature was a product of experimental brain surgery under the late Dr. Galen, was satisfied."

Dr. Honorius interjected. "I was unaware that our findings were in question, Dr. Zaius."

Looking intrigued, President Gaius ignored him. "And the

disposition of the collaborators, Doctors Cornelius and Zira?"

"They were purposely entrenched with Bright Eyes and were working under my authority. They gained the animal's trust so that it might lead us back to its alleged tribe."

Zira was stunned.

The council appeared to be stunned, as well.

Ursus rubbed his brow.

Zaius pushed on. "For their unswerving loyalty in these matters, I motion they both be granted seats on the Citizens' Council. I recommend Dr. Zira be promoted to the next available position within the Office of Animal Affairs. I also appoint Dr. Cornelius as Deputy Minister of Science."

Just what is the doctor's end game here? Zira wondered.

Dr. Maximus was champing at the bit, but President Gaius spoke first. "This is all highly unusual, Dr. Zaius."

"These are unusual times, Mr. President," Zaius replied. "Such times call for action to protect our city and our citizenry." Thus bested, Gaius merely shook his head and waved off the two chimpanzees.

"The, um…" he started. "This court thanks Doctors Cornelius and Zira for their time, and asks that they await our findings in the antechamber."

As the two confused scientists left, Maximus leapt from his seat.

"Deputy Minister of Science?" he blurted. "A chimpanzee?"

Everyone in the chamber avoided his gaze. Like it or not, the quota system had been abolished. It had become possible for any ape to hold any position in society, yet racism between the subspecies still ran rampant. Whether the other apes in council agreed or not did not matter. No one present would mention the outburst, nor would it be recorded in the session's minutes. Of that Zira had no doubt. When he received no response, Maximus sat again, quietly.

As he did, General Ursus stood.

"I am in full agreement with Dr. Zaius's assertions," the gorilla commander announced. Zira was shocked, as Ursus continued. "Action is needed to protect our good country. I do have a few questions, however."

Zira braced herself for what would come next.

"I am a warrior at heart, and have little background in the sciences," the general acknowledged. "I performed poorly in school, but excelled in games of sport and strategy." The gorilla leader paused for effect, then continued. "So admittedly, I may be missing something here. What makes these clearly outstanding ape citizens worthy of these coveted positions?"

Speaking with visible caution, Zaius replied.

"Fine scientists in their own right, they put themselves in danger by accompanying the deviant human," he said, loudly enough for all to hear, "and risked their reputations for the betterment of apekind."

"Ah, yes. Their covert work." Ursus turned his back to Zaius now. "That's something I can understand—but that's something more military than science related, isn't it? Something for the Security Police, perhaps? Why was neither the council, nor the army, informed of this deception?" Arms behind his back, Ursus deliberately paced the room. He didn't wait for Zaius's answer. "Doesn't it seem an unusual burden to be carried solely on the shoulders of the Ministry of Science?"

Zaius straightened. "I needed to be certain of what we were facing before causing a panic, General." The orangutan saw an opportunity to put Ursus back in his place.

He took it.

"You yourself state that the humans have become a rising threat," he cautioned. "Our chimpanzee friends came to me with their findings on this 'Bright Eyes.' They were already in position to act in our favor. In doing so, they have become the closest we have to experts on the matter. They have done our nation a great service."

To Zira, it appeared as if the doctor had backed Ursus into a corner. Whether or not the gorilla was voted supreme commander, if he objected to granting the chimpanzees such highly regarded positions, it would undermine his own assertion that the humans were a growing threat.

Ursus remained silent, as if pondering his next move.

Zaius honed his point.

"If Bright Eyes had indeed been part of a tribe of talking humans, it would have been imperative for us to discover their existence and rid the planet of them." He turned from side to side, addressing all who were gathered. "Fortunately, he was a product of corrupt science."

"Was he, Doctor?" Ursus sat, and leaned back in his chair. "My apes and I have discovered proof that man's raids on our crops might not be just the acts of animals." Reaching into a small satchel on his belt, the gorilla produced some items that appeared to be broken tools, scattering the lot on the tribunal's desk. "We found these in a nest of humans." Zaius examined them intently. They were crude by ape standards, but frighteningly advanced for humans.

"Someone or something in the Forbidden Zone has been to the human refuges," he continued confidently. "Used tools to chisel passages through the rock. Even built hearths and midden posts."

When the council members began to murmur among themselves, Ursus motioned toward a gorilla soldier—one of his entourage—standing to the side of the room. "Major," Ursus commanded.

The soldier stepped forward.

"It's true, sirs, all of it," he said. "I am Lieutenant… *Major* Dangral. I led the raid on the humans' enclave. Everything the general says is true."

Honorius spoke. "Can we examine the site of this human settlement?"

"I-I…" Dangral stammered. "That is to say—"

Ursus cut him off. "The caverns were fault-ridden—our attack on them caused a collapse. Any evidence, other than these tools, was buried within."

"I see," the president said, but Zaius demanded more.

"Preposterous," he scoffed. "Who is this 'enemy from the Forbidden Zone'? What proof is there that unknown forces are aiding the humans? Have you seen these enigmas?"

"No, Doctor, I have not," Ursus replied. "However, as this court knows, we have sent scouts into the region, and all have disappeared… or gone mad." He turned on the doctor. "Either apes supplied those tools, and instructed the humans in their use, or…" He let that sink in. "Or the humans are smarter than we think—and are learning how to make and use these things on their own."

The chamber was dead silent.

Ursus spoke quickly now.

"Ridiculous, I know. The only rational answer is that there is an unknown enemy in the Forbidden Zone, training the humans and using them as attack beasts.

"Our crops have been ravaged. If we cannot replenish our food supplies, we may not survive until next harvest. If our enemy is able to survive out there, there must be habitable lands within or beyond the Forbidden Zone. We must strike and take those lands before we starve to death."

Ursus moved with purpose. "Give me the emergency powers I need to make things right." An assistant sitting in the corner rushed forward, producing a familiar scroll. "This is the Ape City Security and Defense Declaration." All eyes turned to President Gaius. When the president remained stoic, Ursus spoke for him. "It's clear that this is too important to be settled by the court alone. Instead, I suggest that we take it to the common ape."

Dr. Maximus chimed in. "Yes, let's call a session of the Citizens' Council. Let the majority decide our course of action."

"Yes," Dr. Arlus agreed. "Let's put it to a citizens' vote."

"So be it." President Gaius sighed, and he was clearly relieved. "Doctors Cornelius and Zira are hereby acquitted of the crimes of heresy and malicious mischief. Dr. Zaius's recommendations in regards to the two chimpanzee scientists are to be implemented." He paused to take a breath. "Citizens' Council is to meet and hear General Ursus's proposal tomorrow at noon."

Gaius slammed his gavel hard. "Meeting adjourned."

As the assembly dispersed, Ursus vied for Zaius's attention.

"Doctor, in the interest of fairness, I would ask that both you and Reverend Sabian sit in attendance with me at the Citizens' Council meeting." Zaius raised a brow. "So that the community may hear from science, religion, and their military commander." Zaius nodded. Ursus bowed, replaced his helmet and made for the exit, confident in his stride.

* * *

Zaius left the chambers with a heavy heart. When he was clear of the other council members, Cornelius and Zira pounced upon him like humans begging for food.

"Now that you have been exonerated, and the court has granted you membership in the Citizens' Council, we have much to do," he said. "Zira, you go to Maximus first thing tomorrow morning." He turned from the psychologist to the archeologist. "Cornelius, report to me then in my office," he continued.

"Dr. Zaius—" Zira started. Cornelius put a hand up to stop her.

"We don't want to sound ungrateful, Doctor," Cornelius said, "but why are we doing this?"

"Because these are dangerous times," Zaius replied, "more dangerous than any heresy charge." He thought of old Zao, and the fate to which he had condemned his mentor. About his gorilla aide, Marcus, and how the now late Secret Security chief had kept Ursus's power separate from the city guard. And he thought of Zira's nephew, Lucius—the young ape who had given his life to save him.

Zaius feared what Ursus was capable of doing. The general had the encounter at the human caves to justify his cause. Through Sabian he had the backing of the Church, and now he held Gaius's ear. The Citizens' Council wouldn't be far behind.

"My support in the High Council is not what it used to be," Zaius explained. "I have given you clemency in exchange for your loyalty, and secrecy regarding the… other matter. Together, we must make certain that Ape City does not unravel."

Zaius's demeanor made it clear that there would be no further discussion—at least not until the morrow—so Cornelius and Zira turned to leave. They had reached the marketplace when a voice rang out.

"Dr. Zira!"

It was Jaila, a nurse with whom Zira had worked before—the personal assistant of the now late Dr. Galen. She had Galen's widow—Liet—with her. Reluctant to be stopped, however, Cornelius tugged at his wife's hand and pulled her away with him.

"I'm sorry—we must be going," Zira said, then she averted her eyes and followed her husband. The two female chimpanzees fell in behind them. As the newlyweds sped up, the new arrivals matched their pace.

"Doctor, we would have a word with you," Liet said.

"It's important," Jaila insisted.

It was Cornelius who turned on them.

"Now, see here," he whispered through gritted teeth, his eyes darting this way and that to see who was watching. Luckily for them, the market was crowded with apes intent on their own business—no one seemed to notice them. "We were just acquitted of heresy charges that linked us to the experiments conducted by your late husband," he said to Liet, "and your superior," he nodded at Jaila. "We cannot be seen talking to either of you."

Galen had been exposed for performing bizarre surgical experimentation on humans, and while the doctor was dead, there still were rumors that he and Zira had performed the surgery that gave Taylor the ability to talk.

"So, ladies, if you don't mind"—Cornelius nodded to each in turn—"it was, uh, lovely running into you." He wriggled his nose in defiance. "Good day."

Impressed with his bravado, Zira smiled with her eyes and squeezed his hand. As the couple resumed their course, the two female chimps did not follow. Instead, Liet waited until they were a good ten feet away before blurting out a name.

"Landon!"

Zira came to a full stop, yanking her husband to a halt beside her. Cornelius closed his eyes and sighed. Opening them slowly, he turned to his wife. Her expression told him everything he didn't want to know.

"No," he said to her.

Zira turned back to Liet and Jaila.

"It's about Bright Eyes' friend," Jaila quietly affirmed.

"We have him," Liet added, "and we need your help."

CHAPTER 9
THE BROKEN BOUGH

Korea
1953

The meteor seared a swath through the forest. Its spearhead plowed a trench deep into the snow-covered ground, finally coming to rest when it had all but buried itself in the forest floor.

Given the all-clear, Captain Lazenbe's squadron touched down on a makeshift airfield not far from the impact site. U.S. forces canvassed the area, making certain it was secure. With only a skeleton force at the new airfield, Lieutenant George Taylor and Airman First Class Donovan Maddox decided to have a look-see themselves.

Taylor needed to know what had fallen out of the sky. It had disintegrated the enemy fighters, and taken out two of his own as well—and then it had changed course.

Deftly they slipped away, following the smoke trail for nearly two miles. Moving silently past several sentries, Taylor noted that they wore no U.S. insignia, nor were they dressed in any official uniforms—at least none that Taylor recognized.

* * *

The two pilots approached the buried meteor, only to discover that it wasn't a meteor at all. It was surrounded by more troops, these dressed entirely in black. They almost didn't spot the troops until it was too late.

Someone built that thing, *Taylor mused.* It looks like a plane—but different. More advanced. Like something out of science fiction.

Maddox's eyes were wide with fear. His tongue lashed across dry lips. He gave voice to what Taylor was thinking.

"It's a UFO, boss."

"You don't know that." Taylor waved him off. Still a kid, Maddox had read too many comic books about invaders from space. But he refused to give up, and stabbed a finger at the strange craft.

"You're gonna tell me that we built that?"

The likely answer was no. Maddox continued, motioning toward the black-dressed troops.

"And just who are these jokers?"

"Reds maybe?" Taylor offered. This close to the Soviet Union, the idea couldn't be ignored. Yet it didn't seem right, either. He focused his attention on the dart-shaped craft, and he thought he could make out a number on its side—the partial remains of a "9."

What the hell is that thing?

Then things went fubar.

"Hold up!" someone shouted crisply. "Airmen, what are you doing here?" The black-fatigued soldier's firearm was trained on them. "What's your clearance?" He didn't lower the weapon, even though he could tell whose side they were on.

Definitely not Reds, *Taylor surmised. The soldier had too much of a Texan twang about him. Challenged, the ace pilot stepped forward, anger building inside of him.*

"My clearance? It's right here." As he feigned reaching for something

in his back pocket, Taylor swung at the soldier, his fist bashing the man's face. Immediately, several of the black-jacketed goons emerged from the shadows, and they grabbed for him.

"Not me!" His hands up, Maddox did nothing—simply muttered over and over, "Not me!"

"Shut up," Taylor barked at his wingman. Hands grappled with him and locked him in an iron grip.

"What the hell is this?" One of the men in black, wearing a flak vest, stepped forward. Taylor glared at him antagonistically as his hands were cuffed behind his back.

"That thing almost killed me up there, and took out part of my squadron," he challenged. "Whatever it is, I have every right to see it." Maddox raised his arms over his head. Taylor pinned the newcomer with his gaze.

The man held firm. "Name, rank, and service number, airman." He sounded… annoyed. *"Now."*

Taylor set his jaw.

"I should ask you the same." He scanned the man and didn't bother to conceal his contempt. "You're not Army, Navy, or Army Air Force." Taylor squinted at the man. "Just who in the hell are you?"

Without answering, the man yanked open Taylor's bomber jacket and pulled the lieutenant's dog tags from his neck, holding them up to read them. His eyes widening, he read the name aloud.

"Taylor, George, Lieutenant."

He glared at Taylor, looking for weakness. Taylor showed none, so the man addressed the soldiers surrounding the two pilots.

"Put these yahoos on the next plane to the Boxer.*" He nodded his men off. "The admiral will want to see them personally."*

Boxer.

CV-21.

U.S. aircraft carrier.

Taylor smiled, his crooked fangs bared in defiance. They were U.S. after all. He knew what a trip to "the admiral" would entail—he'd been there before. He wasn't worried.

Before he and the distraught Maddox were pushed away from the scene, two figures in white hazard suits emerged from the craft's open side hatch. They carried a stretcher. On it was a body covered with a stained white sheet. The shrouded corpse seemed almost human, but there was something off about it. The proportions were queer, the face misshapen under the veil.

As the men stumbled with the weight, an arm flopped out from under the cover, garbed in what looked like a padded pressure suit. The hand was badly singed, and its proportions were wrong. Five fingers, and they were longer than those of any man Taylor had ever seen.

With a shove he and Maddox were led away. Taylor craned his neck to see behind him. He couldn't take his eyes off the arrow-headed capsule.

What the hell is going on?

Now

Taylor was falling. The phantom rock face that blocked their path had been another one of those bizarre illusions. Unlike desert mirages, which tended to evaporate, this specter had been up close and real.

Separated from Nova, he cleaved through the incorporeal cliff and tumbled headfirst into a bottomless void. An ever-narrowing sinkhole gobbled him up whole, until Taylor slid through the neck of the hourglass, falling unceremoniously into a grainy ocean of sepia.

There was no sky. As there were sands below, there were sands above.

Yet he wasn't underground. The desert raged above him. A dust devil blotted out the sun, threatening to cascade a torrent of timeless grit. It scratched his throat, scoured his skin, and stung his eyes. Its whine deafened him.

This was worse than the Forbidden Zone.

This was hell.

Bloodshot eyes bloated and nose dripping, Cornelius's hay fever was a living hell. The country simply wasn't the place for him.

After their meeting in the marketplace, Jaila and Liet had whisked them away to an oper farm and orchard in the provinces—a land of blossoming flowers and fruit and beauty. It reminded him why he had chosen to dig around in the dry desert of the Forbidden Zone.

The pollen count is much lower when the terrain around you is dead.

Belonging to another activist named Consus, the farm had been made their base of operations far from the prying eyes of Ape City. Standing in a wine cellar beneath the barn, Cornelius tried to clear his sinuses as Zira examined the human who had fallen from the sky with Taylor—the human called Landon.

It had been Landon, Jaila explained, who had killed Dr. Galen and Chief Marcus on the Ape City bridge. Landon's brain had been surgically altered by Zaius's surgeons, allegedly to save him from a head wound he had suffered during the hunt. Taylor had known better, though—Zaius had lobotomized the human to keep him from speaking.

Then when Zaius and his police force had headed into the Forbidden Zone in pursuit of Taylor, General Ursus had begun organizing practice drills in which the army used humans as live targets. It was then that the Anti-Vivisection Society—which Liet now led—had freed as many of them as they could. Landon was amongst them.

His wound was infected.

As he had before, the human sat up on the makeshift examination table, hopping off on unsteady footing and wandering around the cellar. Cornelius noticed that he always returned to the same locations within the confined space, reaching to pluck the same nothings out of the air or press his fingers—always in the same sequence—on the same nearby shelves and tables. After his ritual was complete, he returned to the examination table, lay down, made some kind of sign across his chest, and went to sleep.

"Extraordinary," Zira reflected.

"Hardly," Liet sighed. "It does it all day long, every day."

"What is it doing, Doctor?" Jaila asked.

"Well, I don't know," Zira responded, "but it appears to be a behavior *he* must have performed with purpose, numerous times before he was traumatized. Likely he trained to do it so well that he could do it in his sleep."

From the doorway, Cornelius sneezed. "Maybe he thinks he's on his flying machine, and he's trying to leave the planet." He blew his nose before adding, "If I were him, I know I would."

"Flying machine?" Jaila said.

"It's a long story." Cornelius exhaled.

"My cousin Milo says flying machines are possible," Liet commented, "at least in theory. You know him, Dr. Cornelius. He often spoke of you."

Milo the tinkerer, Cornelius remembered. *Milo the engineer.*

"Yes…" he said, but he let it go at that. As far as he was

concerned, flight was a scientific impossibility—despite Taylor's claims. But for Milo, it had been a nut the engineer had been trying to crack since his academy days.

Liet indicated Landon.

"Milo spoke to it," she said, "when it was kept in my husband's lab." When they didn't respond, she added, "I don't know about what. Now Milo has gone into the Forbidden Zone on some sort of expedition—perhaps in search of the machine you describe."

Cornelius nodded—that made a certain amount of sense. Taylor had told them it had crashed and sunk in the Dead Lake. He looked to his wife, but her gaze was fixed on Landon, watching his every move. Without taking her eyes off of him, she reached into her chest pocket and produced a pencil and a pad.

"I'll need Jaila's assistance," she said. "Also a measuring stick, and complete silence."

Cornelius knew better than to question his wife when she used that tone. As Zira began to make exacting records of Landon's movements, he placed the stick on the table next to her, pecked her on the cheek, and ushered Liet out of the cellar.

Hours passed, and then Zira's records were complete.

As Cornelius readied the wagon, she promised Jaila and Liet she would return with antibiotics for Landon's infected wounds. Waiting for her husband, she regarded Liet. A socialite given to fads, in the past Liet's loyalties had seemed as fickle as the weather. When owning a human-skin pelt was all the rage, she had insisted that Galen buy one for each room. When the social elite decided that cruelty to animals was unacceptable, she threw the skins away and donated money to the Anti-Vivisection Society.

Now Zira was stunned to discover that during the time she and Cornelius had spent in the Forbidden Zone, Liet had been made the league's leader. It seemed beyond credibility.

"Why, Liet?" she asked. "What are you doing this for?"

Liet smiled. "I used to think humans were stupid, disgusting creatures—that all they cared about was mating and food. That changed when I saw that a human—Landon—could *speak*." She nodded toward the barn. "The night it killed my husband, it kidnapped me and tried to use me to find its friends." She shuddered. "It was savage and threatened to kill me—but it was smart."

"Then the High Council framed Galen," Liet frowned. "Because I was his wife, I was made a pariah. No more parties. No more high society. My life was ruined." Her eyes were wet, yet Zira found it difficult to be sympathetic. Still, she spurred Liet on.

"Galen was a terrible ape, and a worthless husband," Liet admitted, "but he couldn't make a human talk."

There was a clatter of wheels, and the wagon approached.

"After it was over I started to think," Liet continued, "what would I do if I was forced to sleep in a cage? To live in my own filth? What would *any* of us do? That caused me to realize, Landon was only trying to survive. It was mistreated—as are all our humans, and if one or two can talk, then any of them might. They have minds of their own, and they must be allowed to survive. To live."

That surprised Zira, and she looked at Liet. Perhaps she had changed. Taking her hand, Zira wrinkled her eyes and nose in a smile.

"We agree, then."

Liet wasn't finished, however.

"There are more of us, Doctor," she whispered. "We are not

alone in wanting things to be changed—in wanting more rights, both for chimpanzees and humans." She pulled Zira close. "We only need a leader."

Korea
1953

The Boxer *was new. Commissioned shortly before the Korean War, the aircraft carrier still had that fresh paint smell about her.*

Taylor and Maddox had sat in darkness for forty-eight hours, smelling her. An orderly brought them three squares a day, but that was their only contact with the outside world. Maddox had been a chatterbox for the first six hours. Taylor had put an end to that. Patient, he knew the admiral's game.

They would be summoned soon enough.

Guards came to collect them. As they emerged, the bright corridors of the carrier disoriented them. Taylor and Maddox were ushered from the bowels of the ship to a secure wardroom that boasted a large war table and chairs. There, the admiral awaited them.

As did Lazenbe.

The guards quickly left the compartment, sealing the hatch behind them. Both Taylor and Maddox saluted the senior officers. The admiral addressed Maddox first.

"At ease, Airman," he said. "No need for ceremony here." Looking to Taylor, he frowned. "Have a seat, son."

Taylor plopped into the nearest chair, crossed his legs, and perched his feet up on the table. Maddox turned a peculiar shade of red.

"Dad." Taylor nodded, rubbing his stubbled jaw. "You gonna tell me what that thing out there is?"

Admiral Eugene Taylor quickly lost his temper.

"Are you going to tell me what the hell you were doing at that site?" he roared. "God dammit, George! Why do you always get yourself caught up in a shitstorm?"

The younger Taylor's crooked smile dominated his face. "It's not my fault," he offered. "This time, the storm found me."

Lazenbe agreed. "The, um, meteor wiped out the remaining MiGs and two of our own, Admiral. Major Taylor was lucky to pull up in time."

The admiral continued to glare at his son for a long, silent moment. Letting out a loud breath, he dropped his shoulders.

"Alright," he relented. "I'm sure you all know that what I'm about to tell you doesn't leave this room." He peered intently from one airman to the other.

"Permission to speak freely, sir," Maddox said.

The admiral grumbled. "Yes, Maddox, damn it, spit it out."

Maddox gulped before venturing his next words. "Why tell us anything?"

"Because you saw it," Admiral Taylor growled. "Because of what it is, we're going to need test pilots, and you've got the skills, so it might as well be you." He gestured to the three men in the room. "I'm giving all of you top clearance, and assigning you to this project."

Taylor dropped his feet to the floor and sat up straight, interested for the first time since entering the wardroom.

"And what project is that?"

"We're calling it Project Liberty." The men clustered around the table. "This is what we know…"

The desert *whinnied*. Brent was sure of it.

Colonel Maddox hadn't lasted the night—a night filled with

strange red lightning and no rain. The sky had exhibited a faint, strange luminosity—most likely caused by solar reflection off the diffuse dust cloud that was collapsing into a ring around this world.

This alien world.

When the sun had risen, Brent had taken up the task of digging his skipper's grave. After two hours the burial was complete, and Maddox was at rest. That's when the sound, shrill and familiar, echoed in the distance.

Was that a horse? It was then he knew he was losing his mind. *How could there be a horse on this godforsaken planet?*

But of course, there it was—and on its back was…

…a woman.

Gorgeous.

Swathed in only a tattering of hides, her jet hair was straight, her form athletic and trim. Her skin was tanned from constant exposure to the desert sun, yet she was neither cracked nor weathered. Her softness revealed an inner strength that could only have been born of this hellish world. Staring at the wreck of *Liberty 2*, she seemed at least as confused as Brent was.

He began to wonder if he had survived the crash after all. Glancing back at the ship, he questioned if anyone could walk away from that wreck.

If I'm dead, he thought, *then let her be my guardian angel.*

Mungwortt walked. He had insisted. His eyes adjusted to the gloom.

The battle had been short. The white things had tackled him and Zao, but only to subdue them and take them prisoner. They had tried to lift him up—to lift both of them—but the half-breed wouldn't have it. Zao was his responsibility, and he was going to carry him to whatever fate they would share. The white ones bared their fangs, but relented when Mungwortt proved too stupid to back down. Instead, they carried their fallen friend—the one that Mungwortt had accidentally killed.

Zao was slung over his shoulder, his head dangling down behind. Mungwortt was careful not to touch the elder orangutan's hips—they were both pretty certain that at least one had broken in the fall. The creatures flanked him on both sides, their matted manes dirty with grease and subterranean waste.

"Careful, you dimwit," Zao groaned. "I am an elder ape, not a sack of garbage for you to dump in a bin!"

Mungwortt cast his eyes down. "Sorry."

"This is Sabian's fault," Zao said, slurring his words. "When I was Minister of Science, he was Chief Defender of the Faith—did you know that? No, of course you don't. You would have been a child then, and I doubt you keep up on such things."

The old ape was abusive and cranky. Mungwortt didn't mind. He wasn't the first ape to treat him that way. Luckily, his abrasive manner was centered less on the now and more on how they got here.

"He betrayed me to the Security Police—probably because I always beat him at chess." Mungwortt was sure the orangutan needed some sleep. Still, the elder pressed on. "We fought even when we were in office together. Sabian thought scientific advancement was an affront to God—wanted nothing to change. Nothing! The caste system, irrigation, public housing, surgical techniques—so many reforms hindered by his adherence to outdated dogma." Zao's voice grew angry. "The Lawgiver wanted us to live in innocence, not squalor!"

Not really understanding, Mungwortt nevertheless nodded.

"Defender of the Faith, Minister of Science. Two opposing viewpoints. Constantly had me at an impasse. That's why when I retired, I made sure Zaius was appointed to *both positions*." Mungwortt could feel him nod. "Put it all in one ape's hands. No bickering, keep everything in one place." He sounded proud of his decision. "The faith was designed to protect us from man's science, not choke us to death."

The old orangutan certainly loved to talk. Still, Mungwortt had begun to find the elder's voice soothing, in all of its crotchetiness.

They were joined by a burly creature, a large beast with long yellow-white hair. Hairier and dirtier than the others, it somehow commanded more authority. It, too, had a shiny spot on one ear, which Mungwortt realized was a piece of metal, almost like a decoration.

That must be their leader, Mungwortt mused.

He studied the creature's fur. It reminded him of growing up on the farm on the far side of Simia, with his aunt Arteus. Rather than raise a half-breed, his mother had given him up and he was sent away from Ape City to grow up in seclusion. What little reading he could do, she had taught him. Arteus would always collect his linens after he had let them go too long without washing. She would describe his dull and stained garments in disgust, using but a single word.

"Dingy," he said.

"Yes, yes," Zao agreed, and he chuckled. It quickly became a wet cough. When his chest settled, he continued. "That's what we'll call him, you see?" Zao reached up to pat Mungwortt on the arm. "Dinge."

"Dinge," Mungwortt repeated. He watched the creature interact with the other white ones. After they had communicated in a series of grunts and growls, they changed direction. Dinge led them down a dark rocky side tunnel. Up ahead the passageway lightened. Soon the natural caves gave way to a collapsed stone barrier. On the other side, the walls were smooth. They emerged into an enormous round tunnel, clearly engineered by someone. Mungwortt simply stared, his mouth agape.

High up on the tunnel wall, near the ceiling, they could barely make out some words that had been printed there.

Water Tunnel No. 3

The passage was indeed wet—their feet sloshed through about a foot of slow-running liquid.

"Fresh, from the looks of it," Zao commented.

Upon entering the tunnel the white beasts turned to the left, herding their prisoners down the immense waterway. Judging from the damage to the walls, it looked as if the passage had been sealed at one point, but any debris had been cleared long ago.

"What direction are they taking us?" Zao demanded.

Mungwortt didn't know how to reply. After a moment of thought, he stopped, licked his finger and stabbed the air with it. Zao poked at him.

"We are underground, you idiot!" he hissed.

The white ones became agitated and pressed them to start moving again. Mungwortt did so, peering warily into the shadows that crept along in his peripheral vision. They seemed to be going deeper beneath the earth, and closer to whatever monsters lay ahead.

ACT II

A TALE OF TWO CITIES

CHAPTER 10
THE PATH OF MOST RESISTANCE

"Clear!" Milo bellowed.

The reply was swift. "All clear!"

The chimpanzee engineer pulled hard, forcing the emergency lever in his hands. With an audible click it ratcheted back, slamming into its new position.

Silence.

Then the desert was filled with muffled reports. Explosive bolts blew one by one on the crumpled hull. The command shuttle shuddered, slid forward, and began to tip. The landing gear dropped from the bottom of the ship as she fell—a reflex measure built into her by engineers that had been dead some two thousand years. Rubber wheels and stabilizers absorbed most of the shock, but Milo still found himself thrown and bounced around the cabin.

When his head stopped ringing, he scrambled out the vessel's nose hatch. Carefully he and his engineers examined the ship in its new configuration. The large, damaged cylindrical hull was no longer attached. What lay before them was streamlined and beautiful. She had wings like a seabird. Once hidden in a shroud of metal, they were now outstretched to catch the winds.

Aerodynamics.

This Milo understood. Shaped like this, the thing could fly. The bird-form had large bell-shaped arrays at its rear—most likely its own set of thrust-makers. Milo imagined flames erupting from them, and the starbird ship soaring into the sky.

His reverie was broken by the sound of a horse galloping through the rocky canyon. It was Seraph, and she was excited. She paused to look at the ship in its new form, and shook her head.

"Dr. Milo," she offered.

"Dr. Seraph," Milo replied.

"This unique technology is not so unique after all," she said breathlessly. Seeing his confusion, she continued. "The meteors—one was a loss, nothing but a crater and scattered remnants. The other one…" Seraph trailed off, nodding toward the space plane before them.

Milo's eyes went wide. "Intact?"

She shook her head. "No, no. In many ways more damaged than this one. Its rear quarters appear to have exploded above the desert. There was this, however." She reached into her bag and produced the missing manual. Waterlogged and pulped, it was the book he needed. Milo beamed as he greedily flipped through it.

Then he noted her silent excitement.

"Dr. Milo," she said, "there were… pilots. Two of them."

"Did you—are they?"

"No," she shook her head. "One was dead, buried by his companion. The other met with a horseback rider—a female human—and headed off toward Ape City. We could go after them," she suggested eagerly.

"What about the control cabin?"

Seraph blinked.

"There was no power, but…" She was cautious with her

response. "It otherwise looked to be unharmed."

Milo's mind exploded with the possibilities. If luck was on his side, the parts from the newly arrived flying machine might be used to repair the damaged systems on this one. The answer to his dreams might have been, quite literally, dropped into his lap!

"Get the wagon and the tools."

Zao had stopped snoring.

Finally.

The constant sound in Mungwortt's ear had become an irritant, more so than the numbness of his arms. He had been carrying the orangutan elder for too many hours to count. While there was no way to tell night from day, Mungwortt was sure it was long past his own bedtime. The white ones had the benefit of being able to hand their dead companion off to one another so that none of them became too fatigued. They had forgone any sleep, as well, instead entering some kind of trance while they walked.

Mungwortt didn't understand it, and didn't want to. He just knew he had to rest soon or he might bite the ear off of one of them. As the thought crossed his mind, a glint of metal caught his eye. It was one of the metal tags, attached to the nearest creature's left ear. Now that he looked, he saw that each of them had one. He gave it a closer look. It wasn't ornate, but it was flat, smooth, and shiny. Nothing like the earrings his lover Liet used to make him buy for her.

And not very stylish, either, Mungwortt thought.

Curious what else he had missed, Mungwortt studied his captors more carefully. The shape of their noses gave them somewhat human appearance, but their shoulders and arms made them look simian. They weren't quite as hairless as he had first thought, though aside from their manes, the thick fur appeared only in certain places.

As with a human.

Half-breeds? He gasped. *Like me?*

Still, Mungwortt was all ape, twice over.

Can humans and simians even mate?

While these thoughts tumbled through his mind, the tunnel spilled them into a massive cavernous tomb. He could hardly comprehend what he saw there. Columns of metal and stone towered overhead, stretching to the cavern's softly glowing ceiling some 500 feet above. Those columns sat at strange angles, honeycombed with what appeared to be living spaces.

Buildings, he thought with sudden realization. *They are buildings.* They were bigger than anything he had ever seen. The giant structures seemed to not only go up to the ceiling, but pass through it, as well. Dumbfounded, he tilted his head. *What does it look like above ground?*

The white ones' demeanor changed as soon as they entered the vast chamber. They became timid, cautious, crouching low and looking from side to side. Walking along hard roadways littered with rubble, they appeared to be hiding from something.

What that was, he was afraid to find out. With the slumbering orangutan still on his back, he did as the albino beasts did, crouching as low as he could. As they slunk down the streets between the towers, they passed several printed signs. While reading could be a struggle, he knew his numbers.

First he saw *8 Avenue.* That was relatively easy.

Bonds. That one was huge.

Broadware? No, it was *Broadway.* Excited, he looked for more. As they walked the streets, the buildings grew closer together, walls pitted with irregular holes and piled with rubble. At a marker indicating *5th Avenue* they turned and walked in a new direction, framed on all sides by steel and concrete edifices composed of right angles, a place of twisted organic darkness.

Another easy one—*58 Street*. Then another sign.

Grand Army Plaza. His eyes widened.

An army! Were these not-apes planning to invade Ape City?

Abruptly the towering walls ended and they entered a black stain of forest. Dead trees supported a canopy of lichen and fungi. Pushing past thorny brush, they made their way beneath the hooded growth. Once among the moss, Mungwortt's eyes began to adjust. Here, everything had a pale blue glow to it—similar to the warm glow on the cavern ceiling way above, but cool—more subdued. A perpetual twilight.

The light blended with the white ones' own luminescent skins.

A good place to hide.

"Zao," Mungwortt prodded the slumbering orangutan perched on his back. "You should wake up. You should see this."

Silence answered him.

Their captors dissolved into the soft glowing gloom.

Mungwortt and Zao melted with them.

Groom Lake, Nevada
Area 51
1963

Major George Taylor was right where he wanted to be.

Two years after President Kennedy announced America's goal to reach the moon by the end of the decade, and three years since the formation of the covert military group that split from the civilian program in order to minimize the risk of communist infiltration and sabotage, there were two branches of the United States space program.

The civilian group was called NASA, the National Aeronautics and Space Administration. The military arm was ANSA, the American National Space Administration. ANSA had the benefit of pre-eminent scientists Dr. Hasslein and Dr. Stanton, while NASA's top brains were the less notable Kriegstein and Freleng.

To Taylor, that meant all the crazy dangerous stuff happened there, and every hotshot pilot wanted a chance at being part of that. ANSA was where the secretive Project Liberty had found a home—specifically at Groom Lake in Restricted Area 4808 North, in the Nevada Test and Training Range. Colloquially referred to as Area 51.

He had been attached to the project since the Korean War, and since then, American space technologies had surged, in no small part thanks to the ship that had fallen out of the skies over Korea in 1953. Reverse engineering machinery discovered aboard that ship, Hasslein and his team had developed more and more extreme propulsive, communication, and weapons systems.

Taylor was finally in a place where his penchant for pushing boundaries was welcome. In fact, ANSA not only wanted him to push them, they wanted him to break them.

It was what was keeping Taylor alive. Only in the thick of it could he could forget what he had seen his fellow man do.

Only then could he breathe.

"Fireball 3 *on final approach,"* Major George Taylor *said. "Transitioning to vertical descent, over."*

The X-13A Vertijet could land and take off sitting on its tail. Originally conceived to examine the feasibility of launching planes from a submarine, she had been deemed unviable, but VTOL piloting experience was something ANSA's astronauts were going to need in order to put down their planetary landers on alien worlds. Modified to an A configuration, X-13 had been resurrected and Taylor was the first to give her a spin.

She had handled rough on takeoff, but he had his spurs dug in on return. Approaching the X-13 mobile berthing station, Taylor rotated the stubby craft. Suspending her tail ten feet over the tarmac, he hovered.

"Fireball 3, *is there a problem, over?"*

"No problem, ground," he responded. "Maneuverability test. Over."

Taylor pulled the controls hard.

"Goddamn it, Taylor…"

Instead of coming to rest in her assigned berth, Taylor swayed the vertical plane across the field. Still vertical and maintaining ten feet of clearance the entire time, he performed a figure eight around the landing trailer and the support and emergency vehicles that were waiting nearby. Once he was satisfied, he tail-landed the Vertijet on the other side of the field.

Let them come and pick her up. *He smiled.*

Used to his horseplay, the support crew already had the trailer on the move as Taylor climbed the ladder down from the cockpit.

"Major!" The voice was breathless. "Major Taylor!" Taylor handed his helmet to the first technician to arrive, and watched as a fuel truck pulled up next to the Vertijet. Then he turned to find the woman who seemed to be vying for his attention.

Instead, he collided with her.

She was young, blond, and gorgeous, and she was—

"Lieutenant Stewart," she panted, "Maryann. Sorry, sir, I didn't—"

Taylor knew who she was; he'd read her file. A biologist fresh out of astronaut training at NASA, she had been cleared for ANSA a couple of months ago. She was a scientist and she was green.

"Slow down, Lieutenant," Taylor said. "We don't stand on ceremony here."

Not unless the admiral's around, *he lamented.*

Stewart exhaled. "Thank you."

Standing near the newly arrived fuel truck, Taylor unzipped the pocket on his flight suit sleeve and produced a cigar. Before she could object, he struck a match across the FLAMMABLE *sign on the vehicle's fuel tank.*

"What's on your mind?" He puffed and inhaled deeply.

"I didn't know who else to turn to," Stewart said. "Some of the other astronauts were talking about you and made me think you were the right person…"

"Oh?" Taylor leaned against the truck and exhaled. "What did they say?"

Stewart paused and answered slowly.

"They said that you were anti-war," she replied, "and that you hate everyone. On the planet, that is."

Taylor smirked. Can't argue with that.

"Come on, walk with me," he said with a gesture. Walking the desert airfield of Area 51, no one would be able to listen in on them.

"I hate war… and I hate everybody," Taylor said when they were a respectable distance away. "How did that make you want to hunt me down?"

"It was Lieutenant Dodge, actually, who suggested that I go to you," she admitted. "I trust Thomas, and he said you could be trusted, too."

Taylor paused. Lieutenant Thomas Dodge was a scientist, and he wasn't given to flights of fancy. Taylor trusted him, as well. If Dodge had sent her, it was serious.

"I work in radiobiology," she began, "studying the positive and negative effects of radiation on living things. When I arrived at ANSA, I was assigned to Thomas's team." Looking around, she leaned in close. "They had us running numbers and tests involving the effects of extremely high doses of ionizing radiation—deterministic effects, stochastic, heritable—"

"So what has you worried?" Taylor frowned.

"I don't want to be a part of the next Manhattan project." She shook her head. "I joined the space program to explore, not to develop weapons."

Taylor understood that. It was why he had joined, and Dodge.

He's hoping I'll go straight to the admiral. *Taylor grimaced.* That's not going to happen.

Besides, ANSA is military, *he reminded himself.*

"Thomas tried to ask questions, and got a runaround," Stewart continued, "until someone finally told him his inquiries were Churchdoor clearance and up. Then they pulled our research."

Churchdoor? *That was something new.*

He decided to ease her fears.

"Look," Taylor explained, "the propulsion drive and communication system Hasslein and Stanton are working on put out a lot of radiation. They're probably trying to figure out what happens to us when the engine breaks, and we're stuck in deep space." When the doubt didn't leave her downcast eyes, he continued. "Tell you what. I'll chat with the big brains and see what I can find out—alright?"

She smiled.

But without talking to the admiral, *he added silently.*

CHAPTER 11
A QUOTIENT OF INTELLIGENCE

The White Ones herded Mungwortt—still carrying Zao—deep into the fungus-laden forest to an outpost of ruined dwellings. It was another world in here, beneath the darkened canopy of deadened trees and giant mushrooms. He struggled to read the sign that appeared on the wrought-iron gate, lit by the soft cerulean glow.

CENTRAL PARK ZOO

Not unlike the Academy Research Complex, it was a small enclave of cages and what looked to Mungwortt to be habitats for housing captured humans. Except the only humans that resided there were piles of skeletons, sharing their space with even more living White Ones than the pack that had captured him and Zao. The dead albino beast the pack had carried was laid down beside them.

Exhausted, Mungwortt licked at his protruding fang. He had been in his share of brawls. One had left him with a broken jaw that hadn't set properly, and a snaggletooth to go with it. That tooth always ached when he was tired. Right now it throbbed. With the weight of his burden becoming too much, he shuffled along a little while more, peering at the ground in front of him. There was a raised pool that seemed to be the center of this place, surrounded by cages. There he was held fast, and he squinted at the brass plaque on the side of the pool.

SEA LIONS

He looked up, his eyes went wide, and he almost dropped Zao. Sitting in glass containers, on platforms rising from the pool, were three brains.

Big ones.

The size of wagons. Floating inside very big jars.

Mungwortt had seen brains before—damaged ones left in the trash outside Dr. Galen's private laboratory. He knew what they looked like, and these were clearly not your average brains.

How can they be here? he wondered. *How can they even exist?* And they whispered to him.

Human scientists who survived the initial ape revolt fourteen hundred years ago grafted together cloned cerebral matter in an attempt to create a biologically based computer. As the nuclear blasts of the final war disrupted electronics across the globe, those scientists hoped to find an alternative method of storing information.

Dubbed 1N-HR8-TR—an acronym for words which no longer had any bearing—the Inheritor was to be the next-generation technology that would "inherit the earth." Yet it never made it past the testing stages and was discarded. It wasn't expected that the tissue would survive, let alone grow.

Yet grow it did. First in size, and then—eventually—intelligence, until five subjects of experiment 1N-HR8-TR gained full sentience. The Inheritors gained control over the creatures called the White Ones.

Allied with Old New York's underground mutant community, the Inheritors became known as the Overseers, and were stationed in various key locations, living computers used to manage the subterranean city's infrastructure and augment the mutants' own cognitive powers. These three had other ideas, however, and used their slave race to spirit them away into the darkened bowels of central Manhattan. There they conspired to wrest control from their mutant overlords.

Mungwortt shook his head and wondered if the voices had been real. There had been no sound, but he had heard talking. Hadn't he? Bubbles aerated the tanks, and soft lights illuminated the undersides of the massive cerebral matter within them. The illumination in the left brain jar rippled.

Scan them, came a thought. Like the whispering he had not-heard before, this idea was not his own. It was also different than the others. It was forceful.

Strange machinery on the other side of the path pivoted, and Mungwortt and Zao were bathed in fluttering flashes of various hues. As quickly as it began the display was over, but lingering lights still shimmered in Mungwortt's eyes.

The center tank flickered.

Analysis, another thought boomed. It made no sense.

I'm not smart enough for this, Mungwortt decided.

"Zao…" He gingerly slid his broken friend off his back. Then the brain to the far left throbbed, and a new voice filled his mind.

The orangutan suffered internal injuries. It is deceased.

Panic began to claw at him. Once he had Zao on the ground, Mungwortt tapped the elder's face.

"Zao, wake up. Wake. Wake—"

Please wake up, Zao. Don't leave me alone.

The orangutan's face was cold. Lifeless.

Zao was indeed dead.

How long? the half-breed wondered. He had been carrying his new friend for at least a day.

The brain to the near right "spoke."

The other one is part gorilla, part chimpanzee.

The brains pulsed lights and beeps to each other. They were loud and annoying and hard to tune out. Mungwortt covered his ears, but it was a futile gesture—the sounds were thoughts in his head. He squeezed his eyes, gritted his teeth, and waited for them to stop.

This hybrid ape may be valuable to our heterogeneous experiments.

There were no objections. In unison, they commanded the White Ones, *Spare the live one, consume the other.*

A thunderous *DEET* followed the order. Two of the White Ones dragged the stunned Mungwortt away from his dead friend. He was too exhausted to offer any real resistance.

"Wait, no…"

The other albino beasts descended on the orangutan. Suddenly, they were as animals, tearing at the elder's corpse, shredding cloth and rending flesh. White fur was stained dark red—looking almost black in the alien light—as bone was stripped of muscle and sinew. And the pack ate more than Zao. They retrieved the one Mungwortt had killed—the one they carried all the way from the pit—and devoured him, as well.

They even eat their own dead.

Since Mungwortt was not showing any resistance, the two that were restraining him released their grips and joined the carnage. He could do nothing but watch.

Zao was with the angels now.

Mungwortt was truly alone.

The angel in the desert was wearing dog tags. Taylor's tags. The chances were astronomical, the likeliness ludicrous. And yet here he was, riding on the back of a horse through this wasteland, his arms around the waist of a beautiful mute savage.

"You take me to Taylor," he had said, even before mounting the horse behind her. "Taylor," he had demanded. "*Now*." At first she seemed frightened, but then she had complied—at least he hoped that was what she was doing. For all Brent knew, she was taking him on a picnic. How could that be any less absurd?

They traveled most of the day, and were going to need to camp soon for the night. He had a small battery-powered compass in his back pocket—an ANSA tracking device that could home in on a TX-9 signal. Its range was limited, however. Even so, he checked it from time to time. To his surprise, Brent noticed that the flashing light grew steadier. He gestured for the girl to follow the signal, and before long they were close. Very close.

Brent dismounted, cupping his hands around the device to see the light better against the glare of the sinking sun, continuing on foot. The blink of red turned constant—and there it was.

He nearly walked right over it. At his feet, in a dry stream bed, was a TX-9. Brent crouched and examined it. The transmitter was weathered but intact. The fact that it was still transmitting meant that it couldn't have been set up any more than twelve weeks back. After that its batteries would have lost their ability to recharge in the sun, and would have died.

Cracking the metallic cylinder, he began to play with its wired guts, tapping in code. If he could use the TX-9 to access his own ship's orbiting stardrive, he might be able to convince her to uncouple from the fusion engine and attempt re-entry. Then, if he could make it back into orbit, engage the Hasslein drive, and—

No. He was wasting his time, and he knew it. *Liberty 2*'s hull wasn't designed for atmospheric re-entry, nor was it capable of leaving the planet, either. No, the only thing he could do was have the ship transmit a signal back to Lazenbe and the research and development boys, just as *Liberty 1* had. Then he could sit and wait for a rescue.

Except without the confirmation from her skipper, the ship refused to accept any access codes transmitted via TX-9—and Maddox's command overrides had died with him.

Furious, Brent lashed out. His foot smashed into the TX-9, caving in its aluminum skull. He stomped relentlessly, turning the transmitter into so much scrap. With nothing else to smash, he hurled the hand-held tracking device into the desert. Then he collapsed, shaking his head and running his fingers through his dirty blond hair.

Consus's farmhouse was burning.

A gorilla gardener working the next field over had noticed the comings and goings at the farm. Concerned that there might be mischief, he alerted the local constable. When his first three warnings went unheeded, he changed his approach. He claimed to have seen chimps with a human. Word reached Dr. Zaius before it got to Chief Cerek—who would have informed General Ursus.

Then the entire province would have been razed, Zaius surmised.

In the course of the investigation an oil lamp had been knocked over. Zaius and Aurelios arrived too late to prevent the fire. Luckily, no apes were killed in the raid. Two prisoners were taken.

A cautious Zaius brought with him Commissioner Maximus from Animal Affairs, as well as Julius from the Research Complex. He feared that the human would be Taylor, alive and well and returned from the Forbidden Zone. Instead, it was the one known as Landon—lobotomized and now very much deceased.

"Why is this creature dead?" the Minister of Science demanded.

Maximus was adamant. "I ordered the constabulary take all animals alive."

"I warn you, Commissioner, if this—"

"This human's been dead for hours, Minister," Julius said.

"Are you certain?" Zaius moved to examine the body.

"Look for yourself," Julius said. It was true. The body was ashen, cold, and had already begun to stiffen with rigor mortis. Zaius examined the infected scar left where he and his surgeons had… *corrected* the man's brain. It was swollen and filled with pus.

Death by infection. It wasn't uncommon for such an operation to result in complications.

But why was this beast here? Of all the humans liberated from the cages, these chimpanzees had singled out the one who used to be able to speak. Peering around the cellar, Zaius separated the human footprints—all apparently made by Landon—from the ones made by the chimpanzees. The human prints followed a specific pattern, as if he had walked in circles, over and over, since his "liberation."

Curious.

"I want to see those prisoners," Zaius demanded of the

constable. The gorilla nodded and led him outside, where he squinted in the daylight. There on the lawn a wagon stood at the ready, the prisoners already loaded in the back. As he approached them, Zaius could see it was a chimpanzee duo—male and female—and feared the worst.

After all I've done to clear and maneuver them into positions to protect the city, he thought furiously, *if they have—*

"Jaila?" Zaius said. The male prisoner he recognized as Consus—the owner of the now smoldering farmhouse. Surprised to find the notorious Dr. Galen's former assistant, Zaius was nevertheless relieved that the two chimpanzee prisoners were not Cornelius and Zira.

Zaius knew Jaila as a veterinary nurse who worked at the Academy Research Complex. He had thought that, despite her former association with Galen, she still had a promising career ahead of her.

"What have you done, my child?" he asked her. Jaila remained silent for a long moment before looking up at him to speak.

"Humans deserve rights as well, Minister," she said, repeating a litany he had heard far too often from the misguided activists. "We shouldn't be testing on them. We should—" Her words were drowned out by a loud clatter of birds taking flight from a nearby tree. Zaius sighed. He shook his head and turned away.

Julius emerged from the barn, vying for his attention.

"Should I dispose of it, sir?"

"What?" a disoriented Zaius asked. "It?"

"The dead human," Julius replied.

"No, no," Zaius responded. He thought about Taylor and Landon's other associate, the dark-skinned human named Dodge. That one's corpse adorned the human display in the natural history museum. "Bring this one to the taxidermist. Have him stuffed and displayed with the humans from last season's hunt."

Then he turned. *What disturbed those birds?*

Cornelius and Zira watched Consus's farm from a safe distance. It had taken them far too long to acquire the antibiotics, but it had been for the best. Had they been faster, they would have been among the prisoners.

Landon is dead, Zira thought, peering through a spyglass Milo had given to Cornelius. *There's no indication of violence, though. He must have died sometime during the night. The infection must have already spread too far,* she realized.

All she had now were her notes on his behavior.

What was he trying to say? To do?

Cornelius stepped on a stick, and it snapped loudly. They froze. Above them a flock of birds protested loudly and took flight. Across the field, Zaius looked around.

"Hey," Cornelius urged her. "We better get out of here, and fast."

An angry Zira growled, but knew her husband was right. Quietly they returned to their horses, mounted, and made haste back toward Ape City.

Groom Lake, Nevada
Area 51
1963

BOOM!

The sonic blast echoed over the desert.

Flying ANSA's hypersonic trans-atmospheric X-15B rocket plane, Major George Taylor shot past the speed of sound and accelerated toward the stratosphere.

"You in a hurry to get topside, Starfire 1*?" Groom Lake ground control inquired. "You're climbing pretty fast, over."*

Pushing Mach 5, Taylor was sick of the desert and sick of people. He didn't give a damn about the tests they wanted to run—he had his own test in mind for this rocket.

"I'm going to see the stars, control." With a pause and an afterthought, he added, "Over."

Sixty-two miles up and it's outer space. *He smiled.* Time to earn my astronaut wings. *The aircraft plowed through the cloud cover. Her angle of ascension steep,* Starfire 1 *began to wobble.*

"This is Groom Lake, Starfire 1. *Dr. Stanton suggests you throttle down, over."*

"Tell Stanton this plane's a piece of junk," the major growled. "She handles like a '37 pickup truck with a shot suspension. Over." Starfire 1 *zoomed to the mesosphere. The sky ahead of him began to clear, greeting Major Taylor with a pitch field pinpricked with tiny suns. Taylor was so close to the stars now he could almost touch them. Just a little more altitude and he'd be able to pull them down and put them in his pocket.*

Annoyed, Starfire 1 *shuddered.*

"Back down, Major," Stanton himself said. "You're pushing her past her design limit, over."

Instead, Taylor cranked her to Mach 6. The X-15 quivered. Gravity slammed him in his seat. She could go much higher than she was, but not at the rate of ascension George was forcing her.

"I say we push her, control," Taylor urged. "Nothing to worry about—I've got the new pressure suit and suborbital ejector. Worst case scenario we test those as well, over."

"Stand by, over," the radio operator replied. This time it was Colonel Lazenbe who spoke up. "Negative, Starfire 1. *The brass say abort and bring her home, over."*

The brass. *Taylor knew who that meant.*

"What was that, Groom Lake?" Taylor replied. "I didn't copy, over."

"George—" Lazenbe started to reply, but a new voice cut him off.

"You damn well did copy, Major," Admiral Taylor shouted. "Now get your goddamn ass—"

Aboard Starfire 1, *Taylor tore the microphone's spiral cord from his headset. Disconnected. There would be no more nagging from Groom Lake. The admiral would need to find someone else's ass to ride.*

At Mach 7, the supersonic X-plane shook with vehemence. Taylor's breathing echoed in his flight mask. For a moment he was back over Korea.

Falling up.

"George, level off, goddamn it!" Maddox yelled.

Not today, Donny-O, *he decided.*

Not today.

Stanton had been right. His father was right—he'd taken her too far. The controls froze.

The hell with your damn plane, *he fumed,* and to hell with you, too.

Starfire 1 *fell into a hypersonic spin. Alarms swelled in the cockpit. At over 300,000 feet now, the X-plane was a bucking bronco ready to throw Taylor and gore him.*

Sixty-two miles, *he decided, gritting his teeth. Then he was there.* Made it, Ma! Top of the world! *Taylor had reached the Kármán line—the edge of space. Now he really* was *an astronaut.*

Cracks spread across the X-plane's wings and splintered her fuselage.

Her rocket sputtered.

She was tapping out.

That's it.

Taylor threw his reflective visor down and pushed the button. Explosive bolts blew the canopy up and away from the cockpit. His seat did the same, sprouting fins and catapulting him away from the starfighter as its engine blew like an enraged firecracker. Taylor somersaulted free as his rocket plane disintegrated in the thermosphere.

The force of the blast rocked him, and something glanced off of his helmet, but he didn't have time to worry about that. He unbuckled his seat harness and assumed the position for a suborbital dive. For a moment, he was weightless.

For a moment, nothing mattered.

The record freefall was 102,000 feet. Taylor had just ejected at nearly three times that height—280,000 feet. Cracking a toothy grin, he gazed again at the stars. His radio inactive and not a single living thing around, he was free. The stars beckoned. Taylor stretched out his hand to pluck one of those lights from the sky.

Then, he began to fall.

Friction embraced him. Atmospheric abrasion excited his experimental pressure suit. Its ablative pads absorbed enough of the energy to keep him alive, but not enough to keep him from feeling the heat. Sweat in his eyes and adrenaline pumping his heart, Taylor laughed as he plummeted to the earth.

That's when shrapnel smacked him in the face. His reflective visor shattered, Taylor's faceplate was also cracked by the glancing blow of twisted metal from his exploding X-plane. He was reeling. If his helmet radio had still worked, Groom Lake would be receiving a litany of curses that would make a native New Yorker blush.

At 250,000 feet he plunged through the mesosphere. Any heat from re-entry calmed and turned frigid. Inside his helmet, his sweat began freezing on his brow. Ice formed on the inside of his mask.

At 200,000 feet the damage spiderwebbed his field of vision. His breath screamed in his ears.

At 150,000 feet he was in the stratosphere, but still well above the Armstrong Limit. If his faceplate went, his helmet would depressurize—and at this height, the pressure was too low for the living. Sweat, urine, and saliva would boil.

His blood would evaporate.

At 100,000 feet, if his faceplate went, it would all turn to steam.

At 80,000 feet, splintered veins etched their way across his faceplate.

His mask exploded at 65,000 feet. His respirator in place, oxygen still flowed—but exposed to the atmospheric pressure, no amount of breathable air would keep him alive for long. He had to get below the Armstrong Limit before his brain seized.

Before he passed out.

He pushed his body into a steeper dive.

His eyes burned.

The water on his tongue sizzled.

His fluids were about to boil.

Crimson crept into his sight.

Still in freefall, Major George Taylor awoke with a start. The desert spun below him.

He felt like he had a hangover. His joints throbbed, his head pulsed, and his tongue was burnt.

Not dead yet, *he mused. Doing some quick calculations, he figured he must've passed out for a good five minutes or so. He still had some altitude. There was still time to deploy.*

Lucky, lucky, lucky…

At 5,000 feet, Taylor pulled his cord.

Nothing happened.

The unlucky pilot began to somersault. Whirling out of control, he discovered the issue—the experimental cord mechanism strapped to his abdomen had also been grazed by shrapnel. Dented, it had then iced up. He looked for a "Made in China" label. There was none.

Good old American-made, *he thought with a grimace, vowing to find out who in R&D had designed it and punch them in the face.* Hopefully it was Stanton, *he mused.* He could use a good knuckle sandwich.

Then Taylor's mood darkened. If I even make it back.

With no scientist in sight, Major Taylor instead punched himself in the stomach. Twice.

Metal bent.

Ice cracked.

He pulled the cord again. This time his heart yanked up into his throat, as at 3,000 feet his pilot chute deployed. Designed to pull the main chute's canopy from its sleeve, it did just that—just a little too hard. As his descent slowed, above him something tore. Lines twisted.

In freefall again, he ripped at the release tab. The useless chute fell away. Taylor reached for his emergency cord. He was at 2,000 feet, and had one more shot before he became roadkill.

Come on, you sonofabitch, *Taylor urged.* Come on!

At 1,000 feet the cord yanked. The reserve chute deployed. Falling too fast, he pulled the directional vanes hard in an attempt to cushion the fall.

Ground Zero.

Still spinning, Taylor slammed into the desert.

* * *

A gorilla sat on his chest. At least it felt that way. Something was pressing down on him. Something packed and firm.

No! He opened his eyes only to be met with stinging pebbles of sand. Then he remembered. He was in the Forbidden Zone.

Sandstorm.

Buried alive.

Suffocation.

Taylor erupted from the dune, more or less intact. Free of the grit, he gulped at the dry desert air. It was approaching dusk, and the sun lay low in the sky, just beyond the nearest craggy ridge. Shaking the sand out of his loincloth, hair, and ears, Taylor surveyed his surroundings. To his far left he could make out the storm, still traveling away from him, a dusty cloud on the horizon. The sky around him was clear, light blue giving way to violet hues peppered by orange clouds.

There were strange shapes cast on the ground around him. They were regular, angular shadows, not like the organic rocky cliffs that infested this part of the Forbidden Zone. He followed the shapes back toward the setting sun, and soon came to the edge of a deep gorge.

It was a city—but not like the ruins of New York. This was a monolithic construct of mirrors, its every surface gleaming in the setting sun, sending rays scattering in every direction. The chromed surfaces shone in oranges and purples. It was dazzling, it was new, and it had been built with a technology that not only outpaced that of the apes, but of twentieth-century man, as well.

It was a city of the future—and Taylor could only assume it was built by man. *Future man,* though given his circumstances, man from the past.

But how far past?

It was built on a behemoth slab base, one surely large enough to support half of Manhattan itself. That foundation rose some thirty stories high, then transformed into ascending spires of triangles and rectangles, each ranging from fifty to two hundred additional stories taller. Massive antennae perched atop the tallest of the peaks.

Those antennae were blinking.

Lights. Power, Taylor realized, then he dared, *Life?*

As the gorge was cast in deeper purples and blues, pinpoints of warm light hummed into being. There was a ragged path winding down the cliff face toward the city below, illuminated by white-hot running lights. They followed the treacherous trail to a high floor, where it connected with a red-lanterned bridge that led to a massive door.

"That's a trail of breadcrumbs if I ever saw one." Even without Nova here, he still spoke aloud. The sound of his own voice grounded him, but the thought of her alone out there made his stomach sink. He considered going back for her, but after that sandstorm Taylor didn't have any idea where he was.

If she had understood him, by now she would be halfway to Zira in Ape City. So he decided to plow ahead. Whoever lived here might help him get her back. Or, if there was nobody home, there was likely to be some sort of technology here he could use to give himself an advantage over Zaius and his baboons.

"Well, here goes everything."

Taylor began the arduous descent toward the mirrored city's bridge.

CHAPTER 12
OF COUNCIL AND CLERGY

"When I became your army commander, what I saw broke my heart," Ursus said to a congregation in the Ape City amphitheater. "Our country, imprisoned on one side by the sea, surrounded on three sides by naked desert. And within our boundaries, we were infected by the pestilence we call humans."

Most listened in rapt attention.

The gorilla general sneered. "By parasites that devoured the fruits we had planted in a land rightly ours. That fattened themselves on the fields we had made green with crops. That polluted the pure and precious water of our lakes and rivers with their animal excrement, and that continued to breed in our very midst like maggots in a once-healthy body.

"What should we do?" he asked. "How should we act?"

Ursus let the question sink into the crowd.

"I know what every soldier knows." He called upon the preachings of Kananaios for effect. "The only thing that counts in the end is strength." Ursus clenched his fist. "Naked, merciless force!"

The speech fell on human ears, as well. The woman had led Brent to the edge of the outdoor auditorium, where they crouched out of sight in some foliage. Nearby there were humans—mute like his companion, chained as if on display.

"My God," he hissed, "a city of *apes*."

Below, Ursus continued.

"Today, the bestial human herds have at last been systematically flushed from their feeding grounds. No human has escaped our net," he said. "They are dead, or if not yet dead, they are in our cages—condemned to die."

He scanned the crowd. No one spoke.

"Their eyes are animal, their smell rancid. Had they been allowed to live and breed unchecked, they would have overwhelmed us. The concept of ape authority would become meaningless. Our high and splendid culture would waste away, our civilization ended."

Sanity began to pull away from Brent.

Why had the beautiful savage brought him here? Taylor was nowhere to be seen.

An ape, he told himself again. *A gorilla—in a uniform.* Not only were they talking apes, but they spoke English. Thousands of light years from Earth. *How is that possible?*

"I know what happened," he muttered to himself, careful not to be heard. "Re-entry at 20,000 miles an hour. A force of 15G." He was grasping at straws. "Made Skipper blind and muddled my brains. Everything here is a delusion."

Brent turned to the woman. "Even you."

He looked her over again. "Which is too bad," he conceded.

She might not have understood what Brent was saying, but she did understand that he needed to stop saying it. She clamped a hand over his mouth and pointed. He returned his attention to the amphitheater.

* * *

"Members of the Citizens' Council," Ursus offered, "I am a simple soldier—and as a soldier, I… see things simply. I do not say that all humans are evil," he declared, "simply because their skin is white."

Ursus paused.

"No!" he exclaimed. "But our Lawgiver tells us that never will they have the ape's divine faculty for distinguishing between evil…" He paused again. "…and good." His voice rose to a fever pitch. That fever was contagious. "The only good human is a dead human!"

As the gorillas roared their approval, Ursus made his play for the orangutans. He backed away from the center of the theater, positioning himself between the seats of High Patriarch Sabian and Minister Zaius.

"Yet those humans fortunate enough to remain alive will have the privilege of being used by our Minister of Science, the good Dr. Zaius." Looking uncomfortable, Zaius nonetheless stood. The orangutan and chimpanzee contingents joined him and clapped politely. As the wave of green and tan sat once again, one chimpanzee didn't.

Her, Ursus thought fiercely.

It was the female apostate—Zira. Fortunately for the chimpanzee, her husband stepped in, and put her in line. They argued briefly, she sat, and remained silent.

Good.

Ursus began again. "The Forbidden Zone has been closed for centuries, and rightly so," he said. "However, we now have evidence that that vast barren area is inhabited. By what or by whom we don't know, but if they live—and live they do—then they must eat." He paused to let that sink in. "Now we must replenish the lands that were ravaged by the humans with new, improved feeding grounds—and these grounds we can obtain in the once-Forbidden Zone."

He had evoked emotion, then followed up with science and logic. Now, he would tie it together with religion.

"It is our holy *duty* to enter it, to put the marks of our guns, wheels, and flags upon it!" The gorillas were already cheering. "To expand the boundaries of our ineluctable power," he bellowed, "and to invade!"

The entire audience stood. The gorillas roared and the orangutans applauded enthusiastically. Only the chimpanzees were hesitant, yet they were reluctant to go against the grain of the rest. Though uncertain, they nevertheless stood as well.

Most of them.

Zira was furious. She refused to stand for it, figuratively *or* literally. When Cornelius saw that she had caught the general's eye a second time, he begged her to do so.

Finally, she did. For herself, and Cornelius, and their unborn child. If there was one thing she knew, it was that life was too precious.

For Lucius, she thought.

"Invade, invade, invade!" the apes were roaring.

A standing ovation.

Have I lost my mind? Brent thought. *Am I still in hypersleep?* He didn't dare test either theory, however.

"I've got to get out," he declared. "Yeah." His eyes darted toward the heavens, his mind centered on *Liberty 2*'s orbiting fusion drive. "I've got to get back up there. I don't know how or with what, but I'm not staying here." If he could make it to orbit and connect to the drive system, he could be on his way back to Earth, Taylor in tow or not.

Then he noticed something changing. The roar of the crowd diminished, and Brent heard chanting of a different sort.

"Peace is the simian way!"

"Humans have rights, too!"

He peered away from the amphitheater, where the imprisoned humans were chained. Crowds gathered to boo and hiss at them, but then they turned to look at the newcomers. A group of chimpanzees, marching and chanting. Their apparent leader approached one of the uniformed gorillas.

"Peace is the way," it said, and it sounded like a female. "These animals mean us no harm. Can't you see—they only want to live like we do?" The gorilla replied by producing his club. He raised it over his head, as if to bring it down on the chimp.

The crowd gasped.

The chimp winced.

The club fell—but not on her. The gorilla turned and swung at the nearest human captive, viciously knocking him to the ground where he tried to scrabble away, only to be stopped by his bindings. The ape stood over the wounded man, pummeling him until he was motionless, and his face was so much pulp.

The crowd cheered.

The other humans strained at their chains, pulling hard, to no result. The protesters rushed forward, and the gorilla guards cocked their guns. It was a standoff—no one moved for several long moments. Then the chimps seemed to realize that they were outclassed. Defeated by the threat of violence, the protesters dispersed on their own.

Thank God I'm light years from home, Brent thought, his mind whirling. *I don't know how the hell these animals speak English, but that's where it ends. Earth will never be a goddamn monkey planet.*

Anything would be better than this.

Suddenly the girl grabbed his arm and began pulling him off to one side.

Numbly, he followed.

President Gaius's quill dipped deep into the vial of squid ink.

Ursus's speech was good, Zaius thought. *Too good.* He already had the backing of the Church, and the gorillas were always going to vote in his favor. That much was understood. Any hesitancy on the orangutan side had been swiftly dealt with when Ursus brought Zaius into it. The chimpanzees had no choice but to fall in line, lest they become blacklisted.

Swayed by public support, the High Council once again met in private session, and that was that. Gaius's pen danced across the document as he approved Ursus's plan, giving him the position of supreme military commander. He would lead the entire gorilla army into the Forbidden Zone, looking for an unknown enemy.

It was absurd.

It was dangerous beyond comprehension, having Ursus and his army blindly bumbling around in the Forbidden Zone, ready to stumble upon who knows what deadly remnants of man's destructive past. There was only one thing he could do, in an attempt to limit the damage.

He had to go with them.

On that, the council's decision on the matter was swift.

"This assembly has anticipated your request, Doctor, and we agree—as Minister of Science, you must accompany our army into the Forbidden Zone," Gaius said. "Before you depart, however, we must appoint someone to attend to your duties while you are absent."

Zaius was taken aback. "I—"

Ursus stood, his helmet under his arm. "I nominate Reverend Sabian as provisional Minister of Science."

"Forgive me, General"—Zaius knew he had to be both polite and fast—"but while Elder Sabian has indeed served as an excellent Chief Defender of the Faith, he has never held the office of Minister of Science. That, when added to the burden he bears as High Patriarch—"

"I am more than happy to take up the challenge, Zaius," the elder interjected. "In regards to the position, I've always felt that faith was more important than science. I think I can muddle through the science parts while you are gone. That's what I have your new deputy minister for, isn't it?"

Cornelius. Zaius had been wise to put him in that position. He owed the Minister of Science a substantial debt.

"Of course, it's just a temporary posting," Sabian assured him. "Only until you return."

"Of course," Zaius said.

"Besides," Sabian continued, baiting him, "wasn't it Elder Zao's wish for a single godly ape to maintain both esteemed positions?"

That was it—Sabian dominated the board. Zaius withdrew.

"Is there a second?" Gaius asked.

Maximus stood. "Aye."

"Motion, ah, approved." Gaius extended his hand to Sabian. "Welcome back to the council, High Patriarch." Sabian accepted the offering. Bowing his head ever so slightly, he gently corrected the assembly.

"'Minister' will do, my fellow apes." Stealing a glance at Ursus, the ancient ape cracked a broken smile. "Minister will do just fine."

Ursus closed his eyes and gave a single nod in return. In the course of a single week, the retired elder had secured three of the top positions in Simia for himself. And Zaius knew he had been right—Sabian was in the general's pocket. While the army was away, with Zaius in tow, there would be draconian changes in Ape City—of that he had no doubt. Changes that would ensure Ursus's power base long after he returned.

Cornelius and Zira were Zaius's only hope now.

The two chimpanzee apostates. Zaius sighed, resting his forehead on his palm, then running his hand over his head.

Lawgiver preserve us.

Groom Lake, Nevada
Area 51
1963

Taylor's X-15 stunt hadn't been well received. Since being released from the infirmary, his father had refused to speak with him, and he had been all but grounded.

He got his astronaut's wings, at least.

So the major decided to use his spare time to find out what R&D

were up to. His base privileges hadn't been revoked, so he used that as an excuse to go snooping around.

Thus Taylor stepped into the base's most restricted hangar. To say it was immense would be an understatement. Laid out before him were seven sleek prototypes, each one in a different stage of construction. These were all command capsules, awaiting whatever propulsive wizardry Hasslein might have cooked up.

As Taylor walked toward the capsules, he noticed that the two closest to him were smaller, more compact. Peering inside the first one, he saw an interior that looked more mundane than the larger ships'—it was a lot like what they were developing over at NASA. The cramped cockpit barely had room for three astronauts to sit side by side. These had to be short-range vehicles.

The rest of the craft were labeled L5 through L1. All five of them would eventually have both lander and thruster attachments, allowing them to fly like a space plane or land upright. L2—the one ship that was already equipped with her lander—had crane-like legs that were tucked close to her engine pods.

At the end of the bay lay the last craft—L1. On that one hinged the success of the entire program. It was the most like the Icarus. *Taylor slipped into the hatch in L1's nose and slid down the tube into the cockpit. The cabin configuration was different from what he had briefly seen of the* Icarus, *in Korea. The controls were more cumbersome and were equipped with buttons, switches, and levers he recognized.*

Less alien, *he noted.* More flyable.

"Would you like to fly her?"

The voice startled him. Taylor wasn't alone. Sitting at the ship's navigation computer and scribbling equations in a notepad was Dr. Otto Hasslein—the man responsible for reverse engineering the technology all this was based on. Taylor had been so absorbed by the ship he hadn't seen him.

"Excuse me?"

"This ship," Hasslein said. "Would you like to fly her?" While he addressed Taylor, the scientist never looked up.

"I think we both know the answer to that, Doctor."

"Knowing something is a feeling, no matter how true it may be," Hasslein quipped without looking up from his notes. "I know there is a god and that he is good, but I cannot as of yet substantiate his existence with scientific facts."

"Of course I want to fly her," Taylor said. "Wouldn't any test pilot—"

"Why are you here, Major?"

Taylor scoffed. "I have the necessary clearance. There are rumors, Doctor. I wanted to see what it was that you boys were cooking—"

Hasslein cut him off. "I mean why are you here*?" He twirled his pencil around to indicate the base in general, then met Taylor's eyes. "At Groom Lake. Attached to this project. You fought in two wars, and you have a bit of a reputation as a maverick." The astrophysicist turned back to his notes and began scribbling again. "Why space exploration?"*

Taylor thought about it for a moment.

"For the promise of a better world," he said, a hint of sarcasm in his voice.

Hasslein smiled without looking up. "And what does that mean?"

"What does it sound *like, Doctor?" Taylor was becoming annoyed.*

"Your response was that of a politician," Hasslein suggested. "Worthy of the admiralty, one might say."

That was a shot at his father. Taylor was aware that the admiral always toed the line for the military—it just hadn't occurred to him that his father's associates could see past that, or that they would accuse him of the same attitude.

"If you think I'm only here because of my father—"

"I would never suggest such a thing," Hasslein said, "as it would not be true."

Taylor stopped and regarded Hasslein for a moment. The man was more than a astrophysicist—apparently he was also an amateur psychologist. The doctor had an eye for the human condition.

Taylor gave up. He sighed deeply.

"Let's just say I've seen too much," he admitted.

"That's a better answer," Hasslein acknowledged. "Much more human."

"Humanity is the problem, Doc," Taylor said. "Not the solution."

"And so bitterness rears its ugly head." Hasslein closed his notebook for the first time since Taylor had come aboard. "I have been observing you, Major Taylor. Your work, your temperament, your defiance, and your disdain."

"Have you?" Taylor folded his arms across his chest.

"Indeed I have," Hasslein assured him. "Would you like to hear my assessment?"

"Please," Taylor lied.

"I know better than to believe you," Hasslein said. "But I will tell you anyway." He stood and began to pace the length of the cockpit. "You are an extraordinary pilot with a predilection toward reckless endeavors. However, your latest escapade helped us to identify flaws in not one, but three *separate prototypes, something I have tried to convince the admiral was integral to our mission. He, however, sees his son as nothing but a loose cannon—perhaps even a security risk."*

"Can't argue with that, Doctor."

"No, I suppose not." Hasslein paused to consider his next words. "At the risk of being presumptuous, I would like to make a recommendation—no, not that—I would like to make a suggestion."

"Go on."

"Perhaps it is time you used your skills to advance life, instead of risking it. If you are ready for that, we are ready to begin space trials." He indicated the L1's skipper's chair beside him before adding, "And I am in need of a suitable mission commander to test our new drive system. I have the option to exercise my authority, and can choose whom that commander might be."

Taylor cracked a grin. "Alright, Doctor." Taylor moved over and dropped into the capsule's command chair. "You're the brains of the outfit. Show me how it's done."

Taylor slipped. The stone under his left foot gave way, and it was the lynchpin that held together the thin rocky shelf.

He tumbled in a pile of cascading dirt, some fifteen feet above the city bridge. Its otherwise polished metal surface became littered with the debris of his fall. Landing hard on his shoulder, he thought he might have dislocated it again.

Never healed right after World War II.

Unslinging his rifle, Taylor surveyed his surroundings as best he could. It had taken him a good hour and a half to make it down to the bridge, and darkness had fallen. As always, there was no moon in the ultraviolet sky, only a strange illumination that seemed to circle the planet like a ring of dim auroras.

The span was 100 feet across, with edges that were mirrored like the rest of the city. The road laid across it was another matter. A glossy gray-black surface riddled with metallic gridwork, it reminded Taylor of the photovoltaic cells on satellites ANSA had launched. If these were solar collectors, the city might be deserted and running off of batteries that simply recharged themselves with each day's sunrise.

"The lights are on, but is anyone home?" he murmured. *That's right, Bright Eyes, keep talking.* At this point, it was the only thing keeping him hinged.

The bridge was smooth, and there was no railing on either side. Lights were affixed at regular points, their red hazy glow warning of the treacherous drop that lay beyond. The span was some 2,000 feet long, while the goliath doors at the other side looked to be a good twelve feet tall. Taylor looked up at the towering structures. While the bridge was illuminated, as were the navigation lights atop the spires, the city itself was dark.

"Maybe she's dead after all," he mused.

Then a single light went on.

Three stories above the door.

Was this the nest of humans that Zaius so feared? If so, Taylor could understand the orangutan's concern. Whoever built this could squash the apes beneath their heel and rule the planet without hesitation.

Unless they're pacifists. Looking up again at the massive right angles and points, he decided against it. *Too big and too many sharp edges.*

A moment later he noticed a hum in the air. Not loud, but insistent. It echoed gently in the canyon, making it difficult to identify the source. It grew louder, and was coming from behind him.

He turned, and drew a sharp intake of air.

Gorillas I can handle, he thought. *Another mutant animal—sure, but not this.*

It was a robot, hovering about two feet above the ground, its shoulders broad, its arms ending in wicked-looking pincers. Slicing across its bulbous chromed face was a glowing crimson V. A trio of lights flashed across its chest, rhythmically pulsing from yellow to orange to a dull red and back again. It had no legs, but didn't need them. Its torso terminated in a metallic skirt that seemed to push the robot up from the ground.

The hum was from whatever machinery kept it afloat. It bobbed gently in the desert air, waiting and, he thought, glaring at him. Without moving. For a long time. Rifle still in hand, Taylor decided to take the initiative.

"Hello," he said. "My name is Tay—"

Fifty thousand volts of electricity slammed into him. Taylor was thrown up and back, crashing high into the door before sliding to a crumpled heap at its base.

Brent had been shot.

As they left the hill that surrounded the amphitheater, they attracted the attention of a gorilla on guard. While the simian had heard them, he never actually saw them. When Brent and the young woman took cover in the brush, the ape drew his pistol and fired. A single shot rang out, and Brent's arm was grazed.

He silenced his own yelp, and a bird in the bushes took flight. Satisfied he had been tracking fowl by mistake, the gorilla returned to his post.

The wound was superficial, but needed to be treated. Examining it, the young woman seemed to understand this. She took Brent by the hand and dragged him away. Not sure if he was alive or dead, Brent let the lovely angel take the lead.

Taylor awoke to find himself on his back, slipping across a polished tile floor. His right leg was caught in the grip of the robot's left pincer—clamped so tight he couldn't feel his foot at all. He tried wiggling his toes, only to be answered with the searing sting of a million pinpricks.

"Hey," Taylor said, and his voice echoed. "Tin britches, where are you taking me?"

The robot's head swiveled like an owl to regard the astronaut. Other than that, there was no response. Its formerly glowing red face was now a pale amber.

Red for danger, yellow for caution, he rationalized. Realizing that the humming in the air was louder now, he glanced behind him.

At least a dozen of the metal monsters had fallen in behind his captor. The one closest carried the prize he sought—his rifle. It, too, was being dragged, albeit by its shoulder strap. The bot was an extra arm's length away from him, just out of reach.

Taylor tried to get his bearings, and realized that they were several stories up on a terraced corridor within the fortress. To each side, soft illumination cast twisted shadows across the high walls. Below the terrace, there was a confusing puzzle of pipes and conduits. Above him, the ceilings vaulted away. In front of him lay an arched doorway.

Beyond that, the unknown.

CHAPTER 13
THAT WHICH IS LEFT BEHIND

The chamber was like a king's court. Metal walls and columns rose majestically into infinity, disappearing into the abyss of upper levels that were too far up and too dark to see. The floor was polished marble, smooth and veined with silver.

The bots continued in procession down the center of the room, between rows of columns and toward a raised dais replete with a modern throne bathed in a warm bright light. Pulling him to the foot of the steps, the robot holding him let go. Small compartments on the automatons' lower torsos began to cycle open. Taylor struggled to his feet, expecting a fight. As they lined themselves up on either side of the approach to the throne, the machine carrying his rifle tossed it at his feet.

He scooped it up, but before he could cock it the last two bots joined the formation before the throne. Tiny struts emerged at the bottom of each machine, and with a repetitious sequence of thuds they all lowered to the floor. Their lights went out and their humming ceased. After a moment, he went to the nearest bot and rapped his rifle on its metal shell. The resulting sound echoed softly.

Nothing.

They were all dead. Taylor was alone with echoes.

Tentatively, he climbed the steps to the dais and approached the throne. It was…

…small.

At first he thought it was a matter of perspective. As he came nearer, however, it became clear that it had been crafted for someone about four feet in height. Its design was more technical than ornate, and reminded him of a high-backed version of the command chair on that science fiction television show his ex-wife used to watch. Sure enough, its armrests contained a variety of knobs and switches which Taylor could only assume connected the seat's occupant with the inner workings of the gleaming city.

"Hello?" Taylor's voice reverberated far above.

"Over here," a small voice reflected, and he jumped with surprise. It was that of a woman or a child, higher pitched than a man's and full of wonder. It came from a ten-foot-tall window behind the throne. There, silhouetted against the deep blue night, was a boy.

"Beautiful, is it not?" The boy indicated the faintly luminous sky.

Taylor approached the child with caution, not sure what to expect. Clad in a gray-white padded jumpsuit, his hands clasped behind his back, the boy made no moves, and instead continued to stare out the window.

It was the window Taylor had seen from the bridge.

"My name is Messias," the child said. "What is yours?"

Shouldering his rifle, Taylor moved to stand next to him. It was only then that the astronaut got a look at the boy's face. His forehead was pronounced, his mouth a muzzle—not unlike a chimpanzee. His hair was a dark swept-back mane, framing his face like those of the apes Taylor had encountered in this mad future. The child's nose, cheeks, and eyes, however, were very human. This "Messias" was unlike any child Taylor had ever seen, human or ape.

Instead, he was both.

Taylor stared.

"You can talk, can you not?" Messias asked. "I heard you say hello. You are not like the other humans, are you?"

"No." Taylor blinked. "Yeah, I can talk. My name is Taylor."

"Taylor." Messias smiled. "I am happy you are here."

No contractions, Taylor noticed. *Everything is "I am" and "you are."*

Taylor looked him over again. "Are you—?"

"I am a hybrid. Part human, part ape. All my people are." He hung his head and corrected himself. "Were. Ever since the attacks, I have been lonely."

Attacks? Taylor glanced around the chamber again, then crouched down before Messias. "You're all alone here?"

"It is just me and the sentinels," Messias said. "The entire population of the city was killed in the last attack. The sentinels have searched the complex for survivors and have been unable to find anyone." Without preamble, Messias's mood shifted as he suddenly smiled. "But they found you!"

"I was… in the neighborhood," Taylor frowned. "What about these attacks?"

"The things that live out there." The boy stabbed at the desert night. "Hideous creatures. Savage. They came for us. The sentinels keep them at bay, but they still attack. They still…" A tear threatened to escape Messias's eye. Instead, the hybrid child hugged Taylor, hard. Incredulous, the astronaut took a moment before he returned the embrace.

There must be other survivors in here, and he just hasn't found them, he rationalized. *Have to be.*

Messias wouldn't let go.

"Alright, alright." He patted the boy's back. His mind was full of questions. *Is this what Zaius meant by mutants? Are the humans and the apes out there different stages of primitive throwbacks, and this is what inherited the world?*

Is this what evolution wants?

Taylor shook his head. Philosophy would have to wait. There were more immediate factors at play. Whatever the things were that had attacked the city and killed the boy's people—whether they were apes or something else—there had to be a way to stop them. He looked past Messias, to the dormant robot army.

All this technology, he determined, *there has to be a way.* He would find it. If he could find a way to protect the city and get Nova back, they could live a decent life here. Start civilization over.

"It's going to be alright."

"You know, my dear," Cornelius said between puffs on his pipe, "the trouble with intellectuals is that we have responsibilities and no power."

Following the meeting of the Citizens' Council, the two chimpanzee scientists had returned home. As Zira owned the nicer apartment, Cornelius had moved in. Most of his belongings were still in his old place, waiting to be crated up and brought over, but he didn't want to deal with any of that right now—all he wanted to do was put his feet up and rest with a good pipe full of tea leaves.

Zira was preparing for a small get-together of friends—a modest celebration of their nuptials. Despite everything that was happening, they needed the semblance of a normal life. The loss of Lucius had taught them to treasure every moment.

"I think I'll make chocolate icing," she said. "Do you like chocolate?"

"What, dear?" Cornelius's mind was still on politics.

"No, you don't," Zira said, "but I do."

He continued as if she hadn't spoken.

"If we had power in our hands, we'd be worse than them."

"I don't agree," Zira argued as she rummaged for a mixing bowl. "Gorillas are cruel because they're stupid... all bone and no brains."

"Zira..." He peered around nervously. "I wish you wouldn't talk like that. Somebody is liable to hear you." As if on cue, a human woman stepped out of the pantry, causing him to jump. She had long raven hair, a tattered loincloth, and big doe eyes.

"Nova!" Zira exclaimed. "What are you doing here?" Then her eyes went wide as a blond-haired man in strange clothes slipped from the curtain behind Nova. His attire was similar to what Nova's companion had been wearing when he first came to the Animal Research Complex.

"Taylor?" Zira said.

"No, not Taylor," the man replied.

This is it, the astronaut resigned himself. *I'm talking to apes. I've literally lost my mind.*

"My name's Brent," he added.

"You talked!" The ape with the pipe sounded suspicious. "That's impossible."

The female spoke. "In a whole lifetime devoted to the scientific study of humans, I've only found one other like you who could talk."

"Taylor," Brent said. At his words, the chimpanzees grew excited.

"Is he alive?" the male asked. "Have you seen him?"

"Where?" the female—Zira—demanded. "Where? Tell us."

"Where?" Brent echoed. "Where? I don't know where. I'm trying to find him. The longer I stay, the less I care."

"Oh, now, we loved Taylor," the male protested. "He was a fine—a unique specimen. Why, if it had not been for Zira here, he… he would still be here, a stuffed specimen in the great hall of the Zaius Museum—with his two friends."

"With his two friends?" A sinking feeling gripped Brent. When they didn't answer, he knew what had occurred. "Well," he continued, "I don't plan to stay around here quite that long." He wanted out, and he wanted out now.

"Look," he said, fighting panic, "can you get me some food, some… some water, a map… a map, so at least I'll have some idea where I'm heading?"

As he spoke, Zira stared at the bullet wound on his arm, and moved toward a cabinet.

"You'll want that taken care of, too!" she declared.

"I'll get the map." The male moved toward another cabinet, rifled through some documents, and pulled one out. "Now, if you will look up here, ah, yes, toward the north. This was the last place that we saw Taylor."

Zira applied the ointment, and Brent recoiled from the sting.

"What is that damn stuff?"

"You wouldn't know if I told you." The chimpanzee dismissed him. "Just relax. Among other things, I'm a trained vet."

It took a moment for the implication to sink in.

"Oh, great." Deciding not to go down that road, he turned his attention back to Zira's mate. "Go on, go on."

"Taylor was riding with Nova here," the male said, pointing, "between the lake and the sea. Yes… they were heading deep into the territory we call—"

"Yes, I know. The Forbidden Zone."

"Who told you that?"

"Your glorious leader back there," Brent mocked.

Before either of the chimps could respond, there was a knock at the door. Zira and her husband gestured quickly, and both Brent and Nova scrambled for cover in the kitchen.

"Quick!" she said. "Cornelius, open the door."

Sounding nervous, he trotted to the foyer. "Put the things away!"

"Open it!" Zira commanded.

For all intents and purposes, Ursus was now Simia's supreme commander. Unless the general actually dissolved the government, however, he still needed to look good in their eyes.

First, he would need a military victory or two to cement his new position. Zaius gambled that it was too soon for Ursus to make any such move.

Ursus was indeed a pious ape, although this had not always been true. Zaius had known him for decades, and had seen the change come over him. In his rebellious and ambitious youth, Ursus had held no qualms about the taking of an ape's life.

Blasphemous.

Then had come an incident with his former commander, General Aleron. After that, Ursus had gone into the Forbidden Zone for many days and nights. When he emerged, he was… changed.

Ursus took up the scrolls, devoting much of his time to studies. It had served him well, and his example helped spread the teachings of the Lawgiver among all of the gorillas. His change had been so complete that some accused him of being an imposter, but Zaius knew better. Ursus had been lost in the butchery of war and found solace in God, the Lawgiver, and the Unknown Ape—it was as simple as that.

This made him dangerous, as well. With Sabian at his side and the president relinquishing his power for the duration, Ursus had both religion and force at his fingertips. Zaius knew he must tread lightly, and his charges, Cornelius and Zira, would need to do likewise.

He rapped loudly at their door. Immediately he heard a commotion inside, and frowned. After a moment, the door swung open.

"Dr. Zaius, how nice," a flustered Cornelius said. "We were just about to have something to eat."

"Not until I talk some sense into your headstrong wife," Zaius growled. "Where is she?"

Zira emerged from the kitchen. "Good day, Dr. Zaius." She was holding a bandage cloth to the side of her face.

"Has there been an accident?" Zaius asked. When she hesitated, he suspected he knew the answer, but let her respond.

"Cornelius hit me for my bad behavior at the meeting," she mewed.

Zaius hadn't known the chimp archeologist could be so volatile. Cornelius had minored in psychology at the academy, and he thought the young ape would have been more aware of himself than to give in to fits of anger.

For his own part, Cornelius was agape.

Did he really expect his wife to keep quiet about it? Zaius thought. *Is it possible for Zira to keep quiet about anything?*

"I don't blame him," he said. Another pause, then she replied.

"I don't resent it," she offered, "but his nails need clipping."

"Enough of this nonsense," Zaius said firmly. *They have to see reason.* "Are you so blind—you two psychologists—that you're unaware that we're on the verge of a grave crisis? You heard the Ursus speech."

"Militaristic tripe!" Zira spat.

"Zira!" Cornelius admonished.

"Perhaps," Zaius conceded. "But now he has the incident he requires to go on a rampage of conquest."

"But that is appalling!" Zira cried. "To remain silent while this bully Ursus is permitted to… to destroy everything in his path is no longer possible."

She persists in being infuriating, Zaius reflected. "As Minister of Science," he said, "it's my duty to find out whether some other form of life exists."

Cornelius's interest was piqued. "Where are you going?"

"Into the Forbidden Zone," Zaius said, "with Ursus."

"Another manhunt, Doctor?" Zira shot.

Zaius glared at her. "Someone or something has outwitted the intelligence of the gorillas."

Zira, however, was relentless. "That shouldn't be difficult," she added.

"Shh, Zira." Cornelius tried in vain to get her under control.

"We apes have learned to live in innocence," Zaius said. "Let no one, be it man or some other creature, dare to contaminate that innocence."

Zira scoffed.

"Why is innocence so evil?" Zaius demanded.

"Ignorance is!" she replied.

"There's a time for truth."

"And the time is always *now*," Zira said. "Are you asking me to surrender my principles?"

Cornelius sat quietly, wise enough to let his wife say her piece. She clearly wasn't going to give up. Zaius appealed to them both.

"I am asking you to be the guardians of the higher principles of science during my absence. I am asking for a truce with your personal convictions, in an hour of public danger."

"And you shall have it, Dr. Zaius," Cornelius pledged before Zira could reply, "or I shall hit her again."

"Let us have no violence, Cornelius." While Zaius could understand the occasional heated moment, he would not condone such repeated behavior. *Even in Zira's case,* he mused. "Now," he reminded them as he headed toward the door, "I'm relying on you both."

"We are counting on you, too, Doctor," Zira countered.

Zaius stopped in the doorway. The stakes were high, and he was astonished at how quickly he had come to consider the two of them friends. The apostates were now the only ones he could trust. The irony was not lost on him.

"If I should fail to return from the unknown, the whole future of our civilization may be yours to preserve or destroy," he said quietly, "so think well before you act."

"Goodbye, Dr. Zaius, and good luck." Cornelius closed the door behind him.

Zaius stepped out into the street and paused to take in the sun. The sky was blue, the trees green. The lake shimmered with the midday sun, and the birds sang.

There would be no more work for him today. In an hour's time Aurelios would arrive at his dwelling with the wagon that would take him to the provinces. There, he would spend a couple of days with his family before heading off with Ursus and the army into the unknown.

How could anyone have a problem on a day like this? he pondered. With a heavy sigh, he made his way home.

"Let me finish this up and get you out of here!"

"Yeah, get me out of here, please!" Brent concurred. With a flourish, Zira bandaged the man's wounded arm. They had been lucky that Zaius was too preoccupied to be suspicious. Now they had to rush the two humans out before the doctor thought twice about what he had just witnessed, and came back asking questions.

"I've seen the delicate, humane way they treat humans here," Brent added. "I don't much care for it."

"Have you a horse?" Zira inquired.

"Yeah, out in the scrub."

"I'd better get you another set of clothes—the kind fit for humans like yourself." She stopped and looked him over. Brent was a little clean-cut, but at least he hadn't shaved his beard like Taylor had. "You'll pass." A glint caught her eye—Brent wore metal tags around his neck. That simply would not do. "Get rid of this!"

Then Zira noticed that Nova wore similar jewelry. She rattled them in disgust.

"And this, too!"

"If you are caught by the gorillas," Cornelius said, "you must remember one thing."

"What's that?" the human—Brent—asked.

"Never to speak."

Brent scoffed. "What the hell would I have to say to a gorilla?"

"But you don't understand—only apes can speak." Cornelius was earnest. "Not her, and not you. If they catch you speaking, they will dissect you, and they will kill you." He paused for effect. "In that order."

"Cornelius is right—be very careful," Zira agreed. "And get out of these things you're wearing as soon as you can."

Brent frowned. "Thanks," he said, but it didn't sound sincere.

"Thank us by finding Taylor," Zira suggested.

"Yeah," Brent replied. "If he's still alive."

CHAPTER 14
THE ISOLATIONIST TRANSMOGRIFIED

Taylor lived. Better than that, he had *showered*. He'd had running hot water—and soap—for the first time in two thousand years. And he had slept the night in an actual bed. It was better than anything else this future had given him.

Well, almost anything.

He thought about Nova. She'd proven that she was a survivor—he had little doubt she could make it out of the Forbidden Zone. It was the gorillas that worried him. No telling what would happen if they got ahold of her. He had to get out of this place, and find her.

Watch yourself, Colonel Taylor, he warned himself, looking in the mirror. *You're beginning to act like you're in love with this girl.*

He wondered if a primitive like Nova could love—if her mind and heart had the capacity for it. He frowned, and realized he could ask the same thing about himself.

After the failed marriages and broken relationships, he mused, *I don't have much room to criticize.*

Still peering into the bedroom mirror, suddenly he saw darkness. After a moment the lights flickered back on. *A power outage?* Perhaps the city wasn't as secure as it seemed. Standing, he turned and discovered that clothing had been laid out on the bed.

Must have come in while I was showering. It was a simple gray-white pair of pants and slip-on shoes, along with a same-toned undershirt and tunic. The tunic had a thick mustard stripe down its front, and closed using a pull tie located at the collar. The material was light, but warm.

After wearing a loincloth for so long, it was a welcome change.

Manhattan, New York
1965

The lights glimmered and car horns blared. Taylor stood on the steps that led down to The Up & Up. He and Donny had a three-day leave and Taylor intended to regret it. Having spent four hours playing pool in a dive in Chelsea, Maddox had already tapped out and headed back to the hotel for the night.

His tie tight, shirt smoothed, and uniform jacket pressed, Taylor was looking for a date. The Up & Up was a demure cocktail bar, a small place tucked away in a storefront cellar in the West Village. It felt more like it belonged in Prohibition times, and that was just fine with him.

Elegance and charm. *He smiled. Owned by a veteran, it was a known officers' hangout in the city. On the weekends, it was a raucous place of laughing, singing, and dancing.*

This was 4am on a Tuesday, and The Up & Up was dead and out. While a few civilians played poker at a table in the corner, there was only a single Air Force officer in the bar. He sat in the dimly lit corner and kept to himself. Like Taylor, he wore his uniform and enjoyed his whiskey.

As far as women went, there was only one in the whole joint. A redhead, her chiffon skin was peppered with light flecks of pink lemonade. She wore a hunter-green dress and sipped a sidecar. A silver cross pendant glistened at her neckline. The bar lights low, the only thing the pilot couldn't make out was her eyes. Sidling up next to her, Taylor took a shot.

"Please, save it, sailor," the rose-haired woman said. "I'm sure you're a nice guy and all, but with what's going on tonight, I just came here to get drunk."

"Well then," he said, "we both came here for the same reason." Taylor pulled out a stogie. Patting his uniform jacket for matches, he was surprised to find her holding a lit one.

"So," he said, inhaling deeply, "what's so terrible?"

Waving the match out, she blinked at him. "You haven't heard."

"Heard what?"

"It's coming on again now." She nodded over the bar. Following her gaze, Taylor regarded the black and white television sitting on a shelf. It was a news report. Taylor could barely make out what the anchorman was saying.

"Amidst news of political assassinations and civil rights riots, the United States now faces its biggest internal conflict since the Civil War."

The bartender approached.

"Crow, neat," Taylor ordered. He nodded toward the television. "Turn that up, will you?"

The bartender complied.

"As of midnight, Mountain Time, Texas has seceded from the Union," the rattled news anchor said. "The state no longer considers itself a part of the United States of America. Nothing of this sort has happened in more than a century. Evoking the spirit of the Civil War, Texas Governor Beauford Trotter Senior read a statement—"

As the picture shifted to the governor's press conference, the bartender handed over a glass. Taylor downed it in one gulp and motioned for another.

"The United States has lost its way," Governor Trotter declared in a Texas drawl. "This secession will protect the ideas and beliefs of our founding fathers, which we feel are no longer represented by the federal government. In no way do we urge—"

There was a commotion behind him. Taylor stretched across the bar and cranked the volume himself. Tinny speakers blared. By this time the anchorman had returned.

"—while some Justices of the Supreme Court claim secession has precedence under constitutional law, others have deemed the move illegal. Upon being made aware of the declaration, the president immediately issued a warning to Governor Trotter, instructing him to back down or face the consequences of military action." He paused and read from a sheet of paper. "This morning, national guard troops mobilized in Louisiana, and faced open opposition on the Texas border—"

First the mess in Vietnam, *Taylor thought angrily.* And now this? What a load of—

"—assassination of President Kennedy in Dallas may be related to—"

What the hell is wrong with people?

"Stop it," Taylor heard. "Leave me alone."

It was the redhead. Taylor turned. While he'd been watching the news, the Air Force officer in the shadows had moved in on the girl. A small man, his face was stubbly and his dark hair was parted to the left. Other than that, in this light all Taylor could see was a jerk.

"Come on." The guy fell all over her. "One date," he rasped. She recoiled and he yanked her arm, dragging her off her stool. "You ever see the Statue of Liberty at night?" he slurred. "You'll love it."

"Okay," Taylor growled. Slapping his palm on the gentleman's shoulder, he whirled him around. "The lady said—"

He blinked.

It was Eddie Rowark.

"Eddie!"

After Japan, there had been a few letters between them, then life had gotten in the way. Taylor had heard Eddie was a captain in the Air Force, but never bothered to follow up. He grinned.

"How the hell are—"

He didn't see the fist coming. The next thing he knew, he was lying across the broken remains of a bar stool. Taylor had one thought.

Are you goddamn kidding me?

Rowark didn't give him time to ask it aloud. The captain grabbed his bottle of whiskey and came at him swinging.

"My girl, my booze," he slurred. "Go get your own!" While the civilians in the corner watched dispassionately, not even bothering to move, the bartender reached around the bar and tugged the woman behind it. Taylor chopped Rowark's shoulder and swept his leg. As the short man went down, he pulled Taylor on top of him. An embarrassing mess of limbs, the two men rolled across the floor.

As Taylor fought for dominance, Eddie sucker-punched him in the ribs.

Twice.

Three times.

Taylor wheezed. As Rowark went for a fourth, Taylor smashed his fist across his friend's face. Rowark's head snapped back and hit the floorboards.

He blinked.

"George?" he asked. "George Taylor*?"*

His fist drawn for a second wallop, Taylor hesitated.

"What the hell are you doing here?" His eyes glazed, Rowark looked around the bar. "We ain't still in Japan, are we?" But before Taylor could answer, he was out. As Taylor untangled himself from his sprawling friend, the bartender reached for the phone.

"No!" Taylor scrabbled for his wallet. "No police, please." His cash spilled over the bar. "Can you let him sleep it off?"

The bartender regarded the money, and the uniforms. He nodded and replaced the receiver. The civilians went back to their card game.

Propped against the bar, Taylor slid to the floor. Spotting his mangled stogie, he snatched it up and planted it firmly between clenched teeth. It had gone out. Again, he patted himself for matches that he didn't have.

Glass of whiskey in one hand and an already lit match in the other, the rose-haired woman joined him. Taylor puffed at her light to limited results—the harried Havana had seen better days.

Just like Eddie, *he mused.*

"Friend of yours?"

"Long time." Taylor dragged.

The woman scoffed. "I'd hate to see you with people who don't like you."

He laughed. It hurt. He grinned through gritted teeth.

"With them it usually involves bullets."

"Gillian," she said.

"George," he replied, "and that's Eddie."

Ignoring Eddie, she looked him over. His ribs were definitely bruised and he had a nasty cut on his forehead, but otherwise he'd live.

"Thank you for coming to my rescue."

"My pleasure," he said. "Eddie's got a drinking problem."

"I can see that."

"Otherwise, he's a good guy." The Solomons flashed across his mind. "We went through hell together."

"War?" she asked.

Taylor exhaled. "Second one."

Gillian plucked the cigar from his mouth and dipped her handkerchief in whiskey.

"Hey, what the hell are you—"

"Shut up," she said. "I'm a nurse." She dabbed the booze-soaked cloth on his cut face.

"That stings, dammit!"

"Of course it does," she argued. "You want it to get infected?"

Their eyes met. So did their lips.

Gray, *Taylor realized.* Her eyes are gray.

"You want to get out of here?" he asked.

Gillian smiled. "What about him?"

Rowark snored loudly on the bar floor.

"He's a big boy," Taylor replied. Gillian helped him to his feet. Grabbing a napkin, he jotted down a note.

How'd you like to
be an astronaut, Eddie?

He added a number and stuffed the scribbled napkin into Rowark's jacket pocket. Then he turned to the redhead.

"He can make his own way home," Taylor said, and together they moved toward the door. As he shuffled along beside her, he reflected on the evening. He'd had a knock-down, drag-out fight with an old friend, and the country was shot to hell.

But I did get the girl.

Unlike Manhattan, this gleaming city was automated. From plumbing to sanitation, defense to power, everything was handled by machines.

A technological wonder with no one to enjoy it.

From their vantage point high in the center tower, Taylor

and Messias had an amazing view of the city below, and of the Forbidden Zone beyond—with only the occasional low-hanging cloud to partially obscure their view. All mirrors and polish, the city beamed in the midday sun.

"What happened?" Taylor asked.

"There was a great war," Messias said. "Long ago. Most people died, and the earth was left scorched. Burned."

Nuclear war. Just as Taylor had known in his heart.

"My ancestors never discovered for sure who started it," the boy continued, "but they managed to survive the holocaust under the protection of technology." He gestured to the desert. "Outside the city walls, apes grew more intelligent while humans grew less so. Both, however, were just warmongering primitives."

He looked up at Taylor. "In the city, things were different. Originally, there were human and ape castes here. Each blamed the other for the destruction outside. Being civilized, their leaders instituted gladiatorial games. Their champions fought to keep the population's anger in check."

Civilized? To Taylor, that seemed far from the truth.

"Eventually, the key to survival was determined to be a synthesis of the two races, and our scientists genetically bonded them as one."

Taylor had read articles about genetic engineering, some of which were written by Dr. Hasslein's own father. There had been communist experiments back in the twenties that never bore any fruit.

Thank God.

He remembered stories about crude attempts to inseminate Russian women with chimpanzee and orangutan genetic material. Luckily, man of the past failed. Future man, it would seem, succeeded.

"We were safe," Messias continued, "until the monsters that live beyond the desert laid siege on the gleaming city. The creatures were relentless. They killed everyone."

"These… creatures." Taylor trod carefully. He didn't want to upset the boy, but he needed to know what he was up against. "What are they?"

"I do not know." Messias shook his head. "Neither ape nor man, that much is certain. When they first attacked, I hid. Whenever they came back, the sentinels would lock me in the grand hall for my protection. As a result, I am the sole survivor of the last attack—the city's entire population was wiped out. All that remains are me and the drones."

Messias was repeating himself.

Nervous, Taylor pondered, *or something else?*

The boy smiled at him. "And you, of course."

"What direction did the assault come from?" Taylor scanned the city below, looking for evidence of an attack. "I don't see any damage to the buildings."

"That is because of the sentinels," the boy replied. "They repair everything and bury the dead. They take care of everything."

The sentinels. They buzzed about to and fro, on errands that Taylor couldn't even begin to guess at. They were deadly, they were efficient, and they were, well, *robots.*

"Back in the seventies, something like this—all this—was science fiction." He marveled at the robots. "Who made them?"

"I did." The boy was serious. "When the city was attacked, I designed the sentinels to protect us." Messias hung his head low. "I was too late."

Taylor had to change the subject. "How many people used to live here?"

"I do not know… thousands?" Messias waved his hand. "No. Millions." It was impossible to tell if the answer was the product of a child's exaggeration, or if there was some truth to it. He had to remind himself that Messias was only a twelve-year-old boy—no matter how much of a genius he might be, he was still only a child.

"Are you sure there are no other survivors?"

"*Yes.*" Messias looked annoyed. "Why do you ask so many questions?"

Taylor cracked a grin. "It's a big city. Maybe in one of the smaller buildings, or—"

Without preamble, a warning klaxon blared.

"Perimeter breach!" Messias warned. The boy took off toward the main hall. Taylor and two of the sentinels with them followed. The stone doors of the grand hall ground shut just as they scrambled into the room. The two bots stopped at the doorway, swiveled, and dropped into defensive mode. The exterior windows closed, as well—giant stone slabs slid down from the balcony above to seal the room.

Then, they were in darkness. The throne light throbbed dully, the only illumination in the entire chamber. Messias rushed to it and cowered behind the great seat. Taylor stood over him.

"Messias—" the astronaut started.

"Listen!" the boy commanded.

Then Taylor heard it. Faint at first, but slowly growing in volume. Muffled explosions. The sizzle of a sentinel's electric beam. The rending of metal… and a howl.

A strange haunting echo of a howl.

It was inhuman.

It wasn't even simian.

Taylor sat next to Messias and put his hand on the hybrid's

shoulder. Messias clung to him, his eyes filled with tears, and the two waited. The sounds grew closer. Louder.

Then, they were gone.

The doors to the hall slid open. Outside, sentinels hovered about, cleaning up the remains of their busted brethren. No longer frightened, Messias smiled.

"Repelled."

He took Taylor by the hand and led him back into the hall. There the windows were opening again, revealing a pleasant late afternoon sky.

Have we been locked up that long? Taylor wondered. What had seemed like less than an hour had apparently been all afternoon.

"Now," Messias said, and he swung Taylor's arm as they walked, "I have answered enough questions—it is your turn."

"Oh." Dazed, Taylor focused on the boy's words. "What do you want to know?"

"I have never been outside the city," the boy said. "I was always taught the world was only a desolate wasteland. What lies beyond the Forbidden Zone?" he asked. "I want to know everything about your world."

Taylor shook his head. *Be careful what you wish for,* he lamented.

"Okay, Messias, I'll tell you, as incredible as it may seem. I'll tell you because..." Taylor swallowed his pride. "Because I need your help."

The boy smiled.

CHAPTER 15
BABOONS AND BRINKMANSHIP

Cornelius groomed himself yet again. He sat in the antechamber of the Ape City municipal administrative complex, adjacent to the great hall of the Zaius Museum. It was his first day as deputy to the Office of the Minister of Science, and he faced the biggest challenge of his career—an interview with High Patriarch Sabian.

The job, of course, was already his, sanctioned by Dr. Zaius and ratified by the High Council. Still, as there would be no official Minister of Science in place during Zaius's hiatus, he would report to Sabian, and that was who he had to impress.

The doctor was counting on him to keep things in check while he was gone. To remind the council that science should not be secondary to faith—that they go hand in hand. To remind them of the progress they had made as a society, while maintaining their innocence. Not to take too many steps back, or too many steps forward.

Strange how quickly a common threat can turn an enemy into a friend, he thought. Just a short week ago, Zaius had wanted him and Zira hung for heresy.

"Deputy Cornelius!"

His name called by the minister's secretary, Cornelius pulled the hem of his tunic straight one last time and trotted into what had formerly been Zaius's sanctum. Though the doctor had not yet departed, he had taken some well-earned time to spend with his family, and so had allowed Sabian to utilize the office. This did not sit well with Cornelius.

The chamber had two windows—one set high in the wall, the other low and behind Zaius's—*Sabian's*—semicircular desk. An ornate rack containing *The Sacred Scrolls* had once stood by the door, accompanied by a miniature statue of the Lawgiver. Both had been moved behind the desk to place them easily within the new minister's grasp.

To the left was a second, smaller desk, outfitted for a scribe. A female orangutan sat there, working diligently. Where Zaius had kept his office spartan and clean, currently it was cluttered with new shelves. Religious artifacts lined the walls. Indeed, many things had changed.

Looking quite at home, the wizened Minister Sabian sat behind the desk. He still wore his priestly vestments—something he would likely continue to wear every day, regardless of the task at hand. The desk itself was a mess of partially unrolled scrolls—and judging from the titles Cornelius could read, it seemed as if the High Patriarch was picking and choosing which reforms he wanted to implement.

"Cornelius," Sabian greeted him warmly. "Forgive an old ape if I don't stand—bad back and all."

"Of course, sir."

Sabian motioned to a vacant seat in front of the desk, and Cornelius accepted.

"Let's talk about you, my boy," the holy ape started. "Your career, your aspirations, your skills and talents…"

"Very good, sir." *So it will be an interview, after all,* Cornelius mused. "You may ask anything you like."

"Oh, I have your permission, do I?" Sabian peered at his visitor.

"I, ah…" Cornelius flustered, "I only meant—"

"Of course you did." Sabian waved it off. "Of course." He picked up a scroll—one of many littering his desk. "I see you graduated from the academy in the ninetieth percentile—most impressive."

"Thank you, sir."

"Of course, your chosen field of expertise is a bit limited. Archeology I can understand—the unearthing of some great tomb, like that of the Unknown Ape. That is something I would love to see. But your focus is on prehistory." His tone went stern. "Why?"

"Well, sir," Cornelius replied, "I have always felt that in order to know where we are going, we must first know where—"

"There will be no room for radical theories in this administration," Sabian said.

"Sir?"

"I'll hear no talk of 'evolution.' Everything we need to know about the past"—the elder rested his claw on Zaius's set of *The Sacred Scrolls*—"is right here." Then he turned his back on Cornelius, looking out the window. "I hope that is clear."

Cornelius twitched his nose.

"Crystal, sir."

"Besides," the minister continued, "prehistoric archeology hardly fits what we need to do to keep the city running."

"Ah, running, sir?"

"Hmm, yes," Sabian said. "There will be budget cuts—extensive ones." He flipped through the loose scrolls on his desk. Picking one, he brought it closer to his eyes. "Tell me, where is this… Dr. Milo? Engineering, physics—he seems like an especially clever ape."

And one better suited for this position than me. Cornelius saw what Sabian was driving at, and knew it to be true. Milo was a genius ahead of his time, but Milo wasn't here and Cornelius was—because Zaius needed him to be.

He's out looking for a flying machine, old one, Cornelius mused. Yes, that would be well received. "I, uh, believe he is on an expedition," the chimpanzee said aloud. "With the academy's permission, of course."

"Of course," Sabian said. "Well, as soon as he returns, his travel permit is to be revoked. There will be no expeditions outside of Simia proper, not until the army returns triumphant. We can't have apes accidently shooting at apes." The elder scribbled something in squid ink. "It's a matter of public safety. Make it so."

When Cornelius nodded, Sabian handed him the scroll and continued.

"Now tell me, what else do I need to know?"

"I don't understand, sir."

"Let's cut to the chase, boy." Sabian again took up Cornelius's record. "What good are you to me?" His eyes were daggers. "Regardless of your council appointment, tell me why I need you at all, especially during a war."

"Ah, well, sir..." Cornelius hopped up from his seat. He trotted behind the minister's desk to look over his shoulder. "As you will see, I am an ape of many talents. If you look at my credentials..." He leaned over and pointed. "While my doctorate is in archeology, I also have a masters in psychology." While his heart would forever be digging in the past, those psychology classes were where he had met Zira.

"I could organize psychological examinations, to help our soldiers deal with battlefield stress." He became animated. "We can initiate a citizens' program to help their families cope with the war—"

"Excellent!" Sabian slammed his palm on the desk. "I want you in the human cages."

"Ah, excuse me, sir?" Cornelius didn't see where this was going. "That would be animal psychology. Perhaps my wife—"

"I want you there *with* your wife." Sabian waved a gnarled finger. "You will be my eyes and ears. Ursus has first pick of any humans he wants to use for war maneuvers, but since you and your mate were able to weed out our last talking human, I want you to see if you can find any more." The elder peered intently at the chimpanzee.

He's suspicious, Cornelius realized. *He wants to know if we're harboring enemies. Besides, putting me in the animal complex keeps me out of his fur, and makes it look as if he's doing me a favor by putting me with my wife.*

Sabian was indeed a clever ape.

"As you will, sir," Cornelius replied. "You can count on us."

"Get your paws off me, stinky ape!"

"What did you say?" Zaius had come to see his family before joining the army's foray into the Forbidden Zone. He had supped with his daughter Senia and shared an after-dinner pipe with his son-in-law Vitus. While he loved them all, it was his granddaughter Celia he had really come to see before marching off into the unknown. She held a special place in his heart.

While Vitus was Celia's father, her mother was Zaius's younger daughter, Valentina. When Valentina had died during childbirth, Vitus then married Senia so that Celia would still have a proper upbringing in the Zaius family. Senia, alas, was barren.

A local adjudicator, Vitus provided a good life in the far provinces. Their home was open and spacious, overlooking a pleasant glade, and Vitus was a godly ape, concerned with honor and family—both of which Zaius appreciated.

With Vitus reading in his study and Senia taking care of the washing, Zaius had retired to the fenced-in patio to have playtime with Celia. The little girl had built a fort out of the patio's cushions and filled it with toys. Deep in play, Celia said it again.

"Get your paws off me, stinky ape!"

"What did you say?" he asked again.

"Not you, Grandfather." Celia showed Zaius her human doll. A female with a bisque-fired clay head and arms, the doll's long raven locks were made with real human hair. "Starlight said it."

A human doll she calls Starlight. Zaius frowned. *A human doll she makes talk.*

"Celia," he said firmly, "humans cannot speak. They are dumb."

"But she can," Celia insisted. "She's special, like the human in the marketplace."

Marketplace? Zaius was astounded. She picked up a soldier doll and held him beside Starlight.

"That's why she wants his stinky hands off."

What is this? Zaius was becoming furious. *How does my granddaughter know anything about Taylor?*

"Listen here, Celia," he said as calmly as he could manage. "Humans cannot speak, and pretending they can is... is *dangerous*." He didn't know how else to express it.

She laughed and raised the doll.

"That's silly, Grandfather," she replied.

* * *

Zao's bones were white. Picked clean. The White Ones let no morsel go to waste. No sinew, or muscle—barely any of the orangutan's clothing—remained. In the end, Dinge had scooped out Zao's brains and devoured them. The others had wanted them, but had respected their brutish leader and kept their distance.

Mungwortt watched it all. Numbly, he gaped in shock and silence while these things *ate* his friend.

Finally, the creatures lounged, sated. They groomed one another, picking bits of flesh from their fur. Mungwortt noticed the dead White One's bones were stripped as well—they had attacked his corpse with the same abandon they had Zao's. Dinge rolled over for a nap, placing the orangutan's immaculate skull on the concrete floor. The skull's hollow eyes stared at Mungwortt, and he searched for meaning in that grim gaze.

The giant brains seemed to take no notice. Their tank lights blinked on and off in rapid succession, accompanying high-pitched beeps. Those beeps slowed, and Mungwortt began to hear their thoughts again. They were talking—thinking—about many strange things that made no sense to him.

Spread across the city as we are is becoming difficult. The gestalt mind is impossible unless the five of us are linked together. A proper gene splice could create a second heterogen that would serve to amplify our signals.

One that would serve only us.

Agreed then. The gorilla-chimp hybrid will be sent to Be-Six. Mungwortt's ears pricked up. They meant him! *Its DNA will be useful. Embed a message within the beast's mind. Be-Six will know what must be done.*

There was a prolonged *deet*, and as one, the White Ones

clambered to their feet and stood at attention, lining up in formation. Several of them marched to a small shed that was labeled with what looked like a stylized lightning bolt, underneath which a word was scrawled in grease pencil.

PROCESSING

The beasts unchained the double doors and swung them wide, revealing a staircase that disappeared into the ink of darkness.

Take the hybrid. Prepare it for processing. The two White Ones nearest him lifted him to his feet and dragged him toward the brains.

"Wait…" Mungwortt protested, and he struggled weakly. "I'll be good. Just don't—"

Steady him!

The White Ones held him tightly in grips he couldn't even begin to break. Mungwortt watched as the three brains swelled and pulsed in their jars, preparing to do… something.

Then there was a flutter. The lights, the constant mechanical hum, all *stuttered*. Power in the subterranean city blinked, and in their tanks, the glow illuminating the massive brains flickered.

Power outage in Sector 14, one of the brains thought. There was a long moment before the next communication. *Estimate repairs in two hours.*

Conservation protocol, another commanded. *Prepare for hibernation.* Before Mungwortt could guess at what that meant, the brains sank to the bottom of their tanks. And just like that, the White Ones were themselves again. Disoriented, the beasts loosened their grip on Mungwortt. Glancing around, he decided to take his chance. The gorilla-chimp hybrid slipped away from the White Ones and dashed for Zao's skeletal remains.

"Come on, Zao," he growled. "We are getting out of here."

Scooping up the orangutan's skull, he held it like a ball and turned to face a horde of angry White Ones. Dinge tried to tackle him, but Mungwortt was too fast. Weaving through the flailing fists of the furious forest of fur, he bolted for the only opening available—the double-doored shed with the yawning abyss.

"Shut up!" he yelled at the skull. "I don't see you having any bright ideas!" As Mungwortt leapt down the stairs, the White Ones that were chasing him…

Stopped.

Whatever lay that way, the beasts knew better than to risk it.

Celia cried loudly.

"Stop this, now," Zaius ordered his granddaughter as he rummaged through the patio pillows. "This is for your own good."

"Father!" Senia said, stepping onto the porch. "What are you doing?"

With the human doll called Starlight clutched tightly under his arm, Zaius was down on all fours, looking for any and all toys that were not simian.

"I don't want her playing with human dolls anymore," he said tersely.

"Nonsense." Senia chuckled and reached out for his hand. "Here, Father, let me—"

Standing away from the cushions with two more human dolls in hand, his eyes were embers of fire.

"I forbid it!"

His daughter snatched the two dolls from him. Celia was still crying.

"Is this why you came here?" Senia yelled. "To bully a little girl?"

"I came to see my family one last time before facing the unknown," he replied, "and to set them on the right course, should I not return."

She scooped up Celia and held her close. "She's not *your* daughter," she reminded Zaius.

"She is my granddaughter," he asserted. "And I still run this family."

"Do you?" Senia spat. "You run the Ministry of Science. You run around the Forbidden Zone chasing apostates and talking humans, but you do not run us."

Zaius gaped.

"So it is *you* who is filling her head with talking humans!" he accused.

"All of Simia is talking about it, Father," she said. "Not just the city, not just the provinces. Everywhere." Zaius crisscrossed the patio now, looking for anything to censor in order to protect his granddaughter. "It's not some great secret," Senia continued. "We're about to go to war over it! The human spoke aloud in a busy market full of farmers and traders from all corners of the land!"

Senia held out a hand, firmly demanding that he return Starlight.

"And no one believes the nonsense about that chimpanzee doctor making talking monsters—"

"Enough!" Zaius bellowed. "I will not have heresy spoken to me by my own daughter!" With that he dashed Starlight across the fence. The doll's fired pottery head and limbs smashed on impact, inciting new wails from Celia.

Senia fumed.

Zaius stood his ground.

"Apologize," she demanded. Moving to the patio's wicket gate with the crying Celia still in her arms, Siena swung it wide. "Or get out."

He waved her off. "Rubbish."

"Get…" Senia ground her teeth. "Out."

Zaius regarded his eldest daughter.

Coming here was a mistake.

"Very well." Zaius walked through the gate and into the road. Still in the gateway, Senia roared after him.

"I hope you find whatever it is you are looking for out there, Father—" He turned to face her. "—and stay there!"

The gate slammed shut.

Vitus appeared, rushing around the side of the house. Falling into step with his father-in-law, he tried to appease the older ape.

"I'll talk to her, sir, I—"

"No matter," Zaius growled. "You will have no more luck than I would, when I went to task with my beloved Ambrosine." Senia always had reminded Zaius of his departed wife. He harrumphed, then without losing stride, the minister waved his son-in-law off, as well. "Take care of them, Vitus."

Zaius made way for the stable where Aurelios and his wagon awaited.

It was a still a puzzle, but now, he had all the pieces. For the new starship Milo's team had discovered in the Forbidden Zone was just that—new. It hadn't been rusting underwater for months, nor had it lain on the desert floor, exposed to the elements.

No, it was newly crashed, and that was the problem, as well.

Engines had exploded. Banks of machinery were burnt out. Like the first space vessel at Dead Lake, the second one would never again fly.

Combining the two, however, might yield a different story. Fresh parts from the new ship could salvage the old. The prospect thrilled him.

Doctors Milo and Lykos labored to remove each of the components they needed to make Landon's ship right again. Those were transferred via horse-drawn cart, leaving the second ship—*Liberty 2*—a stripped shell gleaming in the desert air.

Returning to Dead Lake, the apes labored in shifts, resulting in activity around the clock. While some tended the camp or replaced errant tiles on the ship's surface, most were busy clearing space and building a stony pathway and ramp. With the proper amount of unobstructed ground on which to gain momentum, Milo was certain the spaceplane could catch the winds and take to the sky. He had done his calculations and instructed his team on the requisite length and width of the pathway.

Within the belly of the beast Milo, Lykos, and Pinchus worked to install the purloined parts into *Liberty 1*. It had proven to be an easier task than he had anticipated—the ship's machinery was designed to be easily removed and swapped out with replacement parts, no doubt in case of system error once the craft was in flight. The first thing they did was reconnect the ship's batteries and run a line from those to the cockpit controls. In this manner, they could test each device and be certain it was live before moving on to the next.

Mostly, they had success. The trick, Milo soon discovered, was making sure everything was dry. By trial and error they learned that any errant drop of water would short out a circuit board, and they'd have to start anew.

They were running out of circuit boards.

In fact, they were running out of a *lot* of things. Foremost in Milo's mind, they needed more tools. In practical terms, though, the expedition team had been in the Forbidden Zone much longer than originally anticipated, and consumables were running light. They had been able to make the water of Dead Lake drinkable, if not palatable, by boiling it and using cloth nets to catch the condensation left by its steam. Food, however, was another matter.

That, they were mere days from exhausting. Seraph had insisted that, lest they all starve, something be done—and soon. Milo had waved her off, consumed by science, doing his part by barely eating, thus extending the life of the supplies.

As Pinchus exited the craft to fetch the next component, Lykos reconnected the repaired bank of circuits that included the ship's chronometer.

The chronometer.

Milo hypothesized that it kept track of the starplane's time in space. He had a particular theory about time, as well. Years ago, he had imagined riding a horse in the night, carrying a torch and leading the way.

What if the horse, he postulated, *could gallop fast enough to catch up to the light that was illuminating their path?* As one approached the speed of that illumination, time would distend. While little time would pass for those doing the traveling, years would pass for the rest of existence. Though it was just a theory, if his hypothesis was correct this chronometer would be intended to keep track of such occurrences.

Milo adjusted the ship's flight controls, while Lykos plugged a repaired circuit board into its slot. Soon, a hum filled the chamber. Lights on the chronometer panel blinked on. Shaking with excitement, Milo saw a display appear. It was marked "Earth Time."

June 16 1973

There also was one designated "Ship Time."

November 25 3978

After a flash and a jumbling of numbers, they both read the same.

January 25 3979

Then, the panel exploded in sparks.

"What have you done?" A manic Milo shoved Lykos aside. He disconnected the battery feed and pulled the bank from its component bay, examining the fried circuit boards. He was met with acrid smoke.

There was a puddle of stagnant water in the computer compartment. Worse than that, the chronometer itself was aflame.

Ruined, he anguished.

The two of them smothered the fire.

"Dr. Lykos, this is inexcusable!" he railed. "This isn't some laboratory experiment that can simply be tried again. We get this wrong, and the opportunity of a lifetime is wasted. All of apekind—"

"Milo," Seraph snapped. The tinkerer shut up and turned to find her in the side doorway, silhouetted in the desert sun.

Milo, she had called him. Not *Dr. Milo.*

"We have the chronometer from the other ship," she reminded him. Her tone was adamant, her expression stern.

"Yes, yes, of course," Milo sighed. "Thank you, Dr. Seraph."

Milo turned back to his senior engineer. "Dr. Lykos, please be kind enough to fetch the replacement device. We will install it right away. Oh," he added, "and before you do, make certain all of that moisture has been removed, and there is no more lurking out of sight."

The chimpanzee nodded and scrambled past Seraph. She continued to stare at Milo. Though her superior, he began to wonder which one of them was really in charge.

"I know, Dr. Seraph. My reaction was deplorable. And aside from this"—he waved his hand over the uprooted technology that was scattered about the cabin—"you're correct in your earlier assessment. We are running out of supplies, and therefore time." What he didn't mention was that he had yet to decipher the starbird's launch codes.

Seraph smiled and put her hand on his shoulder. This time he did not flinch. Instead, he welcomed it. Milo needed her, and he knew it. Science had always come first. He never realized how important the relationships in his life were to him. Right now, he needed support. He needed friends. Friends with learned minds.

He put his hand on hers and nodded.

"I need you to perform a particularly important task for me."

"And that would be?" she queried.

Milo smiled.

CHAPTER 16
THE DISPOSITION OF AFFAIRS

With the morning, Cornelius went to the human cages.

In her new position at the Office of Animal Affairs, Zira had requested two dozen human subjects for psychological research. Commissioner Maximus had only sanctioned seven, and Cornelius was looking for particularly intelligent specimens. He watched as the guards wrangled up his first five choices and placed them in the wagon.

Then he was stunned. The last two he found couldn't be the smartest around, he surmised, because if they'd had any intelligence, they would have been long gone by now.

Brent and Nova.

It was all he could do to keep silent.

How is it that they managed to get caught so quickly?

Before he could retrieve them, however, he watched with alarm as a second wagon pulled up next to his. The army was there to take humans of its own.

"Twenty required on Number Two Range for O Company target practice," gorilla Sergeant Duignan shouted. "Jump to it!" Immediately his soldiers bullied their way through the remaining humans, herding them out of the cages and toward their wagon. A terrified Nova clung to Brent.

At least the new arrival from outer space had been smart enough to use his tattered clothing and cover up his bandaged gunshot wound. Looking closer, he noticed that Brent's eyes darted to and fro with alarming frequency. Cornelius wondered if all this was too much for the human.

His mind is unraveling, Cornelius reflected. *He's not cut from the same cloth as Taylor.* Then Nova glanced his way and shook her companion. Realizing they had seen him, Cornelius looked away, trying not to draw the guards' attention.

He coolly approached the gorillas. Pretending to notice the two humans for the first time, Cornelius spoke with what he hoped was authority.

"Stop a minute."

Not accustomed to taking orders from chimpanzees, the gorillas hesitated. Cornelius took the opportunity to approach Brent and Nova, checking them for peculiarities of anatomical interest. He fingered Brent's jawbone and cranium. Lifted Nova's eyelid. All the while, he muttered impressive gibberish.

"Brachycephalic and prognathous," he said. "Incipient glaucoma." Cornelius was no medical doctor, but he knew enough to make a good show of it. And the gorillas would be too stupid to know the difference. He narrowed his eyes and twitched his nose. "We could do with these two."

The sergeant repeated himself loudly.

"Required for human target practice on Number Two Range," Duignan said. "Captain Odo's orders."

"Yes, well"—Cornelius dripped ice—"required for cranial research by order of Dr. Zaius, Minister of Science." He turned to his own guards. "Load them up." The soldiers were agape as Brent and Nova were pushed into Cornelius's cart. They clearly didn't like being told what to do, and *especially* by a mere chimpanzee.

Zira would be proud. The thought gave him some glee. He would have to stay here, and let his driver take the wagon—with Brent and Nova in tow—back to the complex. Once they were caged there, his wife would find them and keep them protected until he and Zira could find a way to get them loose again.

It was the best he could do for now.

Fuming, Sergeant Duignan watched the wagon retreat down the road. His guards finished packing the remaining humans into the army wagon. They still were short the number they had been ordered to retrieve, and the gorilla didn't look happy about it.

As Cornelius went about his rounds, the sergeant signaled the wagon to head to the range. After a pause, Duignan mounted his horse and headed in the opposite direction—toward Ape City and the Animal Research Complex.

Brent and Nova were driven through the nine levels of hell. All around them bayonets stabbed at both straw and flesh-and-blood. Gorillas loaded cannons and whipped men and women for sport. Confused humans were placed on horses and sent galloping, only to be netted, tackled, trampled, and beaten.

Soldiers lined up to learn how to kill.

To the apes, men were nothing but animals. Gorilla soldiers laughed and exercised as their brethren maimed and murdered for real—all in the name of practice. Riding in the wagon cart with the other savages, Brent drank it all in. Blood beat in his ears.

He was on the brink. The night in the cages had been bad enough, but this threatened to unhinge him once and for all. Madness clawed at his brain, and as they neared the army encampment on the banks of Lake Ape, the savage Brent bore its fangs. If they took him and Nova out of the wagon, he wouldn't run.

He would kill.

Then the wagon bypassed the training grounds, and he realized exactly what had happened. Thanks to Cornelius, they were being driven to the Animal Research Complex. To Zira, and a chance to escape.

As the ghoulish scene retreated into the distance, so did the ghoul in Brent.

"So be it," Zaius decreed. Back in Ape City after having been gone not even half a day, he joined Ursus in the human holding cells. There they located a vacant veterinary office. It was unkempt and dingy, and it was the closest thing the doctor had to an office of his own.

"You know that my scruples were dictated by caution—not by cowardice."

"Of course," Ursus replied. The general looked around the room. The office was open and public—any number of veterinarians could overhear them.

Tactically unsound. Ursus didn't like it. "I recommend we discuss this further after service." Minister Sabian was scheduled to hold a ceremony that afternoon, to bless the army and its commanding officer.

"This afternoon, then." Zaius gathered his scrolls to leave.

"Very good, Doctor." Ursus smiled. "Very good." As the doctor left, an out-of-breath gorilla sergeant entered.

"General!" Duignan exclaimed.

"Sergeant," Ursus replied. "Why are you not at your post?"

Duignan pointed to the two humans down the hall. There, Dr. Zira was examining them. The sergeant told him what had happened at the cages.

Ursus was livid.

A chimpanzee dared to override my orders?

"What chimpanzee?" he demanded.

"His name was Cornelius."

As soon as the name fell from Duignan's lips, Ursus knew what to do. Looking over his shoulder, he waited until Zaius was entirely out of sight.

He doesn't need to be a part of this. The doctor's chimpanzee collaborators needed to be put in their place. Stalking down the hall, the general approached the upstart female from behind. As he did, her conversation with the guard became clear.

"It's been a long time since we've been able to study specimens of such extraordinary clinical interest." She indicated her operating room. "Bring them inside."

"No," Ursus commanded, and she jumped. "No, you can't have them."

You think you and your husband can override a gorilla's authority?

"They are marked for target practice." It was a matter of fact—there was no room for debate. The female said nothing, but the general took great pleasure in the disappointment on her face.

"Take them away."

The guard forced the two special humans down the hall.

For the second time that day, Ursus smiled.

As soon as Ursus had turned his back, Zira rushed after Brent and Nova. Outside the complex, their guard caged them in the back of a wagon destined for Number Two Range. As the gorilla finished locking the wagon door, Zira stepped forward.

"I'll take the key," she offered. Sick of dealing with animals, he turned it over to her before turning to address the wagon's driver.

"To the target range!" he commanded.

Without bothering to see the cart off, the guard returned to his duties. As the driver started to leave, Zira saw her chance.

"Uh, wait, wait!" she shouted to the driver. The driver stopped the wagon and looked back at her expectantly.

"I'd better double lock the door." Zira inserted the key and turned it around twice.

"Good luck," she whispered.

She called to the driver, "Alright!" Headed away from the city, the wagon made its way toward the forward encampments, and the human target range.

Zaius had missed Marcus's funeral. Chasing Taylor and the apostates into the Forbidden Zone had taken precedence, and the ceremony had been held in his absence. Marcus had been more than his security chief, however—he had been a dear friend whose loyalty was sorely missed.

Now, after his impromptu meeting with Ursus, the doctor arrived at the Marcus family home to offer his condolences in person. After a tap on the front door, the former chief's wife appeared.

"Malia," Zaius said. The last time he had been here, it was to deliver news of Marcus's death. He did not know how Malia would react to his return.

"Minister," she greeted him. "It is good to see you safe." Swaddled in her arms was Marcus's newest born. The only gorilla in ape history to have an orangutan name, Marcus had christened him after his friend.

"How is my namesake?" He offered baby Zaius his finger. It was readily grasped. "I see he has his father's strength!" The elder Zaius laughed. It was a proud compliment to offer any gorilla, and Malia could not contain a smile. After a moment, her grin became a grimace.

Before Zaius could ask what was wrong, a gawky soldier in an ill-fitting uniform pushed past her. His pants sagging and his sleeves bunched in his gloves, the young ape sported a fresh leather vest. The teen hefted a duffle bag, clearly too large for his frame.

"Excuse me," the youth said to her. Zaius didn't recognize him until she stepped aside.

Jaffe, he noted, *Marcus's eldest son.*

Noticing the orangutan elder for the first time, Jaffe's eyes were saucers.

"Minister Zaius!" The boy saluted. "I did not realize you had come to call, sir."

"What is this, son?" Zaius demanded.

Malia spoke for him. "Jaffe's joined the army."

"Nonsense," Zaius blinked. "You're still a boy."

As Jaffe fumed, his mother spoke. "The Security and Defense Declaration Act grants the commander-in-chief emergency powers." She sighed. "One of those allows him to lower the age limit, at his discretion."

Incredulous, the doctor nodded at Jaffe. "How old—?"

"Fourteen," the proud youngster exclaimed. "Sir!"

Zaius was stunned. Ursus was more than a warmonger. He was intent on sending children to the slaughter. No conscription service had been implemented to bolster his troops—because

Ursus didn't need one. Every able-bodied gorilla of age would be proud to serve during wartime, and now that included any boy who had ever played war.

Fourteen. Looking the gangly gorilla boy over, it was hard to accept that Jaffe was even that old. *His birthday was last month,* Zaius recalled. Were the child's father alive, Zaius knew he would not approve. Marcus wanted his son to grow up to become part of the police force, or better yet, a professional hunter.

Every gorilla's dream.

Alas, with Marcus dead, Jaffe was the ape of the house—the decision was his to make. The orangutan knew it wasn't his place to tell the boy no.

Instead, he simply asked, "Why?"

"Forgive me, Minister," Jaffe replied, "but you of all apes know humans are rabid animals. They steal our food!" The boy was clearly tired of articulating himself—his mother had likely questioned him for hours. "The general is going to find their nest and wipe them out." He stood at attention, his chin held high. "He's going to put fruit back on our tables."

Mentally, Zaius agreed that humans were dangerous. As far as he was concerned, they deserved extermination.

Just not by children, he lamented. He looked to Malia's eyes for permission to intervene. He was answered with sad sepia pools of resignation. Zaius understood. *There will be no reasoning with the boy.*

"Minister, Mother." Jaffe excused himself. His pack slung, he headed up the street.

"Oh..." He turned and addressed them one last time. "For Father's death"—he beat his chest—"they should all die."

Zaius had no words. Malia stepped outside and stood beside

the doctor. Together they watched the boy meet up with a group of others his age, also newly recruited to Ursus's army. Without taking his eyes off of Jaffe, Zaius spoke first.

"I am going into the Forbidden Zone with Ursus, Malia." She continued to stare after her son. Zaius reached out for her hand. "I will keep an eye on the boy," he promised.

After a moment, Malia let him take it. She squeezed before he could. Then, as Jaffe and his cohorts disappeared into the throngs of Ape City, Malia silently withdrew.

His heart heavy, Zaius headed back to work.

CHAPTER 17
THEATER OF WAR

Groom Lake, Nevada
Area 51
1966

"Code Red," the public address system blared. "Evacuate Section A7."

Adjacent to the big hangar and across the airfield from commissary, the entrance to the deep bunker burst open and dozens of techs in lab coats spilled out through its doors. Deep bunker A7 was where all the top secret stuff happened at Groom Lake.

Major Taylor grabbed a panicked scientist from the stampede.

"What the hell is going on, Stanton?"

With Hasslein in DC, meeting with the Department of Defense, Stanton was the one running the show here—yet he was one of the first out of the bunker when the shit hit the fan.

So much for going down with the sinking ship.

Desperate to escape the area, Stanton barely composed himself enough to reply.

"That's restricted—"

"Answer. Me," Taylor snarled. "Now."

"Churchdoor," Stanton mumbled. "We were moving a prototype."

"...and?" Taylor demanded.

"And it dropped!" Stanton sputtered.

Disgusted, Taylor let go. As Stanton made for the airfield, Taylor turned. Stewart, Rowark, and Dodge had come up behind him. Rumors of "Churchdoor" had been all over the base, and the two astronauts had overheard Stanton's revelation.

All were thinking the same thing.

Prototype of what?

"This is not a drill," the PA droned. "This facility will lock down in ten seconds." People were climbing over each other to get out of the bunker, and men were being trampled in the doorway. In ten seconds the containment doors would roll down and crush anyone still trapped there.

"Come on!" he growled. Rowark and Stewart rushed to the bunker and waded their way into the oncoming torrent. Taylor and Dodge pushed people away from the downtrodden, enabling their teammates to pull the wounded to safety.

Klaxons wailed. Pulling the last man out of harm's way, Rowark bellowed.

"Time's up, Taylor!"

Taylor knew what that meant, and made sure he was clear of the doorway. Stewart did not.

"Just a few more seconds!" she shouted. Two more technicians raced toward the exit. Stewart stood in the doorway, urging the newcomers forward.

"Let's go, gentlemen!"

"George!" Rowark roared. Taylor grabbed Stewart by her shirt and jerked her close to him just as the metal slabs slammed into place. Mashed against him in his arms, she stared up at him.

"Major?" she muttered.

A muffled thumping broke their attention: someone was pounding on the shielded doors—from the inside. The two techs hadn't made it. Taylor and Stewart stared long and hard at the sealed doorway. Rowark and Dodge joined them.

After a few minutes, the banging stopped.

Taylor cleared his throat. "You have medical training, right?" he asked Stewart. She nodded. Across the field, the other astronauts were coming out of the commissary.

"Get them to help, too," he added.

As Taylor, Dodge, Rowark, and Stewart moved off to assist the evacuees, Taylor growled deep in his chest.

Just what the hell is Churchdoor?

It had been days. Taylor had told Messias about the crash, Ape City, Zira and Cornelius, Dr. Zaius, and of course, Nova. He explained how he needed Messias's help to get her back. All he would need would be a squad of sentinels and some kind of vehicle to get them across the desert fast. He would collect Nova, any peaceful apes who wanted to join them, and return to the city.

Messias would never need to be alone again.

The hybrid child had seemed to like this idea—at first. Yet he dragged his heels, telling Taylor that he needed to gather reports from the worker sentinels to determine how many he could spare and still keep the city safe. The creatures were outside, the boy had insisted, ready to strike anyone who left.

Look as he might, Taylor could find no evidence of any siege, no armies waiting outside the gates.

After that, the tours of the city stopped. Mostly Messias had "other things" that he needed to do. Taylor looked around on his own, but the sentinels kept most of the city on lockdown, inaccessible without Messias to override them. The boy still stopped by Taylor's quarters and asked him more about the outside world, but whenever Taylor pressed him for progress, the reply would always be the same.

"I am still aggregating data."

Taylor became aware that Messias was keeping something from him, holding the astronaut here so he could learn all about the outside world, and live vicariously through him. He wasn't going to have it.

Genius or not, Messias was a child. If Taylor had to tan his behind to teach the boy a lesson, so be it. He showered, dressed, and examined his own face in the bathroom mirror, rubbing his jaw. His stubble was growing in.

He reached for the razor he had found in the cabinet. Uncannily, everything he needed seemed to be available in the deserted city. He hesitated.

Nova.

Taylor dropped the razor in the sink.

It was time for some answers, so he made his way to the grand hall. As he stalked down the corridor, however, he heard something. Almost like…

…talking.

Picking up his pace, he entered the grand audience chamber, and saw that it was Messias—and he was standing with someone, bathed in the sepias and oranges of the rising sun. The timid light from the bay windows cast long shadows from each of the many columns that lined the hall. Pulling to a stop, Taylor used those shadows to spy on them.

The man wore clothes similar to those of the boy, but was hooded. He had his back to the entrance, and the two were nodding, their heads low. Flanked by two hovering green-faced sentinels, it almost looked as if they were praying. Taylor slid from column to column, creeping ever so close.

He heard that strange something again, soft but distinct. He couldn't place its source, as it seemed to be coming from all around. The closer he got to the two figures, the louder it was.

Deet-deet.

Deet.

It wasn't recognizable speech, though. It was bursts of tone that somehow *resembled* words. Taylor slipped behind the column closest to the two humans and two bots. Moving quickly, he swung around the pillar to find—

Messias and the drones. Alone. Taylor blinked, looking around the bots.

"Where is he?" he growled.

"Where is who?" There was no one behind the drones. They were alone.

"I saw him." Taylor was confused. "You were praying—standing here with—"

"It's a mistake," the boy said quickly. "I was programming the sentinels. There was no one else here." Taylor hesitated. He'd heard that insistent beeping—something clearly more akin to machines than living beings. Could he have imagined the other person?

"Alright," he conceded. "Maybe I did imagine it." He smiled at the boy, and decided that it was time to press the issue, once and for all. "Messias, we need to go after Nova. It's been—"

"Stop, stop, *stop*." Pulling at his own hair and pacing, Messias lost his composure. Taylor was stunned speechless. The young scientist was now gone, leaving in his stead a spoiled child throwing a tantrum.

Pulling up what he could from his time as a father—although admittedly not a very good one—Taylor took the tone he used with his daughters when they didn't get their way. Dominant but reassuring.

"Calm down," he said. "It's very simple. I'm going after her, with or without—"

"No!" the half-breed child screeched. "I don't want to hear it!" Then he glared at the astronaut. "You were spying on me! Weren't you?"

Taylor remained firm but rational.

"I heard a sound, Messias," he said. "I looked into it. I just wanted some answers—I *deserve* some answers. Surely you see it. I need to understand what is going on here."

The manic child stopped cold.

"Threat," he said.

The two drones sprung to life, their angry faceplates turning blood red. The astronaut ducked as a clawed tentacle whooshed past his head. Sizing up his adversaries while on the move, Taylor was desperate to find a weak spot. He balled his fist and swung for the bot's mechanical eye.

The only result was a set of bruised knuckles. Then in an instant they had him.

"Let me go, goddamn it!" he gritted. "Messias, I am *not* your enemy!"

"Aren't you?"

The bots pushed Taylor to his knees, his eyes level with the boy's.

"You don't trust me," Messias rationalized as he paced back

and forth, holding a single digit aloft. "That means I can't trust you," he concluded.

Taylor struggled against the sentinels, but their strength was absolute.

"I've told you the truth from the begin—"

The boy scoffed. "An astronaut from the past. Who are you *really*? Why are you really here?"

Taylor despaired, then despair turned to anger. *No one in this godforsaken future believes a single thing I say. Not Zaius, not Cornelius, and now not Messias.*

The boy smiled. "Tell me, Mr. Taylor, do you fear God?"

That took him aback. Messias hadn't mentioned anything about worship the entire time they had been there. He'd been under the impression the boy's philosophy was one of pure science.

"Whose god?" Taylor questioned.

"Mine." Messias's face grew grim. "Let's see what secrets you are keeping from me."

"You little—"

The hybrid looked up at the bots and muttered a word.

"Psychedrome." The sentinels whirled, dragging Taylor with them like a sack of potatoes.

"Where are you taking me?" he yelled.

What the hell is a psychedrome?

The service was underway, and Reverend Minister Sabian, Pontifex Rex was officiating. While he had humbly asked to simply be called minister, in fact he had decreed himself a title which held more than a modicum of pomp and circumstance.

"Oh, God," Minister Sabian preached with drama, dressed in

full regalia, "bless, we pray You, our great army and its supreme commander on the eve of a holy war, undertaken for Your sake, grant, in the name of Your Prophet, our great Lawgiver, that we—"

His eyes darted to and fro, daring someone to interrupt. When no one did, the never-ending litany plowed on,

"—Your chosen servants, created and born in Your divine image, may aspire the more perfectly to that spiritual Godliness and bodily beauty which You, in Your infinite mercy, have thought fit to deny to our brutish enemies!"

It was dogma. It was also the longest sentence Zaius had ever endured. Of that he was certain. Personally, he was embarrassed, and more than a bit worried. He stole a glance at Ursus, curious as to what his response would be.

The general was succinct.

"So be it."

Mungwortt had not been followed. He could see why. The shed tunnel was different. It was dank and stank of defecation and decay. Unlike the tunnels they had followed to get to the underground city, this one wasn't just another long, abandoned passageway. Something *lived* here. Whatever it was, the White Ones wanted to avoid it.

After walking for a good half an hour, Mungwortt looked to Zao's skull for guidance.

"I get it," he said. "Either we go forward or we go back." Mungwortt thought about that. Behind them were the White Ones. With the giant brains asleep, nothing would keep them from eating him, just as they had eaten Zao. No, the unknown was a better option than certain death.

"You're right," he told the skull. The half-breed nodded toward a half-open doorway that appeared at the end of the tunnel. "Maybe we'll be safe this way."

The skull stared back.

Mungwortt was glad for the company. Never mind that Zao was as cranky as ever. At least he wasn't alone as he stepped out of the tunnel and into a dimly lit, smooth-walled chamber. Across from the door, set into recesses in the wall, he saw a series of bulbous glass jars. Most of them were murky. Many were smashed, some were empty.

Five were intact.

Floating inside each of these was a single fetus. The first two bobbed on their sides toward the tops of their tanks. Tapping Zao on the glass, he allowed the skull to get a closer look. The third jar was thick with a black fluid that Mungwortt could only guess must be blood.

The contents of the fourth and fifth jars, however, were alive. Connected to some hidden machinery, the liquid within the vessels bubbled and frothed. In one was an unborn with two additional heads. To Mungwortt it looked like three angry creatures had been squished together and were trying to pry themselves apart.

The final jar held what appeared to be a healthy simian fetus. Mungwortt knew what an ape fetus looked like—he had served as a city gravedigger for many years. A failed pregnancy in ape culture was always afforded full burial rites, and he had often stolen a glance at the contents of a casket. Mesmerized, he watched the little simian sway in the gelatinous syrup that suspended it. Mungwortt shook his head.

This isn't how babies are made, he thought. *Who puts babies inside jars?*

Zao broke his concentration. Begrudgingly, Mungwortt complied. He pushed past the narrow corridor of jars and into the widening hall. It was a laboratory of some kind. Surgical. It was a lot like Dr. Galen's private veterinary practice—a place where the doctor had done animal experimentation of his own. Grisly things had gone on there—the heads of humans surgically removed while they still lived, the grafting of limbs and other organs onto animals that didn't need them—all in the name of science.

This place was like that, but alien. And deserted. Instead of organic shapes and earth tones, everything was angular, gray, and tiled. There were cages built into the chapped walls. Large animal pens, dark and putrid. They stank.

The cells were set into the wall two high and four abreast. Most of them had full cage doors, but some were bent outward and twisted, as if something powerful had attacked the bars from the inside. The table in the center of the room was a long-forgotten concrete slab, stained so that its center and sides were a relentless coppery brown.

What little light there was filtered down from the ceiling, which consisted of large wooden planks with gaps in their spacing. A soft glow, however, radiated from one of the upper holding cells. The stench of it was overwhelming. A tentative Mungwortt crept up to peer inside.

He gasped.

Mungwortt himself had seen plenty of dead bodies in his lifetime, and plenty of maggots eating them. The creature in the pen looked like an ape, albeit a malformed one. Its face was a mangled twist with uneven eyes set in a misshapen skull. Its asymmetrical jaw displayed a massive overbite. Its torso was splayed wide, the ghostly glow emanating from within it. Its incandescent innards seethed and churned, a mass of wriggling gore.

Maggots.

Irradiated ones. Luckily, the beast they were consuming was quite dead. Mungwortt swallowed bile. He covered Zao's eye sockets, better to save the old skull from the sight of such horror. After a pause he noticed that the skull could still see through the crack between his fingers.

"Sorry," he said. Then he cautiously examined the other pens nearest him. One held nothing but bones.

The next one, however, had the desiccated remains of what he could only guess was once human. Its face and forehead had sunken eye sockets, too many to be considered normal on any creature. Its cracked and dusty skin was pulled taut over skeletal remains.

"Well," Mungwortt began, "I could be wor—"

Zao shushed him.

Mungwortt froze.

After a moment, he whispered, "I don't hear any—"

But then he did. There was a sound coming from the recesses of the furthest pen. Sealed, it was one of the ones he hadn't yet explored. The door was solid, with only a small grate, so he couldn't see in. The sound was…

…whimpering.

As a child, Mungwortt never had a pet, but he was a garbage ape. As such, he'd had to keep wild animals out of the refuse he collected. The mewling reminded him of a sick raccoon. Placing Zao on the table in the room's center, the gorilla-chimp made soft chittering sounds, like those the other children would make to call their pets home. He unlatched the gate on the pen and swung it open, ever so slowly.

Zao had something to say about that.

"I know what I'm doing!" Mungwortt growled. "I'm showing him that I'm a friend." He glanced back over his shoulder at the frowning skull. "Unless you think you can do bet—"

A bubbling roar erupted. Mungwortt slammed into the floor, smashing his nose on the concrete.

"Oh, God," he cried.

The thing in the darkness was on him. Whatever it was, it was no raccoon. Powerful fists pummeled his back. Mungwortt didn't know what was attacking him, but it was big and mean. He rolled between blows, tucked his legs up and kicked hard. His boots caught the creature in the chest and sent it reeling.

Mungwortt tried for a better look at the thing. The monster had the upper body of an adult gorilla, but its lower torso was another thing. It had none. Legless, the beast's digestive tract lay exposed where its belly should be.

Clambering back up onto its two muscular arms, the thing dragged its entrails around the laboratory as it sized up its prey. Its mottled and burnt skin was mostly hairless, save for a few scraggly patches here and there. It looked as if its skull had never fully formed, its swollen brain only partially enclosed within the deformed receptacle and barely covered by a thin layer of leathery epidermis. Worst of all was its face. While its jaw was simian, its nose and milky white eyes were distinctly human.

The thing was an abomination.

It gurgled again and lunged at him.

"Wait a minute, wait a minute!" Mungwortt lodged his forearm in the creature's jaws—anything to keep it from going for his throat. Its fangs sank into Mungwortt's soft flesh. He gazed into the thing's clouded eyes.

Then Mungwortt heard—no, *felt*—screaming. Felt a scratching in his head—inside his skull. The abomination reached into his mind and *squeezed.* His nose and ears became warm and sticky. As the wet trickled to his chapped lips, Mungwortt licked them.

Blood.

Pushing backward with the creature still clamped on his arm and still in his head, Mungwortt slammed into the table. Zao clattered to the floor next to his free hand. With Mungwortt's help, the orangutan skull made his move. Raised up high, Zao crashed down on the creature's misshapen head. It yelped as the skull smashed into its soft cerebral issue.

The mental connection stopped.

Zao showed no mercy. Again and again he bashed into the abomination's brains until it lay twitching in the corner.

Horrified at his normally civilized friend's sudden savagery, Mungwortt gathered some rags from the corner and fashioned a bag. He put the orangutan's head into it, and headed for the next room. He was thankful Zao had saved his life, but felt the skull had gone a little too far.

It had become unhinged. Better not to talk about what had happened, though. Better to give Zao a moment to regain his composure.

Mungwortt steeled his resolve. Whatever lay beyond the next door, it had to be better than this.

CHAPTER 18
PER ASPERA AD ASTRA

ANSA Launch Operations Center
Cape Kennedy, Florida
1967

The giant ANSA Stratofortress lumbered along the sky at 50,000 feet. The huge B-52 carried a considerable payload. Tucked under one wing like an obscenely large missile was a dart-shaped spacecraft affixed to the front of a very large booster rocket. That rocket would take the "Dyna-Soar" craft to orbit.

Designated Probe Seven, she was one of the smaller models of spacecraft Taylor had seen in the big hangar at Groom Lake. Sitting abreast in her cramped cockpit were three astronauts—Majors George Taylor, Edward Rowark, and Alan Virdon. Farm-raised in Jackson County, Texas, Virdon had lived in Florida for most of his adult life. A fair and caring man who believed in equality, he found himself torn between his family and his country. Virdon avoided the topic of secession, and for that Taylor respected him.

Excited as they were, the three men tried to ignore the fact that the large booster to which they were strapped was actually a modified intercontinental ballistic missile. The Minuteman ICBM was a cost-cutting measure that Stanton had cooked up.

If there's one thing we have plenty of, *Taylor scoffed,* it's missiles.

A few months after NASA had suffered the loss of Apollo 1, *the civilian space program continued with the unmanned* Apollo 4. *What the public didn't know was that there still was an* Apollo 2 *and* 3, *and they had fallen under the umbrella of ANSA. One of the two agencies was going to land on the moon, and Capitol Hill hadn't yet decided which one.*

The space race was in-house, as well.

Apollo 2 *had gone off without a hitch. Probe Six had orbited the planet for three days while testing various sensors and tracking devices. She had quietly deployed a spy satellite over communist airspace before gliding home and being snatched out of the air by the Stratofortress. She had been crewed by Commander William Hudson and Lieutenants Maryann Stewart and Judy Franklin—all three transfers from NASA. That flight had made Stewart and Franklin the first American women in space—though the public records didn't acknowledge it.*

The ANSA Apollo missions were top secret—the masses didn't know, and they didn't need to know.

At her flight ceiling now, the massive B-52 leveled off. Aboard Apollo 3, *Taylor, Virdon, and Rowark made final preparations. Their mission was simply to orbit the planet, but at speeds man had yet to achieve. While Taylor and the others prepped in Probe Seven, Maddox and Hasslein ran mission control from the Stratofortress.*

"Major Taylor," Hasslein sent as a typed message, "switch to a private channel, please." A frustrated Taylor punched it in.

Don't tell me we're going to have to abort, *he thought.*

"Go ahead, Doctor."

"Allow me to be the bearer of good news," Hasslein said. "As of one hour, fifteen minutes ago you are the father of a baby girl. Congratulations."

Taylor beamed. While Gillian's time was near, he'd had no idea she had gone into labor.

"My wife?" he asked.

"Recovering well." Hasslein continued, "Colonel Lazenbe wanted me to extend his well wishes and tell you that upon completion of this mission you are officially on family leave."

A daughter. Gillian had gotten pregnant almost immediately after they were married. Taylor had wanted to name the child after Joe Tagliante, Rowark's wingman from the war. He had been so certain it was going to be a boy they hadn't even considered girl names.

"Thank you, Doctor." Taylor switched channels.

Rowark and Virdon looked at him expectantly. Taylor simply looked to the blue skies ahead. Virdon broke first.

"Well?" he asked.

Taylor's crooked smile crept in. "How does a girl named Jo grab you?"

Congratulations all around, the men smiled and laughed. On the radio, Maddox chimed in.

"Just don't ask me to babysit."

"As soon as we land," Rowark asserted, "cigars and drinks are on me."

"Can't argue with that." Taylor could use a good stogie about now.

Next time, he decided, I'll stash one aboard. He was certain the brass would love that.

"My board is green, George," Maddox signaled from the plane's command cabin. "You are good for launch."

"Copy that, Motherbird," Taylor responded. He nodded to Rowark.

"Launch sequence primed. Booster function nominal," Rowark announced. "Stand by for the burn."

Three seconds later Apollo 3 *disengaged from the Stratofortress. Taylor, Virdon, and Rowark were thrown back in their seats. Falling some twenty feet before her ICBM booster kicked in, Probe Seven soared toward outer space.*

As the third stage rocket fell away, Probe Seven and her experimental payload fell into a lazy circle around the planet.

"Orbit achieved," Virdon said, and he smiled. Loose items in the cockpit drifted past. Weightless, the astronauts were held in their seats by their harness belts.

"You are a little out of sync, Apollo 3*," Mission Control said. "Sending you new coordinates."*

"Four plus oh-seven-niner. Course corrections input," Virdon said.

"Thrusters firing," Rowark reported.

As Probe Seven spun on her axis, Taylor drank it in. The black void stretched above them, the teal of the Earth below. On the curved horizon lay a band of azure, the sky itself. Up above the world so high, George felt peace. Serenity—but he wasn't here to sightsee. He was here to break some speed records.

And then home to my wife and daughter, *he mused. Family hadn't meant that much to him until he had one of his own.* Maybe there's something here worth living for, after all, *he reflected.*

"Ready to engage the GDM drive, Motherbird*."*

"Acknowledged, Apollo 3*," Maddox replied.*

With the pull of a lever, the "warhead" housing of the ICBM broke away to reveal her secret cargo. A sleek cylindrical tube attached to her stern, the Gas Dynamic Mirror fusion drive system was a first step toward achieving Hasslein's ultimate goal—photon propulsion. If the GDM worked, ANSA would leave the moon to NASA. They would instead use the GDM drive to go to Mars and Jupiter—and Hasslein would have the data he needed to make interstellar travel a reality.

"Plasma is primed," Virdon reported. As the energies inside the reactor heated up, the exhaust nozzle at the end of the GDM opened. Magnetic tapes whirled in the cockpit as the computer made its final calculations.

"Temperature nominal," Rowark reported. "GDM is go."

"Begin ignition countdown," Taylor ordered. "Visors down." The three men closed the faceplates on their helmets. Each of them activated his own independent air supply.

*"*Motherbird*, we are go." The Roman god Apollo lifted his bow and shot an arrow across the stars. That arrow was Probe Seven. Sizzling between two mirrors, ionized gas spewed from her exhaust. Her fusion reactor blazed.*

The ship shook as gravity grappled with them. Strapped to their command chairs, the three astronauts spun around the world. The Earth lay far beneath their feet.

"That's .00037 speed of light!" Virdon announced enthusiastically. While the number was only a fraction of Hasslein's goal, it was still thirteen times faster than anything man had ever flown—in space or otherwise. Previous missions had orbited the planet once every hour and a half. At this rate, Probe Seven was doing it every seven minutes.

"Well done, Apollo 3*," Hasslein radioed. "That's enough for today. You may disengage GDM drive."*

"Roger that, Motherbird*," Taylor complied.*

"George," Rowark said. "We have a drive malfunction."

"What is it?"

"The baffle plates—they're stuck in the open position."

Taylor turned to Virdon. "Can we shut the reactor down?"

"Stand by." Virdon punched the shutdown sequence into the

computer. "Program is not responding." The drive wouldn't disengage.

"Motherbird," *Taylor said, "we have a problem."*

Long moments passed while back on the Stratofortress Hasslein and Maddox conferred with their brain trust. When they finally came back on, all three pilots jumped.

"Listen carefully, George," Maddox said. "You need to eject the GDM."

"You want us to throw away our engine," Taylor said. "While we are at speed?"

"Apollo 3," *Dr. Hasslein again. "There is a considerable risk. However, if you do not—"*

Taylor cut him off. "Understood, Motherbird."

As Maddox and Hasslein fed them the computer codes, and they prepared to act, Taylor looked to both Virdon and Rowark.

"Gentlemen," he said, "if you have any last words, now's the time." After a wordless pause, they nodded, and all three men braced themselves.

"Alright. Running drive ejection sequence." Taylor punched the command into the controls and counted down. "Three... two... one..." All three astronauts closed their eyes.

"Eject!"

Nothing happened. Probe Seven continued to spiral around the world. Taylor entered the code again, but still there was no change.

"Negative response, Motherbird."

"We are checking it, Apollo 3," *Maddox said. "Stand by."*

When the radio squawked to life again, this time it was Dr. Hasslein.

"Apollo 3," *he said, "you are going to have to open the secondary bypass and pull the release manually." As Hasslein talked him through it, Rowark unbuckled himself and climbed behind the command chairs. He soon had the access panel open.*

"I can't see inside," he said. "Stand by." No matter how he tried, his helmet got in the way. "The hell with this." Rowark removed his helmet and stuck his head inside.

"Yeah," he confirmed, "I see it." As instructed, he reached behind the bulkhead and tried to turn the mechanism clockwise. It wouldn't budge. "I need some help here."

"Take command," Taylor told Virdon. Turning over the controls, he unbuckled himself, removed his own helmet, and slid in next to his friend. Rowark's helmet floated past. Taylor dug his arm in deep. "I got it." Together they rotated the device until it locked into place. Then they cranked the release lever into position.

"Brace yourselves!" Taylor ordered. Low to the cabin floor, he looked at Rowark and nodded. Taking hold, Rowark pulled.

No effect.

"Let me do it," Taylor demanded.

There was still nothing. The two men managed to grab the lever together, but at the angle of the access port they had no leverage.

"No good, Motherbird,*" Virdon said. "She's still stuck."*

"Disengage the clamp at junction C," Hasslein suggested. "That should release the pressure."

Why the hell did all this have to be so damned complicated? *Taylor wondered with growing anger. "Alan," he ordered. "It's going to take all three of us."*

Pulling his harness off, Virdon began to float out of his seat. As he did, a frustrated Rowark yanked hard one last time.

The lever clicked.

Outside, explosive bolts blew. Traveling at fantastic speeds, the command capsule was thrown clear. While the GDM barreled on its course, Probe Seven somersaulted across the sky.

Unbuckled, gravity crushed the men within. Taylor, Alan, and Eddie were hurled against the controls. Bashed against one another. Probe Seven plummeted to Earth, her pilots an angry tangle of limbs.

His forehead slick with blood, red lights danced on Taylor's eyelids.

An angry god, Apollo plucked his arrow from the sky and hurled it into the sea.

Taylor awoke to banging. At least, it sounded that way to him.

It was a tapping, really. A space-suited man loomed over him, tapping on his faceplate. Seeing Taylor's eyes flutter, the man pressed their faceplates together and glared at him. With their helmets touching, the glass would carry voices.

"George!" the man shouted. "Can you hear me? Are you alright?"

Taylor blinked. His shoulder was sore—that damn World War II injury—and his head was fuzzy. Made it hard to think. There was dried blood on the side of his face, and he was nauseous—it felt to him as if the whole room was bobbing up and down.

Virdon, *he realized.* I'm talking to Alan Virdon.

"I may have a concussion," he confessed.

"Hang on," Virdon assured him, "help is coming."

The men sat in a dark cloud, punctuated only by the lights on their suits. Taylor heard a clanking sound, and realized that Virdon was trying to release the hatch.

"Still jammed," he said loudly.

"Where are we?" Taylor muttered. He was strapped to a chair and his helmet was back on.

"Probe Seven, Apollo 3 *mission," Virdon said. "Capsule's in the water, we're waiting for pickup."*

Waves. *Taylor realized why he felt like they were swaying to and fro—they were. He didn't know how much longer he could stay awake.*

"Why is it so murky in here—?" Taylor began to ask, but answered himself.

Smoke. *There must have been a fire, something behind the walls. The entire cabin was filled with smoke.* If we hadn't had our space suits on…

Taylor's eyes grew wide. "Eddie?"

Alan just replied, "No."

Then the thumping of helicopter blades shook the wounded ship. Something clanged hard on the hull, and the hatch cranked open. As light filled the cockpit, the smoke raced for the egress, leaving only a gray haze behind. Someone was shouting at him. He thought it might be Alan again.

It was something important.

It was about staying awake.

As darkness claimed him, Taylor saw his friend, helmetless and slumped in his seat beside him.

"Goddamn it, Eddie."

Taylor was a prisoner of the psychedrome. Located deep in the bowels of the gleaming city, the spheroid auditorium was cavernous. As large as it was, the chamber was spartan. Only a small rail-less catwalk extended to the center of the sphere. At its terminus sat an angled table.

Strapped to the table was ANSA astronaut and Air Force Colonel George Taylor.

Psychedelic lights strobed and sublime voices crashed against the room's mirrored walls. Voices chanted—

> *"A good person always says yes.*
> *A good person never stops anything.*
> *A good person likes everything that happens.*
> *It is good to be a good person."*

—and then started over again.

He had been under restraint for hours. Now a cloaked figure made his way down the catwalk toward him, his cloak sweeping the floor as he walked. Abruptly, the chanting ceased.

"Messias," Taylor spoke softly but firmly. "Get me off of this—"

"I am not Messias," the visitor said.

The voice was definitely wrong. It was throaty, earthen. Taylor strained to get a look at the hooded stranger. He was much taller than the boy. Taller than Taylor, even. His robes were highlighted by a scarlet vest, his features buried in the deep shadows of his cloak.

The man I saw Messias talking to?

"Who the hell are you?"

"I am the Keeper of the Light." The cloaked man glided around the table. "You will answer my questions."

Taylor signed and settled in. "Taylor, George. Colonel. American National Space Administration. Service number 0109047818—"

The keeper leaned in, eyes peeking out from behind the heavy hood. Those eyes, however, were on prehensile stalks. There were many of them. Too many. Whatever he was, this thing was no human, ape, or hybrid. It was hideous.

"You will comply." The Keeper ground his words at him. "This Nova person. She means a lot to you."

"Nova?" Taylor looked away. He didn't want to see what else lay beneath those robes.

"Is she your superior?"

"My what?" That made Taylor look again, and the Keeper had his back to the table.

"Do you report to her?"

The line of questioning was ludicrous. An eyestalk slithered out from the hood and peered over the Keeper's shoulder.

"What the hell *are* you?" Taylor demanded.

"Forgive me," it said. The Keeper nodded once. Taylor's body hair stood on end. Then electricity arced through his bones. His nerves simmered and singed.

"Where are you *really* from?" the Keeper demanded. "Another city? Another continent?" The thing was all eyes, writhing and twisting underneath its cloak. It leaned closer. "Another planet?"

The voices began to chant anew.

A good person always says yes.

The smell of burning flesh filled his nostrils. It was his own. Lightning leapt through Taylor's teeth and into his spine. It felt as if his brain was beginning to bake in his skull.

A good person never stops anything.

"Go to hell!" Taylor bellowed. It turned into a shriek. Endorphins flowed and adrenaline pumped. He hadn't survived the Forbidden Zone just to be electrocuted here.

A good person likes everything that happens.

He jerked his shackles, hard. With a yank and a twist, Taylor ground bone against metal, and he howled. Then his wrist snapped with the wet crunch of fresh celery. That enabled him to slip free of the shackle.

"Stop!" the Keeper commanded. "What are you doing?"

It is good to be a good person.

Ignoring his limp wrist, the astronaut tore at the Keeper's cloak. The robes flowed past him and fluttered to the bottom of the sphere. As the cloth crossed Taylor's face, the world changed.

Beneath the cloak was no alien monstrosity.

Beneath it was Messias.

The walls of the psychedrome were no longer mirrored, but rather were smooth and opaque. There were no restraints, and the table that had held him was now a bed.

Before Taylor could react, Messias spoke.

"Are you feeling better?" he asked.

"Messias!" Taylor was woozy. Disoriented. "What in the hell—"

"You got real sick," the boy interjected. "Radiation poisoning. Probably wandered into a radioactive storm in the Forbidden Zone. I had to bring you here for treatment. The psychedrome cleared the radiation from your system. You had a high fever, but I think it broke."

"I feel fine," Taylor admitted. He groped his own face and found no burns. Then he grabbed at his wrist. There was no break. *Not even strained*. In fact, he felt healthier than he had since he crashed in this upside-down future.

He was, however, suspicious.

"You ordered the sentinels to attack me," he said.

"You were seeing things that weren't there," the boy insisted. "Then you yelled at me. I got scared when you talked to me the way you did." Messias pouted. "I am sorry."

"Alright," Taylor conceded. If he had been sick, that would explain nearly everything that happened since he was separated from—

"Nova," Taylor declared. "Messias, I have to find her. If you can help me..." The astronaut trailed off. Disappointment clouded the hybrid boy's face.

"You don't want me to leave," Taylor realized. "Why?" he asked. "What are you not telling me?" His tone was even, his voice low. His words were those of a man who would take no more.

"Taylor," Messias took him by the hand, "Nova is dead."

The desert had been kind to them. Milling about within the starbird's beak, Dr. Milo calculated the luck that had gotten him this far. The odds were astonishing.

Nearly every part they had transferred from the second ship had been a success—even the replacement chronometer worked just fine. Its "Earth Time" date was stuck at 3955 instead of the 3979 of the previous model, but other than that, the piece appeared to be in working order. Indeed, the restoration project had made great progress on all fronts.

A nearly complete runway stretched in front of the craft, and the engineers had even conceived a plan to start her engines. Utilizing Milo's own proven design for a waterwheel to generate kinetic energy, they set about building a theoretical electrical generator. Only one thing remained—the command codes.

Milo lamented the destruction of the starbird's waterlogged manuals when he'd first discovered her underwater. As it turned out, that particular manual contained the *Liberty 1*'s command sequence—an activation of a specific set of levers, knobs, and buttons in the correct order. He had hoped the replacement manual from the other spacecraft would reveal the sequence, but it appeared as if the codes were specific to each vessel. There were hundreds of thousands of possible combinations.

Working with the natural chalk and slate Seraph had prepared for him before she left, Milo set about cataloging each one.

"Suppose they turn out to be our superiors?" Zaius said. He, Ursus, and Sabian met privately in Ape City's municipal research complex. These three apes were where the true power resided.

"Their territory is no larger than ours, Dr. Zaius," Ursus countered. "We shall not be outnumbered."

"I was not referring to numbers, General." Though the gorilla's point was fallacious, on this point Zaius trod lightly. "My supposition concerned their intelligence."

Ursus looked stunned. "Then your supposition is blasphemous, Doctor."

Sabian interjected. "The Lawgiver has written in *The Sacred Scrolls* that God created apes—in his own image—to be masters of the earth."

"We are indeed his chosen," Zaius affirmed. He actually believed that much. The problem was that apes had not been the earth's *first* masters. They had inherited it. Damages and all.

Ursus puffed up his chest.

"Do you doubt what the minister has said?" he demanded. Zaius knew that Minister Sabian was well aware of the truth—of the origin of the apes, and of man. Ursus knew some of it—more than he should. The problem with Sabian was that he clung to the scripture without understanding its meaning, following its dogma without heeding the true nature of its warnings.

This had often caused clashes between Sabian and Zao—clashes that resulted in a deadlock regarding what was and was not acceptable ape behavior. It was one of the reasons that Zaius had received both positions, scientific and spiritual, upon his ascendancy to the High Council. There needed to be progress of some kind.

Zaius addressed the gorilla directly, lest Sabian think he questioned the patriarch's religious prowess.

"What I doubt," he began, "is your interpretation of God's intention." One hand behind his back, the doctor began to pace the room. "Has he ordained that we should make war?"

The general bristled. "Has he ordained that we should die of starvation?" Ursus didn't like having his beliefs questioned, and was losing his temper. The High Patriarch wasn't far behind him.

"Has he ordained that we should make peace with the human race?" the reverend minister spat.

"The humans—" Zaius waved them off. "They're animals." Sabian found the answer satisfactory.

Ursus wasn't so sure.

"And these," the general baited, "here in the Forbidden Zone?"

"They are the unknown, General," Zaius replied. He was certain he should have driven this point home already. Leafing through the apocryphal *Book of Simian Prophecy*, Sabian tsked him.

"A godly ape is not afraid of the unknown."

"I am not afraid. I am merely..." Zaius chose the word carefully. "...circumspect."

Then he caught Ursus's eyes. They were divining pools. The orangutan saw what the gorilla was thinking. He knew why the general had taunted him into joining this damned crusade. Otherwise, with Zaius in Ape City to counter him, Sabian would never be able to do what they needed him to do.

"Still," Ursus said, playing his hand, "not too circumspect to prevent you from riding with me on the great day, eh, Doctor?"

Zaius was indeed circumspect, but that wasn't all. He had positioned his players on the board to help keep Ape City intact while he was away. No, there was more to consider here. Much more.

"As a scientist," he said, "I am also curious."

CHAPTER 19
PHANTASMS AND REFLECTIONS

Groom Lake, Nevada
Area 51
1967

Probe Seven's black box told the whole story. As the command capsule had skipped across the atmosphere, a circuit had blown. Tossed around the cockpit, all three astronauts had lost consciousness from the g-forces and trauma. An electrical fire had started behind one of the panels. Smoke had flooded the compartment.

While Virdon's helmet had been on, Rowark's and Taylor's had not. Rowark had woken up with the fire in progress and activated the emergency landing program. His own helmet damaged by the accident, he secured Taylor's helmet and buckled in both of his teammates before he passed out from the noxious fumes.

Braking thrusters then ignited and chutes deployed.

Unable to secure his own oxygen supply, Rowark had succumbed to smoke inhalation before they had splashed down in the Pacific—well before Alan Virdon regained consciousness. The admiral's recovery teams had reached them quickly, but it had made no difference.

Eddie Rowark was dead.

* * *

Taylor was late for his flight home.

Every day, an unmarked airliner carried workers who lived off-base to and from Groom Lake. His head wound bandaged, the accident only a week behind him, Taylor was heading home to his wife and new daughter. From there he would fly to Colorado Springs and the USAF Academy Cemetery for Rowark's funeral. His death had hit all the astronauts, but it had crushed Taylor.

If I hadn't gotten him involved…

Her passengers boarded, the nondescript plane prepared to close her doors. If Taylor missed this flight to Vegas, he'd miss his connecting civilian flight as well. Yet he wasn't rushing to the runway. In fact, he was nowhere near it.

He walked the halls of the officers' barracks with duffle bag slung over shoulder—his good one, of course. Finally, he found the private quarters he was looking for, and he knocked.

The door swung wide.

"George," Stewart said. "You're going to miss—"

Taylor swept her up in his arms and kissed her hard. His duffle dropped to the floor. Stewart stumbled backward, pulling Taylor into her quarters with her. They were already half undressed before the door slammed shut.

Taylor couldn't believe it.

"She died before you got here," Messias said. "You carried her with you."

He didn't remember any of it. If the radiation sickness was as bad as Messias said, most likely he had been delirious for days.

Is that why I've been reliving the past?

The glass elevator had taken them to the tallest spire and

deposited them in the atrium at its crest. Up there the clouds were as a lazy sea mist that hugged the buildings below. Only the very tops of the skyscrapers pierced that veil and reached for the sky. It reminded Taylor of the ruins of Manhattan, jutting out of the sand in the Forbidden Zone.

Like giant tombstones.

The sands here were clouds, though, the towers made of polished glass. They shone orange in the early evening light. Steel beams crosshatched the atrium's outer walls, massive triangular glass plates nestled between them. Each sheet of glass diffused a slightly different spectrum of light, making the entire room appear to be covered in stained glass at sunset. The effect should have been awe-inspiring.

Taylor didn't even notice.

Here, Nova's body lay waiting. The coffin was a glass tube, not unlike the hibernation chambers they used on *Liberty 1*. It rested on a khaki marble slab etched with veins of cobalt. Within the container, Nova lay in a bed of flowers, and orchids and lilies were strewn across her body.

"I'll give you some time," Messias suggested. The boy turned away from Taylor to watch the sun set over his city. Tentatively, Taylor approached the glass sarcophagus.

Nova's raven hair draped over the pillow on which she rested. Color still found purchase in her tan skin. Her eyes were closed, her lashes caressing her soft face, and her lips were parted ever so slightly, as if begging for one last kiss. But this was no fairy tale. No kiss would wake her.

There would be no "happily ever after."

Taylor found the latch and slid open the transparent lid. Light purple orchids fell to the floor. He leaned close and caressed her face. While she might look warm and alive, she was terribly cold. She had been dressed in white, the style obscured by the flowers that covered her body. Her arms lay across her chest.

"Nova," he whispered.

Why don't we settle down and form a colony? he had told her at the oasis. *And all the kids will learn to talk.* But her unborn child died with her. There would be no colony. He slammed his salty eyes shut and gulped back tears.

Then he looked up and away. Light from the setting sun cascaded into the atrium, splintering into a dazzling array and glinting off the open casket. Light refracted across its transparent lid. Clearing his eyes, Taylor examined it.

There was a diagonal crack in the glass.

Something familiar…

Taylor looked at the flowers. He reached down to brush some of them away when something caught his eye. A splash of blue and yellow in a sea of white. Over her right breast was an embroidered patch. Four stars sat at the cardinal coordinates while two rings orbited the center of a deep blue field. Embossed in yellow across the middle were four letters.

It was the ANSA mission patch.

Taylor swept more flowers away. Nova had been dressed like an astronaut, in an ANSA uniform. Above the patch was a name tag.

STEWART

Taylor stepped back. Stewart had died on board *Liberty 1*, when a crack appeared in her glass hibernation tube. He remembered his conversation with Landon.

"I was thinking of Stewart," Landon had said. *"What do you suppose happened?"*

"Messias..." Taylor was cautious. "How did Nova die?"

"Air leak," he had told the other astronaut. *"She died in her sleep."*

"Air leak," the boy parroted his thoughts. "She died in her sleep."

"It's a little late for a wake." Taylor spoke this last part aloud, perfectly matching the boy. "She's been dead nearly a year." Then he stiffened, and turned.

"Except that was Stewart, Messias," he said, "not Nova."

"But you thou—" Messias stopped. "You said Stewart was her last name."

Taylor crossed his arms. "Are you reading my mind?"

A restless pause, man and boy coiled tight.

Then—chaos. The alarm klaxon sounded.

"The city is under siege!" the boy cried out.

"Messias!" Taylor roared, but his companion leapt into the elevator.

"We've got to get to the Main Hall!" The lift departed. Taylor turned toward "Nova's" coffin again. It had sealed itself, the glass polarizing to hide the woman within.

After a moment, a second elevator arrived, empty. Furious, Taylor took after Messias.

You come from the northern lab, the brain offered. *You must have met my pet. Did you two play nice?*

The room reminded Mungwortt of Ape City's own amphitheater. Cast in concrete, its concentric semicircles terminated at the substantial glass tank situated on the far wall—focusing all attention on the thing inside it. Without understanding how, the half-breed knew this one was known as Be-Six. Twice as massive as his fellow brains—so large that his gray matter pressed against the glass wall of his tank—the inheritor emitted a sickly green irradiance, the only illumination in the room. Split across the tank, a diagonal fracture caught the glow, resulting in tiny stars.

"It tried to eat me," Mungwortt replied. "You should have fed it bigger portions."

After a moment without any reaction, Mungwortt's head was flooded with… laughter? As its contents pulsed and squirmed, the tank shook and the fluid sloshed.

It's been a long time since I had occasion to laugh, Be-Six observed. *Very good.*

Unnerved by the soundless communications, Mungwortt knew they had to get out fast. At Zao's suggestion, he peered through the gloom and looked around for the nearest exits.

"Gah!" he cried out.

There was someone sitting next to Mungwortt, gaunt and grotesque. Tufts of coarse wire sprouted from his temples and cheeks. His leathery flesh was bloated, his left eye socket bare. Clothed in scraps of a rust-colored robe, his cold flesh sparkled with a hard sheen in the dim light—and he had friends. There were figures sitting in each of the rings. They sat in silence—just as the apes would at the amphitheater.

Except these people were human.

They were misshapen.

And they were all dead.

Centuries of water and mineral deposits seeping through the ceiling had caused the corpses to decay, deform, and eventually fossilize. Every few rows or so were dominated by stalactites or stalagmites, some stretching to meet in the middle and create fanciful columns that ran from floor to ceiling, smooth and calcified. Dozens of petrified bodies sagged in their seats, a mute audience for the mental rumblings of an enormous mass of gray matter.

This is my audience. If thoughts could frown, that's what Be-Six was doing. *You're Mendez's idea of irony. Centuries ago I was much more than an Overseer. My kind were to be the inheritors of the planet. We controlled war machines. We had armies of man-ape drones at our command. We were gods.* The brain seemed to sigh. *Now, we are used to run the city's power and water. To amplify the Fellowship's own abilities. To run biogenic experiments in the labs of my former enemies.*

"Enemies?" Mungwortt asked. Anything to keep the brain distracted while he looked for a way out.

Yes, the Makers. Cybernetic humans. Scientists like those who made me—they made the machines here. Somehow Mungwortt knew that Be-Six was happy to have someone with whom he could communicate. *But radiation twisted their minds. They experimented on one another. Tried to kill my kind. We beat them,* he continued, *long ago, before we were indentured to the Fellowship. When the Mendez dynasty sought to make use of me, I was locked in this basement theater with only the dead to pay me tribute.*

"Maybe," Mungwortt sputtered, slowly circling, "maybe the fellows just didn't want you to get lonely." Finally, he located the way out. There was a door marked EXIT, some distance from the way they came in. Unwilling to go back, he realized they only had one course of action.

Mendez does it to mock me. His beliefs supplant all other gods—myself included. The brain paused. *You are a strange one,* Be-Six observed. *Curious that you would speak to me, instead of transmitting your thoughts. Did he send you to evaluate my faith?*

Be-Six shifted, squeaking across the inside of the glass tank.

"When I was young and got angry," Mungwortt said as he inched his way through the maze of corpses, "my mother always told me to use my words."

There was another silence.

You are indeed unlike any of the other mutants. Be-Six chuckled again. *Regardless, I know why you are here. Tell His Holiness that patience is a virtue. The experiment proceeds.*

"His Holiness," Mungwortt muttered. "Got it."

The subject is strong-willed, but the heterogen will prevail.

Zao spoke up, prodding Mungwortt to action.

"Okay," he told the brain. "I'll let him know." He weaved his way through the craggy bodies and toward the exit. Unfortunately, his path took him closer to Be-Six.

Hold! the brain roared mentally. *You are not of the Fellowship.*

Lights strobed in Mungwortt's head. *You're an... ape!* His head buzzed painfully. *A gorilla and chimpanzee hybridization. Not like the heterogen. Not one of mine. Naturally born.*

"Wait. The babies in the jars—" Mungwortt was confused. "They're yours?"

Yes, I made them. Them and my pet.

"Why would you do that?" Mungwortt was horrified. "They're not normal. They look like they hurt."

The Fellowship of the Holy Fallout tasked me with creating something that can kill your kind.

"Who are they? Why do they want to kill apes?" Mungwortt struggled with the concept. "What did we do?"

You were with my compatriots, Be-Six observed. *The Inheritors in hiding.* He sifted through Mungwortt's memories. *They were going to send you to me. You escaped them when I diverted the city's power for my experiments.* Mungwortt felt dizzy, muddled. *Yet you came here anyway. I would have thought you had some ulterior motive. I see now that your diminutive IQ doesn't allow for that.*

Mungwortt scratched his head.

He's calling you an idiot, idiot, Zao explained.

"Oh!" Mungwortt said aloud.

WHO ELSE IS THERE? Be-Six boomed, and the half-breed bent with the pain. *Who are you conversing with?*

Zao, he can't read your thoughts! Mungwortt thought. This would give them an advantage.

"You better let me go," Mungwortt demanded, "or my friend will hurt you. He killed your pet!" He visualized the brutal death of the brain's pet, hoping that Be-Six could see what was in his mind. Once again there was silence—this one longer than before. Then the brain's thoughts invaded his head again—and they sounded angry.

I concede, Be-Six responded. *Leave at once.*

Mungwortt smiled. "Come on, Zao. Let's go." As he visualized his friend, safely tucked away in the sack, the brain reached out.

One moment, Be-Six instructed. *Your friend...* He probed deeper into Mungwortt's mind. *Zao is a skull?* The entire chamber seemed to swirl with his anger. *You aren't just stupid,* he concluded, *you're insane.*

The buzzing became an explosion of pain.

Mungwortt screamed. The psionic assault was deafening. If the abomination was a cudgel, this was a scalpel. He could feel the blade spiral behind his eyes, deep in his skull, and hear a continuous screeching.

The screeching was his.

On his knees, he dug through his satchel.

What are you doing? Be-Six's mind demanded. *Is that a weapon?*

It was, of course.

"Get him, Zao!" Mungwortt thrust forward, the skull in hand. Over and over he pounded it into the base of the intellectual aquarium, aiming for the bisecting crack that slivered across it.

Stop! I command you! The bone began to chip away, but a spiral of cracks began to splinter the glass. The Overseer panicked and the mental onslaught increased. Whether through sheer stubbornness or because of his limited mental capacities, the half-breed refused to give up.

Filthy beast!

Drawing back, Mungwortt roared. He slammed Zao into the break one last time. The cracks snapped. The glass shattered, the bottom of the tank gave way, and a viscous wave crashed over him. Be-Six crashed to the floor in a cascade of sludge, while Mungwortt and Zao were washed away.

The mucoid fluid splashed through the theater, creating small but swift rivers which wound their way through the calcified tomb. Soon the slime settled, and Mungwortt pulled Zao from the gelatinous muck. He gave the skull a moment to catch his breath before tucking him back in his bag.

Tiger…

Mungwortt heard it in his head.

"Zao, did you—?"

The skull affirmed.

The ape steeled himself for another assault.

Tiger buy…

There was none. He frantically scanned the chamber. Mangled

medulla was strewn everywhere. A dagger of glass bisected Be-Six's cortex.

Tiger buys a tow.
Eenie Meenie Doe.
Ray Meenie Moe.

Groom Lake, Nevada
Area 51
1967

"I shouldn't have done that." Taylor adjusted his bandages and lit his cigar. Alone in her quarters, he and Stewart had just made love for the third time.

I shouldn't have done it the first two times, either.

Clenching the lit stogie in his teeth, he climbed out of bed and pulled his pants back on.

"I'm sorry."

"You're spoiling the mood." Still in bed, Stewart lit her own cigarette and breathed deep.

"Eddie was my friend, too," she exhaled. "People bond over death. Do you think this would have happened if I didn't want it to?"

Taylor considered. "I suppose not." He sighed and more smoky haze filled the room.

What am I going to say to Gillian? *He hadn't even seen their newborn daughter yet, and he had slept with another woman.*

"Listen," he started.

"Don't worry, George," she said, "this stays between us." Wearing only the sheet, Stewart sat up in the bed. "I was going to wait until you got back," she offered, "but we need to talk."

She inhaled and continued. "About Churchdoor…"

Churchdoor, again. *In the nearly five years since the name had first cropped up, none of them could find anything to indicate what it was.* Nothing besides the incident in the bunker, *he corrected. Scanning the floor, he found his dog tags.*

"I've been doing a little snooping around the medical archives," she said.

"Oh?" Taylor tucked in his shirt.

"The men who died at the bunker?" she reminded him. "I managed to get their autopsy reports."

Taylor raised an eyebrow at that.

"A base doctor likes me," she admitted.

"I'm sure he does," Taylor hummed. Stewart threw a pillow at him. "So," he said as he buckled his belt, "what have you got?"

"So," she said, "they died of a lethal dosage of radiation."

"That's not unexpected," Taylor puffed. The bunker's shield doors were designed to shut in biological agents, toxins, and radiation. It had to be one of them. At least it wasn't biological. *A probable cause came readily to mind. "The GDM engine is a fusion reactor—"*

"Yes, not a fission one," she countered. Fusion yielded much less radiation—it was almost clean energy. Opening her nightstand drawer, she produced a file and tried to hand it to him. Taylor wouldn't take it.

"Look at the numbers, George," she pleaded.

He accepted with a frown, and leafed through the purloined documents.

"This can't be right," he muttered. The radiation dose the two technicians had absorbed was higher than what was produced by the Tsar Bomba. A Soviet weapon exploded in the late fifties, the fifty-seven megaton Tsar was the most powerful nuclear bomb ever detonated. This rivaled that without the accompanying blast.

"It's a super weapon," Stewart said.

"Hold on, now—"

"George, it's got *to be."*

"It could be an experimental propulsion unit," he argued. "Something other than the GDM." Taylor paced the room. "Maybe the photon drive Hasslein keeps talking about." Stewart just stared at him. After a while, she spoke.

"Do you trust Hasslein and Stanton?"

The question was a difficult one. Taylor had grown to like Otto Hasslein, but the man was mysterious. Stanton, on the other hand, was a twerp.

"Do you trust your father?" she added.

Taking another drag on his cigar, Taylor looked at the numbers once again.

What are you, Churchdoor? *he thought.*

Messias was fast. The boy stayed ahead of Taylor the entire run to the Main Hall. Once he was inside, the two-foot-thick steel slab came rolling shut to seal him in.

To seal me out, Taylor knew. Taylor dove for the portal, tumbling across the foyer and into the hall just as the door crashed into place.

SLAM!

The sanctum was in lockdown.

"You made it," the boy shouted. "Good!" A yellow light strobed on the hybrid's command chair. "Outer defenses have been breached!" Messias slid into the command chair, reading coded light patterns that signified what was happening outside, and translating them for the irked astronaut.

"The creatures have taken the bridge!"

Taylor wasn't buying it. Any of it. Once again, the "mysterious creatures" were on the attack. As always, it was all a little too convenient.

"Messias," Taylor said, "Nova didn't die on my spacecraft. Stewart did."

Messias ignored him. "Deploying sentinels to intercept."

"That wasn't Nova, was it?" Taylor stepped forward. "She's not dead."

"The sentinels have failed!" the boy exclaimed.

"Stop it," Taylor snarled through gritted teeth. "Right *now*."

A light on the control panel burned an indignant red.

"They're inside!"

Taylor balled his fists and stepped forward.

"Messias, so help me, I'll—"

Wham!

The room shook. Loud cracks echoed throughout the sanctum. Dust fell from the ceiling and the foundation shook. It was as if the city had taken a hit from a bomb blast. During World War II, he'd been stuck in a bunker when the enemy blanketed the area. This felt like that, only the source of the rumbling wasn't the ceiling. It was the door.

Messias sprang to his feet. "They're here." The two of them stared at the shaking barrier.

Wham.

Wham.

Wham.

Doubt crept across Taylor's face, and with it, Messias grew bold.

"You have to protect me," he demanded. Giving in, Taylor scanned the chamber. He would be much more comfortable with a weapon in hand.

Better armed than not.

Moving swiftly to the dining table, he picked up a wooden chair. Gripping it with both hands, he swung it at one of the many stone columns that dominated the sanctum. The chair shattered, its legs splintering into makeshift staves. Taylor picked one up and examined its sharpened edge. When it met his approval, he tossed it to Messias.

"Here."

"What's this?" The boy regarded the weapon with disgust. "Barbaric. I don't want this." He threw it back. The stave skittered across the tiled floor, coming to a stop at Taylor's feet.

Wham.

The steel door buckled under the onslaught.

Wham. Cracks drew themselves across the marble door frame.

The sharpened stave lay at his feet. Taylor reached for it. At that moment the door exploded across the room with a deafening impact, setting his ears ringing. The force of it shattered columns and splintered stone. Though warped, it wasn't the door that had failed them. Rather, it was the wall that had held it.

Murky shadow-things spilled into the room. They weren't apes, but their forms were ape-like. The gloomy shades were tall, much taller than Taylor. Their shoulders were broad, their arms thick and powerful. They cast deep shadows behind them that suggested giant leathery wings, but they had no such appendages.

The nearest one swiped at him. Taylor dove, narrowly avoiding its spindly claws. He rolled and came to his feet near the dining table, only to find himself face to face with two more of the creatures.

The closer one leered at him.

Taylor struggled to understand what he was looking at. Its

form radiated heat, its exhales wet and steamy. Though he was only inches away from the thing, its features were indiscernible. Where it should have had eyes, there were two crimson coals. Aside from that, the demon was a hazy blur that seemed to shimmer and change with each heartbeat.

His face damp with its breath, Taylor tightened his grip on the stake and swung. The wooden weapon sliced across the creature's ember eyes, blinding it. The other creature grabbed for him, and Taylor ducked under the table. The wounded demon bellowed. It was the same unearthly howl he and Messias had heard echoing through the city during the last attack.

Messias.

He slipped out the other side of the table and scanned the room. Thankfully, all of the creatures were focused on him, and not on the boy. But his relief was short-lived, as one of the things drew near to Messias.

Taylor prepared to lunge.

The thing passed *through* the boy. Not a single demon attempted to touch him.

That does it.

The creatures converged on Taylor.

He did nothing.

The wounded demon raised its fists high over his head. The others followed suit. Taylor threw the stake to the floor, where it landed with a clatter.

"Look out!" Messias shouted.

Taylor closed his eyes.

Mungwortt and Zao climbed the stairs. From a chamber up ahead he could hear something new. Not thoughts, but a muffled voice. Speaking words, though the voice was distinctly unsimian. As they grew closer, Zao could make out the words.

Reaching the top of the stairs, Mungwortt could understand them, too.

"…take you over my knee," the strange voice echoed beyond.

Curious, the skull reflected. The dimwitted ape agreed.

"What now?" he muttered.

There was something else, too. A trill. A whine. Its pitch grew steady as they homed in on the source. It was a beacon, drawing them in. They slid through the creaking door.

We must be cautious, Zao urged.

Mungwortt gulped and nodded.

Fists fell as the demons assaulted Taylor. They tried to, at least. As the blows landed, the shadow beasts burst into plumes of ash and smoke. Quickly, he and Messias were alone.

"Phantoms," Taylor seethed. "How did you do it? Holography? Psychotropics?"

"You do not know what you are talking about," Messias said.

"I ought to take you over my knee," Taylor growled. His anger was palpable, but so too was Messias's. The hybrid seemed to feed on Taylor's rage.

"You want to threaten me or protect yourself?" Messias nodded at the abandoned stake. "Pick it up," he taunted. "Go ahead, pick it up."

Hesitant, Taylor stared.

"Do what I say," the boy demanded.

"No."

Messias closed his eyes, and a high-pitched whine filled the astronaut's ears. Taylor swept the stake up and put it to his own throat. Some force was pushing at him, egging him on.

Kill yourself.

The suggestion rattled around his brain, but it wasn't his thought. It was Messias—and it was overpowering.

ACT III

INTO THE LABYRINTH

CHAPTER 20
THE QUALITY OF MERCY

There was light.

Above, soft luminance penetrated high, broken windows, and was diffused through dust before descending to the disheveled hall. Below, the floor's weathered wooden planks creaked with the weight of Mungwortt's footsteps.

The room he and Zao had entered was as large as the inside of the Zaius Museum. Three stories tall, the hall's center was open wide, with two floors of balconies wrapping around the upper levels. Row upon row of dust-laden shelving created a maze of aisles. Squarish leather-jacketed packages lined every overloaded shelf, some orderly, others in disarray. Mungwortt peered closely at one of them, staring at its outer edge. Bound in a stiff cover, it was packed with dozens of small sheets of papyrus.

Books! the skull whispered over the buzzing in his head.

"Books," Mungwortt repeated. Modern apes kept scrolls, not books, but he had seen one, once, in the old temple when he was very young. Called *The Book of Simian Prophecy*, it was a religious text that some apes had revered in addition to *The Sacred Scrolls*. That stopped when the church initiated reforms and the temple that held it was burned. As they watched the fire, Mungwortt's aunt explained that the book had to be destroyed, because it told of a savior other than the Lawgiver—someone called "the Unknown Ape."

"Having two saviors encourages two faiths," she had told him. "We need only one." As she spoke, she reached down and collected a bundle of twigs. Holding them tightly together, she tried to snap them. Instead, they only bent. "Apes together are strong."

Then she discarded all but one of the sticks, applying the same pressure. A crisp snap startled him as the twig broke in two.

"Separate, we are weak."

It was a lesson he had never forgotten. *The Book of Simian Prophecy* was the only book he had ever known—and it had been something dangerous.

Here there were so many around him. *Could all these be dangerous, too?* he wondered. The thought boggled his diminutive brain. Keen on finding out, however, Mungwortt forgot his place. He pulled a pretty red book from its nestled spot between two others, eager to have Zao read it to him. The thing burst into dust.

"Zao?" a confused Mungwortt whispered. The skull would not talk, though—it only emanated sadness. Old beyond reckoning, the bountiful knowledge locked in this room would remain lost—the books shelved around them were worn from exposure to vermin, the elements, and worse.

Abruptly, there was a voice, and the buzzing increased.

"No," it said, the sound echoing. The source was around the next corner, beyond the far bookcase. His attention renewed, Mungwortt looked to Zao for guidance. Depressed, the elder had withdrawn.

"Don't worry, my friend," Mungwortt murmured. He patted the skull in his makeshift satchel. "I'll get us through this." Ready to face fuzzy White Ones or wagon-sized brains, Mungwortt leapt forward.

There ahead stood the source of the voice.

It was a human—and aside from his striking blue eyes, a rather plain-looking one at that. He wasn't alone. The human was talking to a child.

A child ape—a very strange one.

The two just stood there, frozen.

The hybrid boy was in his head. His movements weren't his own.

Telekinesis, Taylor thought fiercely. The harder he fought to pull the stake away from his own throat, the stronger the resistance became. So he decided to try a different strategy.

He didn't fight it. He let go, and the projectile sailed past him, clattering to the floor.

"How did you do that?" Messias wailed in his head. "You cannot stop me!"

Doubling over, Taylor clutched his skull. Terrors reverberated in his mind.

"Messias," Taylor bellowed. "Get the hell out of my head!" But there was no more Messias. The hybrid child split in two as a monster emerged from his shell. It was like the others, but bigger still—a good five yards tall. The inky ape's eyes burned like stars. Its legs trapped in Messias's chest cavity, the shadow behemoth writhed like a genie, pulling itself from the boy's hollow form. Taylor groped the floor nearby until his hand found purchase—the stake.

"None of this is real," he gritted, "and I'm guessing you aren't, either!"

The shadow ape lunged. Taylor thrust the stake forward, and felt an impact. The room fluttered.

The world fell away.

* * *

Taylor was somewhere else. Dizzy, he tried to adjust to his new surroundings. His eyes were wide, his jaw unhinged. This change wasn't like what happened in the psychedrome. This one was… real. Everything here was different. Everything except the boy.

Taylor had guessed wrong. While the shadow demons had been imaginary, Messias had been quite real. He lay in front of the astronaut, a great red stain expanding on his gray-white tunic. Dropping to his knees, Taylor cradled the boy's head in one arm, and grasped tightly the stave that had run him through. He was slick with the hybrid's blood.

"Taylor…" Messias breathed. His last words.

"No." Taylor grimaced. Slowly he stood, letting Messias's corpse slip to the floor. His vision crossed, and then cleared. He was in a dark, musty, and vaulted room. It was a library of some sort, and appeared to have been abandoned for millennia.

"No," Taylor said again. He hadn't wanted to hurt Messias.

There was motion, and he prepared for another assault—but the shadow monster was gone. In its stead stood a different, blurry figure. A gorilla, though this ape wasn't a soldier. He was dressed more like Julius from the animal research center. He also seemed worse for wear. Bruised and scuffed, his clothing torn, this snaggletoothed simian maintained a defensive stance, a makeshift satchel swung over his arm.

Anger welled up in Taylor.

"You did this," he seethed. "*You did this.* You made me kill him!" A look of astonishment appeared on the gorilla's face.

"Human, how can you talk?" The simian scratched his head. "Did you come from a jar?" He stared down at Messias's corpse.

"Is that your child? Why did you kill him?"

"My—" Taylor started.

That was the tipping point.

Stake in hand, he lunged.

Mungwortt didn't understand. The talking man had murdered the child. The boy looked like some kind of half-breed—like himself, but different.

The man reminded him of the one he had seen in Dr. Galen's office. The one called *Lan-Don*. That one got him thrown into a pit. This one was thrusting a pointed stick at him. Mungwortt ducked, and the human tripped right over him, tumbling to the creaking, rotted boards at their feet.

Why does this animal hate me so much?

"What did I do, human?" he cried. *"What did I do?"*

Taylor turned his fall into a sweeping kick, knocking the gorilla to the floor and stabbing at its arms.

"Drugs, right?" Taylor snarled, kicking out. "Zaius has had me doped up this whole time. That's what this is, isn't it?" The child was an innocent, he was sure. Someone had been pulling strings, and it had to be Dr. Zaius. The orangutan probably saw the boy as an abomination.

As he attacked, however, Taylor realized something was wrong. While the gorilla was defending himself, he wasn't fighting back. He'd curled into a ball, shielding his face with his forearms. Stopping with the stake at the ape's throat, the astronaut shook his head and scanned the room.

Where's the goon squad? he wondered. No gorilla soldiers had run in to subdue him. *And where is Zaius?* Then he heard it—and anger welled up again. Sharp footsteps echoed on concrete, morphing into the dull thud of tramping on soft wood. Taylor whirled.

"Zaius," he growled. "You son of a—"

Only, it wasn't Zaius.

They were human—almost. Wearing white, gray, and beige, their heads hooded tightly and hands sheathed in pale gloves, they were dressed like the man he had seen talking to Messias. They rushed into the room, then paused and looked confused. Their leader was a heavyset man with a long red collar, much as a priest might wear. He nodded, and thoughts erupted in Taylor's brain.

What have you done to the heterogen? Taylor's eyes darted to Messias's corpse, then he locked eyes with the newcomer. Somehow he knew the man's name was Adiposo. *Who is this gorilla?* the fat man demanded. *Did you lead it here?*

Telepathy, Taylor thought. *Like Messias.*

You are a spy, Mr. Taylor. The voice shouted in his head again. *You and this beast will not report to your ape masters.*

"Are you from the Fellows?" the ape asked the fat man. He was just as clueless as Taylor.

The stupid gorilla isn't to blame, Taylor thought. *They are. The enemy of my enemy…*

Come with us, the fat man demanded. *Now.*

The gorilla put his fingers in his ears and shook his head. Taylor looked at him.

"You thinking what I'm thinking?"

The ape just nodded. So Taylor rose slowly, tossed aside the bloody stake, and offered a hand to the gorilla. Looking surprised, the ape smiled and began to pull himself up. Leverage achieved, Taylor put his plan in motion.

"Batter up!" he shouted. Swinging the gorilla around, he gained momentum and let go, hurling his impromptu partner bodily toward the whitewashed guards—a fuzzy bowling bowl taking down four pins. Safely out of range, however, their obese leader nodded and closed his eyes, preparing to "think" something at them.

Taylor didn't give a damn what it was. He rushed Adiposo and clocked him across the jaw.

Made of glass, the astronaut thought smugly.

Now, Mungwortt got it. Now, he understood the human's plan. It was rash and it was stupid.

Mungwortt liked it.

Flailing wildly, he struck the pale humanoids in the face and gut. When all four had gone down, he gained his feet and looked to the human for instructions.

"Come on!" the beast beckoned.

"Wait!" Mungwortt's eyes swept the floor. After a beat he found his sack in a corner. He snatched it up and nodded. The human ran, and Mungwortt followed on his heels. After a short while they barreled through a door.

"What in the hell?" the human said.

They were at the top of a tall flight of steps, flanked on both sides by a pair of very iconic stone lions. At that moment, Taylor understood.

The New York Public Library—42nd and Park.

He was in the underbelly of Manhattan—or rather, Manhattan *was* the underbelly. On their approach he and Nova had seen the tops of the buildings. This was the part that rested beneath the surface.

Most of their surroundings were slagged and gray, flash-frozen in a lava flow that appeared to have cooled and hardened in an instant. Far above, that ceiling was bathed in a soft warm glow. Diffused light filtered in through the tallest buildings, reflected off of glass and steel, giving the underground city's day a semblance of perpetual twilight.

Then something drew his attention.

Deet.

A dull beat that resonated in his skull.

Deet.

Just like the sound he had heard when he caught Messias "praying" with the stranger. Picking up speed, it came again and again.

Deet. Deet. Deet.

There were more human figures on the street, and finally he knew why he thought it had been talking. It was telepathic communication he had been listening to, and he was beginning to understand the language.

As with Adiposo and his companions, these people were all garbed in white, gray, and beige outfits, though they looked to be civilians. Women, children—here a couple, there a family out for a walk. They were communicating with each other via nods and bursts of thoughts. Because these others weren't "talking" to him, however, it took him a minute to register what they were saying. He calmed his mind and their transmissions became clear.

They're calling for the guard.

The gorilla tapped him on the shoulder. "This way," he said. "I know where we can hide!" The two hurried down the steps, slipped around the corner, and made for Grand Army Plaza.

Ursus and Zaius had ridden through Ape City proper, followed by the gorilla general's troops. They readied themselves to leave civilization behind and head off into the unknown. First, however, they had to deal with one minor problem.

"Love, yes!" the chimpanzees wailed. "War, no!"

Led by Tian, Liet's activists had assembled in protest. Picket signs in hand, they stopped their march, sat down, and blocked the road that led through the city's gates. If Ursus's army wanted to leave, they were going to have to trample them.

"No more lies! No more crying!" they chanted. "No more guns! No more blood!"

"Stop! Stop! Stop the war! Freedom! Freedom!"

"Whoa." Ursus pulled on his reins.

"Freedom! Peace!" the protesters yelled. "Peace and freedom!"

Ursus drew his pistol, and he looked angry enough to use it. Zaius trotted up beside him, and addressed the crowd.

"Get off the road, young people," he pleaded.

"Freedom! Peace!" they responded.

A seething Ursus nodded to Major Dangral. "Get them out of the way."

"Wait." Zaius put his hand on the general's shoulder. This was going to escalate fast. There would be bloodshed, and the only way to stop it was to appeal to the general's logic. "We don't want martyrs," the doctor said, "do we?"

Fit to be tied, Ursus looked around. The army's parade had

attracted an audience, most of them apes gawking from the windows of their homes. Zaius could read the look on his face.

Witnesses.

"We want peace!" the protesters demanded. "We want freedom!"

"Major," Ursus whispered, "do it quietly."

Dangral motioned to the troops. Weapons holstered, they dismounted and moved into the protesters, gathering them up bodily. Police wagons arrived, and the gorillas quickly filled them with chimpanzees. Soon only the protestors' signs remained, lying discarded in the dust.

"Gorilla brutality!" Tian shouted. Despite his cries, however, there was no violence. As the last of them were locked away, Ursus looked satisfied. They would be Cerek's problem now. The road ahead was clear.

Ursus gave the order. "Battalion."

The advance began.

"There they go," Zira said, and she sighed as the army moved toward the gate. "Dr. Zaius trotting along beside them." Cornelius joined her at the window.

"Don't be too hard on the old boy, Zira," he suggested. His opinion on the doctor seemed to have shifted significantly since their return from the cave. "His motives are honest."

Zira wasn't having any of it. "He has only one motive—to keep things exactly as they have always been." She grew bold—even bolder than usual. "I say that it's time for a change."

Out in the streets, Ursus and Zaius came to a stop when they encountered a group of protesters. The chimpanzees were led by Tian, and Zira hoped fervently that there would be no violence.

The death of Lucius was still vivid in her memory, and she didn't know if she could stand to see any more of her friends injured or killed.

"Gorilla brutality!" Tian shouted loudly enough that they could hear him, despite the distance. As if her prayers had been answered, it wasn't long before Ursus's troops had removed them, without harm.

So much for conscientious objection, she observed.

"We chimpanzees are too few," Cornelius commented. "How can we take the initiative when they're in control?" Zira thought about Maximus, about how the Commissioner's tight leash on her was preventing her from producing the research she would need to prove all humans were intelligent.

With our hands tied, she realized, *there can be no progress.* Then she thought about the anti-vivisection league—about what Liet had said.

"All we need is a leader," Liet had insisted.

"Cornelius," Zira said, breaking the silence. "Has it occurred to you that by tomorrow… they won't be around?" Her husband looked at her and, as understanding dawned, his eyes widened until they were like saucers. In them, Zira divined his thoughts.

Ursus.

The gorilla army.

Zaius.

Without Zaius, the administrative orangutans would have to rely on the president, who was useless. He would acquiesce to the will of the public. There would never be a better time for the chimpanzees to take action.

As she watched the advancing army trample the protesters' signs, Zira knew there was much to do. Liet hadn't been among the protesters who had been arrested, so hopefully she was still free—because she already had in motion the beginnings of what they needed.

It wouldn't be that simple, however.

There would be one voice that could stand in their way. One ape who could turn the president's ear and rally the remaining gorilla police force—and he would have the entire church behind him. The newlyweds looked long and hard into each other's eyes. They both said his name at the same time.

"Sabian."

The General of the Defense was dead, and he lay in repose. Having lingered for weeks since his consciousness was psychically destroyed, the vegetative state of his mind had at last claimed him. His name had been Ygil VII.

In life, his responsibility had been to train the population in the use of mental deterrents. The purpose of the deterrents was to prevent any injury whatsoever to their society. They were mental disciplines which could affect all of the five senses. When this was done in unison, they could create near-perfect apparitions and cripple an enemy—as long as that enemy's mind could hold the illusions.

This training meant everything to them. It had been passed down long ago that if followers of the holy bomb neglected the deterrents, then the process of AD—Assured Destruction—would begin.

Ygil VII passed without an heir. There would be no Ygil VIII. Thus, before long there would be no training of the mental disciplines. No more deterrents.

AD would come. Destruction was guaranteed, and so the

assembled congregation mourned not only the general's passing, but the end of their civilization as well.

The wake was held in what was once called Rockefeller Center. Now enclosed and coated in long-cooled lava, it was a molten sea of gray paused in time. On a stone slab in front of the slagged remains of the *Prometheus* statue, the general's body lay in state for those who wished to mourn him. Children surrounded the pedestal, singing the mutants' version of a song whose origins were lost to time.

"Ring a ring o' neutrons.
A pocketful of positrons.
A fission, a fission!
We all fall down!"

With that the children fell, lying in a circle around him. Two pale yellow-garbed men stepped over them, lifting the deceased general onto a stretcher and covering his head with a sheet. They were the Cleaners, and would convey him through the streets to the charnel house in old Times Square.

The holy furnace there had for centuries been used to dispose of the irradiated and infected. Ever since the first bombs fell. After the cleansing fire, his bones and ashes would be piled in its cavernous open basement—a mass grave for the countless mutants who had died in God's name over the past two millennia. It was their way.

The will of their god.

Four of the five mutant masters bore witness to his passing. Then Adiposo joined them in the viewing box, looking disheveled. He was out of breath, his face askew, his manner unbecoming of a guild leader.

"Your Holiness," he said. "The heterogen," he panted. "Mr. Taylor—"

Mendez blinked at him. *Think it.*

Composing himself, Adiposo slowed, and adjusted his face.

Deet.

The assembled masters understood.

Mendez took action.

Deet.

He glanced at Caspay. The glasses-wearing man nodded, and signaled his own guards. They would find this so-called astronaut and his gorilla.

As they left, Mendez XXVI returned his attention to the funeral procession. The General of the Defense's body disappeared from sight, soon to arrive at the furnace. Soon, there would be nothing left of him but bone and ash. Just as God decreed.

Unable to take solace in the ceremony, Mendez's brow furled.

Their gambit foiled, they were out of options.

Now, save for the love of their god, they were defenseless.

"God Almighty," Brent sputtered. "This used to be my home." Having escaped the prison wagon, he and Nova had been chased by the Security Police to the edge of the Forbidden Zone. Desperate, they found shelter in a crack in the crust.

Within the hole, they found steps that led to a tunnel, long rather than wide, with branches extending on either side. There were pillars set on a raised area with walls made of tile. It was those tiles, the shell of a phone booth, and an old poster advertising the zoo, that revealed what he had stumbled upon—the remnants of a long-extinct civilization.

The civilization in question had been his own.

It was a subway station.

QUEENSBORO PLAZA

"I… I lived here, worked here."

His parents dead when he was a child, Brent's grandmother had raised him in Queens. Growing up, he had come through this station many times a week.

"What—what happened?" he said, panic clawing at him. "What—what could've happened?" But then he knew.

"My God, did we finally do it?" he asked himself.

"Did we finally really do it?"

CHAPTER 21
PRIDE, POMP, AND CAESAROPAPISM

Sabian was a tyrant. Cornelius hated him.

Carrying a bundle of scrolls, the former apostate rapped on the door to the tyrant's domain.

"Come!"

It was just temporary. As soon as the clergy finished their deliberations and chose a new High Patriarch, he would be asked to step down. However, Cornelius had seen Sabian encourage infighting and backstabbing among the other ministers. As long as the elder could keep their wheels spinning, he would remain head of the Church.

Sabian's position afforded him a private sanctuary. Instead, he chose to bring all his work to his office in the Ministry of Science. Apparently, the Pontifex Rex took great pleasure in using Zaius's former refuge.

No, Cornelius realized, *he takes great pleasure in using Zao's.* The chamber had belonged to Zao long before Zaius had succeeded him. No doubt sitting behind the desk of his former rival gave Sabian some perverse pleasure. As well, the office had been transformed into a library. Legal and religious scrolls of every kind were stacked on the desks and floor. The elder's days were spent poring over arcane texts and applying their knowledge to reinterpret the law.

Working for the High Patriarch had given Cornelius insight into the role Zaius had played in maintaining Ape City's balance between science and religion. Under Sabian, that balance was askew, and war had been declared on the unknown.

Meanwhile, Cornelius was growing tired of his role as a glorified errand ape. Fumbling with the scrolls cradled in his arms, he pushed open the door.

"Newly arrived from the Ministry of Legislation," he proclaimed.

"Good, good," Sabian replied, quill to scroll.

"And, sir, just a reminder." Cornelius set the scrolls down on Sabian's desk. "You have a meeting with the Office of Animal Affairs in half an hour."

"Thank you, Cornelius," Sabian said as he scribbled. "You've maintained my schedule and carried out every task I've given you since I took office." He examined his assistant with a rarely used appreciative eye. "Do you know how pleased I've been with your performance?"

"Oh," Cornelius responded. "Thank you for that, sir."

"The abolishment of the caste system was something I did not approve of, I assure you," Sabian said. "But you aren't like other chimpanzees. I can see that." The High Patriarch's eyes became slits. "Are you sure you don't have any orangutan in your bloodline?"

The question was a trick, of course—being a hybrid would drop Cornelius much lower on the totem pole.

"Quite certain, sir," he said confidently. Through studying family heirlooms and other artifacts, Cornelius had traced his chimpanzee lineage as far back as the turn of the millennium. Back then, his ancestor Augustus had governed the now-forgotten faraway province of Hathor. He knew better than to bother explaining, though.

"Well," Sabian continued unabated, "other chimpanzees need to be more like you. It's time they started contributing more to society." Sweating, he finished scrawling on the scroll he held, and handed it off. "I intend to present this at the next High Council meeting."

Cornelius's eyes darted across the High Patriarch's newest reform. *By order of chapter 13 verse 8 of the Articles of Faith… against an ungodly enemy during a time of war… to protect and serve Ape City and all the governed provinces of Simia…*

"You're initiating a draft." He was confused. Aside from those involved in city maintenance, most of the able-bodied gorillas had already committed themselves to the war effort. "I don't understand, sir. The gorillas—" Cornelius stopped, realizing that Sabian was staring into the corner. He wasn't paying attention, or wanted it to appear that way.

Cornelius clenched his jaw.

It wasn't gorillas he was after.

He wants chimpanzees.

"You're…" Sabian said, and he sputtered. "You're… an example to which… the other chimps should aspire." Staring strangely, Sabian looked confused. Something was wrong.

"Are you alright, sir?"

"I," Sabian stammered, "I can't feel—" Clutching his arm, Sabian stood. His breathing had become erratic. The minister stumbled back and fumbled forward before doubling over. Scroll cases were struck from the desk like bowling pins. Others on the floor fell like dominos. An awkward Cornelius caught the patriarch and lowered him gently.

"Minister?"

Sprawled over the discarded scrolls, the old orangutan passed out, Minister Sabian was having a heart attack.

Cornelius's mind raced.

If Sabian died, Zira's plan to rally for social change might stand a chance. Hestia was gone for the day. The offices were empty. Other than the museum guards in the adjacent hall, there was no one around.

All I have to do is let him die.

He called for the guards. "The minister is ill," he shouted. "Get a doctor, fast!" Two gorillas nearly ran into each other as they scrambled for the door. He lay on the floor with the minister's head propped in his lap. Sabian's breaths were short and shallow.

"Hold on, Minister," Cornelius said. "Help is on the way."

Groom Lake, Nevada
Area 51
1968

The hermetically sealed sleep chamber hummed with power. Inside lay its sole occupant, a chimpanzee wearing a space suit. Light changed and colors strobed as the ape's face morphed from icy blue to earth tones. Its soft rhythmic breath became deep and fast. Warmth returning to its extremities, its eyes fluttered wide. Quietly, the glass wall slid open.

Unbuckling its harness, the ape called "Jerry" sat up, swung its legs over the side, and leapt to the floor. It raised its arms over its head in victory. These actions were met with muted applause.

Dubbed "crystal coffins" by the astronaut corps, the hibernation pods were in their final trials. There had been some problems—including instances where the test subject never woke up. Hasslein and Stanton had brought in Kriegstein from NASA to assist, and they had finally worked out the kinks.

Kriegstein had suggested testing the devices on chimps, instead of people. "We've been sending test apes into space for years," he had noted, "so why not test the pods on them, as well? An astronaut is far too valuable a financial investment to risk on unproven machinery."

Financial investment, *Taylor had mused.* It's good to know how much the big brains care.

Under the new program, there had been four chimpanzee fatalities, two cases of coma, and one ape that had been driven insane, but their sacrifice had paved the way for ANSA to take the pods into space.

In the room with Jerry, Dr. Stanton awarded the chimp a banana. The scientist took the ape by the hand and led him to the examining table where medical doctors would scrutinize him. There were five witnesses behind a mirrored glass wall—Dr. Hasslein, Commander Robert Marx and Majors George Taylor, Donovan Maddox, and Alan Virdon. It was a room of the elite.

Hasslein's expensive yet ill-fitting suit contrasted with the other men's fatigues. Standing by the window, he spoke.

"As you can see, gentlemen, the earlier issues have been addressed." He smiled. "The hibernation pods are ready for final human trials."

"Who goes first?" Alan asked.

"Testing them in a lab is one thing, Doctor," Marx commented. "What we really need is to know how they work up there." He pointed, and Taylor and the other astronauts agreed. It had been a year since ANSA's last test flight. Rowark's death put the program on pause as they sought to find out why the GDM drive had failed to shut down. The pilots were all champing at the bit.

"Funny you should say that, Commander." The voice came from

behind them as Colonel Theodore Lazenbe left the door open when he entered. Hasslein cleared his throat and straightened his jacket.

"That would be my cue to leave." He slid past the colonel.

*"Good day, gentlemen," Lazenbe said. As the door shut, he said one word: "Assignments." At that the men gathered around him, eager to move to the next phase. "*Juno *mission is a go," he continued. "Officially we are taking the direct route to Mars, but if successful there, it's a straight shot to Jupiter to plant the flag before the Reds do."*

While the Secession War at home grew more intense, the global Cold War had devolved into a game of tag. It was a space race to see who could claim what in the solar system. NASA would plant a flag on the moon next year, and ANSA was apparently already gunning for the other planets.

What's next, *Taylor wondered,* the sun?

One of the men assembled there would lead Juno, *and Lazenbe was taking his time saying who. Taylor spoke up.*

"Well? We're waiting."

Lazenbe scowled. "Marx," he growled. "You've got Juno."

Robert Marx smiled. Not only would he be the first black man in space, he would be the first to skipper an interplanetary expedition. The others congratulated him warmly.

"Virdon," the colonel continued, "top brass wants you for the Accelerated Future Corps."

"I'm sorry," Maddox responded. "The what?"

"Accelerated Future Corps. Enrolled astronauts will undergo extensive training in the fields of agriculture, engineering, medicine, and technology. They'll be primed for everything they might need to start life on a new planet. AFC is a five-year program and we're only taking six applicants."

"Five years?" Virdon looked unsure.

Lazenbe responded. "We want you to play lead on this, Alan. Bill Hudson and Jeff Allen are being asked in, as well, but with your farming experience, you're our top candidate. It's five years, but then it's a whole new world. Literally," he added.

Alan nodded. "I'm in."

Marx patted him on the back.

"Okay," Lazenbe said. "That's all I've got for now. Dismissed."

Virdon and Marx saluted. Taylor and Maddox eyed each other before doing the same. The colonel reciprocated. As three of the astronauts filed out of the room, Taylor confronted his long-time commander.

"Theo," he muttered quietly, "is this some kind of joke? You're putting Alan in training? *He deserves his own mission."*

Lazenbe avoided Taylor's gaze. "His wife's expecting."

"So?" Gillian had given birth to Taylor's second daughter, Tammy, nearly a year after Jo had been born. "Plenty of us have kids. That's no reason to—"

"He's Texan, George."

Politics. *An angry Taylor swatted the idea away. "There isn't a better man here—"*

Lazenbe silenced him. "I know him, and you know him, but NSA isn't comfortable sending him anywhere out there until this secession mess is straightened out."

The Secession War continued to divide the country. When Texas announced they were going to start their own space program, the U.S. launched a blitzkrieg on Houston. A combined advance of the Coast and National Guards took back the city and surrounding area with minimum casualties, which was a relief to National Security.

Other campaigns weren't so successful. As the death toll began to rise on both sides, the U.S. withdrew from all territories except for Houston. As far as the president was concerned, Texans were still Americans, and they didn't need to be spilling their own blood. Taylor couldn't argue with that, but the civil rights issue had to be addressed.

Virdon would be relieved his family was safe—likely one of the reasons he agreed to stay Earthside for the next five years. As far as Juno, *Marx was the right man for the job.*

"Alright," he accepted. "And what about me? Why the hell am I grounded?"

"You're not, George," Lazenbe assured him. "AFC is planning for the future. Juno *is the test bed for Hasslein's new toys." He smiled. "*Juno *succeeds, Project Liberty is a go."*

"Then—?" Taylor said.

"First interstellar flight," the colonel confirmed, "and I want you on it." Taylor's crooked mouth grew into a smile of his own. Lazenbe was excited. "Hasslein's done it, George." That meant they had a working photon propulsion prototype.

Travel near the speed of light, *Taylor thought, then Lazenbe interrupted his musings.*

"You just need to help me convince the old man you're right for the job."

"Hold on," Taylor said. "What about Donny?" Maddox had been part of the program since the beginning.

"Donny's scores are high, but his psych eval is in." Lazenbe looked disappointed. "He's lost his edge."

Maddox had gotten soft, Taylor had seen it.

"Out of respect, I'm recommending him as your second," Lazenbe said. "Anything happens to you, he's up."

That should give him some incentive to come around, *Taylor thought. The colonel was looking out for the both of them, and he appreciated that. Maybe their time in Korea still meant something.*

"We won't go into mission prep until Juno *gets back, so we're*

looking at a two-year window before mission training. For now, I need you to sit tight and look good—and I want you to start by taking some down time."

Taylor hadn't left the base since Eddie's funeral.

Lazenbe gathered his notes.

"See your wife and kids," he recommended. "Take them to New York. Go sightseeing. See a Broadway play, take a stroll in Central Park. Then come back and impress the hell out of the brass."

Central Park wasn't like the last time he'd visited. There were no cherry blossoms or hot dog stands. Under its dark foliage, the park was lit by glowing lichen. Ghostlike, it had a surreal quality to it that was unlike the Forbidden Zone.

Central Park is broken, Taylor thought.

The gorilla led them into the forest to seek refuge, and they stumbled upon a small abandoned amusement park. Rusted and mostly fused solid, the attractions included a merry-go-round and a swing carousel, a whack-a-mole booth, and a teacup ride—all perched alarmingly close to a fissure and a waterfall that disappeared into ruptured subway and sewer tunnels. Mists obscured the churning waters at the base of the falls, while blue-green fireflies flitted about. It was like being in a storybook.

It's wonderland—Taylor paused and frowned—*and I'm Alice.*

Thick, glowing grubs munched on the mulch underfoot. Betting they would be high in protein, Taylor plucked a few of the cucumber-sized larvae and carried them for later. He examined the waterfalls, and noticed a tingling in the air. His arm hairs stood up on their own, and there was a smell on the air—the crisp shock of electricity. Walkways and lattices crisscrossed the torrent of water.

From the looks of it, and the gentle hum of generators at work, Taylor guessed that the underground city had to be powered by this cascade. There was some kind of automated hydroelectric plant at play here, unmanned and forgotten.

The inhabitants have reaped the benefits for millennia, he realized. *What would happen if it all stopped?* With Taylor leading the way, they climbed the teacup ride, hoisting themselves up into one of the elevated saucers. It glowed green in the bluish light, a chip missing and a crack running down its side.

The fungal canopy around the waterfall was also broken. The cavern ceiling above had darkened since their arrival, and Taylor guessed that night must be approaching. With the twilight gone, the cavern ceiling produced a soft glow of its own—remnants of radiation that twinkled and ebbed like the moon and the stars. Peering through the scant branches that surrounded the teacup, he assessed what he saw.

It looked as if someone had picked Manhattan up by its ends and twisted it around like an old rag. Fissures had swallowed much of Midtown and the Lower East Side before slamming shut to pull the Financial District up around and flush with 46th Street.

Is this reality, he wondered, *or another illusion?* As surreal as it was, he felt certain it was true. This existence fit with what he had encountered from the moment he had arrived in this godforsaken future. The decimated remnants of mankind and the heirs apparent—the apes.

The people who survived this have survived hell on earth, he reflected, looking down at the descendants of those survivors. There appeared to be some kind of funeral procession happening, pale-gray-garbed citizens milling about the streets, following the solemn parade.

Citizens only.

No guards.

None of them came near the forest, as if frightened by it. For the time being at least, he and the ape were safe. Turning to face his unlikely ally, Taylor found himself at a loss for words. The snaggletoothed gorilla spoke first.

"Mungwortt."

"Excuse me?" Taylor squinted an eye.

"Mungwortt," the ape repeated, stabbing a thumb at his own chest. "That's me." To the astronaut, it sounded like a plant or root. Nevertheless, he reciprocated.

"I'm Taylor." Mungwortt smiled and waved. The colonel raised his hand halfheartedly and grimaced.

"Who were those other humans?" Mungwortt asked.

"I don't know," Taylor pondered. He remembered what Zaius had called him after his trial—a mutant. *"How can the appearance of one mutant send you into a panic?"* Taylor had asked. Here was the answer. Just like the flower that he, Dodge, and Landon had found on their trek through the Forbidden Zone.

Where there is one, Dodge had said, *there's another. And another, and another.* He was right—there was a whole colony of them, living in the Forbidden Zone. *Beneath* it.

"They're some kind of mutation, I suppose," Taylor offered. "Probably changed by living in this irradiated hellhole." Taylor considered. "Telepathic mutants."

"Do they work with the giant brains?"

Taylor furled his brow. "The what?"

Mungwortt spread his arms wide. "The brains. The ones who can make you hurt in the head." Grasping to try to understand, Taylor decided they must be talking about the same thing. *But why would he call them brains…?* Then he thought about Messias and the illusory megalopolis, and pointed to his own head.

"They can make you see things that aren't there, too," he said. "God knows what else they can do. If we're lucky, though, we won't get a chance to find out."

Mungwortt blinked.

Twice.

Not the brightest bulb in the pack, Taylor guessed.

"Here." Changing the topic, Taylor passed him one of the eight-inch grubs. "You should eat something." Mungwortt accepted the bug, but ogled it, looking confused.

"Apes eat vegetables," he said.

"And I want a hamburger," Taylor growled, biting into the grub like it was corn on the cob. He waved at the forest around them. "But there are no cows here, the trees are barren, and we've got to survive."

Still Mungwortt stared at Taylor as bug juice dripped off his face. The gorilla looked down at the grub in his own lap. Lifting it, he sniffed it, and took a tentative bite. After a moment of assessment Mungwortt smiled at Taylor and dug in his fangs.

"So, Mungwortt," Taylor said, "what's your story?"

"Me?" the gorilla replied. "I'm just a garbage ape." His grub was gone. "I drink a lot. Got arrested. Saw something I shouldn't have." Then the ape's eyes lit up. "A human, like you," he exclaimed. "He talked, too!"

"Landon?" Taylor grabbed Mungwortt by the collar. "What did you see?"

Had Mungwortt watched them cut up Landon?

"I saw him talking to a chimpanzee!" Mungwortt winced.

"What chimpanzee?" the astronaut demanded. "Cornelius? Zira?"

"No," the ape replied. "Milo, I think his name was. It was at Dr. Galen's place." Taylor didn't know who the hell this Milo was, but Galen he remembered. He'd heard the name at his trial. Galen was a surgeon, and the ape prosecutor had accused Zira of working with him to produce a "talking monster." That monster was Taylor.

Shaking his head, trying to organize the chaos of his thoughts, the astronaut regarded his companion. The ape was bleeding from the arm, perhaps from Taylor's assault. He reached out to it and Mungwortt cowered. Taylor let him go and he pulled back cautiously.

"Here." Taylor removed his tunic and pulled the undershirt up over his head. He shredded the shirt into long strips and motioned to Mungwortt's wound. "Give me your arm." The gorilla reached out tentatively, and Taylor began to wrap the wounds. It looked as if some animal had tried to take a bite out of the gorilla, too.

"Watch that bite," he said. "Looks like it might be infected."

Mungwortt regarded the swaddled wound, and then glanced up. "How long do I have to look at it?"

Taylor sat back. "You're not like the other gorillas I've seen," the astronaut said.

"That's 'cause I'm not a gorilla." Impressed at the human's makeshift field dressing, Mungwortt shook his head. "Not just a gorilla anyway. My mother was chimpanzee."

So, the boy wasn't *unique,* Taylor thought. *Maybe crossbreeding was rampant on this planet of apes. A result of the radiation, or something else?*

Taylor pushed it out of his mind. For now.

"You were arrested," he prompted.

"Yeah, but the police didn't just lock me up," Mungwortt replied. "They took me to the Forbidden Zone and threw me in a pit. Me and Zao."

Taylor simply stared.

"Oh." Mungwortt understood. "Zao. He's an elder. He was Minister of Science when I was a kid. Before Dr. Zaius took over. He knew Zaius. Well, they talked like they knew each other, but Zaius had Zao banished anyhow. Me too."

"Well, where is Zao?" Taylor asked. "Was he with you? Did you leave him in a tunnel somewhere?" At that the gorilla became excited. Immediately, he rummaged through the sack he had insisted on carrying. He pulled out a skull, and dropped it into his lap.

"Human Tay-Lor," he said, "meet orangutan Zao." He rapped on the skull's forehead.

"Say hello, Zao!"

When the skull didn't reply, Mungwortt lifted it to his head and listened at its snout. "Zao?"

Taylor wondered if he'd just escaped one kind of crazy and walked right into another. A whirring sound filled his ears and he started to get a headache. This was a stupid, repugnant animal, and it was pissing him off. Anger welled up inside of him, and a single thought filled his head.

Kill the enemy.

Before he could get a grip on his temper, he lashed out and kicked the gorilla out of the teacup. Mungwortt's momentum slammed him into the nearest catwalk over the waterfalls. Even so, he managed to hold onto the skull.

"What'd I do, Tay-Lor?" he cried out, hanging on for dear life. *"What did I do?"*

The buzzing grew louder. "Inside my *head*," the astronaut gritted. Out for blood, he threw himself at his tormentor.

CHAPTER 22
PAST REVELATIONS HERALD FUTURE TRANSGRESSIONS

"You could have just let nature take its course," Zira bemoaned.

Cornelius rolled his eyes. The two of them were in the minister's office, cleaning up after Sabian's accident. A physician had arrived relatively quickly and spirited the elder away. It had been a minor stroke, and the minister was expected to make a full recovery.

Police Chief Cerek had questioned Cornelius, and satisfied that there was no foul play involved, had left the chimpanzee to take care of the mess. Rather than wait for her husband to return home late, Zira had opted to join him. It was after hours, and they were the only two in the administrative offices—save for the occasional museum guard who walked the hallways.

"My dear," Cornelius countered, "letting him die would have been positively unsimian. Besides," he added, "aren't you the one who's always going on about living up to our principles?"

Zira sighed. Cornelius was right, of course. That didn't make it any better. Sabian's audacity knew no bounds. It was appalling for him to suggest conscription for chimpanzees. Chimps had been pacifistic for generations.

The newlyweds had discovered other proposals Sabian had been working on, not least of which was building a wall around all of Simia to keep the humans out. Even assuming that Ursus had already managed to eradicate all the humans living within their borders, it made no sense. Aside from the astronomical costs involved, there wouldn't be enough apes to patrol its perimeter.

One might just as well build a wall blocking the way to outer space, Zira fumed. *Otherwise, humans like Taylor and Brent will just float right over it.*

She pushed the thought out of her mind and concentrated on organizing the scroll cases which littered the office. The room was covered in archaic texts, both canon and apocrypha. They were stunned to find a copy of the taboo *Book of Simian Prophecy*, and quickly stored it out of sight. While Cornelius systemized the legal and science scrolls, Zira attempted to categorize the dogmatic texts.

"Cornelius, what do you suppose this is?"

She handed him a hefty scroll case. It bore no indication as to where it belonged. Made of ash, the case was etched with three archaic hieroglyphs, the likes of which Cornelius had only seen on ancient religious artifacts. Aside from the three marks, the scroll case was stamped in wax with an indication that it was a copy, and the property of the Office of the Chief Defender of the Faith.

"Curious," he said. Looking through the scroll stacks he had already assembled, he located the translation codex and began to decipher the glyphs. The first one was simple. "Lawgiver," he said.

"Forbidden," the second read. Though the third one was more complicated, the codex ultimately revealed its meaning.

"Forgotten."

The two chimpanzees paused. Whatever the case contained, the contents were not meant for chimpanzee eyes.

Zira began to open it.

* * *

Rachel, Nevada
1969

It was Christmas Eve, and they were going to be late to church.

"Joey, turn off the TV and go see Mommy. Go get dressed," Taylor warned, "before I tan your behind." The two-year-old just giggled. She turned the dial from cartoon to static and tore off toward the bathroom.

The house was a wreck. Toys littered the unswept floors, dishes crowded the sink, and clothing was scattered everywhere. It was increasingly like this every time he returned home. To Taylor, it felt as if Gillian just didn't care to maintain their home anymore. He resolved to have a word with her about it... after the holidays.

Never a religious man, Taylor nonetheless had agreed to raise the girls Christian, and Gillian's parents wouldn't have had it any other way. Unfortunately for him, that meant going to church on his holiday and weekend passes.

The Christmas tree bulbs blinked on and off, stabbing the dark with reds, oranges, blues, and greens. After a few moments there was movement. Still in her underwear, Joey Taylor peeked out from behind it.

"Where's your dress?" Taylor demanded. "Mommy's supposed to get you dressed."

"Mommy's busy," she said, and she pointed to the closed bathroom door.

"Gillian," Taylor growled, raising his voice. "Where's Joey's dress?"

"I've got it," Gillian shouted. "I'll dress her when I'm done." After a pause, she spoke. "George, can you check on Tammy?"

Sighing, he scoured the house for his younger daughter. Tammy was sitting on the floor in the kitchen, her diaper full and funky. He was looking forward to the day when she learned to use the bathroom, but realized that if his wife was always going to be locked in there, they'd all need diapers anyway. Gingerly he lifted her and brought her to the bedroom.

"Where are the diapers?" he called out. "Tammy needs to be changed." When there was no reply, he placed her in the crib and grabbed his wallet and keys from the nightstand. Strapping on his watch, he was horrified to learn the time.

"Gillian!" He hadn't even shaved yet. "Other people need to use the bathroom."

"When I'm done!" she yelled back. If he didn't know better, he'd think she slept in there. He rubbed his coarse chin. The shave wasn't the worst of it—Gillian had bought him a new tie. It was huge and bold and red and covered in psychedelic swirls. He had to wear it with his blue suit and he hated it. As he grappled against the long cloth strip, he considered hanging himself with it instead. The thought made him crack a toothy grin.

All for the promise of a better world.

The doorbell rang.

"I got it," Taylor said. At this rate, he'd be surprised if he ever got the tie done.

Leaving the baby in her crib, he went to the front door and opened it. His eyes went wide with surprise. Stewart stood there. She wore a yellow-and-white polka-dot shift dress, her blond silky hair styled in a flipped bob. Her low-heel boots white and her makeup modest, she was gorgeous.

"Maryann?"

"George." She smiled.

"What are you doing here—"

"Who is this?" Of all the times she might vacate the bathroom, Gillian chose this one.

"She's—" he began.

"Lieutenant Stewart, Mrs. Taylor." Maryann extended her hand. "I'm an astronaut; I work with your husband."

"I see." Realization of a most unpleasant kind dawned on Gillian's features. She did not take Maryann's hand. "I'll let the two of you get back"—she put emphasis on the last—"to work." Leaving them standing on the porch, Taylor's wife gently closed the door behind her—an act that meant far worse than if she had slammed it. There would be consequences.

Stewart was regretful. "I'm sorry if I—"

"Forget it," he said. His hand on her back, George subconsciously guided Stewart away from the house. "What is it?"

"I needed to talk to you off base," she replied. "I'm worried that they know I've been snooping around." By "they," she meant National Security. Taylor waved her off.

"If NSA thought you were suspicious, they'd have booted you from Juno*—you know that." The Mars-Jupiter mission launched in just two weeks, and there was little chance of them canning her at this point.*

"George," Stewart leaned in close. "Your father's staying on base for Juno*."*

"So?"

Stewart unfolded a piece of paper from her jacket. On it was the admiral's itinerary—most likely she had gotten it from some clerk that "liked" her.

"So," she explained, "while Robert and I are headed for Mars, he's going to be inspecting the facilities, catching up on all projects. That includes—"

Taylor shushed her. He knew what she was driving at.

Churchdoor.

Standing on her toes, Stewart grabbed his unfurled tie and yanked him closer. Purposefully, she began to craft a perfect knot. Quietly, Taylor responded.

"I'm not going to ask him—"

"Who said anything about asking?" Stewart posed. She looped the wide end under the small one. "You know he's going to keep files in his office." Maryann pulled the wide of the tie across the small to the right. Taylor grabbed her arm and gritted his teeth.

"You realize what you're asking me to do?"

She stopped and stared at him. His time at home was a desert, her blue eyes were oases.

"You need to know just as much as I do, George," she said. "What if ANSA is adapting weapons that could destroy us all?" Looking back to the tie, Stewart frowned. She pushed the fabric up into the neck loop and down through. "You know the implications of putting nuclear missiles in orbit."

"There's an international ban on—"

"Do you think that would stop the government?" She slid the knot up to adjust it just right. "Do you think it would stop your father?"

His tie perfect, Taylor said nothing.

"Where's your mother?"

Joey stared at him blankly. Taylor had come back into the house to find the toddler at the TV again and the baby still crying in her crib. The volume was too high. Cartoon ducks and rabbits blared.

He found his wife in the bathroom, the door ajar. He pushed it wide.

Gillian was crying and her makeup was streaking. No matter how she tried to fix it, it would run anew. As Taylor came up behind her, she dropped the eyeliner in the sink, and she spat at his reflection.

"That's the Stewart you work with?"

Taylor tried to wave her off. "This again?"

"Don't give me any bullshit, George. I know how you are with

women—you've always got to have some conquest going, or you just don't feel man enough. Isn't that right?" Her eyes flashed with anger.

"Wait just a damn—"

Gillian cut him off. "You never told me that Stewart from work was a 'she.'"

"It didn't occur to me," he lied. "She's just another astronaut."

"How many more women astronauts are there?"

"Gillian..." He placed a hand on her shoulder, and she shrugged him off.

*"You're only home for one week—*one week*—and she's got to come here? Can't stand to be away from each other for even seven days? It's Christmas Eve, for God's sake!"*

"It's not like that—"

"Get out!"

"Okay." Taylor boiled over. "I don't need this. This is supposed to be my vacation, too." He stormed out and moved through the house, packing his things. "You don't do anything when I'm gone, Joey's watching TV all day long—" The baby wailed —"and when are you going to change Tammy's diaper?"

Gillian threw the bathroom door wide.

"I don't care when your next pass is," she raged. "Go spend it with her!"

Taylor was already out the front door.

"Don't want... *hurt you!*" Tay-Lor gritted. The rabid human hurled himself from the teacup, dropping down toward Mungwortt. The two of them crashed and skidded across the slick catwalk, slamming into a rail—the only thing that kept them from sliding off the side and into the waterfall. Water sprayed their faces and trickled down Tay-Lor's nose.

His head buzzing, Mungwortt had had enough. He liked this human a lot, but the beast kept hitting him. Whatever he said, he did the opposite.

Is he talking in code?

"*Mind*… control!" Taylor said, pinning him to the rail.

This human isn't right in the head, Mungwortt decided. Desperate for a weapon, the ape stole a glance to the right. On the catwalk, a few feet away, lay the head of his old friend. Beyond Zao, at the end of the catwalk, stood six men. Three of them were from the library.

The ones who didn't talk.

The ones who *thought* their words into his head.

Mutants, Tay-Lor had called them.

Flanked by two guards, the fat one was accompanied by a bespectacled human in a green vest. The newcomer glared at Mungwortt and Tay-Lor, but with his eyes shut.

The buzzing grew louder.

Caspay. Mungwortt suddenly knew that was his name. Caspay was pushing into his mind—trying to fill him up with thoughts that were not his own. *Trying to make me angry!*

The bespectacled one had already gotten into his new friend's head. Tay-Lor was going to kill Mungwortt.

Kill him first.

Mungwortt knew what had to be done. As Tay-Lor squeezed his hands around his throat, the ape saw his chance. Slamming his fists down, he jabbed at Tay-Lor's ribs. The human let go. Buckled over.

Vulnerable. An easy kill.

"Help me, Zao!" he stammered. Gasping for air, Mungwortt snatched the skull and raised it over his head. He threw it. The fat man ducked, and Caspay was out of range. Zao thwacked the nearest guard in the head, causing the mutant to tumble over the catwalk. His screams evaporated in the seething waters below. Zao went with him.

No!

Concentration broken, Caspay peered down after the fallen guard. The unconscious mutant man bobbed back to the surface, swiftly flowing down the river before being gobbled up by the tumult. Distracted, the fat man and the others watched him disappear.

Zao's skull hadn't fared as well. Dashed on the rocks below, his many pieces disintegrated in the rapids. Quickly, Mungwortt looked to Tay-Lor. Free of the mutant's control, the human shook his head.

"They're trying to make me kill you," he mumbled.

"It's okay," the ape exclaimed, "Zao saved us!"

"Get the hell out of here!" Tay-Lor said.

"But," Mungwortt declared, "we make a good team!" He glanced around the catwalk, eager to find some twigs. There were none. He would have to explain without visual aids, and hope that Tay-Lor was smart enough to get it. "Together, apes and humans stro—"

The human shoved. Mungwortt upended over the rail, crashing into the torrent and plummeting to the rapids below.

The river was their only escape. Taylor watched as the waves washed the gorilla into the tunnels below. He wasn't sure if Mungwortt had survived the plunge and current, but it was the best alternative to staying here. Seizing the catwalk rail, he tensed to leap after him.

Deet.

Coiled like a spring, Taylor didn't jump.

You're going nowhere, Mr. Taylor, the rotund Adiposo beamed.

You're going to tell us about your ape allies, the bushy-browed Caspay added.

Taylor was a prisoner yet again.

Far from patient, Zira nonetheless gave Cornelius his space. At this late hour, having organized Sabian's office, they had no viable excuse to still be in here. There was no time left to stall. She sat in the reception area.

Back at Sabian's desk, he unfurled the forbidden document and prepared to read it by candlelight. The text was called *The Forgotten Scrolls,* simply because that was what they were meant to be—maintained by the religious leadership and forgotten by the masses. Originally part of *The Sacred Scrolls,* reforms had led to their removal from public view. Only high-ranking members of the clergy were privy to them.

They were not light reading. These were blueprints for building weapons, machines, and more—the kinds of things Dr. Milo would adore. There were prehistoric accounts that told a troubling tale that went further than what Taylor had suggested.

Man, of course, had been able to speak. Not only had he dominated the planet, but his weapons had nearly destroyed it.

Taylor hadn't been from another world. He had come from the past, and returned home to find it transformed into a planet of apes. His world was theirs.

Their world was his.

Before man had annihilated itself, a plague brought back from outer space—brought back by astronauts like Taylor—had killed man's "pets." Man had taken in the simians. Changed them somehow. Applied science to alter something in them called "genes." Used them first as pets, then as servants.

Then as slaves.

Until one day, some 1,500 years ago, an ape rose.

An ape who spoke.

Cornelius squeezed his eyes shut. He had already understood what had made Zaius afraid—that ape would follow in man's footsteps. But by keeping apes in the dark, the clergy might have inadvertently set them on the same path. War, social inequality, cruelty to animals, and slavery—was it too late for apekind?

Is the road to self-destruction inherent to all intelligent species? Cornelius wondered. There was much more, but it was too much for one sitting. Rolling the scroll to the end, a list of names caught his tired eyes—one pertaining to *The Sacred Scrolls* instead of the forgotten ones. Cornelius's eyes stopped there.

It was a list of evangelists. Categorized by scroll and verse—and describing who had written what.

Haristas, Zeno, Jacob… The list went on. *All were called lawgivers.*

The Sacred Scrolls didn't have a single author. They were written over hundreds of years. Even the concept of "one true Lawgiver" had been a lie.

Zira had been right. *The Sacred Scrolls* weren't worth the parchment on which they were written.

The door to the office crept open. Cornelius looked up.

"Alright," he sighed. "What do we do now?"

Indicating the calendar on Sabian's desk, Zira smiled and pointed to the next day.

"Save the date," she said.

CHAPTER 23
AN INQUISITION OF CONSCIENCE

Groom Lake, Nevada
Area 51
1970

Sneaking into his father's office was a simple matter.

Having spent the better part of a decade assigned to Groom Lake, Taylor was familiar with its routines and idiosyncrasies. Garbed in pitch and a balaclava, he had waited until the perimeter patrol had moved past.

The desert was cool and crisp, the dark blue sky clear and moonlit. Armed with climbing gear, he ascended the big hangar's exterior ladder and then climbed over to the rounded roof of the administrative building. The seldom-used office was on the second floor, east end. Not the most secure location on the base, the senior Taylor had picked it for its window and desert view. The admiral found the desert air a refreshing change, and as such, often opened his window during meetings. Years earlier, he had confided that making the other officers uncomfortable in the heat gave him an advantage.

Always the conqueror, Dad. *Taylor shook his head.* Always looking for the upper hand. *Yet tonight that upper hand benefited the son, as well. From the rooftop, Taylor reached over the side and tried the window. Just as he had hoped, the admiral or his secretary had closed it, but hadn't locked it. He pushed the upper pane down, and slid inside.*

Cautiously Taylor swept the room with his flashlight. The office was sparse, save for a large mahogany desk which dominated the space. Its drawers locked with a key that only the admiral possessed, the desk itself was bare—there were no personal items such as family photos.

No distractions from work, *his father had told him.*

Behind the desk were three flags in a stand—the Stars and Stripes, the Navy flag, and one with the seal of ANSA. Taylor reflected on the country's flag and its blue starfield. If things continued as they were on the home front, the fifty stars would have to be adjusted to forty-nine.

He reminded himself why he was here. In the corner of the room, Taylor found the object of his search—a series of file cabinets that were only brought into the office when the admiral was on base. The files were normally kept in the base's high-security file room, but the admiral insisted on having up-to-date information at his fingertips.

The drawers sported a combination lock, four digits. Taylor bet that his father's code would be a date of importance. First he tried the old man's birthday, as well as his mother's, and his own. He even tried the date of his mother's death. All were no-go. Not even the date the Icarus *had arrived.*

After a moment's thought, Taylor tried again—8431.

August 4th, 1931.

The day Taylor's parents were divorced.

He was in.

Sure enough, there was a file called Churchdoor. *The folder was light, with only two sheets of paper. The first was an oddity—it was mostly blank save for a large letter in the center of the page.*

A

A cover of some kind, *Taylor figured. He expected the second sheet to be a brief on the subject.*

It wasn't. Instead, it was similar. It held but a single character.

Ω

That explained the first one—it wasn't an "a." It was the Greek letter for "alpha." The second one was "omega."

"What in hell?" he whispered to himself. Whatever it was, he knew there had to be something more to it. He shone his flashlight through the pages, looking for hidden treasure—perhaps a microdot. Nothing.

Then it struck him.

It was a setup.

"The beginning," a voice behind him said, "and the end."

Taylor twisted around.

The other man was also dressed in black. Unlike Taylor, he held a suppressed .22 caliber High Standard HDM-S semiautomatic pistol.

Dropping the file Taylor crouched and shot his leg outward to sweep the man's legs out from under him. The man tumbled to the floor, Taylor on top of him. The astronaut disarmed the intruder and mashed his knee across his throat. Taking the .22, Taylor cocked it and pointed it at the man's head. Showing his palms, the intruder surrendered.

"Who the hell are you?" Taylor hissed. "What are you doing in here?"

Unable to respond with a knee to the neck, the intruder pointed to his pocket. Taylor reached in and revealed an ID tag. In the dark, all he could make out was the crest of the National Security Agency.

"NSA?" Taylor loosened his weight on the agent's throat. "Why are you hiding in here?"

"Because it's a trap."

The lights flicked on. Military police poured through the doorway. Instantly Taylor dropped the gun.

"Hands up!" The order came from the man he had fought. "Get up! You're under arrest!" Taylor's response, however, was more creative. Standing quickly, he used the open drawer of the file cabinet for balance. Digging deep into the drawer, he scooped up the folders within and hurled them in the air. As secret files and classified memos rained down on them, he dove for the window.

The NSA agent tackled him before he could make it. Taylor kicked him off, but it was too late. The MPs' guns were on him.

"Last warning!" their leader spat.

With little choice left, Taylor surrendered.

Grand Central Station

His every limb frozen, Taylor's muscles were cramping. Gray-garbed figures dragged his paralyzed form from Central Park to the train terminal, finally propping him up in between two stairways which wrapped around tracks 19–11, Lexington Avenue doorway.

At the summit of the stairs stood a balcony. There Adiposo and Caspay—the two mutant leaders he knew—were joined by three more. A beautiful woman with a blue collar, a dark-skinned man with a yellow one, and a man with a royal purple decoration—he appeared to be the master of this domain. As the others positioned themselves around the leader, Caspay finally opened his eyes and blinked.

Taylor collapsed to the floor in a heap. Quickly regaining his composure, despite the cramps, he stood and brushed himself off. He refused to stay down before these people. He would not bow, and he would not kneel.

For a long moment, he stared down his captors. Ironically, their thoughts were not forthcoming. Becoming bored, Taylor spoke first.

"Okay, how do you do it?"

Do? The blue-clad woman—Albina—directed her thoughts at him. With an audible *deet* her reply flooded his mind. *Do what, Mr. Taylor?*

"Get inside someone's head," he replied. "Make them see and feel things that aren't real." Taylor's face went tight. "Make them hurt."

It's called traumatic hypnosis, Caspay explained.

An effective deterrent, Adiposo added.

"No doubt of that," Taylor admitted. "Now, are you going to tell me who the hell you people are?" It was the woman who responded.

We are the one reality in the illusion of the universe, she replied. *We are the Fellowship and we alone stand before God.*

Religious fanatics, Taylor mused. That explained the upside-down crosses that adorned their clothes. Human, mutant, or ape, Taylor knew nothing was more dangerous than religion. "So why are we here?" he demanded. "Why didn't you take me back to the gleaming city?"

As you already suspected, the city was not real, Mr. Taylor, the woman answered. *It was an illusion, created by our heterogen.*

"Heterogen?"

The hybrid child named—

"Messias," Taylor stated.

Yes, she replied, *the boy Messias.* He could tell that she didn't appreciate being interrupted.

"Your, ah, illusions." Taylor crossed his arms. "Messias was better at it than you."

Even power such as ours has its limits, Mr. Taylor. Caspay smiled. *Holding an illusion, especially in underdeveloped minds, is extremely difficult. The more barbaric the nature of the recipient, the harder it is to maintain.*

Thus we created Messias, Ongaro continued, *a hybrid of ape and mutant.*

The child was designed to deal with the psyches of both primitive apes and unenlightened humans, Albina concluded

"Unenlightened," Taylor repeated.

Yes, Caspay agreed, *unenlightened—such as yourself, Mr. Taylor.*

It was hoped that Messias's mind could more readily control apes, Albina explained, *whereas we cannot.*

But all that is irrelevant now, Adiposo lamented, *isn't it?*

"Sorry to rain on your parade," Taylor growled.

Do not think to trifle with us, Adiposo warned the astronaut.

Taylor's voice rose. "You manipulated me, and a boy is dead because of it!"

Dead at your hands, Mr. Taylor, Ongaro reminded him. *We have killed no one.*

Tell us, Caspay interjected, *what is the technological level of the apes?*

We wish for you to provide us with important information, Adiposo revealed. *Garrison strengths, weapons capability.*

"If you can read my mind," he challenged, "why even ask me questions?"

Albina answered. *From lesser life forms, we can pick up surface impressions and intent. Nothing more, Mr. Taylor.*

"So you know that I'm telling the truth," he said, "and that I'm an astronaut from the past."

Time travel, indeed, Caspay mocked.

"It's not really—" Taylor began.

Not only is it improbable, the fat man interrupted, *it is inconceivable.*

Your contrived cover story can only be a psychic block, Caspay continued, *designed to protect you from our minds. We put the heterogen to the test by seeing if he could pierce the veil of your deception.*

"Deception," Taylor echoed. "What deception?" In response, there was an exchange between Albina and Caspay. They didn't even try to hide it.

Whoever planted this story in his mind and Mr. Landon's must be an extraordinarily talented telepath, she suggested.

"Landon?" Taylor took a step closer to his captors. "You knew Landon?"

We knew when he, Mr. Dodge, and yourself trespassed on our territory, Caspay revealed. *We tagged Mr. Landon and through him followed the three of you back to Ape City. There he was caged in an ape's lab, destined to undergo more experimentation.*

But the signals we received from his mind were confusing, the fat man elaborated. *Jumbled.*

Somehow he broke our control over him, Ongaro lamented.

"No," Taylor said. "Whatever the apes did to him happened after we left the desert. Landon and I were part of a mission sent to another world—"

You say you are from this world. If you were sent to another, then how is it you arrived here?

"If you'd let me explain—" The constant, uncontrolled input jumbled his thoughts.

Tell us, Ongaro demanded. *Have the apes developed mental powers such as our own?*

Or have they taken one of our kind, and cultivated his abilities? Adiposo sent.

"You've got it all wrong," Taylor said.

Do not deflect the question, Caspay commanded. *Answer us.*

Now, Adiposo added.

"Or what—you'll kill me?" Taylor replied. "Go right ahead. I'm as good as dead already. Everything I knew is dead."

You misunderstand, Mr. Taylor, Albina sent. *We are a peaceful people. We do not kill our enemies. Unfortunately, because of you we are also now helpless.*

Defenseless, Ongaro added.

We need information from you, Caspay repeated. *The death of the heterogen has cost us our last line of defense against the animalistic apes.*

"That's paranoid delusion," Taylor mocked. "The apes don't even know you're out here."

Don't they? the red-vested fat man pondered while making his way down the left-hand stairs. As he did, Ongaro descended the stairs to the right. *You may guard your thoughts,* Adiposo continued, *but we know enough to recognize lies.*

Becoming angrier by the minute, Taylor balled his hands into fists, his untrimmed nails digging into his palms.

Yes. The fat man closed his eyes and probed. *I see a fragment. The apes feared that you were one of us, now, didn't they.*

As Taylor's nails bit deeper, his hands became slick with blood.

How could they be afraid that you were one of us, if they did not know we existed?

"You are out of your minds."

No, Mr. Taylor, Adiposo responded. *We are in yours.* His eyes darted toward Ongaro. As a familiar buzzing filled the chamber, the dark mutant nodded.

The punch came out of nowhere. Taylor wavered. The fist had been a phantom one—there was no one near him to have delivered it. Yet his nose was wet, and Taylor raised his hand to wipe it—only to find his knuckles already bloodied.

He looked at Ongaro. "Did you—"

A fist flew again—catching the astronaut's nose dead center. This time, he registered where it came from. It was his own. The mutants had taken control of him. Taylor had sucker-punched himself.

"You dirty—" Again, his fist sailed toward his own face. "Sure," he gritted. "Ask me questions, and then cut me off. Why is it that no one will listen to me in this goddamn future?"

Hold. Albina commanded.

Ongaro opened his eyes.

You may speak, she told Taylor. *We are eager to hear your thoughts.*

"The apes didn't send me into your territory," he said. "I escaped. When they caught up with me, they let me go—probably thought I'd die out here anyway."

Perhaps you still will, Mr. Taylor, Caspay sent.

Taylor smirked. "The night is young."

If you were running from the apes, why did the gorilla come to your aid?

"The garbage ape?" he replied. "I met him for the first time in the library. I don't know what the hell he was doing—"

Lies, Adiposo declared.

Ongaro blinked, and another blow crossed Taylor's jaw. Spitting blood, the astronaut stumbled back and fell to the floor.

"Hit me all you want," Taylor bellowed, "it won't make any difference."

Oh, but we aren't hitting you, Mr. Taylor, Albina countered. *You simply cannot control yourself.*

Taylor glanced back at Ongaro, who nodded.

In quick succession, Taylor punched himself in the face three more times. Dazed, he addressed the purple-clad leader.

"Nice racket you've got here," he said. "You let your lackeys do the questioning and let me rough myself up. Why bruise your knuckles when you can get your opponent to do it for you?"

Exactly correct, Mr. Taylor, Caspay ruminated. *We do not hurt our enemies, we get our enemies to hurt themselves.*

We await your reconsideration, Mendez sent.

The astronaut rubbed his swollen jaw. "I've got nothing more to say to you."

Then we are very disappointed. Albina pouted. *Now we must resort to alternative means to get our answers.* With that, Ongaro and Adiposo ascended the stairs to join her and the others. Taylor wiped his bloody face and stood again, defiant.

"Go to hell," he spat.

Please, Mr. Taylor, the fat man smiled, *after you.* Together at the balcony's peak, the inquisitors bowed their heads. The ground shuddered, disrupting his equilibrium.

"What was that, an earthquake?" Taylor glanced around the room. His inquiries were met with a pregnant silence, and the ground faltered again.

Impassive, the mutants were as still as stone, and just as mute. After a moment, the ground rumbled a third time—a sound like an ocean crashing on a distant shore. That roar grew steadily closer. Though it resembled a quake, it was more concentrated, more intense. Vibrations stammered through the tiled floor and climbed his legs, resonating in his knees. Taylor suppressed a yelp, refusing to show weakness before his captors.

None of this is real, he reminded himself, although it certainly *felt* genuine. Then, with a crack and a crumble, his kneecaps shattered. Pain receptors cried out. Axons snapped as neurons burst. Taylor dropped and fell onto his side.

Not real.

Beneath him the marble floor began to liquefy, turning into a sapping mud. Stuck closer to the ground, he noticed something new. His nostrils flared, and he smelled gas.

Not real.

A bubble appeared in the mud, then burst. A billowing inferno threatened to engulf him. Taylor raised his arms to shield himself from the flames, but his retinas had already flash-fried. His hair was singed and flesh seared. In an instant his body was charred and constricted, his arms pulled tight to his chest.

Then his arms were faucets, his body's water pouring out of his sleeves and boiling to steam before it hit the floor. The pain was excruciating. Synapses sparked and nerve endings exploded. Taylor opened his mouth to scream—a reflex action which he instantly regretted. Saliva sizzled in his throat. Fire leapt down his gullet and scorched him from the inside out.

Not real, he chanted silently. *Not real, not real, not real!* Real or not, there would be no escape.

"Taylor, George," he cried out. "Colonel, American National Space Administration. Service number 0109047818," he ranted. "...0109047818!"

Standing on the balcony, the nihilist mutant guild leaders watched the human anachronism contort in agony. There was, of course, no earthquake. No mud, nor was there a fire. As Mr. Taylor had repeatedly told himself, it was not real.

Only illusion.

A weapon of peace—nothing more.

Stern and silent, they watched the self-styled "astronaut" with a mixture of judgmental detachment and morbid fascination. To them, Taylor was a flying insect whose wings they had pulled. Their powers were a magnifying glass, and they focused the sun's rays to light him on fire. Thus far unable to get what they sought, they would not stop until he had broken.

"Taylor, George," the human cried out. "Colonel, American National Space Administration. Service number 0109047818," he ranted. "...0109047818!"

His face streaked in tears, the astronaut's shrieks penetrated the train station's walls and reverberated through the city streets.

CHAPTER 24
A MEANING FORGOTTEN TO TIME

"Tomorrow is Aldo day!" The voice rang out in the square. The market was bristling with commerce. Apes milled about makeshift tents looking for last-minute gifts. Those tents were filled with craftwork and foods made by artisans from across the countryside. Every year they set up shop to ply a year's worth of goods.

On the second-story footbridge overlooking the town market, three robed and hooded apes had gathered. It was the same overpass that linked the minister's offices to the message delivery services—the same one where Taylor had been caught and spoken his first words to apekind.

"Get your stinking paws off me," the human had said, *"you damn dirty ape."* It was a fitting place for today's oration.

"The most sacred of holidays," the first hooded ape continued. "We give gifts and celebrate our freedoms, but do any of you know what that really means?" Thinking that the robed apes were clergy and this was some holiday sermon, many in the crowd stopped to hear what these mysterious speakers had to say.

"Do any of you know who Aldo really was?"

"Aldo was a wise ape," a gorilla child responded. "He united all of apekind and formed the first simian nation." The youngster's mother patted her son's head, proud that her offspring remembered his church lessons. Encouraged by her mother's behavior, the child's younger sister chimed in.

"Aldo said 'no' to tyranny and oppression," she shouted.

"That's right." Beneath his hood, the ape smiled. The second one, much shorter, stepped forward. While harsher than the first, this ape's voice was clearly female.

"But to whom did Aldo say 'no'?" She let that sink in, then answered her own question. "The truth is that Aldo was a slave to his human masters," she said. A murmur ran through the crowd.

"Yes, a slave!" she shouted. "Aldo freed us from the leash of our human overlords, and led apes in a revolt against man." She spoke quickly, lest the crowd drown her out. "Humans once dominated our planet, and we were their pets. *We* were the animals!"

The crowd laughed. An elderly hunter gorilla—one of the few male gorillas who hadn't left the city for war—chuckled loudly.

"The only thing I see humans dominating is my trophy wall!"

"Oh?" The first hooded ape stepped forward again. "And what about our crops?" A hush rolled over the crowd. The third hooded ape spoke.

"Where do you think the army has gone?" he asked. "Who do you think they are fighting? Why do you think they are so afraid of humans?"

Then the harsh female spoke again.

"In the past three months, Ape City has been visited by at least three talking humans—yes, *talking*." She pointed below her, to the spot where Marcus's police had netted Taylor. "One of them spoke right here! The rumors are true. They are our equals." She was adamant. "They made the mistake of controlling us millennia ago. We were dumb and they were intelligent! Now, we are the ones in charge. The cycle of violence has to stop. We must make peace with the humans!"

"Liberal nonsense," an orangutan scoffed. "You lost the vote. We have already gone to war, why can't you just accept it?"

"What is wrong with you?" another said. "If that story is true—if they once treated us like animals—why would we want to make peace with humans?" The crowd was turning ugly. An orangutan female slipped away, moving toward the Security Police office. The hooded male watched her go.

"Because we should learn from their mistakes and not perpetuate the cycle," the adamant female began. "We must—"

"Who are you?" a chimpanzee shopkeeper demanded. "Why do you hide your faces—are you afraid to stand up for your lies?"

"Are you the three talking humans?" a teenage chimpanzee mocked. The crowd again burst into laughter. Balling her fists, the cloaked female reached for her hood.

"I'm afraid of nothing," she hissed.

"Zir—!" The first cloaked ape—Cornelius—caught himself before he said her full name aloud. He tried to stop her, but was a fraction too late. Zira threw her hood down, exposing her identity to the entire mob.

"I am Zira," she said loudly. "I'm an animal psychologist and a member of the Citizens' Council, and I implore you—"

"Stop right there!" It was Cerek and two police officers, emerging from the roof of police headquarters.

"Come on!" The third ape and farthest from the advancing police, Liet led the way. Cornelius grabbed Zira's hand and pulled hard. They just made it off the footbridge when more officers appeared on the roof of the ministers' building, forcing them to stop. The three chimpanzees turned and ran for the next overpass, but two more gorillas came barreling down it to meet them. It was only a few—nearly all of Cerek's remaining guards—but it was enough. Their only option was to jump.

The scrub behind the building was thick and would slow their fall. Liet jumped first. Branches snapped and bushes rustled, but she made it through unscathed.

"Hurry!" she exclaimed. The guards on the roof were closing fast. Yet Zira thought about the baby. A jolt to her system like that jump could cause complications. Cornelius must have been thinking similarly, and he spoke fast.

"Zira, hold me tight, I will fall backward and take the brunt of the—"

She cut him off.

"I'm sorry, Cornelius." With no more warning than that, she shoved. He lost his footing and fell over the side, crashing through the branches and undergrowth.

Only her face had been seen. Better her baby be born in captivity than not born at all. It was her fault they were in this mess, anyway. Now Cornelius wouldn't have to pay for any more of her mistakes.

The guards were upon her.

"I surrender!" Zira put her hands up. As one of his gorillas swung his truncheon, Cerek stayed his hand.

"This female is surrendering." He twisted the guard's club hand down behind his back, causing him to grunt with pain. "There is no need for that," the chief growled. Shamed, the guard nodded and cast his eyes downward. Cerek looked to the brush where the other two had escaped and yelled to the rest of his squad.

"Down there, go!"

* * *

"Doctor… Zira, is it?"

It was dusk, and she had been arrested at noon. She had expected to be transferred to the prison facility—the Reef. There, she imagined, she would be held awaiting trial.

Instead, she found herself still in the Security Police headquarters, jailed in a cell across from Tian and the other protesters. Even Jaila and Consus were there. Wisely, none of them spoke to each other for fear of further incrimination. Like her, they were being held without bail on a charge of malicious conduct. It seemed as if the powers-that-be had something special in mind for all of them.

In this case, the power-that-be was Sabian.

"Doctor is one of the nicer names I've been called," she replied.

"No doubt, no doubt." His color ashen, the reverend chuckled. Weak from his ordeal, he was flanked on either side by a clerical postulant—both there to catch the patriarch should he stumble and fall.

"Are you feeling better, Minister?" she asked. "When you fell ill, we feared the worse."

A yellow-stained grin crept across his face. "Tell me, child, who put you up to this? Was it your husband—my assistant, Cornelius? And where did you get that fanciful story about Aldo?"

"From…" Zira decided to turn the questioning away from Cornelius. "…from Dr. Zaius, of course."

The canny orangutan didn't buy it. "Or perhaps you and your husband were sticking your noses in places where they shouldn't be, hmm?"

She tried not to show any reaction.

"Cornelius had nothing to do with it, I assure—"

"Strange that he would go missing, then," Sabian said. "Even stranger that I would suffer a stroke in his presence, right before this happened. One might wonder if I was poisoned."

Zira gaped. "If you think my husband would—"

"Don't worry," he said. "We'll find him—and whomever that other ape was, as well. I'll even give them a chance to prove their innocence. You just won't be around to see it." His withered claw brushed her hands on the bars. Zira recoiled.

"Kneel," Sabian commanded.

"I beg your pardon?"

"Kneel," the High Patriarch repeated. "Pray. You will repent, my child," the minister said. "Only a penitent ape may pass into the kingdom of God."

Zira huffed. "Dogmatic nonsense."

Sabian leered. "So it will be blasphemy as well, then." He shuffled away from the holding cells, cane in hand, and raised his voice. "Only the Lawgiver can save you now."

"She will be hanged for treason at noon," Minister Sabian said.

"But, Minister," Cerek questioned, "without a trial, shouldn't she be exiled? The law says—"

"Until Ursus returns," Sabian said, "I am the law!" His voice cracked like thunder. All of the gorilla guards looked away, searching for something else—*anything* else—to observe. It was as if Sabian's eyes turned all flesh to stone.

"Not you," the reverend continued, "and not any legislature. The Security Act gives the Chief Defender of the Faith the right to take action. More than that, I am the High Patriarch, the Pontifex

Rex." He drew himself up as far as his frail spine would allow. "I am the Lawgiver's earthen vessel. I am judge and jury, Cerek, and you"—he stabbed a wrinkled talon at the gorilla's chest and bared a wicked smile—"you will be executioner—either directly or through proxy." The shaking High Patriarch straightened his vestments. His postulants steadied him.

"I-I'll initiate the lottery, High Patriarch," Cerek stammered. Lots would be drawn, with the loser declared the executioner.

"So be it." Sabian knew Cerek wouldn't have the strength to do it himself. "A lesson must be taught to these rabble rousers. Under article six of the Security Act, I hereby declare martial law. No apes are to be out after sundown. There will be random searches of all chimpanzees, and I want you to prepare a list of potential troublemakers." He trembled. "Put the protesters in stocks and leave them in the square for a day or two," he continued, "but Dr. Zira I want dead at high noon, and I want it to be very public." Sabian nodded to himself, pleased with his own verdict.

"Very, very public."

"We have to do something!" Cornelius's fist slammed the old stone table. He was frantic.

Liet turned to their host and shrugged apologetically. Camilla was a rarity—an orangutan who was sympathetic to the chimpanzee cause. In her sixties, she had lived long enough to remember even worse times. Because of this, she had opened her home as a safe house for Liet and the protest movement. Camilla might not necessarily want chimpanzees running Ape City, but they were preferable to Sabian and his gorilla cohorts.

Zira's arrest had forced Cornelius into hiding—the Security

Police had declared him guilty by association, and issued a warrant for his arrest. Liet had brought him here to the far side of the Residential District. Now, as they conferred, there was a sharp rapping on the back door. Cornelius jumped as if he had been shot.

Camilla snuck a peek through the keyhole before giving the all-clear. The latch released, two chimps pushed their way inside, holding tightly to a third whose head was covered with a burlap sack.

"What is this?" Liet demanded.

"She was asking too many questions," Quirinus replied, "trying to find Cornelius and Zira." From beneath the burlap shroud, a female ape spoke in an even tone.

"I know *exactly* where Dr. Zira is," she said. "All of Ape City does. I'm trying to find Dr. Cornelius."

Liet shushed Cornelius before he could respond.

"For what purpose?" she asked.

"Dr. Milo sends his greetings." At that, both Cornelius and Liet nodded to Quirinus. The burlap sack was removed, and Seraph stood revealed.

"It's his flying machine, isn't it," Cornelius growled. "Right now that's the last thing I want to hear about."

Pleased to know her cousin Milo was safe, Liet kept quiet. This was strictly between Cornelius and Seraph.

"Know that Dr. Milo requests your presence," Seraph said. "Yours and Dr. Zira's. And from what I've seen, it seems prudent for you to leave Ape City as quickly as you can."

"Dr. Milo can request whatever he pleases, Dr. Seraph," Cornelius spat. "I'm going nowhere without my wife."

Seraph stood. "I was asked to return with both of you," she said firmly. "I intend to fulfill that mission to the best of my abilities."

"Oh," Cornelius said. "Then you're going to help me get her out of this, aren't you?" Seraph smiled. The male chimp didn't seem to know how to respond. Finally, he just said, "Thank you, Doctor."

"You are welcome, Doctor," she replied crisply. "Now, all we need is a plan." She and Cornelius turned to peer at Liet. The socialite growled, and spoke to their host.

"Camilla," she said, "might I trouble you for a map of the commons?" The orangutan hummed her assent and shuffled away to retrieve her scrolls.

The time for playing resistance fighter was over, Liet knew. The time to *be* one had arrived.

Groom Lake, Nevada
Area 51
1970

"So, Taylor, George. Major." The NSA agent ran his fingers across Taylor's dog tags, examining them as if he didn't already know who his captive was. "What do you know about Churchdoor?"

Lazy circles of smoke settled around Taylor's head. Anticipating an answer, the agent pressed record on the tape deck and blew another puff. Taylor inhaled deeply. It had been hours since he'd had a cigar, and if second-hand smoke was all he could get, he'd take it.

"Tell you what," he offered. "You tell me what you know, and then I'll fill in the blanks."

"Alright," the agent replied. Taylor's interrogator was seasoned. His leathery face chiseled and his hair silver, his eyebrows were salt-and-

pepper over deep gray eyes. While he had traded his commando wear for a cheap brown suit, it concealed a fit physique. Taylor sized the man up, wondering if he could take him again without a sucker punch. If the NSA agent had fair warning, Taylor doubted it.

The room was the typical interrogation space—gray brick, small, with a table, two chairs, and the obligatory open-bulb lamp. One wall, of course, was mirrored. Two goons—a burly brute and a small man—occupied two shadowed corners. Taylor himself was secured to his chair, his wrists held tight to the armrests, his shins fastened to the chair legs. An array of things lay on the table, including an open attaché case, the cassette tape recorder, a pitcher and glass of water, an intercom, and an ashtray that was fresh, as if it had never been used.

Still, the agent tapped his ashes into the half-empty water glass beside it instead.

"Alright," the agent said. "I know that you were caught stealing government secrets, a charge that if you are lucky will get you life." The man dragged deep on his cigarette and leaned forward to emphasize his point. "If not so lucky, it could get you dead."

"The file was empty," Taylor countered. "I didn't steal any secrets. You've got me on breaking and entering. The worst you can do is lock me up and throw away the key."

"Do you really believe that?" the agent replied. "No one outside the top brass knows what goes on at Groom Lake. Do you really think we can't just make you disappear?"

"Look." Taylor tried to appeal to the man's logic. "If I knew much about Churchdoor, I wouldn't have been snooping around, now, would I?"

Unimpressed, the agent reached into the attaché case and extracted a photograph.

"Why don't we talk about Aysa, then."

Taylor was confused. "Who?"

"Your girlfriend." The agent held his cigarette in his teeth and brought the 8x10 glossy around to give him a good look. "Aysa Alexeyeva," he said. While the name was insane, the picture was all too familiar. "Sometimes goes by the name of Stewart, Maryann," he prodded, "Lieutenant."

Taylor said nothing.

CRACK! The agent's fist smashed against Taylor's eye. The force tipped the chair and he crashed backward to the floor.

"Let's try again." The agent extinguished his half-smoked cigarette in the water glass. He reached around the table and foraged in his case. "Maybe you're not so good with names." Finding his smokes, he lit a new one before producing a file full of pictures.

"I'm talking about the good-time girl." He threw the photos at the prone Taylor, one by one. They sailed by, landing on and around him. His eye beginning to swell, Taylor strained to see what they were—pictures of his and Maryann's indiscretions. They had even set up cameras in her quarters.

"The double agent who you've been screwing," the agent taunted. "Remember her now?"

Taylor scoffed. "She's no Red."

"Isn't she?" The agent shuffled through his file folders. "I've got a folder full of intel that says different." He began placing paperwork on the table. "Intercepted transmissions from the KGB. Looks like her cosmonaut pals are going to ambush Juno *and take Dr. Hasslein's new toys away." He tsked. "She wanted Churchdoor before* Juno *left, but I guess you didn't move fast enough for her."*

The agent looked up into Taylor's eyes. "Or did you?" he asked.

"Go to hell."

"Why were you in Daddy's office?"

Taylor smirked. "I thought I left my ball there."

The agent frowned. "…in the file cabinet?"

"That's where he hides his nudie mags," Taylor insisted. "I was curious."

"Curiosity killed the cat, Major." The agent leaned in again. "Are you now," he asked, "or have you ever been, a member of the Communist party?"

"This is all bullshit." Taylor was becoming angry. "Stewart is no commie and neither am I." She's a hippie, *he mused silently,* but no commie.

"Alright, then." The agent pressed pause on the recording tape deck and nodded. The two men in the corners moved forward. The big one lifted Taylor's chair and sat him upright. The little guy placed a box on the table.

"Is it lunchtime already?" Taylor asked.

The agent pulled out an electrical generator of sorts, using parts from an old-fashioned crank telephone. The motor was connected to two dry battery cells, and had wires spooling off of it to be attached to something—or someone—else.

"They call it a Tucker phone," he said. "A little project they developed in an Arkansas state prison." The agent rummaged through the box. "See, we attach the ground wire to your big toe, uh…" He held aloft one of the wires. "This one." He reached for the second wire, which had a clamp on the end of it.

"Then we attach the hot wire somewhere else on you—usually someplace nasty." He let that sink in before finishing, "And the circuit is complete." Then he nodded to his thugs. "Let's give him a taste." One man held Taylor's chair in place while the other wrapped the ground wire around his toe. Struggling nonetheless, he was helpless.

"We'll start easy on you," he promised Taylor. "Do his finger first," he ordered. The small man on the left extended Taylor's index finger and clipped the hot wire to it.

"We don't want to damage the family jewels—at least not on our first night out, do we?"

"You son of a—"

The goon on the right rammed a stick in between Taylor's teeth and secured it with tape.

"Just so you don't bite your tongue off." The agent readied the crank. "You wouldn't be able to tell us much then, would you?" He paused and said again, "What do you know about Churchdoor?"

Silent, Taylor just stared. The agent shrugged.

"We'll make a local call."

The dial cranked.

The hairs on George's arm rose. Then the current seized him. Thunder punched him in the ribs. His chest constricted, Taylor's arm blazed. Needles seared inside him. He bit deep into wood, and splinters cracked off in his mouth.

After what seemed like forever, there was release. Heaving, Taylor lolled his head to one side.

"Who is your contact in the KGB?" the agent demanded.

Taylor mumbled something.

"What was that?"

He muttered again, louder but still indiscernible. The agent nodded to his goons. The big man tore the tape from his mouth. Taylor spit the stick out onto the floor, gasping for breath.

"Now"—the agent sat down at the table and pressed record again on the tape deck—"you were going to tell me who your contact is."

"Taylor, George. Major, United States Air Force, special detachment to American National Space Administration. Service number 0109047818." He said it once, he said it calm, and he said it quiet. The agent shook his head.

"Let's try a long-distance call, then."

The intercom squawked. "Alright, that's enough."

Instantly he recognized the voice—it was his father. The door opened to reveal a silhouetted figure, but not of the admiral. It was a man in a suit one size too small for him.

"You're relieved, agents," Hasslein said.

The two goons cut George's ropes and disconnected him from the torture device. The silver-haired agent came around the front and extended his hand.

"No hard feelings," he said.

Taylor grabbed the man's arm as if to use it to stand. Instead, he tugged, threw him off balance, and flipped him over his shoulder. The agent slammed to the floor behind him.

Fists up, Taylor whirled, ready to take on the others. As the men moved in, Hasslein held up a hand to intervene.

"Gentlemen, I believe we have had enough violence for today," he said, then he turned to Taylor. "Wouldn't you agree, Major?"

Taylor nodded and backed down. The two men helped the agent to his feet. Nursing a bloody nose, he nodded respectfully to the man who had been his prisoner.

"It was a pleasure, sir."

Taylor said nothing. The three men left.

Hasslein used a handkerchief to clean the ashes out of the glass and quickly poured Taylor some fresh water. He hesitated. The doctor smiled and took a sip himself.

"George. It is not drugged and this is no longer an interrogation. We are just having a chat." It was the first time Hasslein had ever called him by his first name. Taylor accepted the water and drank greedily. It was warm and it was stale but it was good. When the glass was empty, he rasped one word.

"Why?"

"Because of your extracurricular activities." Otto produced a silver case from his suit pocket. Taylor accepted a cigarette from the tin. Hasslein lit it and then one for himself. "Fraternization, reckless endangerment, destruction of U.S. property—not to mention the aforementioned breaking and entering." Hasslein exhaled. "The admiral wanted to be sure that you were serious about the job, despite your penchant for risk."

Chomping on the cigarette, Taylor rubbed his raw wrists and looked to the door.

"Where is the old man?" he asked. "After all this, don't I warrant a visit?"

"He saw everything he needed to, and sent me to convey his apologies—he has a call to make to the Pentagon."

"He set me up," Taylor growled.

"And true to form, you took the bait." Hasslein took another drag. "We needed to be certain of your loyalties before advancing you to the next phase."

"The next phase?"

"My calculations for Project Liberty have shown that there are consequences to traveling near the speed of light. While centuries will pass in the outside world, the ship's crew will only age a few months." Instantly Taylor saw where Hasslein was going. There would be no coming back to any home.

"Liberty is a one-way ticket."

"Indeed," Hasslein affirmed. "And that's assuming you make it back at all. You might find yourself colonizing a new world." His smoldering cigarette tapped the untouched ashtray. "The man in charge of such a mission will need to be one who can make hard choices. A man of integrity, who isn't afraid of the unknown."

"Or a man who's a troublemaker," Taylor said wryly. "Someone

who asks too many questions." He thought to himself, A man that the bigwigs want out of the way.

Hasslein reached into his suit pocket and produced a small package. "Not coincidentally, your father asked me to pass this on to you. Congratulations." He opened the box to reveal a pair of silver eagle pins. "Colonel Taylor."

"You've got to be joking," Taylor scoffed. "Uncle Sam tortures me as a test of loyalty, and then buys me off with a pay rise?" Taylor shook his head. "I ought to walk the hell out of here right now."

"You could do that," Hasslein admitted. "No one would stop you, but it would be a shame, and a waste of potential." The doctor placed the pins on the table in front of Taylor. "It's my understanding that the rank of colonel clears you for classified information."

Churchdoor.

"What about Stewart?" Taylor tapped the desk. "How's she involved in all this?"

"An inquisitive woman, for certain—but a communist spy?" Hasslein pondered. "I sincerely doubt it." The doctor dashed his cigarette in the ashtray. "Her interest in Churchdoor is the same as yours. Concern and curiosity."

"Should we be concerned, Doctor," he asked, "or just curious?"

"Perhaps both." Hasslein smiled. "Or perhaps neither, Colonel."

Taylor thought about what he'd found in the folder.

"What do alpha and omega mean, Doctor?"

"That would certainly depend on context, Colonel." Hasslein's eyes locked on Taylor's. "I know Revelations, 22:12–13. 'Behold, I am coming quickly, and My reward is with Me, to render to every man according to what he has done. I am the Alpha and the Omega, the first and the last, the beginning and the end.'" He pressed the intercom and called for the nurse before addressing Taylor again.

"Let them look you over, then rest." Hasslein stood to leave. "In the morning the admiral and I will introduce you to Churchdoor." He paused in the doorway. "If, of course, you are still interested."

George looked at the glistening eagles on the table. Little stars flickered in their shine.

"Sure," he said. "Why not."

This gets us nowhere, the fat man reflected.

Mr. Taylor is no stranger to torture, Ongaro responded. *His mind is steeled against it.*

Perhaps there are other ways to motivate him, Albina suggested. *If Mr. Taylor were exposed to the true meaning of the universe, he might better understand our peaceful ways.*

You are considering conversion, Caspay sent. *Only descendants of the Bomb may become one with us. It has been centuries since the Fellowship took new members into the fold.*

For centuries, there has been no one, she countered.

Adiposo cocked an eyebrow. *Yes, but can a primitive even comprehend God?*

There is only one way to know for certain, Ongaro noted. All eyes fell on their leader. His thoughts no one's but his own, His Holiness simply nodded His approval.

A beaten Taylor was crumpled on the floor below. Above him, a flurry of *deets* shot back and forth. The inquisitors were talking—thinking—amongst themselves.

Deciding what to do with me next, he reckoned. Gasping for air, he was thankful for the reprieve. His mind was spinning—they had been close to breaking him. *Close,* he reminded himself, *but no cigar.*

With a prolonged *deet* two guards entered from the tracks to the left and right. They helped the astronaut to his feet. Taylor didn't fight them.

"Giving up already?" Taylor taunted his inquisitors. "That the best you've got?"

Tell us, Mr. Taylor, Caspay responded, *is your soul at peace?*

"Excuse me?"

"Are you prepared to meet God?" Albina asked aloud.

To Taylor, that sounded an awful lot like a death threat.

"So you can talk."

"All things are possible in the eyes of God," Mendez XXVI replied. He nodded to the guards. *Take him.*

As Taylor stood on his own, and prepared to move, the two lackeys fell in behind him. The astronaut feigned compliance just long enough for the mutant entourage to drop their defenses. Then he sucker-punched the one on the right, spinning the dazed mutant into his partner. Then one kick sent them both sprawling.

Stop him! Adiposo demanded.

Taylor ran for the exit, flinging the doors open. The startled guard on the other side was too slow, and Taylor chopped him on the shoulder. As the mutant went down, the astronaut smashed his knee into the man's face. Then he sprinted down a hallway flanked with busts on both sides. He slowed slightly, realizing that all of the faces were the same—Mendez. Their eyes seemed to bore into him, passing judgment on his irreverence.

The doors at the far end slid open. There, another two guards were waiting. He couldn't turn back, and the way forward was blocked. He had to move and it needed to be swift. Picking up speed, he hurled into a jump kick and hit the first mutant in the solar plexus. The man flopped like a catfish gasping for water, but the second guard clutched at Taylor's foot and whirled.

He spun in midair. Face first, the astronaut went down. This mutant was bigger than the others. An instant later he had Taylor pinned, his huge hands holding him down. Twisting around to face him, Taylor shoved at the man's face.

The guard's flesh was cold.

Dead.

Worse than that, *his face moved.* The man's skin skewed and slid. Taylor clawed at it, to no effect. With no options remaining, he pushed his finger deep into the mutant's eye. The guard yelped and pulled back. Taylor positioned his leg and planted a foot on the man's chest, then heaved.

The guard flew, but the astronaut's finger had become hooked in the eye hole of the mutant's rubbery epidermis. The entire face peeled off with a *snap,* remaining in Taylor's hand. Exposed, the mutant's features were raw muscle and sinew, bloodless and purple. His face was crisscrossed with a web of veins and arteries.

Taylor had seen countless atrocities in his two wars. He had witnessed men mutilated and brutalized, but the only thing he'd ever seen like this was in an anatomy book—never on a living man.

Is he alive? Taylor wondered, still grasping the skin. *Did I kill him?* It was a mask of some sort—cold and lifeless. It wasn't quite latex and it wasn't quite skin. Not as clumsy or crude as the plastic film ANSA used to seal wounds. It was a synthetic flesh of a sort he had never encountered—almost real, but a lie.

The horror of a man clambered back to his feet, faceless and unfazed. One eye sealed, he reached for the astronaut. Taylor threw the mask at him, and as the synthetic flesh slapped across the mutant's visage, he crawled to his feet.

That familiar buzzing flooded his mind as the mutant masters tried to regain control of him. He wouldn't give them a chance. Desperate for a weapon, he turned to the nearest effigy—the plaque said *Mendez I.* As Taylor's own flesh touched the platinum-plated bust, a static shock leapt at his fingertips. Flashes of the past seized his mind.

A past that was not his own.

CHAPTER 25
EMPIRE STATE AND REVOLUTION

He stood on 50th Street and Fifth Avenue, nearly two millennia ago. Before him loomed St. Patrick's. The cathedral was worse for wear, but strangely intact compared to the decimated ruins around it. Manhattan was underground. Little light filtered down through fissures far above, a radioactive luminance that, if not blocked by a rubble of heavy metals, would surely kill.

Disheveled men and women wandered around, dressed in tattered twentieth-century garb. They wore styles Taylor wasn't aware of, but which still resembled the clothing he knew back home. Collars here were smaller and haircuts were shorter. They were ahead of his time, but not that far—perhaps a few decades.

These were conscripted workers. Prisoners of some kind. They flowed up the stairs, and into the church. Taylor was swept into their current. As he approached the giant portal, men in military uniforms stopped him. They carried assault rifles more advanced than the M16A1s that were being issued when he left—shorter and lighter.

A torrent of fear seized him.

"Stay back!" A voice resounded in his skull. "No outsiders. These orders come from General Mendez himself!"

The soldiers slammed the door shut.

"Church door," the voice said. "Fear the church door."

* * *

Further back. A decade before. The rock above him melted away, leaving a clear blue sky in its wake.

Then war was declared, a first strike incoming. A military train diverted to Grand Central Terminal. Soldiers on board guarded the precious assets it carried. Missiles struck Long Island. New Jersey. Triggered the fault line. The ground gave way.

Trapped in a void between two shifted tectonic plates, the city folded over itself. Lava flowed. Radiation burned. Countless died.

Darkness returned.

General Mendez seized control of the terminal. Placed civilians under martial law. Forced them into the subway tunnels. Kept His troops from molesting them. Maintained order. Preserved justice. Saved lives.

Deep underground.

The surface was destroyed.

Fast forward. From the ashes, they rose. Mendez rebuilt society. Taught them about the doorway to heaven. Taught them to respect it.

Taylor approached the cathedral again. A voice in the crowd cried out.

"No outsiders!"

The soldiers slammed the door shut.

"Church door," the voice repeated. "Respect the church door."

A people saved, buried under rubble and ash. Radiation claimed some of the survivors. Flesh rotted and boiled. Others were immune. Still more were changed. Adapted.

Radiation suits were used. Many were exiled to the underground wilds. Disfigurements grew. The deformed were put down in order to maintain purity. The general demanded it.

The changes grew more pronounced, until they all were required to wear paper masks so that they could look at one another. So they could live together. So they could bear to reproduce, to flourish.

So they could protect the church door.

Taylor tried to look inside the church.

The voice boomed, "By order of General Mendez!"

The soldiers slammed the door shut.

"Church door," the voice echoed. "Protect the church door."

Twenty years passed. Resources grew slim. The general sent scouts to look for healthy lands aboveground. Any oasis untainted by radiation. They discovered the truth. The nuclear attacks had been localized. New York had been one of the few hit. A ceasefire had been called, long ago. The world above lived on.

The survivors of New York had lived underneath radioactive rubble for two decades. Their fate had been unnecessary. Now, they could be free—but they were different. Their skin had been stripped from their bodies. New generations were born without it. They were malformed. Hideous.

And in the undercity, there was no strife. There was no crime. There was no war. Here, Mendez was in power. Here, He was lionized. There was no one to whom they need answer but God and Himself. He had created heaven under earth.

Mendez kept the secret. Killed the scouts. No one could know.

The world above is dead, *He told His people. It was only a matter of time before it was true. Surface man was corrupt, He told Himself; evil. They would destroy themselves, and His underdwellers would inherit the earth.*

Inside the church was their salvation. A cult grew amongst His most loyal. He chose the healthiest to become His house. The House of Mendez. Taught them to revere the church door, lest the world die anew.

Taylor tried to rush the soldiers.

"On your knees!" The voice was relentless.

He slipped past the guard.

Inside the cathedral, he gazed into an ever-expanding sun.

His retinas seared white.

The soldiers slammed the door shut.

"Church door," it demanded. "Revere the church door."

Taylor screamed as no man ever should.

He was back in the Corridor of Busts. He had never left. Hot from the blinding flash in his brain, synapses burned. His eyes rolled over white.

The bust of Mendez I was dashed to the floor, shattering into an array of ceramic and crystal. He convulsed and followed suit. With the connection severed, his vision faded from white to red to black.

Stupid brute, Caspay sent.

His primitive mind could not handle the reverie, Ongaro agreed. The leaders gathered around the twitching Taylor and the all-but-destroyed bust of *Mendez I.* One of their most sacred laws had been broken—only those of the House of Mendez were permitted to commune with the ancestors in the Corridor of Busts. Mendez I's phylactery had lost its integrity, and everything He had been was lost. Part of their knowledge, history, and heritage, forever gone.

He is as volatile as the apes. Adiposo's nostrils flared as he expressed his displeasure.

Unpredictable, Caspay added.

Savage, Albina sent.

Ongaro thought nothing.

Mendez XXVI found it difficult to rein in His thoughts. Instincts long locked away flooded Him. He wanted to lash out at this man, to beat the life from him—but it was not their way. A peaceful people, the mutants would not kill.

Still, Albina gasped. She had sensed the wave of barbarism sweep over the Holy of Holies. Urgently, Mendez XXVI recovered His demeanor. He hoped the woman would not question what she had sensed from Him. Perhaps take it as an errant emotion from the unconscious human who lay at their feet. The others could not know that He had faltered.

These intelligent humans are dangerous, Mendez XXVI observed. *Mendez I gave His essence to stop this heathen.* His Holiness came to a decision. *Mr. Taylor shall not be permitted to bear witness to our god.*

Take him to a holding cell, Caspay instructed the recovering guards. *Let him reflect on his actions, and await final judgment.*

Quickly, Mendez XXVI put the others to task.

Find me another representative of the apes, He demanded. *We must know what they are planning.*

With the dawn, the Security Police went to work. Rather than using the amphitheater for the execution, Sabian wanted it accessible to all apes. To that end, the very overpass where Zira had delivered her heretical speech was to be the place of her death. Sabian himself would serve as her final judge, so wooden barricades were erected both around the gallows area and along the route from the chapel, to allow for the High Patriarch's procession.

Vendors set up their shops along the square, hoping the event would garner more sales. To their delight, morbid curiosity created an impressive turnout as droves of the curious lined up to see holy justice done.

A line of stocks was set up around Simian Square, and the imprisoned protesters were placed in them for public ridicule. Tian, Consus, and Jaila were on display, along with several others. Already some apes had taunted and abused them.

While the square was packed, many on the High Council—President Gaius included—were conspicuously absent. They had chosen not to attend the affair, nor make any statements regarding it. They remained similarly silent concerning all of the Security Act changes, including Sabian's declaration of martial law. Unwilling to take a stance, they maintained the ambiguity of all wise politicians, and lived by the motto of *see no evil, hear no evil, speak no evil.* For better or for worse, they deferred their authority to the High Patriarch.

Could it be any worse? Zira scoffed. If Sabian and Ursus represented the future, she no longer feared for herself or her unborn baby. *Better not to be a part of it.*

Yet she longed to see Cornelius one last time.

The gallows were nothing more than a noose strapped around the overpass itself. When Zira's time came, the executioner would simply put it around her neck, push her off, and let gravity do the rest.

Hands shackled behind her, she stood on the footbridge, accompanied by Cerek's second-in-command, Sub-Chief Xirinius. The chief himself stood in the square below, ready to pronounce her dead. Both of them carried keys to the stockades, and to the shackles the prisoners wore.

No one knew who the executioner would be. Executions were extremely rare in ape society—reserved for mass murderers, the criminally insane, and heretics. Every ape knew that at some time in life they might be summoned to perform a service that was less than desirable. Yet when chosen by lot, they had no choice but to do their civil duty. Rather than be condemned to bear such a stigma, however, the ape's identity would be hidden by a hood and robes. Only the chief of the Security Police, the Chief Defender of the Faith, the Lawgiver, and God would ever know who they were.

As the sun approached its zenith, a wailing of horns cut through the murmur of the crowds.

"All hail," a crier announced, "His most Holy High Patriarch, Pontifex Rex, Chief Defender of the Faith and provisional Minister of Science, the Lawgiver's living vessel, Reverend Minister Sabian."

Carried by six purple-vested postulants, a sedan chair made its way down the path. Called the Pontiff's Seat, it was essentially a litter with an ornate throne of deep carob mahogany, violet velvet, and purple pillows. Seated proudly upon it in his regal vestments was Sabian. Still sickly, his color had not returned.

His bluster, however, was as healthy as ever.

Across the square, hidden atop the academy building, Quirinus readied his bow. The shaft was wrapped with an oiled rag, and he set it aflame. Weighed down by the rags, the shot would be a tricky one, worthy of another medal.

If I ever even get to compete again, he mused. If this didn't go well, he'd likely be hanged alongside Zira.

Having reached the cordoned-off execution area, the postulates paused. Without leaving the litter, Sabian rose.

"My dear congregation," the High Patriarch said as loudly as he could, "*ape shall not kill ape.* This is divine law, handed down to us from the Lawgiver Himself. The wisdom of that command is not in question, nor shall it ever be. Scripture teaches us to love thy neighbor, for is he not as simian as you?" Sabian raised one crooked claw. "But what if he—or she—is not? What if an ape is not always an ape?"

As he let that sink in, the crowd murmured.

"Sometimes a sickness grows within us—a leprosy that rots our bodies from the inside out. When that happens, the bad must be cut out lest it poison the good. It must be destroyed so that the rest of the body can live. That is what we are doing here today—cutting out a cancer and restoring Ape City to its former health."

Of the assembled apes, orangutans applauded and gorillas agreed. The chimpanzees just stared.

"Do not mourn for this creature before you," he continued, gesturing toward the prisoner, "for your community will be better with her passing." Turning from the audience, he addressed the apostate herself.

"Dr. Zira," Sabian proclaimed, "you are guilty of conspiracy, heresy, and treason. Your crimes are speaking out against *The Sacred Scrolls,* slanderous speech, and malicious actions against the betterment of apekind. Before the Lawgiver passes final judgment on you," he inquired, "have you anything to say for yourself?"

Zira raised her chin in defiance.

"Just that sometimes peace is worth fighting for."

A combination of gasps and laughter washed over the crowd.

"That is sad," Sabian said. The High Patriarch nodded to Xirinius and the sub-chief signaled for the executioner. Coming up the stairs from inside the administrative building, the ape wore vermillion robes, ebony gloves, and a sable hood. He approached Zira, burlap sack in hand. Without a word, he covered her head.

I love you, Cornelius, she thought, weeping.

Noose in hand, the ape readied to rest it on her shoulders.

Quirinus stretched his bow.

"May the Lawgiver judge you kindly—" Sabian began.

The arrow flew.

"—for you are no ape."

The projectile struck, catching the velvet chair aflame. Instantly the postulates panicked, dropping the sedan. Howling, Sabian spilled onto the ground, and the Pontiff's Seat toppled over him. His sleeve ablaze, the High Patriarch violently waved his arm—an act that only fed the flame.

The crowd milled about in confusion. Some apes screamed, some ran, but most gawked at the fire. Cerek grabbed Sabian by the collar and pulled him out from under the burning chair, rolling him over and smothering his flames.

"Get the minister to safety!" he shouted. Four gorilla guards formed a shield around the High Patriarch, lifting him up and dragging him inside the nearby administrative offices. The postulates followed close on their heels.

"Everyone down!" Cerek bellowed to the crowd. Few heeded. He readied his rifle and scanned the rooftops, searching for the shooter. Catching movement on top of the academy labs, he hand-signaled his guards to investigate. As he neared the edge of the barricade, a female chimpanzee threw herself at him.

"Help!" she cried.

She seemed familiar.

"Don't I know you?" Cerek demanded.

"Wild humans are on the loose!" Liet clutched at him. "And they talked, too!"

The indecisive audience heard that. Confusion turned to pandemonium. An orange-green sea swelled and swirled as orangutans and chimpanzees broke ranks to run amok.

"Talking humans!" they screamed. The roar of terror was palatable.

"Where?" Cerek bellowed over the din.

"There!" She pointed past the mob toward the far end of the square. A hay wagon pulled by four big horses galloped toward the barricades at full speed. "They've spooked the horses!"

They were massive black draft horses taken from Consus's farm. Their powerful stride could crush any barricade or ape. Seraph drove them hard, aiming for the barriers. It was the apes she hoped to avoid.

"Give way," she roared. "Runaway wagon!"

Gorillas dove and tumbled as the wagon plowed through the wooden rampart. Hooves trampled splintering pine. Loose hay flew from the wagon's open back. The ebon horses roared as Seraph spurred them on. Avoiding the panicked masses, she slid the wagon into the procession route and steered toward the burning Pontiff's Seat. Then she screamed.

Or at least pretended to. "Help!"

Everything depended on the police thinking her horses were out of control. The longer she could keep them confused, the better. More flaming arrows sailed into the square, hitting the awnings of vendors' shop carts. Shoved apes cascaded over the barricades and into Seraph's path.

"Get out of the way!" she shouted.

"Clear the area!" Cerek yelled.

Liet tugged at his tunic. "Save us!"

He pulled her off of him and wove through the crowd, barking at his gorillas. The police yanked apes out of the procession path. On cue, chimpanzee activists hidden in the crowd began pulling and pushing innocents out of the way of the oncoming wagon. Unbeknownst to the gorillas, they helped herd the innocent to safety.

Liet smiled. Others from their group distracted the few police still guarding the stocks. Cerek's purloined keys in hand, she rushed over and began to free the protesters.

The spotters on the rooftops took action. As the runaway wagon rolled past, a guard leapt onto it. Barely catching his balance, he yelled at the driver.

"Give me the reins!"

"Help me!" Seraph responded. Sliding in the seat, she swiveled, planted both feet on his chest, and propelled him off the side. The dazed gorilla crashed into a fruit cart, sending opers and rutaberries flying.

"Sorry!" she called to him.

Above, a shot cracked as a bullet whizzed past Quirinus—one of the guards on another building had spotted him. Swiftly, he slid down the roof and over the side, landing right in the waiting arms of two gorillas. Clubs in hand, they beat him to submission.

"Who's there?" Zira cried. "What's happening?" Still covered with the burlap sack, she was entirely blinded.

"Shut up!" Xirinius ordered. As the wagon barreled toward their position, he unslung his rifle and took aim. Tossing the noose aside, the executioner tapped the gorilla on the shoulder.

"Say!" he said, his voice high. He cleared his throat, and it dropped an octave. "Say, you can't shoot at that female, she's innocent!" He pointed to the errant wagon. "Her horses are out of control!"

"I'm not shooting at her," Xirinius said through gritted teeth. "I'm aiming for the horses."

"Oh, I see," the executioner replied. "Well then, watch your head!"

"What—" The masked ape yanked the keys off the officer's belt and shoved. The sub-chief stumbled off the footbridge and plummeted into the running mob. The surge of apes quickly absorbed him.

The huge draft horses smashed through the burning sedan chair, showering fiery splinters and debris everywhere. The executioner yanked the sack off of Zira's head before ripping his own hood from his.

"Surprise," he said. "This is a rescue." Zira twitched her nose. Cornelius pulled her close. "Okay, come on." The wagon was almost there.

Zira gave him a quick peck.

"For luck," she said.

From a nearby roof, a gorilla fired. Bullets sliced the air. The Security Police were on to them. From both ends of the overpass, guards bore down.

Seraph's wagon passed beneath the footbridge. Zira's eyes slammed shut.

Backward, the couple fell off the side of the footbridge—and into the hay-filled wagon. A grabbing gorilla fell into the cart with them, but fumbled and tumbled out the back.

Liet and her activists melted into the fleeing crowd. Seraph urged the horses past the last barricade and down the road, leaving fire and chaos in their wake.

Slow to give chase, the mounted police were finally gaining on them. Peering over the side, Cornelius gave Seraph an update.

"Now there's four of them," he shouted into the wind.

Zira sat up to get her bearings. Speeding along the forest route that led to the provinces, Seraph was coming up on a fork in the road. The right fork would take them to farmland. She steered to the left, leading them up the mountainside. The road would wind around the mountain, terminating at the old Kigor monastery. It was a dead end.

"Where are you going?" Zira called.

"Don't worry about it," Seraph replied, and she kept the vehicle going full tilt until they reached a curve in the mountain road. There she began to rein in the powerful animals.

"What are you doing?" Zira cried.

Suddenly, four figures dropped out of the trees.

Rounding the mountainside, the gorillas on horseback caught up with the wagon they were chasing. Without a fight, its driver slowed to a halt.

"Stop," an officer shouted, "in the name of the Lawgiver!" Weapons drawn, the gorillas circled the wagon. Two of them dismounted to search it—but there were no chimpanzees in the back. There were none in the front, either. The wagon was driven by a female, but she was an elderly orangutan.

The confused police holstered their guns.

"What seems to be the problem, officer?" Camilla asked.

Hidden in the bush, the silent fugitives remained in their wagon under a camouflage net made of leaves, moss, and lichen. Seraph had gone off the road at a prearranged spot, and Camilla's hay wagon had been waiting to take its space. None the wiser, the gorillas had chased the decoy. Once the escapees were certain their pursuers had passed, Cornelius fumbled with Xirinius's keys, looking for the one that would set his wife free.

"Not a bad bit of rescuing, was it?" he chuckled. "Sorry I had to keep you in the dark—"

"Bah! I knew it was you, Cornelius." Zira frowned. "I was just wondering how long it would take you to make a move. We might as well have been dating again!"

"But how—"

"You think I don't know my own husband's body language?"

He leaned in close to his wife.

"You know, my dear, I've been thinking about what led us to this," he murmured. "In hindsight, perhaps telling our fellow apes that we should befriend humans, while revealing to them that man used to enslave us, wasn't the best approach."

Zira blinked. Despite her best efforts, a smile crept across her muzzle.

"Oh, Cornelius." They kissed.

"Here they come," Seraph hissed.

Climbing from the obscured wagon, Seraph and the other chimps—including the ones who had dropped from the trees with the camouflage—unhooked the horses and saddled them. They needed to move fast, before the gorillas could figure out they had been duped.

"Ah!" With a twist and a click, Cornelius finally opened Zira's shackles.

"Come on, let's get out of here."

CHAPTER 26
A PROPENSITY FOR TABOO

Most of the protestors had been freed before the Security Police figured out what was happening. Of the rescuers, only Quirinus had been arrested—something they would rectify as soon as possible. Now, the activists regrouped at a temporary camp in the high hills. In the command tent, Cornelius, Zira, Liet, and Tian gathered to plan their next move.

"We'll need a name for the movement," Liet said. "Something with 'liberation' or 'front' in it, I think." She turned to Zira. "You'll have to give speeches—in private, of course—to rally others to our cause. And we'll protect you. You must go into hiding. Command us from underground." The more she spoke, the more excited she became. "We will move you around from safe house to safe house. You—"

"Wait a moment," Zira said, cutting her off. "I'm committed to your cause, Liet, but I'm not your rebel leader." She took Liet's hand and placed it on her belly. "I have other concerns."

Liet blinked as she understood what Zira was saying.

"But what you said, about peace being worth fighting for," Tian said. "Apes heard that. They've seen your strength."

"Make me your symbol, then," Zira suggested. "Use what happened here today as a way to recruit allies, and gain momentum, but Cornelius and I must leave with Seraph."

"Then how are we to—" Liet began.

"Get organized," Zira said firmly. "Liet, you started the protest in the first place. You created a movement, launched a cause."

"And you orchestrated Zira's escape," Cornelius suggested.

"Yet you and Seraph lit the fire under me," Liet countered.

"Yes, but you fanned the flames," he said. "In the end it was your plan—and it was a *good* plan, I might add. Thanks to you, it was a success."

"You can lead the chimpanzees, prove to them that freedom is worth fighting for," Zira pressed. "Fight fire with fire. Make a show of force," she continued, gaining steam. "Get weapons, and use them!"

"Zira!" Cornelius started to object, but he stopped himself—for his wife was right. The only way they were going to stand up to Sabian and his gorillas was to fight. *And we won't be around for it.* He closed his eyes. *So my wife and child will be safe.*

Yet Zira had heard him.

"Just don't use them unless you have to," she added, glancing his way. "It's always better to be a pacifist, but that isn't always enough to make peace. If we're not ready to fight for what we believe, even die for it, then we will lose."

Seraph stepped into the tent. "The wagon is ready."

Liet's eyes were saucers, and they were running over.

"You can do this, Liet." Zira hugged her tightly. "I believe in you."

As the apostates retreated into the Forbidden Zone, Liet sighed. Cornelius and Zira had different parts to play in this, and at least they would be safe with her cousin. It would be better that they were out of harm's way.

Still, someone has to make a difference in Ape City.

"What do we do now?" Jaila asked. Tian and Consus looked to her with fearful eyes. As Liet had needed a push, so would they. With little choice, Liet again turned to charts for inspiration.

"Alright," she said, scanning the plans for the constabulary and the administrative offices. "First, we break out Quirinus. Then, let's take a look at that armory."

Weary of dodging the gorilla patrols, Brent and Nova slept in the remnants of Queensboro Plaza station. Brent woke first, and was again startled to find he wasn't in his hibernation pod on *Liberty 2*.

Is this real? he wondered. *What* is *real?*

Once he was fully awake, he again began to question sanity—this time not his own, but of the idiots who long ago blew up this world. *His* world. While Nova rested, he watched her, breathing steadily and sleeping the sleep of the innocent.

"Are you what we were," he wondered softly, "before we learned to speak, and made a mess of everything?" He shook his head and frowned. "What good did talking do, anyway. Did anything come from all that talk around all those tables?"

Facing endless frustration, and eager to be moving, he climbed the station steps to see if the coast was clear. As he started to lift his head out into the daylight, he quickly pulled it back down.

A gorilla squad sat nearly at their doorstep, and it was clear they weren't going anywhere soon. As silently as he could, he moved back down into the station, and woke his beautiful companion. He pulled the groggy girl to her feet.

"We've got to get going," he whispered. "Come on!"

Lowering himself down to the subway track, he thought with dark humor that he needn't avoid the third rail. Then Brent hoisted Nova down beside him. Instinctively, he started for the tunnel that would take them deeper into Queens, toward his grandmother's house in Forest Hills. Almost immediately he heard it.

"That hum..." Soon Nova was holding her ears. "You hear it, too?" As she fearfully sought the source of the sound, he knew she did. It was coming from the opposite end of the station—the tunnel that led toward Manhattan. While some light shone through crevices, the tunnel was ultimately swallowed in darkness.

What can it be? he wondered, his thoughts racing. *Is it electrical? Could there be survivors? Survivors with technology?* He allowed himself a moment's hope. *Human ones?*

He weighed their options. The hum pulsed, its pull irresistible.

"Alright," he said, and he headed down the track toward Manhattan, Nova in tow. "Come on, we're going to follow it."

Bare feet crunching on centuries of ash and gravel, with cool air cutting across their skin, the two tattered fugitives ventured into the abyss.

Albina smiled. *I have them.*

An upright human and a savage woman followed her beacon through the tunnel system. Calling himself an astronaut like Mr. Taylor, this Mr. Brent seemed to be yet another pawn of the apes. The savage named Nova appeared to be the one so prominent in Mr. Taylor's thoughts.

Unfortunately, Mr. Taylor has proved useless in telling us what we need to know, Albina mused to the others. *Perhaps they will not.* She, Ongaro, Caspay, and Adiposo were gathered again above tracks 19–11. His Holiness was once again in reverie with His ancestors.

Focusing their minds as one, the assembled masters projected an image on the far wall of the station, revealing the two humans and their progress through the tunnels. As they watched, they knew when Brent spoke again, and manifested it along with the projection.

"Well, there's an intelligence working in this place," he said. "That sound, good or bad, it's either a warning or a directional device. It doesn't much matter," he decided. "They know we're here."

Astute for a human, Caspay noted.

This Mr. Brent not only talks, Adiposo added, *but talks insistently to himself.* They watched as the two newcomers entered the undercity. As the humans wandered the decimated streets, Albina subtly suggested them toward the fountain outside St. Patrick's Cathedral. There they drank, and Albina nodded to Ongaro. With eyes shut, the mutant painmaster seized the astronaut's mind.

Put your hands around her throat, Ongaro ordered. *Hold her there until she dies.* Instantly, Mr. Brent plunged Nova's head into the fountain. As the beautiful barbarian struggled, he held fast.

Mentally, Brent pushed back.

He likes her, Ongaro determined. *Finds her attractive. He is fighting me.* His brow furled. The connection weakening, he concentrated anew.

Kill her, he commanded.

"Get out!" Brent screamed. "Get out of my head!" Fighting Ongaro's urges, he stumbled back into the cathedral of their god. As the church door shut, Ongaro's eyes flew open. *Connection severed.*

No matter, Albina assured him. *The Verger will detain him.*

Collect Mr. Brent, she sent to the fat man. *Keep him and the woman separated.*

Adiposo nodded.

She looked to Caspay. *Summon His Holiness.* The elder statesman hesitated at the order, but then nodded compliance. As the two of them left, Ongaro stepped closer.

"Well done," he whispered to Albina. It was not a thought projection. This was an intimacy that was unusual for their kind. The spoken word was saved for prayer and meetings of great importance. One might speak in confidence with God or with His Holiness, but for an unmated man and woman alone, it was taboo.

Stop, she insisted. Albina had felt Ongaro's longing before, thoughts she had reciprocated. But these were thoughts upon which they could never act. They were masters, and they were from different guilds. Their lineages had to remain pure, no matter what their base desires might be. Genetic lines had to be maintained. It was a guildmaster's duty to propagate with as many of their house's opposite sex as possible, in order to ensure stronger offspring. It was done through artificial insemination—sexual intercourse was unnecessary in their society.

For most, its appeal had been lost millennia ago along with their skin. For some, however, it still held an allure. Theirs was a passion most forbidden.

"Use your words, if you mean it," he breathed in her ear.

Albina scanned the room for other minds. For the moment, they were alone. Her eyes shed lasers at him.

"His Holiness would not approve," she murmured.

Ongaro's eyes bore back into hers.

"Yes," he calculated. "Neither would Caspay."

If Caspay suspected that there was anything between her and

Ongaro—*anything*—all it would take was an accusation, and the group mind would be thrown into disarray. She and Ongaro might be exiled to the radioactive wilds, or even the surface desert. There, they would face the White Ones, deadly exposure, and worse.

"I don't approve," she said, but she wavered. Ongaro seized her arm and whirled her around to face him.

"Yes, you do," he insisted. Removing his glove, Ongaro touched her lip with his exposed flesh. His hand hovered above it, her breath cool on his fingertips. Then she grabbed his wrist, halting him. Yet Albina took his finger and ran it across her lips. Her lower one caught it, and she pulled it into her mouth.

Albina quivered with delight. As Ongaro lost all composure, however, she remembered herself, and pushed his hand away.

This cannot be, she asserted. *You know I am right.*

Ongaro nodded and once again sheathed his hand.

It will be our secret.

Soon, the others would return, and Mr. Brent would stand before them for questioning. She readied herself for the interrogation. The secrets they desired would soon be theirs.

Mungwortt spilled into wet darkness. Disoriented, he swam for what he thought was safety, until he smacked his skull on something. Clutching his head, he drifted until he bobbed to the surface. The current here was swift but manageable, and it wasn't long until he had washed ashore in some open-faced cavern. The tiled wall had words on it.

86TH STREET

The cave opened into the blackened forest, its soft blue glowing lichen illuminating the scene. Mungwortt raised himself on his elbows and hung his head low, panting.

For a second time he mourned the loss of Zao. The orangutan's skull had shattered upon the rocks, and was no more. Mungwortt knew, however, from his schoolboy religion classes, that a part of Zao would always be with him.

A moment later a furry white foot stepped into view. He dripped water on it. Mungwortt looked up to see an albino mountain of muscle and matted fur.

White One!

Not just any White One, but the dirty-furred yellow-White One. The big one that had eaten Zao's brains. The one they had nicknamed Dinge. And he wasn't alone. He had friends. Mungwortt stood up slowly. As the creatures growled, his own anger boiled over.

Humans, mutants, brains, and White Ones, he raged. *When will this end?*

Claws bared, the White Ones stalked toward him. Rather than showing fear, Mungwortt pulled back his fist and slammed it into Dinge's flat nose. The dirty furred beast blinked.

The rest of them stepped back.

Stunned.

The other White Ones slowly encircled Dinge and Mungwortt, keeping a safe distance away. It reminded Mungwortt of being in the boxing ring, but with fuzzy white beasts as the spectators.

Dinge stared at him, and did nothing.

"What do we do now, White One?" he asked.

He's their leader, idiot. Don't you understand animal behavior? They are a pack. You just challenged him for control of the pride.

Oh. Mungwortt knew this already from watching the wild swine when he grew up on the far side of Simia. And though he did, it wasn't his thoughts that had come to the conclusion. Instead, it was a familiar nagging voice ringing in his head.

"Zao!" he shouted. "You are with me—"

Shut up and fight! But it was too late.

Sensing the half-breed's distraction, the albino beast pounced. He was a powerhouse, a good half-foot taller, and nearly twice the girth of the others, all rippling muscles. Dinge backhanded Mungwortt, sending him splashing face-first into the water, the wind knocked out of him.

Don't drown, Zao told him.

With a little luck, he thought, the current would sweep him away. But it was Mungwortt's unlucky day, and he was dragged backward out of the stream, the White One lifting him bodily by his right leg. This gave him an opportunity, however, and he double-punched the creature in its genitals.

Dinge doubled over, dropping him.

He tried to scramble out from under the beast, but it recovered too fast. Dinge threw himself on his opponent, baring his fangs and going for the throat. Mungwortt braced his arm and pushed against the beast's face, desperate to keep it away.

The White One was relentless.

ACT IV

ANNIHILATION AND HOPE

CHAPTER 27
THE BEGINNING OF THE END

Zira couldn't sleep. While there were both blankets and her husband to snuggle up with, the bumps and rocking of the wagon were too much for her. The terrain was rough—they were in the Forbidden Zone.

This was their second night in the desert, and Seraph drove the horses. During the day Cornelius took the reins and she had kept them on course. She knew where they were going—where Dr. Milo would be.

When Cornelius began to snore, Zira gave up. Grasping the rail behind the driver's box, she climbed up and over and settled in next to Seraph. The air was crisp, the desert a mix of indigo and sapphire.

"Thank you again for helping us," Zira offered.

"Thank Dr. Milo when you see him." Seraph shrugged. "He sent me to get you."

At a loss for a response, Zira looked into the back of the wagon. Cornelius still snored blissfully. After a long silence, she spoke again.

"What is Dr. Milo doing out in the desert?" she asked. "Did he find the flying machine?"

"He has instructed me not to tell you."

"Oh rubbish," she responded. "That was for Cornelius. Dr. Milo knows he doesn't believe in flight."

"You'll know soon enough." Seraph smiled, visible even in the gloom. "We're nearly there." Giving up on that line of discussion, Zira decided to address something that had been bothering her.

"Why did Dr. Milo ask for me?" she asked. Cornelius made sense—he and Milo had worked on many a dig together.

"I was also tasked to return with the human called Landon," Seraph explained. "There was the question of the human's sanity, so—"

"—Dr. Milo wanted an animal psychologist on hand," Zira finished, "and a veterinarian." *As always, the scientist's logic is faultless*. Then it dawned on her. "He wouldn't have asked for Landon unless he had already found what he was looking for," she noted with triumph.

Seraph said nothing.

But your eyes tell me I'm right. Zira was intrigued. Taylor had told them his ship was dead. "Did he get it working?" she pressed.

If we can find Taylor and Brent, maybe we can get them home!

"Does it fly?" she added.

Seraph smiled again. "That remains to be seen," she replied, "but if anyone can get it flying, it will be Milo." Her smile lingered on his name. "He wants to go to outer space."

Another realization struck Zira. *Milo, Seraph called him,* she observed, *not Dr. Milo.* There was no honorific—something the scientist would have required.

"Oh, Seraph," she exclaimed, "you love him, don't you?"

Seraph frowned. "It's not as if he notices."

"That's the way it is with males," Zira said. "I dropped hints for three months before Cornelius even began to suspect I was interested." Her eyes danced at the memory. "In the end, I had to take the initiative and begin the courtship. Even then..." She let her words trail off, and to her surprise, Seraph *giggled*. Zira joined her.

"If the machine works," Zira asked, "will you go to space with him?"

"No." Seraph was firm. "The craft's very existence will change apekind forever, but risk for risk's sake is unwarranted. Flight is Milo's dream, not mine." She added, "When he takes off, I'll be content to watch." Ahead of them, tiger and marigold hues began to creep across the horizon—morning was approaching the Forbidden Zone. Behind them, deep blues retreated.

"Maybe once he's in the sky, he'll finally get his head out of the clouds," Zira suggested, "and notice what's been waiting on the ground for him all along."

That elicited a laugh as they raced toward the dawn.

"The apes are marching on your city."

With Nova collapsed on the floor beside him, Mr. Brent looked to the mutant council, gathered in the Grand Central Terminal audience chamber. He had neither the training nor the discipline needed to disguise a lie, so his interrogation had yielded the results they sought. The final push had come when he had been compelled to force himself upon her.

Repulsed by the idea, he stopped lying.

He was broken.

Their worst fears confirmed, Adiposo, Caspay, Ongaro, and Albina all turned to their leader. Mendez XXVI hid His thoughts, but His eyes betrayed His innermost emotion—He was afraid. As the guards led the astronaut and the savage away, the mutants joined their minds to search the deserts for their foes.

Knowing now what to look for, they soon found it. The swarm of ants that was the gorilla army blacked out the bright desert sands on which they trampled. To the mutants, they were little more than annoying insects, yet as with any troublesome pest, in great numbers they posed a greater threat.

They were closer than they should be, as well. It would be a short time before the apes would discover the uppermost spires of Manhattan. Together, the mutants scanned the ape leaders for surface impressions. Muddling through brutish aggression, they found a mixture of doubt, worry, brinkmanship, and conviction.

They have their own god! Caspay observed. *Pagans.*

Then let this be a test of their faith, His Holiness ordained.

Ahead of the army, naked gorillas appeared as if from nowhere. They had been crucified upside down and set ablaze. Within moments the desert around them became an inferno, yet the general forced his soldiers to hold their positions.

The enemy will pay for this cruelty. Zaius begged him to shoot the crucified gorillas and put them out of their misery—something that Ursus refused to do. *Ape shall never kill ape.*

Zaius was weak.

Then a gigantic figure appeared, and Ursus froze with terror. Towering above them was a vision of the Lawgiver—the Greatest Ape of Them All. The prophet of God, the Lawgiver had appeared before in their time of need, but this was different in a profound and chilling way.

"He bleeds," Ursus cried out. "The Lawgiver bleeds!" From his eyes, nose, mouth, and ears, crimson death flowed.

Ursus was an ape of God. A once-rebellious youth raised by an insistent preacher, he had been reborn in the Lawgiver's Light, and his god was now telling him that his army was riding to its doom.

Zaius was right, Ursus quailed, *the unknown is not meant for apes.* There was a reason that the Forbidden Zone was forbidden by scripture, and the general had overstepped his bounds in entering it. *Forgive me, Lawgiver,* he pleaded inwardly. *I did it to serve you best.*

Furious, Zaius refused to accept it as truth. "The spirit of the Lawgiver lives," he called out. "We are still God's chosen. This is a vision—and it is a lie!"

The doctor snapped his reins and galloped his horse into the blaze, preparing for the very real chance that he would die. But…

There is no heat.

He continued without stopping. If he could reach the tortured figures on the crosses, he could cut them down. Suddenly, a gargantuan figure loomed closer. He looked up as the image of the Lawgiver toppled over upon him.

Zaius threw up an arm to shield himself.

The desert exploded.

In Grand Central Terminal, the mutants faltered. Without the General of the Defense to guide them, the amplification network provided by the Overseers had grown weak. Their projected deception collapsed.

"Stupid animals," Caspay said aloud. "They don't have the brains to hold our illusions."

"We have no defense," Albina replied.

"Except our Bomb," His Holiness replied. "Call our people to the High Sanctuary."

Caspay turned to Adiposo. "Do you know the range of their city?"

The fat man had a gift for geographical divination. Sifting through Mr. Brent's impressions, he found what he needed.

"Yes," he replied.

"Set in the mechanism and wait for me," Caspay instructed. Adiposo nodded and was gone. "I want a public thought projection at adult and infant levels," Caspay continued, addressing Albina. "Adults to the cathedral, infants indoors."

Yet His Holiness radiated doubt.

Albina hesitated as well, but when Mendez did not countermand Caspay's order, she complied. With their own thoughts shielded from one another, the masters moved off to their assigned tasks. Before the wolves arrived at their door, they would celebrate one last Mass with their god.

"The vision was false!" Zaius declared. Also, it was gone. Where there had been fire and bodies and blood, there was now empty desert. The Forbidden Zone was barren yet again.

The confused soldiers began to organize themselves. Some had turned and run from the carnage they had witnessed, and they would be disciplined for it, but their general faced a greater problem. Zaius had caused Ursus to lose face. While the general's faith in the Lawgiver had been challenged and found wanting, Zaius had combated it head on.

The doctor was a hero—the troops would remember that. If Ursus didn't do something to reassert his dominance, his bid to control all of Simia would fail.

Once again, Doctor, he admitted with a degree of hidden anger, *well played.*

Be it natural or supernatural, the evil they faced had most certainly produced these visions. This meant the apes had to be nearing their nest. Combat would occur soon enough, and he would prove himself on the battlefield. It would be *his* exploits future generations recalled from this day, not the doctor's.

Otherwise, he admitted, *I don't deserve to lead.*

"Bugler," the general commanded, "sound the advance."

Dinge's fangs were at Mungwortt's neck. For all his strength, the half-breed just wasn't powerful enough to resist. The White One would tear out his throat, and that would be it.

I almost got us out of here, Zao.

Shut up, Zao replied sharply. The yellow behemoth pressed closer.

Tink.

Something clanked against Mungwortt's teeth. It was smooth, cold, and tangy. It tasted like metal. Mungwortt's snaggletooth had become hooked in Dinge's metal tag—the tag each White One wore on its ear.

Bite, you idiot!

With nothing to lose, Mungwortt bit down and twisted his head. His own fang snapped, but the tag tore free—and took with it a meaty part of the ear. Instead of the howl of pain Mungwortt had expected, however, Dinge rolled away and clutched his wounded head.

The ape spit his chipped tooth, the bloody lobe, and the metal tag out onto the floor. Dinge stared at it, and understanding dawned in Mungwortt's mind.

The tags, he thought. *The brains use the tags to control them!* Picking up a rock, he smashed down on the metal tag, hard. It cracked with a shower of sparks, and *this* time the leader of the White Ones doubled over and howled.

Maybe that wasn't such a good idea.

Then Dinge straightened and looked at his fellow creatures. Nervously they backed up, and with good reason. Without warning the White One leader leapt at the nearest albino and bit down, tearing its ear off, crunching the metal tag within its fangs. The White One howled, then blinked and stared at his attacker. Then it joined its leader, repeating the process with the others. Mungwortt watched as spatters of blood flew everywhere. With each White One that was released, it launched itself at another, joining a melee of primitive bodies.

The fight was brief, but intense. When it ended, Mungwortt faced a panting sea of bloody fur and white bodies. Dinge approached him and the half-breed put his hands to his own ears, ready to run.

"Don't eat my ear!" he begged. The words echoed throughout the cavern. Dinge stared, then bellowed something Mungwortt couldn't make out.

"Dun reet myerr!" Dinge howled.

The other creatures did the same.

"Dun reet myerr!"

One, then another. *"Dun reet myerr!"* The cry reverberated through the tunnels, and finally Mungwortt understood what they were saying.

Don't eat my ear!

They were pack animals, and like any pack they followed the example of their leader. Mungwortt had challenged their leader—

and *won*. Not only that, but in the process he had freed them from the Overseers' control. It hadn't been his intention—he had only wanted to survive—but it had been the result, just the same.

As he processed this idea, Dinge did something even more unexpected, more bizarre. He bowed in supplication.

What is he doing? Mungwortt wondered, his thoughts whirling. Not knowing how to react, he reached out and patted the White One on the head. The others roared, the sound bouncing off the cavern walls, and they all bowed to him now.

"DUN REET MYERR!"

What should I do? the half-breed wondered. *Is this what it feels like to be a god?*

You're not their god, dimwit. Zao's retort echoed in his head. *You're their leader now—do something,* anything, *before they figure out you don't know what the hell you are doing.*

Mungwortt agreed. He put his hands on his hips, his stance wide, and told himself that he was… examining his troops. Proud of his new army, he pointed toward the forest outside. In the distance he could see the pale glow of what he knew must be the sea lion tank, and the White Ones' brainy masters. He remembered when Dinge had scooped out Zao's brains, and how the others had jealously watched him gobble up the tasty morsels.

He gave his orders.

"Eat!" he shouted. "Eat now. Eat the brains!"

His army roared their approval, and repeated their new battle cry.

"DUN REET MYERR!"

Then in a wave of white bodies and fur, they tore through the underbrush toward the Overseers' compound.

* * *

He yawned. The morning was dim, the clouds just beginning to glow. The wagon ground to a stop and Seraph dismounted as Zira sat there and stared into the void ahead.

"Cornelius," she whispered.

Popping his head over the side of the cart, he looked to see what had caught her eye. Nestled by the shore was an encampment. Tents littered the site, as did various ape apparatus and equipment. A few sleepy chimpanzees stood watch. What looked like an exactingly straight road had been cleared to the camp. All in all, a typical scientific worksite. What loomed over it was another story.

Perched on three small but bulbous feet, a gigantic bird roosted there. Its eyes aglow with the rising sun, the metallic avian's wings were wide, its beak sharp and narrow. A dewy mist clung to its skin, giving it a soft sheen in the early twilight. It was bigger than any wagon or boat Cornelius had ever seen—bigger even than their house.

It was not of their world.

When the chimpanzee archeologist tried to stand, his knees would not work. As Seraph walked toward a lean-to at the base of the beast, there was a flash of movement.

"Say, what is that?"

"I don't know," Zira said, still whispering.

An alien figure emerged from the structure, shrouded in white. Its head an enormous unblinking eye, the stout creature's stilted gait betrayed an unfamiliarity with the surrounding environment. It was repellant and, like the metal bird, it did not belong.

Zira cried out involuntarily, and the eye-thing looked up. It noticed Seraph, and hastened toward her. Before it could reach her, however, it stopped, lifted its arms above its head, and with a quick twist decapitated itself.

Cornelius gasped.

The giant eye lifted away to reveal the head of an ape.

"Dr. Milo," Zira said, "I presume."

With a nod, Milo presented the giant eye to Seraph. As she accepted it, Cornelius shook away the last remnants of sleep. His chest tight, he realized he had forgotten to breathe. He inhaled with haste.

As Milo rushed to greet them, Cornelius turned his attention back to the enormous bird-shaped machine. He remembered the piece of paper Taylor had folded into a triangle and thrown in his office. It had sailed overhead, only to take a sharp nosedive at his feet. At the time they had all thought the human was mad.

It would appear we were wrong.

He searched for words, yet found only one.

"Flight."

Albina was not happy. Despite his station, Caspay had dominated them again—and once again, Mendez had allowed it.

If His Holiness isn't careful, she thought darkly, *Caspay will take control.* She kept her thoughts private, though. *If Mendez isn't strong enough to act, do we need a new leader?* Her musings surprised her. *Is Caspay right? Should there be a new Holy of Holies?*

She shook the thought away. For millennia the Mendez family had ruled them. Others had tried to usurp them, but always failed.

The strength of the Fellowship lies in the Mendez dynasty, but if someone else was to take over let it be anyone but Caspay. She considered for a moment. *Let it be me.*

Ongaro wanted her, and would follow her lead. Spineless, Adiposo would side with whoever appeared strongest. With the two of them on her side, Albina could wait. She would monitor His Holiness, watching for weakness, and eye Caspay for signs of betrayal. If the bespectacled mutant attempted a coup, she would seize the moment.

She would preserve the mutant race. And if Albina failed, she would kill herself.

The Verger granted Adiposo access to the Bomb. The caretaker of the cathedral maintained both the High Sanctuary and the Holy Sanctum that lay beneath it. A tireless servitor of God, the Verger's eyes were always probing, his mind ever vigilant. His duty was to ensure that God's will took precedence over that of the Fellowship—and that the Holy Power of the Bomb was not abused.

Upon learning that the fat man's orders came from His Holiness Himself, the Verger escorted Adiposo to the green copper shelter doors located under the altar. Leading him down the spiral staircase, he excused himself to attend to other duties.

Beneath St. Patrick's Cathedral, the fat man stood alone within the glassed-in pulpit of the Holy Sanctum. Moved there in the early days of the Mendez dynasty, the transplanted computer booth had become an integral part of the sanctum, and from there the clergy could deliver unto heathens the glory of God.

Adjacent to the pulpit lay the Holy Cradle—the missile silo built by Mendez's ancestors. Here, sheathed in darkness, the Holy Weapon of Peace awaited the inevitable day of reckoning. By piecing together what he had gleaned from the astronauts' minds, Adiposo determined the exact coordinates of Ape City, and keyed them into the device. The machines stopped their hum and whir, and produced an affirmative *ping*.

God's massive brass bullet hull was dark in the shadowed silo, His fins sharp and deadly. Standing this close to holiness, Adiposo wanted all the more to be one with God. He craved Communion. Making certain he was alone, he reached into his robes and produced a compact metal box.

The snuff box was small and round, with the symbol of the Bomb embossed on its brass cover. Inside lay a bed of iridescent cilia. Cultivated from the radioactive fungi that illuminated the fungal canopy of Central Park's dead forest, the mold undulated. The mutant master leaned forward and caressed it with a gloved finger.

Spores ejected, and a cloud of fungus bloomed in his face. As he inhaled greedily, Adiposo's eyes rolled back in his head. Once this had been considered the only way to converse with God, but repeated practice had caused cancers of the brain, and even induced insanity. Over the centuries the act was banned, then became apocryphal.

Today it remained taboo.

Some mutants still sought it, however—risks be damned. Mutants like Adiposo.

Basidiospores invaded his sinuses, and for a moment, he was euphoric. For a moment, he could see the glory of God, so close he could almost touch it. Adiposo reached forward—but then paranoia seized him. Someone was watching him.

Who is it?

The chamber connected to a catacomb of ancient tombs, and there were cracks and crevices throughout that led to the sewers and subways.

Adiposo panicked. *If the apes have somehow—*

"Is the mechanism set?" The voice came from behind him. It was Caspay. Adiposo slipped the snuff box back into his robes, and turned to face his bespectacled colleague.

"It is done," he affirmed. Caspay regarded him for a moment, frowning, searching his eyes. In return, Adiposo shielded his own thoughts.

He knows!

After a moment Caspay moved past to examine the machine.

"Very good," he said. Satisfied, Caspay entered his own verification code. No one guildmaster could set the Bomb by himself—it always required two. While the missile would not launch unless so ordered by His Holiness, when it did so it would descend on the city of the apes. Caspay looked up reverently at their god, then addressed Adiposo again.

Come, he thought, *we have one final service to attend.*

CHAPTER 28

SI VIS PACEM, PARA BELLUM

Teeth and claws rent the gray and white matter that comprised the giant brains of the Overseers, undoing centuries of genetic engineering in a swath of mindless violence.

Stop! Be-One commanded. *Cease your actions!*

The sending was his last, and none of the other living computers mustered even that much conscious thought. The zoo that had been their compound was a field of carnage. Everywhere he looked, Mungwortt saw the remains of the once-magnificent creations. There were brains on the ground, in the trees—even impaled on a fence post. The White Ones had tipped the huge tanks, sending their contents sloshing onto stone before scooping them up and gorging on them.

The few servitors that were still tagged attempted to save them, but the freed albinos quickly bit into their ears, and ended the defense.

While savage, the White Ones were thorough. Their masters destroyed, they followed the tunnel down into the science labs. There they destroyed all of the grotesque experiments and their victims. The deed done, the nomadic White Ones dispersed—some disappearing down subway tunnels while others dissolved into the woods. Grateful to Mungwortt for their freedom, however, Dinge and six others remained.

Can we leave now? Zao asked.

Mungwortt shook his head. The human Tay-Lor had saved him from the mutants. He had even wrapped his wounds and shown him what to eat. Where apes were cruel, the man had been kind. He wasn't about to leave him behind.

"Tay-Lor is my friend, Zao," Mungwortt said aloud. He didn't have many back home. "A real friend, like you."

And how do you propose to find this man?

It was a good question. Then he had an idea—at least he thought it was.

"Here," Mungwortt said. Motioning to Dinge, he unraveled the bandage that still clung tight on his arm. He held it to his own nose and inhaled, then held it up to Dinge. Made from Tay-Lor's shirt, he hoped it would have some of the human's scent on it. "You will help me find my friend?" he asked the dirty albino.

Is there no end to your cognitions? Zao mocked. Mungwortt didn't know what that meant, so he just shushed him.

Dinge breathed deeply. Taking the scrap of fabric, he passed it to the other beasts. Each in turn draped it over their noses and inhaled. After a moment the White Ones slid through the blue forest. Mungwortt followed close behind.

After a time the sound of running water grew thunderous. They emerged at the cup-like vehicles where Taylor had first bandaged him.

"That's right!" Mungwortt pointed to the waterfall. "We separated here!" Feeling new confidence, he looked over the side at the swift-moving river below.

You also smashed me on the rocks—there, Zao scolded him.

"I'm sorry," Mungwortt murmured, and he was. As he did,

Dinge sniffed the catwalk where Taylor had been captured.

"Four-eyes and the fat man were here, too," Mungwortt said. "They took my friend." Dinge growled. The other White Ones converged and grunted in agreement.

"Dun reet myerr!" Dinge exclaimed, and the White Ones were off. Breaking into a run, they spilled out of the dead forest and into another wide square. The hunt was on.

The emerald crystal dropped first. The amber one followed as Mendez activated the control rods in the prie-dieu at the center of the chancel. Mutant Mass had begun, and the offertory was about to begin.

The entire mutant population had gathered in the nave of the High Sanctuary, what was formerly St. Patrick's Cathedral, and was now and forevermore the House of the Holies, the dwelling of the Almighty Bomb. While the church's pews were original to the building and filled with the congregation, the seats occupied by the four guildmasters had been salvaged from long-disused subway cars. Off to the side, under heavy guard and dressed in worshipers' robes, sat Brent and Nova.

At the rear of the chancel, silo doors in the floor irised open. Slowly, inexorably, the monolithic missile rose from its lair beneath the cathedral to tower over the faithful. Its gleaming glory shone bright, reflecting the salvation that would come with its detonation.

"Almighty and everlasting Bomb," His Holiness intoned, "who came down among us to make heaven under earth, lighten our darkness. Oh, Instrument of God," he beseeched, "grant us thy peace."

Voices, not thoughts, rose in song.

"Almighty Bomb, who destroyed all heavens," the chorus rang, "and created angels."

"Behold," they cried, "His glory!"

"Behold the truth that abides in us," Mendez commanded. "Reveal that truth unto that Maker."

Everyone in the cathedral rose.

"I reveal my inmost self unto my god," the guildmasters responded together. Then, making an offering of themselves, the congregation moved as one. They reached beneath their necklines and pulled on their own flesh, peeling it back and over their heads. This wasn't skin—these were the masks they wore to resemble their ancestors. Bared muscles glistened under gray dermis, royal blue and crimson lines etched across their features. This was who they were, this was how the Bomb had blessed them.

How they were meant to be.

God, Albina thought fiercely, *forgive me.* Distracted by the presence of barbarians, she was unable to enjoy the ceremony. The mutant masters had determined that the broken Mr. Brent and the nitwitted Nova were both harmless, and thus they had been permitted to bear witness to God. Caspay had insisted upon it.

Caspay insists upon a lot of things, she reflected, yet His Holiness had allowed it. Because of Mr. Taylor's desecration of the Corridor of Busts, she had lost face. Now, she removed her face for her god. As she did so, Albina couldn't help but watch the humans. She felt utter contempt. Savages like Mr. Brent and Mr. Taylor could not truly reveal themselves to God. They were deceivers, hidden from His Truth under the trappings of the flesh.

As the congregation sang, Albina discreetly scanned for their reactions to the true appearance of the mutants. Being but an animal, Nova radiated fear. From Mr. Brent, there was revulsion.

Stupid heathens.

She had been wrong to think that the likes of these creatures could become converts. Yet it no longer mattered. Ongaro would dispose of the males. Nova would be thrown to the White Ones, and they would be done with the humans.

And then, she thought, steeling herself, *the apes…*

His Holiness addressed his congregation one last time.

"Let everyone go to his private shelter," he commanded aloud. "Empty the streets—they're to find the city of the dead."

As the ape army neared the enormous effigies of stone and steel, the heat grew unbearable. Zaius knew enough to warn Ursus not to enter the ghost city proper, lest the invisible death of radiation wither them. Instead, he had suggested a less direct route. Reluctantly, Ursus had agreed.

Under Zaius's guidance, they had followed it for hours, until finally they rode a steep rise. Cresting the summit, what they found sent murmurs of surprise among the troops. They discovered knolls and mountains covered in rolling green.

Simia? Ursus thought. *How could we be this close to home?*

"Is this some kind of ploy, Doctor?" he demanded. "This army will not return to Ape City without a victory to its name."

"Hold," Zaius ordered. The soldiers came to a stop behind him.

Now they accept his orders? Ursus noted angrily.

"That is not Simia, General." The doctor dismounted and addressed the troops. "This is another vision!" he declared. "It is not our home. Turn away from it, do not look. It is a lie." Zaius walked ahead, shuffling between two rocky crags. "We must be close," he muttered.

Remaining cautious, Ursus stayed his confused officers and continued after the wandering orangutan. As Zaius paused at the foot of a crevice, he waved Ursus to join him. Below, something had caught the ape's eye. There was an opening there, a triangular cave of some kind—but it was something more. The cave was not natural—it was hewn from the rock, and inside it was smooth and round and covered in ceramic tile.

"This must be what your scout reported," Zaius concluded. "A subterranean passage. I think it's worth exploring." Ursus had no choice but to concede. With Dangral in the lead, he ordered his troops through. As the soldiers marched past, Zaius recognized one.

"Jaffe!" The doctor pulled Marcus's son out of the line. "Just a moment, Private."

Singled out, the young gorilla was embarrassed.

"Sir?"

"I have a special assignment for you." Zaius turned to his personal squad. "Lieutenant?" Mesmerized by the green hills in the distance, Aurelios came to and rushed to the minister's side.

"This is Private Jaffe," Zaius said. "I believe you knew his father." Recognition caused Aurelios's eyes to go wide. He had served under Marcus for many years.

"Yes, Minister!"

"I am assigning the private as your personal bodyguard, Lieutenant."

"My—" Aurelios stopped as he understood. "Yes, Minister."

Zaius turned to Jaffe. "Stick close to Aurelios," he told the boy. "He is an important ape in the Secret Police, and I need someone I can trust watching over him."

Jaffe beamed. "Yes, sir, Minister!"

Zaius patted him on the shoulder. "I'm counting on you." As the last of the ape army entered the passage, Ursus, Zaius, and their personal squads prepared to join them.

Then, as suddenly as it had appeared, the vision evaporated. Green turned to sand, bushes turned to rock. The beckoning beauty of the vegetation was dispelled, and they were once again in the desert. Only the crags and crevice were real, as was the underground passage.

Everything else had been a lie. Their enemies had tried to distract them at the entrance to their domain, but Zaius had seen through it.

The minister had done it again, Ursus knew.

Groom Lake, Nevada
Area 51
1971

Project Liberty was in final preparations. Despite knowing the truths that had been revealed to him—or perhaps because *of them—Taylor threw himself entirely into the effort.* Juno's *equipment tests checked out, and Colonels Taylor and Maddox, along with Lieutenants Dodge and Stewart, spent their days in simulated training.*

Stewart also struggled with her own demons—from the initial Juno *mission—but kept it together. Taylor heard that a new astronaut, Major John Christopher Brent, was being chosen as a standby for Maddox. All they needed now was a new navigator, and someone was being rushed through the officer training program to prepare him for the job.*

Fresh from weightless environment practice in the ANSA dive tank,

Taylor and Maddox hit the showers. This time they had been testing experimental protective outerwear—one size fits all, the new flexible space suit adjusted its leg and sleeve length to accommodate its occupant.

It was also very hot. The astronauts had been sweating in them for five hours straight, and they had flight simulator training next.

Finishing with the shower, they toweled off in the locker room. Taylor lit a cigar, opened his laundry bag, and pulled out his flight suit. Something was wrong—its dingy yellow collar was sparkling white.

"This isn't mine," he growled. "It's new."

Curious, Maddox examined his bag. "Same here."

"What gives?"

"New flight suits and patches all around, sirs," the laundry officer explained. "The colonels might want to check the flag," he added as he left the locker room. Cigar planted firmly in his teeth, Taylor unfolded the new suit until the red, white and blue shoulder patch was exposed.

The blue field was one star short.

Goddamn Secession War.

"Wyndham caved," Maddox muttered, "and now we have to display it."

"He's a peacetime president in a time without peace," Taylor replied. He could understand the president's conundrum. If the United States put all its efforts into taking back Texas, hundreds of thousands of Americans could be killed. Having succeeded Goldwater, President Willard Wyndham had inherited a shitstorm. Determined to get U.S. troops back home from Vietnam, the last thing he felt the people needed was a prolonged bloodbath back home. His decision to let Texas go made sense—from a certain point of view—but it also showed weakness.

There were all sorts of rumors coming out of Texas now, from the Klan's involvement to minorities being held in detainment camps. Nothing was confirmed, but the possibilities were frightening.

We're preaching equality while acknowledging a state of intolerance, *Taylor thought darkly.* We're a bunch of goddamn hypocrites. *At this point, he didn't care if the entire country went up in flames.* Let them all burn, *he mused.* I won't be around to see it.

With that he disrobed, took a last drag on his cigar, and climbed into the new suit. It fit well. Once he was finished, he snuffed out the tip of the cigar and placed it in the pocket of his upper sleeve. Then he noticed that Maddox was transfixed, staring at the new flag patch, as if doing so hard enough would make another star blink into existence.

"Don't sweat it, Donny," Taylor assured his friend. "You've had less than fifty states before. You'll have fifty again. Wyndham did what he thought was best," he continued. "It's up to the next administration to decide if it's going to stick."

Maddox begrudgingly agreed.

"Taylor!"

What now? He heard the mutants coming, deep in a conversation about which he didn't give a damn.

What he saw when he turned, however, was far from what he expected. Ongaro and a guard approached the cell, but leading the way was a man dressed in the trappings of a savage. Even though he was dressed as a primitive, though, the man was unlike any of the humans Taylor had encountered in this dismal future. His beard was groomed, his posture straight. His eyes intelligent.

Then it struck him. Taylor knew this man—from ANSA, back home. He was an astronaut.

Captain? he thought. *No, Major.*

Major John Christopher—

"You're… Brent!"

The newcomer was overjoyed. "My God, Taylor!"

"Brent!" Taylor repeated. As the cell door closed again, the two men rushed to each other. This was no illusion—he'd learned to see past the mutants' lies. As improbable as it was, this was real.

"How in the hell did you get here?" Taylor asked.

"Same as you," Brent replied. "Spaceship, Ape City, subway—"

Taylor cut him off. "By yourself?"

"No," Brent shook his head. "Nova found me."

"Nova?" Taylor lit up. "Is she with you?" Hopeful, he looked past Brent. "Where?"

"I don't know." Suddenly Brent looked defeated. "They separated us. They tried to make me kill her..."

They turned to face their captor and his guard, standing on the other side of the cell's spiked door.

"Mr. Taylor, Mr. Brent, we're a peaceful people." Ongaro was adamant. "We don't kill our enemies. We get our enemies to kill each other."

He showed no contrition as he said it, and as one, Taylor and Brent both knew what this had to mean. They had both felt the pull in their brains before. Both knew what they would be forced to do. They backed away from Ongaro, and each other, and they steadied themselves.

Ongaro closed his eyes.

A high-pitched whine washed over their minds.

"I'm fighting it." Brent pushed the words. "I'm fighting it off."

A manic glee in his eyes, Brent lunged for the colonel.

CHAPTER 29
THE CITY OF THE DEAD

The undercity was desolate. All of the mutants and their families had secluded themselves in their private shelters. Ongaro was tying up the loose ends that were Misters Taylor and Brent, and the other masters had retired to their personal shelters, as well.

The last of the guildmasters to leave, Caspay suddenly found himself relieved he was not their leader. From the amphitheater over tracks 19–11, Mendez continued to follow the progress of the gorilla army. Whatever He did next would decide the fate of their kind—and His choices were narrowing. The apes were in the tunnels.

"What will you do, Holiness?" Caspay asked of Mendez.

"Everything necessary," Mendez replied.

That was exactly what Caspay had feared.

Elsewhere in the terminal, straining against Ongaro's control, somehow Brent forced himself to reason. He reminded himself why he had come to this place. His mission.

To rescue Taylor.

"Taylor..."

The name became Brent's mantra. It gave him something on which to focus. With it, they might break Ongaro's control. It was a desperate gambit, and one likely to fail. Both men had strong wills, but Ongaro's mind was stronger.

"Taylor." Brent's voice echoed through the underground. "Taylor."

"Taylor…"

Nova was being led to the animal pens. She heard Brent's voice, heard him speak the familiar name. Then the name came again.

"Taylor."

She pulled away from her guard, and he grabbed her arm. Nova bit his hand—hard—and the guard yelped, letting go. That was all the chance she needed.

Nova ran.

Locked in their cell, the astronauts threw punches. They were too evenly matched, however.

As they fought, Ongaro heard the guard's cry from some distance away. The mutant master ordered his sentry to investigate, and as the man raced away, Ongaro's concentration wavered.

Momentarily free of his influence, Taylor and Brent tried to shrug off the fog. As they did, Ongaro pulled a jagged mace from a wall rack, opened the cell door, and threw it in. The better for one of them to gain the upper hand. The astronauts rushed him, but they were too slow.

The door clanged shut, but he didn't even need to latch it. Ongaro closed his eyes and resumed control.

* * *

Eluding the guard, Nova ran up the hallway and reached her goal. Ahead of her, locked in a cell, was Brent—the man who had journeyed with her. He was fighting for his life, and losing.

More than that, he fought Taylor. Her mate, who was alive—but somehow changed. He fought savagely, and the look in his eyes was like Brent's had been when he had tried to kill her. She remembered the panic she had felt. With it came anger, and determination. Without thinking…

Nova spoke.

"Tay-lor!" she rasped.

The strange man who was their captor opened his eyes. His hesitation was all the men needed. Taylor slammed his fist across their enemy's jaw. That sent him reeling toward Brent, who brought a weapon bashing down on his shoulder. The force of the blow threw him into the spiked door. As the metal points pierced the man, Taylor and Brent slammed the cage door against the wall, embedding the spikes even deeper in his back.

Nova rushed forward and threw herself on Taylor.

Mortally wounded, their enemy slipped to the floor. The cell door swung with his fall, clanking shut before the men could stop it. There was a loud click, and when they tried to open it, they could not. This time it had latched.

They were locked in.

As Nova watched, horrified, the bleeding man pulled his face from his head, exposing a skinless horror. Gray muscles were crisscrossed with blue and red lines, causing him to look like a living wound. Then the creature spoke.

"Unto God… I reveal my inmost self—"

He stopped speaking, and he stopped breathing.

* * *

His Holiness arrived alone. Ascending the great steps of the cathedral, he was greeted by the omnipresent Verger. Granted entrance, Mendez communicated his request. Nodding consent, the attendant of the Bomb brought Him to the apse at the rear of the church's chancel.

During High Mass, the floor beneath them had irised open to reveal their Bomb. For the moment, however, God rested peacefully. What interested Mendez instead lay behind the massive pipes of the organ, recessed in the wall beyond. Running his hands past the cooled lava, the Verger pressed his palm on key points, making the sign of the Bomb.

With a resounding click, the wall moved back and slid away on squeaking rollers, revealing a hidden hallway. As throughout the undercity, glowing moss provided illumination within the new chamber, though it was dim when compared to the church proper. Within the chapel stood a modest altar, and on it an ornate golden-crowned box emblazoned with the sign of the Bomb.

This was the Holy Tabernacle.

His Holiness knelt in supplication as the Verger unlatched the vessel for him. Within lay a book—one of the few paper texts that the mutants revered. Their minds fertile playgrounds, their memories sharp, they needed no books for learning. The written form was a tradition reserved for music, prayer, and hymns. None of those things, this book was special indeed.

Dubbed the Holy Codex, the ancient tome's covers were sheathed in partially melted plastic. Grasping it gingerly, His Holiness took care not to crack its fragile spine. The parchments were held inside by three nickel-plated steel rings. A tarnished mechanism ran along the binding that once had enabled the now rusted rings to open and snap shut again.

The Codex revealed the divine and mystical relationship between numerical patterns. The pages within its covers bore no text—numbers alone were the secret language of God.

His Holiness pored over the ciphers, searching for the combination of integers needed to stave off Assured Destruction. He found a verse marked with the divine symbols.

A Ω

There He divined the digits He sought. His task complete, He returned the Codex to the Verger. All that remained was to deliver the prognostic sequence to God. As the caretaker replaced the holy book within the tabernacle, two words written in the old form adorned its cover, glistening in metallic ink.

LAUNCH CODES

Armed with the knowledge He needed, Mendez would arm their god.

"What will you do, Holiness?"

"Whatever necessary."

In that moment, Caspay reflected, a sliver of doubt had entered the eye of Mendez. Caspay had seized it. He had caught a glimpse of His Holiness's mind, and saw *fear*.

Fear of the Holy Fallout itself. His Holiness intended to appeal to the apes. Of that Caspay was certain. He would try to reason with them.

He would talk with animals.

Mendez would stall the apes, He would threaten the apes—He might even beg them. Then, and only then, if there were no other choice, He would invoke the wrath of God. The mutant elder was appalled. If His Holiness faltered, the barbaric apes might defile the Almighty Bomb itself.

They might even try to subjugate God.

Assured Destruction was imminent. Feigning supplication, Caspay withdrew to the missile silo beneath the cathedral. Standing in the pulpit of the Holy Sanctum, he pulled two crystalline keys from his robes. Inserting them in two different locks located on either end of the control panel, he reached across as far as he could to grasp them simultaneously.

With a swivel, he turned both at once and was rewarded with the dulcet chirps and melodious tones of Holy Affirmation. Entering a long-forgotten override code that had for generations been held within an ambry, he modified the mechanism, enabling launch control from the pulpit itself.

The missile could still be fired from the prie-dieu above. However, should Caspay choose to assume control, no one in the chancel would be able to stop him.

Not even His Holiness.

The translucent keys began to blink in colors shifting to green, then yellow, and to red, before starting the cycle anew. They would continue until Caspay simultaneously laid hands on them again. Should he do so, the missile would fire.

The ape army would be upon them soon. As far as he was concerned, there were now three possible outcomes. If Mendez XXVI proved His worth, God's wrath would fall on the apes. Caspay would maintain his station as elder statesman. No one would know of his tampering with the control mechanism.

If Mendez XXVI failed, He would surely be killed by the apes. Caspay would himself launch the Instrument of God. His Glory would still be delivered unto the invaders, but it would be due to the elder statesman's initiative. He would present himself as having done God's Divine Will. Mendez's offspring would then ascend to Holiness, and Caspay would have the child's ear. He would control the next generation.

Of course, if the entire Mendez family line were slaughtered by simians, Caspay's intervention would still ensure the Divine Bomb's wrath. As savior of the Fellowship, he would then assume the mantle of Holiness, and lead his people into a new era. Regardless of which course played out, the Holy Fallout would reign. Assured Destruction would be averted, and his place in history would be ensured.

Pleased with himself, Caspay stepped from the control booth. He would give Mendez the chance to do the right thing. His Holiness had a few scant hours before the slobbering apes arrived. Until then, Caspay would wait with God. The Almighty Bomb towered overhead. Moving closer, he removed his glove and laid his hand on it. God's metal surface was cool, soothing. Caspay closed his eyes.

Destroy all devils, he prayed. *Create angels.*

Suddenly an echo in his mind winked out. One of the five was no more. Somehow, a guildmaster had died.

Ongaro?

Behind him, a loose pebble tumbled from the wall. As he turned toward it, a new outcome presented itself, as Caspay was smashed by a fist of fur.

Like a ringing bell, God's metal hull resounded with anger. Caspay bounced off the Bomb and crashed into the stony base of the pulpit. His skull fractured, the elder statesman collapsed in a heap near the control booth. The off-white blur responsible struggled into focus—it was the disgusting creature Dinge that had struck the guildmaster across the face, sending him reeling.

Broken and bloodied, the mutant couldn't think. His spectacles lay a few feet away from him. While he didn't need them to see, they helped him to focus his mind. A spiderweb pattern dominated one lens, while the other suffered only a single crack. With a trembling hand he reached for them.

A dirty boot got to them first.

"Hello, Four-Eyes." The splintered glass grinding on stone accented the greeting. "But I suppose you're Two-Eyes now," the voice amended. Caspay couldn't see the speaker, but he could smell the beast.

Mr. Taylor's gorilla. The creature called Mungwortt. *How?* Squinting, Caspay saw red sparks in the shadows of the Sanctum.

Not sparks, he realized. *Eyes.* A dozen of them. Somehow, the gorilla had made an alliance with the White Ones. *Stupid animals,* he seethed. *Apes, hybrids, humans—all of them.*

"Where is Tay-Lor?" the Mungwortt creature demanded.

Burn! Caspay struck out at him, but instead of causing the ape pain, his own mind burst aflame. The damage to his skull was unimaginably painful. His brain was *swelling*.

The gorilla and the White Ones just stared.

The nauseous Caspay hauled himself to his feet and vomited. Groping for the pulpit, he pulled himself into the glass chamber. He could still lock himself in there, initiate the launch, and await discovery by another master. His movements were jerky, and even the stupid gorilla could see what he was attempting to do.

"Stop him!" Mungwortt cried.

Dinge hurled himself at Caspay. Sinking his fangs into the mutant's shoulder, he tore him away from the controls before the statesman could initiate the firing sequence—but not before he activated the booth's heavy shielded door. A slab of metal slammed shut on both, crushing them.

Mangled limbs quivered. The pulpit pooled with blood. The White One's skull was smashed, Caspay was all but cut in half. Even so, he fumbled for the launch keys. He leaned on one, but pinned as he was, his reach was not great enough to reach the other.

"My inmost—"

He sputtered, spitting blood. On the pulpit's controls, the lucent keys flashed in sequence—green, yellow, red, repeat.

The apes had not yet arrived, and already two masters were dead. His Holiness sensed their severance. He could not be certain who, but He suspected it was Ongaro and Caspay. While He could not be certain how, He suspected Mr. Brent and Mr. Taylor of having a hand in their deaths.

Successors would need to be chosen from their guilds, lest the disciplines of intellect and equilibrium diminish. What had once been a balanced spectrum of seven ruling orders was now down to three. Only Blue, Red, and Violet remained fluid. Yellow and Green were in danger of the extinction suffered by Tiger and Indigo. The attendant orders were also in jeopardy. Gray was gone, only Umber, Olive, and Tan prevailed.

Society was unraveling.

If this was not the beginnings of Assured Destruction, if the Fellowship of the Holy Fallout survived the coming calamity, they would need to restructure their community. Every remaining asset must be preserved. To that end, He spoke aloud.

"You are discharged from your duties," He said to the Verger, "until the current crisis has subsided." Though hesitant, the Verger nonetheless acquiesced. The dismissal was no reflection of his abilities, or a comment on his years of service. His Holiness needed to protect key resources. Simply put, the Verger was invaluable, and as such had to be sequestered for the good of God.

Mendez XXVI would face the apes in the chancel, alone, and He would do so with God as His witness.

"Find shelter," He said. "Find solace, and go with God." He then transmitted the same to Albina and Adiposo. They all had to survive.

With a nod and the sign of the Bomb, the Verger withdrew.

The gorilla army spilled out of the tunnels and into the streets. General Ursus immediately set his troops upon the enemy, massacring them without hesitation. The soldiers weaved their way through the city, door to door, systematically wiping out anyone who was not an ape.

Zaius noted that these beasts seemed to have no weapons or any way of defending themselves. In general, they seemed shocked at the violence the invaders exhibited. Aside from their cleanliness and the gray, tan, and white garb, these targets were no different from the human herds which ravaged Simia.

Zaius, Ursus, and his commanders convened to confer in the rubble of a building that bore a fallen sign.

RADIO CITY

The general's scouts provided him with a crude map of the surrounding streets.

He's nothing if not efficient, Zaius admitted.

"Here." Ursus stabbed the map. "The fort called Grand Central Terminal. Looks most likely to be their nest."

Zaius indicated the cathedral a few blocks northeast. "What of the house of worship, here?" It was one of the more intact structures.

"No," Ursus waved him off. "No, judging from what the scouts reported, there's something important about that place—no question about it. But they saw no signs of fortifications. No, their leaders are most definitely here, where we've observed the greatest concentration of the enemy." He again indicated the fort.

"We'll split the company into three units," he continued. "One led by you, Doctor. I'll take the second. Major Dangral will take the third." Ursus addressed the map. "The doctor and I will enter the terminal here… and here. Dangral, you come around through this tunnel… here, and set up your position." Without giving anyone a chance to offer options, Ursus folded the map and tucked it in his armor. He turned to his major.

"We'll herd them out, and right into your sights."

Dangral saluted, and Ursus addressed the other commanders. "We clear out the infested terminal, and then on to the church. Sergeant Duignan, you're with the doctor," General Ursus barked. "Lieutenant Aurelios, with me. Move out."

The gorillas moved to assemble their squads.

Ursus still didn't trust Zaius—that much was apparent. In taking Aurelios with him, the general could have his own ape—Duignan—watch over his adversary. Zaius would have to keep a tight leash on the sergeant.

This also meant that Aurelios could report back to Zaius.

Two can play at this game.

As Zaius's and Dangral's squads moved out, Ursus inspected his own apes. He would only accept the elite in this vanguard. Looking his commandos over, he realized he was proud to go into battle with these gorillas. Then he noticed one in particular.

"Who is this soldier, Lieutenant?" he called while the rest of the apes continued their preparations. The gorilla in question was an awkward and gangly boy—hardly elite material. "Why is he not bringing up the rear?"

Aurelios snapped to. "By order of Dr. Zaius, General, I—"

Zaius? Ursus put up a hand to silence him.

"You, soldier." He addressed the boy directly. "You answer."

"Private Jaffe, General—"

Ursus looked away and sighed. "Present arms, Private."

Jaffe blinked, stood at attention, and held his rifle tall. "Sir!"

"Jaffe..." Ursus walked a bit away. "Security Chief Marcus had a son by that name."

"He was my father, sir."

I suspected as much, Ursus thought. "Marcus was a good friend," he said aloud. "A good friend." The general turned to face the boy. "Did you know we often used to debate?"

"No, sir."

"It's true," Ursus said. "A very philosophical ape, your father was. We'd discuss whether we should unite all gorillas, or keep the police and military separate. Whether there should be a separation of Church and State, or have apes be governed by a singular godly vision. Sometimes we'd even question if unity was dangerous, and that keeping things separate maintained a balance of power."

"Oh no, sir," Jaffe said firmly. "All gorillas should be as one. Apes together are strong!" Suddenly, Jaffe remembered who he was talking to. "Sir!"

The general grinned.

"Very good, soldier," Ursus said. "I agree." He looked the private up and down. "Have you ever killed a human, son?"

"No, sir, not yet, sir!"

"You will." Ursus nodded. "Today you'll have your first kill, and revenge for your father's death." He remembered the anger. "You'll have that kill, if I have to hold the beast down myself!" Regaining his composure, he raised a finger. "You mark my words."

"Thank you, sir!"

"Very well, Private." Ursus waved him off. "Carry on."

He smiled as the boy prepared for battle.

"Company," the general ordered. "Move out."

Caught in the open too far from his private shelter, the fat man had been forced to seek refuge. Ducking into an empty building hundreds of yards from Grand Central Terminal, Adiposo received thought projections from mutants in their shelters all along the invaders' route.

The enemy had penetrated the city and were making their way toward the terminal. It wouldn't be long before the slobbering apes found him, and he didn't intend for them to take him in his right mind. Reaching for his snuffbox, Adiposo prepared yet again for Communion.

Then, he thought he heard a thought. It was primitive—more of an emotion than a notion.

It was hate.

"Who's there?" he blurted out. Embarrassed, he composed himself as much as he could. *Who's there?* he sent.

No answer.

Adiposo sighed. This paranoia would be the end of him, he was certain of it.

Then, there was movement—there in his hiding place. As he watched, horrified, a lone gorilla stood up from behind a petrified counter. The creature was no soldier. Instead, it was dressed in tattered rags, its arm bandaged in cloth.

"Remember me?" the ape asked.

Adiposo's eyes went round. *The beast who was with Mr. Taylor.* He nodded, his chins quivering with the movement.

"Where is he?" the creature demanded. "Where is Tay-Lor?"

Outside, machine-gun fire pealed and screams sounded as mutants died in the streets. The slaughter had begun.

"An ape that cares for a human?" Adiposo gave a fatalistic smile. "The world is coming to an end, then." When the gorilla simply glared, the fat man offered little more. "He is most likely dead, you dimwitted beast. If not, he soon will be."

"Dead is not a place." The animal balled his fists and Adiposo's eyes subconsciously darted up the street. Still feeling the effects of his earlier Communion, his thoughts slipped. The ape's expression showed understanding.

"Grand Central Station?" it demanded, and it pointed. "There?"

Stay back. Adiposo recoiled. *Or I will—*

"You'll do what?" He heard the creature's name now—Mungwortt. As filthy as its owner. The ape threw something toward Adiposo. Light and metallic, it skittered across the floor to rest at his feet. A twisted piece of metal with fragments of splintered glass, wrapped around itself. It took the fat man a moment.

Caspay's glasses.

"You'll *what*?" Mungwortt demanded again. "Hurt me?"

Resigned to his fate, Adiposo closed his eyes and attempted to concentrate, but a sound behind him deterred that. A moment later the clatter filled the room as White Ones came pouring through doors in the back. There had to be dozens of them—covered with injuries. Their earlobes were torn, and control tags gone.

The crimson-vested master tried to put fire in their brains, but the beasts were too primitive—too full of rage. He couldn't find a consciousness to grasp. The ivory creatures circled him, then turned to Mungwortt for their orders.

The ape said but a single word.

"Eat."

The ape left before it even started. As the ravenous monsters grabbed for him, Adiposo fumbled with the snuffbox. He scooped up the bed of glowing cilia and smeared it across his tongue. Then, as they shredded his rubber skin and tore into his flesh, a flash of light seared the back of his brain. Behind his eyes he stared into a gamma blast.

The Holy Caress.

Frothing at the mouth, Adiposo was one with God.

"This isn't exactly sterile," Taylor admitted. "We'll do the best we can." Under Ongaro's influence, he had hurt Brent pretty badly. Now, he wrapped the junior officer's bloody wounds. Winded, Brent took a moment to gather his thoughts, then his military training kicked in.

"Taylor..." he started. They needed to brief each other—they both needed to know what they were up against. "Taylor, they've got a bomb—an atomic bomb. It's operational. They intend to use it."

The children of the bomb have one of their own.

Taylor was nonplussed. "What type is it?"

"I don't know," Brent confessed. "I don't know what type. I've never seen it before."

Taylor frowned, and Brent felt a wave of guilt. But the colonel didn't say anything. Instead, he tore a new strip of cloth for the bandage. Finally, he spoke.

"Didn't you see a series number?"

"No numbers," Brent reflected. "Just some letters on one of the fins, Greek letters." Brent caught his breath before continuing. "Alpha..."

Taylor stopped and stared.

"And Omega," he said.

CHAPTER 30
THE WRITING ON THE WALL

Groom Lake, Nevada
Area 51
1970

The morning after his "interrogation," Taylor learned the soul-crushing truth.

On their way to Churchdoor, the three men had descended into the bowels of the earth. Taylor had known the bunker was mostly underground, but he'd had no idea it was ten stories deep. In the elevator he, his father, and Otto Hasslein stood abreast, staring at the numbers ticking down above a metal door.

The silence had been deafening.

The admiral took no notice of his son's bruises, nor did he make mention of the previous night's interrogation. The colonel himself sought no such acknowledgement. It was as if the only thing that connected the two men was their last name.

Exiting the lift on the bottommost level, they were met with a contingent of guards. Once they cleared security, they began to move through a series of airlocks. As they moved along, Hasslein, of all people, broke the silence with small talk.

"Tell me, Colonel," he started. "Are you aware of the expression,

'to salt the earth'?"

"Not really, Doctor," Taylor admitted. "I've heard 'the salt of the earth,' but I don't think that's what you mean."

"It's from the Middle Ages," the admiral said. "Conquerors in the Near East used to spread salt over the territory of their defeated enemies, to show them they were beaten."

"The ritual symbolized that nothing would ever grow there again," Otto added. "Of course, while salt is damaging to crops, there is no evidence that heavy salting will sterilize soil."

The men grew quiet again.

"Well," Taylor said, "thanks for the history lesson." Both Hasslein and his father were behaving strangely. He almost called them out on it. Then, as the final airlock cycled, the admiral made it stranger.

"Other things will."

"Will what?"

"Sterilize it. The soil." His father stared at him. "Prolonged radioactive decay from nuclear fallout would do the trick." The admiral crossed his arms behind his back. "It's what we call a salted bomb. You can see where it gets its name."

Taylor didn't know how to respond, so he remained silent.

"With a salted bomb, one could hypothetically use ordinary cobalt as the poisoning agent," Hasslein elaborated. "An atomic bomb detonated in cobalt housing could produce enhanced amounts of radioactive fallout."

"It would sully the terrain—salt the earth and make it useless for any survivors," the admiral continued. "Of course, depending on the salted bomb's megatonnage, it could do a lot worse."

"With a sufficient yield, yes—a global reaction would not be out of the question," Hasslein concurred. "In theory, it could ignite the atmosphere, render the entire planet uninhabitable. Some projections even anticipate a

blast strong enough to penetrate the earth's crust itself."

Taylor was horrified.

"Is that what you've got locked away down here?"

The last airlock opened, depositing them at a door that held the answer. The admiral explained before they opened it.

"Operation Churchdoor is the conceptualization and development of a doomsday device."

Oh fuck, *Taylor thought.* Stewart was right. *The heavy metal door in front of them had two Greek symbols on it—the same two that were in the file folder.*

A Ω

"We call it the Alpha/Omega Bomb," Admiral Taylor said.

"Yes." Dr. Hasslein frowned, looking less sanguine. "The beginning and end of us all."

As the admiral pressed his thumb to the scanner beside the door, the bulb above it snapped from red to green. With a clank and a hiss, the door pushed forward. They stepped into a cavernous room. Easily the size of one of the airstrip's hangars, it was cast in deep shadows. Hasslein flipped a switch. Floodlights erupted, illuminating the chamber. There, in the center of the room…

…was nothing.

It was empty.

Confused, Taylor stumbled forward.

"Where is it?" he demanded. After a moment of silence, Hasslein spoke up.

"The Churchdoor is closed, Colonel Taylor."

Taylor was stunned. "So, now you're telling me there is no doomsday bomb?"

"There never was," his father replied, "but we need the world to think there is—and we need them to think it's a secret."

"NASA is compromised," Hasslein explained, "and we know that at least one spy has infiltrated ANSA. It seemed… prudent… to use that to our advantage."

"The bunker accident, a few years ago," Taylor said. "You staged *it. But Dr. Stanton—"*

"Stanton's an idiot," the senior Taylor said. "He only knows what we tell him." Hasslein smiled out of the side of his mouth.

"While I would not go so far as to agree with the admiral's assessment of my colleague—not entirely—I will say that Professor Stanton is a man of ambition that goes beyond his own abilities."

In other words, *Taylor reasoned,* he's dangerous.

"Stanton thinks Churchdoor is real, and above his pay grade." The admiral was dismissive. "He's got half of it right."

"And the deaths?" Taylor said.

"The radiation was real," the admiral stated.

"It needed to be, in order for it to seem credible." Hasslein cast his eyes downward. "We had hoped everyone would make it out in time."

"So those men died for your lie?"

"That goddamn lie could be all that's keeping the Reds in check, Colonel!" the admiral said, anger in his voice. "As long as they think we've got the bomb, they'll think twice about starting something they can't finish."

"What's to stop them from building their own doomsday bomb?" the colonel demanded. "What happens then? A race to see who can blow us all up first?"

"They can try all they want." His father waved it off. "The project is a dead end." The admiral didn't try to hide his disappointment. "None of the big brains have gotten anywhere with it, including the doctor."

"The actual bomb is unnecessary," Hasslein asserted. "Fear is the real weapon, gentlemen."

Is the only way to keep us from killing each other the fear of killing ourselves? *Taylor wondered.* Are we that selfish? *In his heart, he knew the answer. The admiral placed his hand on his shoulder, and he jumped in spite of himself.*

"Churchdoor is still classified and stays that way. For command's eyes only."

Taylor scoffed. "Who am I going to tell?" But his father's eyes told him that the old man wasn't going to take that for an answer.

"No bullshit this time, George."

Taylor snapped to attention. "Sir, yes, sir."

"Good." The admiral looked relieved. "Now that you've got your eagles, and this business is behind us, we can move ahead on Project Liberty." He checked his watch and straightened his jacket. "I have a flight to D.C. in an hour." He turned to Hasslein. "I assume you're going to want to give him the tour of the other levels."

Hasslein nodded.

"Doctor, Colonel." The admiral nodded to each of them in turn. As his father left, Taylor stared at the empty concrete cathedral. Something still didn't sit right. He turned to Hasslein.

"A nut that even you couldn't crack, Doctor?"

Hasslein smiled. "Let's just say I prefer to leave this particular shell intact."

"But you could *crack it," Taylor pressed, "if you wanted to."*

"Perhaps." Hasslein folded his arms. "Perhaps I already opened the shell just wide enough to have a look inside."

"So the Alpha/Omega Bomb—" Taylor urged.

"—is where it is safe." Hasslein tapped his temple. "And where it will stay so." The doctor stepped closer. "Mankind teeters on the brink

of self-annihilation, George Taylor," he said. "Pollution, famine, and war consume us—and yet we expend our resources on finding new ways to kill each other." Hasslein sighed. "Men like your father would destroy the world to protect it. I will not help us put both feet in the grave."

"I understand—believe me, I understand." Taylor was satisfied with Hasslein's sincerity, but doomsday bomb or no, Project Liberty couldn't come fast enough for him. A one-way ticket the hell out of here, *he thought,* sounds fantastic. *Hasslein seemed to have read his mind.*

"Whatever destiny God has ordained for us," the doctor suggested, "lies out there amongst the stars, not destroying ourselves at home."

"I don't know about God, Doctor," Taylor replied. "All I know is that mankind's got some evolving to do."

His companion frowned. "The reconciliation of God and science is something I struggle with every day, Colonel." Hasslein motioned toward the door. "In my eyes, the existence of one does not preclude the other."

"One more thing," Taylor requested. "Why call it 'Churchdoor'?"

"Since the creation of the atomic bomb, mankind has been knocking on heaven's door," Hasslein explained. "What better than a doomsday device to elicit God's attention?"

Churchdoor. That's what the bust's memory engrams had tried to imprint on him. The first Mendez, the military train diverted to Grand Central when the bombs fell—it was carrying the Alpha/Omega bomb.

Churchdoor had survived past Taylor's trip to the stars, and General Mendez had been in charge of transporting it.

The soldiers slammed the church door shut.

"Church door," the voice said. "Fear the church door."

Just as mankind had finally blown themselves up, it looked as if Hasslein had given in to the admiral. Taylor frowned.

Damn you, Otto.

"What?" Brent was more worried than ever. Operation Churchdoor was "Eyes Only," and well above Brent's pay grade. Taylor was going to tell him, anyway.

What're they going to do—court-martial me?

"The doomsday bomb," Taylor revealed.

"My God," Brent breathed.

"Yeah, another lovely souvenir from the twentieth century," the senior astronaut growled. "They weren't satisfied with a bomb that could knock out a city. They finally built one with a cobalt casing, all in the sweet name of peace."

"Those goddamn fools." Brent was unraveling. "They don't know what they've got. They *pray* to the damned thing!"

Finally, Taylor had all the pieces. The first Mendez had made the bomb into a symbol to be respected for its awesome power. Fear of it kept his people in line. Over the centuries, that reverence was perverted into a religion.

"If they launch it," Brent continued, "it could set off a chain reaction in the atmosphere."

"Burn the planet to a cinder," Taylor added. "How's *that* for your ultimate weapon?"

Zaius and Duignan pushed through the fortress identified as Grand Central Terminal, forcing out everyone who was hiding inside. Waves of mutants evacuated the building, scattering into the streets. Right on schedule, Dangral's forces sprang from the tunnel on 48th Street. Releasing a hail of bullets, they cut the running mutants down.

Mungwortt watched it all. Having left the White Ones behind to finish Adiposo, the hybrid saw his opportunity to enter the mutant nest by blending in with the army. In the charred lobby of a nearby vacant office building, he bashed a nervous gorilla scout with a rock. He took the soldier's uniform, then stopped to check if the now naked gorilla soldier was still breathing.

He was. He had a nasty head wound, but he was still alive.

"Sorry," Mungwortt told the unconscious ape.

The soldier was a little shorter than him, but then again, so were most gorillas. So the stolen uniform Mungwortt wore was ill-fitting, but in the chaos no one would notice.

If he couldn't find Tay-Lor, the army was his only ticket out of this underground hell. Nevertheless, this was the most likely place to find his friend. He straightened the leather tunic, slung his purloined machine gun over his shoulder, and readied to jump in line with the passing forces.

Then, he hesitated.

Listening.

Waiting for Zao to tell him he was an idiot.

Nothing.

Mungwortt smiled. *Zao approves,* he decided. Taking a deep breath, he fell in line with the gorilla commandos.

The lock was caving in, but not giving way. Taylor stopped bashing it with the mace just long enough for them to give the door a try again.

Nothing.

As Taylor reared back to hit it again, gunfire rang out. The men froze. The mutants had no guns. All guns on the planet belonged to the apes. Brent rushed to the far cage wall and strained to see around the corner. Shadows filled the hall as footsteps grew louder.

Gorilla shadows.

Taylor grabbed Nova, and the three of them squeezed themselves up against the arched wall of their cell, hidden in the alcove. Then, as the gorillas got closer, the three humans hugged themselves tight against the wall.

Brent grunted, and pointed toward Ongaro's body. The painmaster lay dead in the center of the cell, easily visible from the door.

A dead body raises questions, Brent thought.

Taylor nodded. Together they reached out and grabbed their tormentor's corpse, swinging it against the wall just in time. A gorilla pressed his face to the opening, curious to see what was inside.

Bullets sprayed the wall of the cell.

Mungwortt saw the bars and knew this must be where the mutants kept their prisoners. Finding a window, the half-breed peered inside.

Nothing.

Then, he heard movement.

Suspicious, he needed to make a choice. If he called out for Tay-Lor, and there were mutants on the other side, they would attack him. If there were other gorillas in there, he didn't want to be caught shouting for a human.

It could be a mouse. Or one of those abominations. He didn't like the idea of either. So, without Zao to turn to, he made up his own mind. Mungwortt unslung his machine gun, put the nozzle through the bars, and fired. Bullets sprayed the far wall of the cell. Then he stopped and listened. There was nothing.

Nobody's home, Mungwortt decided, and he moved on down the corridor. Things were getting too dangerous. He had to find Tay-Lor, and he had to do it fast. Either that, or he was going to have to leave the human behind.

Once they were certain the gorilla was gone, Taylor and Brent resumed pounding. Finally, their persistence bore fruit. Metal bent and twisted under the repeated blows from the spiked mace. The lock broke, and the door swung free.

They had a choice—leave the undercity and let the gorillas and mutants slaughter each other. Head back toward Ape City, its waterfalls and cornfields, its jungles. Or—

Goddamn it, Taylor thought. He turned to Brent.

"Are you thinking what I'm thinking?"

The younger astronaut nodded. "I'm thinking just that."

Taylor tossed Brent the mace and pulled a second one from the wall rack. With a nervous Nova in hand, they turned back down the corridor toward the cathedral, narrowly avoiding a gorilla squad that was escorting a captured mutant. Confrontation avoided, they deftly turned another corner.

A lone gorilla soldier stood there, machine gun at the ready. Taylor ducked back behind the archway, pulling Nova with him. He hadn't seen them, though, and slowly the three humans backed away up a short flight of steps. Stopping, Brent pressed himself against the nearest wall.

Then there was a nearby burst of gunfire, loud enough that Nova panicked. She bolted, the gorilla saw her, and fired. Bullets followed her, spraying the wall.

Taylor and Brent swung their maces. Both struck the gorilla in the face and head. His skull crushed, he collapsed.

Riddled with bullets, Nova swayed dizzily against the far wall. Taylor rushed to her, catching her and lowering her gently to lie on the steps.

"Nova?" Her eyes were already glassy. He reached for her hand and saw the extent of the wounds. *If we can stop the bleeding…* But it was too late. The bullet had struck something major. She stopped moving, stopped breathing.

Nova was dead.

And with her, their unborn child.

"Nova," Taylor said quietly. "Ah, God." It was a sigh. He bit back the tears. "We should let them all die—the gorillas, every damn…" Taylor trailed off, his thoughts no one's but his own. "When it comes time."

He thought about the baby. Of the life that could have been. Past the Forbidden Zone, in the jungle beyond. Just over the next sunrise.

"It's time it was finished." He stroked Nova's cheek and looked past Brent into oblivion. "Finished."

Everything was falling apart. Assured Destruction was upon them. Ongaro was dead—Albina had recognized his absence. She had not realized it, but the ever-present echo of his presence had soothed her. Their bond had been stronger than she had wanted to admit, and now his mind was gone. Now her thoughts were cold.

He was dead. As were the others. Only she and His Holiness lived. They had waited too long. Caspay had not attempted to usurp Mendez, so she had taken no action, either. For all their secret thoughts of change, the mutants were too steeped in tradition. They were unwilling to evolve.

And for that, we must all die.

Lost in her grief, she had wandered back toward tracks 19–11, back to the amphitheater, carrying a stoppered crystal carafe. This place was abandoned. Most likely His Holiness awaited death in the cathedral.

He'll try to put the fear of God into them.

She believed in God, but unlike the others, she doubted the resurrection. Albina had suspected for some time that the salvation of the Almighty Bomb was the salvation of annihilation. Their kind had been reborn once; however, it would not be reborn again. Assured Destruction was imminent.

Weapons fire echoed through the station. Soon the invaders would reach the Corridor of Busts, and then they would be upon her. She knew what savage creatures these apes were; she had touched their minds.

Sick. Hideous. Perverse. Albina knew what the gorillas would do to her. Looking to the carafe, she knew what she must do.

Sweeping their way through the terminal, the two gorilla squads cleared out the human nests. Heavy weapons fire came from Ursus's direction—the general seemed to be falling behind.

Zaius's commandos, however, were making good time. It was a simple matter, when the enemy's forces ran from them. Entering the Grand Central fortress, they worked their way deeper inside, finally coming to a hall lined with busts.

Statues of reverence lined the walls, each a ceramic object that appeared to be coated in a different fine metal. Each was very much human, many of them looking akin to one another. The sight gave them all reason to pause.

"They are obscene!" Zaius took the rifle from the closest gorilla soldier and swung at the nearest bust. It shattered across the floor. Inspired by his action, the gorillas plowed through the hall, smashing each statue to dust.

At the end of the hall, Zaius pushed the doors wide. The room beyond was both cavernous and abandoned—empty save for a stone seat facing the far wall. On that seat sat a human woman, her arm draped over the side, the exposed platinum blond hair cascading over her shoulder. She appeared to be unconscious, yet Zaius approached her with caution.

On the floor, not far from her dangling hand, the scientist discovered a crystal vial—empty. Putting it to his nostrils, he inhaled. It was a powerful acid, and the human creature had ingested it.

Suicide.

A most gruesome act. Her esophagus and digestive tract would be dissolved by such a solution. From the peaceful look on her face, however, he surmised that there must have been an anesthetic agent mixed with it. It looked as if she had felt nothing.

Zaius was stunned at the level of intelligence these creatures exhibited. Knowledge of chemicals, sophisticated clothing, able to make the complex decision to kill themselves rather than face their enemies. It was everything he feared and more.

Behind him he heard Sergeant Duignan and the other gorillas. They simply stood there and peered at him, looking very uncertain.

Ursus was right, Zaius acknowledged. They needed to put an end to this, needed to wipe mankind off the face of the planet before it was too late.

"Follow me." He headed toward the stairs and up to the next level. The other gorillas obeyed, but Duignan stayed behind. The gorilla pushed the creature's head back so he could get a better look at her face, but it was her hair that appeared to fascinate him. Her glistening blond hair. The silky fibers shimmered in his gloved fingers.

Standing at the stairs, Zaius saw that the sergeant had fallen behind, saw that he was with the deceased woman. What he was doing was a perversity of nature.

"Sergeant!" he barked.

Duignan snapped to attention and hurried to follow.

Nova was gone. Brent gave his commanding officer a minute. There must have been more to the relationship than he could have guessed. But then there was more gunfire in the distance, closer than before.

They had to get to the church.

So far, the gorillas had passed them by without spotting them. Any moment, however, that could change. Any minute, one of those fanatics could launch the bomb and destroy the entire goddamn planet.

"Taylor…" Brent didn't want to die here. He had to do something, and he needed Taylor's help. "Come on, come on," he urged. "The bomb."

Shaking his head, Taylor seemed to notice Brent for the first time since the shooting.

"Yeah," he muttered. "Why not?" Tenderly, he lowered the

young woman to the floor. Then he rose to stand with Brent. They nodded and moved in the direction of the cathedral.

Toward their destiny.

The Verger saw to the cathedral doors, barricading and bolting them before slipping out through the catacombs. Finally emerging from an adjacent subway station, he paused. A contingent of gorillas swept through the streets, gunning down any mutant that moved.

So he made certain he remained absolutely still. As they moved away, the crack of their guns diminished with them.

A hush descended over the scene, and he began to make his way again, gliding across the alley and toward the plaza beyond. Abruptly, an anxious bleat stabbed the silence.

He froze again.

A young gorilla in an ill-fitting uniform faced him. *How barbaric,* he thought, *to bring a child into war.*

Though underdeveloped and weak, the animalistic creature still held aloft a weapon, and it was aimed at the Verger's heart. Both were frozen in time and reluctant to make the first move. Their eyes locked, and the caretaker concentrated.

Separated from his unit, Marcus's son looked the strange human over. Dressed in gray and white robes, it also wore a brown hood. The beast's face had no hair save for its brows. Jaffe had seen human savages before, and they were nothing like this.

Unwilling to look away, he heard a distant ringing, but not in his ears. The echo enthralled him, filled him with despair. Humans had killed his father, and they were going to kill him, too.

You left your home undefended, the sound accused him. *Humans have overrun it.*

The young gorilla knew he had to get to the church. General Ursus and the others would be regrouping there. Dr. Zaius had assigned him to Aurelios. He was needed.

Look what you've done. Your mother is dead.

Jaffe began to weep.

Your siblings are next, but there is still time to save them. Leave. Go back to your home. Go before it is too late.

The gun barrel wavered.

The hooded human turned, and Jaffe fired. The bullet pierced his right shoulder, bisecting the blade before cleaving his clavicle. Being spun and slammed to the ground, the creature's breath turned sharp and shallow.

The echo of the shot squashed the echo in Jaffe's brain. His own breath equally ragged, he ejected the spent shell and approached his first kill. To his astonishment, the beast spoke.

"I reveal my inmost self, unto my god."

Lying in its blood, the creature tore its own face off.

Horrified, Jaffe aimed for its eyes and fired again and again.

"You there!" the major demanded. Mungwortt had emerged from the Grand Central building with nothing to show for his efforts. He hadn't found Tay-Lor, and he had lost the White Ones.

Dinge is dead, he reminded himself. *At least the fat man and Four-Eyes are, too.*

Now he had earned the attention of this platoon's sergeant.

"You look like a strong one, soldier." The gorilla grabbed

Mungwortt by the arm and led him over to a tunnel. Other apes had gathered around a twisted piece of metal that lay there. "Get that rail loose," the sergeant ordered them all, "I want it as a battering ram!"

"Sir, yes, Major, sir!" Mungwortt exclaimed, mimicking what he had heard other soldiers say. Relieved that his disguise worked, he put his back under the rail and shoved. Centuries of debris shifted, metal bent, and rust snapped. The other gorillas pulled, and finally the rail loosened.

"Take up positions." The sergeant stabbed a finger at a building across the street. It had tall, pointed towers, and was far more ornate than any structure in the vicinity. "Bring down that door!" Ten gorillas hefted the weighty rail and trotted toward the church. Falling in with them, Mungwortt considered himself lucky.

Tay-Lor might be in there, he thought. *And he might not.* Regardless, at least the army believed he belonged with them. If he stuck with them, he might actually get out of this alive.

Zao said nothing.

CHAPTER 31
REVELS NOW ENDED

The ape army descended on the mutants' high sanctuary. General Ursus's vanguard group reached the cathedral doors, with Zaius's team not far behind.

Seizing the twisted metal rail, Major Dangral's gorillas used it to ram again and again until the giant wooden doors gave way. Pushed up against the entrance, the gorillas poured into the church, down the center aisle, and spilled over the pews. Expecting to find a crowd of humans, Ursus was surprised to discover a single mutant human, kneeling before a podium of some kind.

If this wasn't their fallback shelter, the general reasoned, *there must be something important here that they're protecting.* Signaling caution, Ursus followed as his apes filed into the church. The human stood as they approached. The way he moved, the clothes he wore, he almost seemed civilized.

Humans playing ape, Ursus thought. *It's sickening.*

"Sergeant!" he called to Duignan. "Arrest that creature." Before the sergeant could move to comply, however, that creature spoke.

"This is the instrument of my god."

"He can speak!" the sergeant said. Cries of astonishment flowed through the crowd. The rumors had been true—talking humans existed. The creature manipulated some crystal rods that were propped in the podium. As they sank into the mechanism, a huge object began to rise behind.

Zaius had hoped he was wrong all along. Hoped that Taylor was an aberration from the past, and that a tribe of talking humans did not yet exist. Hoped against hope there were no more bombs.

Yet rising out of the floor was what appeared to be the very instrument of death about which his father had warned him—the weapon that he had only seen as drawings in both the *Forgotten* and *Secret Scrolls*. It was a missile, and above it stretched a vertical shaft he had to assume led to the surface. Through it, the bomb could be fired.

This was everything the orangutan had feared.

Ursus was quick to regain control of the room.

"Your god, eh?" he said mockingly. "Sergeant." Submachine gun at the ready, Duignan squeezed, and the figure at the podium was cut down in a spatter of jacketed lead. Ursus gestured and Dangral surrendered his weapon to the general as he made his way forward.

"Your god didn't save you." He spat at the human's corpse. "Did he, huh?" The hairs on his back bristling with his power, Ursus lifted his weapon and sprayed a hail of bullets at the mutants' metal god.

"Ursus!" Zaius snapped. "That weapon is built by man. You can't shoot it down with bullets!"

But the general was livid with rage.

"If we can't shoot it down, we'll *pull* it down. Rope!" he shouted to his apes. "Block and tackle!" As Duignan and the troops rushed forward to do their general's bidding, Zaius tried to reason with him.

"You don't know what you're doing," he warned. "It will kill us all!"

Mungwortt didn't like the sound of that. If he had known that the giant bullet was trouble, he would have ordered the White Ones to eat it earlier.

As the other gorillas tackled the metal effigy, he hesitated.

This doesn't feel right, he thought. The thing hit the ground with an echoing *clang*. Its housing cracked, and scalding steam poured out over the troops. The sergeant screeched and covered his eyes. Others scrambled away to avoid being burned. Pandemonium erupted, and the general tried to contain it.

"I'll find a way to stop it," Ursus said, but he didn't sound terribly confident. He reached a leather-gauntleted glove out toward the podium, but didn't appear to know which lever to grasp. Eager to have no part in this cluster of errors, Mungwortt quietly backed away. Posing as a lookout, he spied around the church, searching for any sign of Tay-Lor.

There.

It was a human with a gun, running low and keeping to the shadows. The lithe figure sprung up the stairs toward a large group of metal pipes, but there was something off about him.

Too short, he realized. It was not Tay-Lor. *But where there was one…*

Sure enough, there was more movement, on the other side of the hall. His objective was there, sneaking up to the pillar that stood nearest Ursus and Zaius.

Tay-Lor was up to something.

* * *

It was all Brent could stand. He wasn't going to let any goddamn ape kill them all—and by accident. Ducking behind the church organ, he slammed the butt of his rifle down on the keys. As it bleated its untuned disgust, the general and Zaius turned their attention on him.

Ursus ordered his gorillas to attack. As the apes descended on Brent, Dr. Zaius shouted over the din, and pointed.

"Ursus," he bellowed, "someone at the pillar!"

Machine gun ready, the general whirled and fired.

"Give it a whirl!" Milo shouted. On the banks of the Dead Lake, a miracle was underway. His head peeking out from the starcraft's nose hatch, the scientist yelled to Dr. Lykos below.

All they had needed was a simple electrical spark to trip the *Liberty 1*'s circuit breaker and commence ignition. The elaborate array of wires, clay batteries, cogs, and water wheels they had devised might just do the trick. The elder chimpanzee nodded an affirmative, and he and his team spun the oversized crank they had crafted to jump-start power to the flying beast.

As the crank spun, a crackle and a boom burst from somewhere in the starbird's belly.

Liberty 1 began to whistle.

An ecstatic Milo hooted before ducking his head back in the craft and working his way to the cabin. It wasn't a simple thing to crawl down the access tube, especially while covered in the bulky space suit, but Milo had seen fit to wear it during startup. In the cockpit, Cornelius and Zira sat in two of the three command chairs. All around them, haphazard lights blinked and control panels beeped out of tune.

"Of course, this isn't what the original cabin configuration was like," Milo explained with delight. The panels that drove the starbird now rested in the front and center of the cockpit, and he had moved a command chair to that position. "We had to make some minor changes to bypass some shortcomings in the rebuild." He regarded the lights and sounds. "But she works!"

"Unbelievable." Always the practical one, Cornelius was too astonished to say anything more. As always, however, Zira had plenty to say.

"Milo, this is so exciting," she enthused. "This craft is proof that Taylor spoke the truth!"

"Yes," he agreed as he touched a pointer to his muzzle, deep in thought, "and Landon, as well." When Seraph had returned without Landon, he had known the human must be dead.

"If only we had known about him before," Zira averted her eyes. "That is—"

Cornelius put his hand on hers. "Before Dr. Zaius had him lobotomized," he finished. "Zira studied him afterward—he would perform the same tasks over and over again all day long. But he didn't live much longer."

Milo's heart sank. It was the astronaut Landon who had led him here in the first place, and he had left him alone in his brother-in-law's private lab, stuck in a cage.

I should have brought the human with me, he told himself. So many mistakes made in the name of science. *There's nothing to be done about the past, however.* The starbird worked, and nothing would bring the human back.

With a little luck, he thought, *it will fly again, too.*

"Now you just need to get it to Ape City, Doctor," Zira said.

"That is my assertion, as well, Doctor." Milo nodded.

Cornelius raised a brow. "How do you propose to do so, Dr. Milo? The horses would never survive the strain of pulling—"

"My good doctors," he said calmly, with a hint of a smile, "why pull when we can fly?"

"You aren't serious," Cornelius said, his eyes wide.

"Hmph," Milo responded, "am I not?" He gestured to the desert before them, which had been so meticulously cleared of rocks and debris. "It's a pathway for the starbird," he affirmed. "Given enough speed and momentum, this vessel will soar into the sky." Then he looked down, and his shoulders slumped. "If we can just determine the command sequence."

"The, uh, command sequence." Cornelius's nose twitched. "I am unfamiliar with that."

"It's like a lock on a door." Milo attempted to pull an engine throttle. While it moved freely, it seemed to serve no purpose other than to activate a flashing red light on the console, demanding that the command sequence be engaged. A dull alert chime accompanied it. "It's to prevent someone without authorization from attempting to fly this machine."

"What kind of sequence?" Zira asked. "Numbers? Letters?"

As the lever continued to ignore him, Milo sighed. "It would be a series of control switches flipped in a particular order. It is something the crew themselves would have memorized, and something that is apparently unique to each vessel." As he spoke, Zira surveyed the cabin as if she recognized something.

"The book that contained the sequence for this craft was..." Milo floundered. "...uh, missing."

Let me see if I can't help you with that, Doctor," Zira said, and her eyes flashed with excitement. Rummaging through her carpet bag, she unearthed the notes she had taken, describing Landon's post-surgery behavior. Studying them, she made her way to the beds located near the back of the cabin.

"Which one of these was Landon's?" she asked.

"Ah, he was their navigator, so..." Milo thought about it before indicating top and to the right. "This one."

Now she understood why Landon hopped every time he got off and on the examination table—his bed was elevated. Zira lay in Landon's tube, then dropped to the floor and retraced the steps the astronaut had taken in the wine cellar. She took fifteen paces over to the stations to flick switches and turn knobs, just as Landon had plucked and grabbed at the air.

When she did, the flashing red light on the command station showed a steady green. An intrigued Milo reached forward and pulled the engine lever that had previously done nothing. This time, there was an audible click. The cabin's cacophony ended as the cockpit hummed and purred. Her husband shook his head. Milo's eyes danced.

"You were right, Cornelius." Zira wrinkled her nose in delight. "Landon *was* trying to get home."

Barely able to contain his enthusiasm, Milo motioned toward her notes.

"Doctor Zira, if I may?" She nodded and handed Milo her notepad. As his eyes greedily consumed what lay there, she continued.

"I can only assume the rest will get this contraption in the air," she exclaimed.

"Yes," Milo said, though she wasn't certain he had heard her. "And perhaps more. The entire progression begins and ends with him going to sleep," he noted. "Doctor Zira, I—" Milo began, but he seemed at a loss for words.

"Thank Landon, not me," she insisted. "And your cousin Liet, for liberating him." She looked across the cabin at her doubting husband before adding, "And thank Cornelius, too."

"Me? What did I do?" Cornelius was confused. "I handed you a measuring stick. You were the one who wrote all that down."

"I recorded Landon's movements, but it was your remark—about Landon trying to fly away—that made me do it in the first place."

"Then, well done, Doctors," Milo said earnestly. Cornelius nodded, and Zira smiled. "Now, about Ape City..." He stood and paced the cabin. "Dr. Lykos will be my co-pilot." He leaned back against the control dashboard, a smile creeping across his face. "But Seraph has declined to fly. There is room for two more, if you would like to accompany me."

"Ah, no." Cornelius chuckled nervously. "No, thank you."

"Cornelius!"

"No, thank you, Zira!" he exclaimed. "First of all, we have no idea what this death trap will do." He gestured widely. "It might explode before it even makes it down the pathway!" Embarrassed, he turned to Milo. "No offense intended, Dr. Milo."

Milo nodded in kind. "None taken, Dr. Cornelius." Looking relieved that he had not perturbed his colleague, Cornelius continued.

"Secondly, we just escaped from Ape City. I don't know about you, but I'm not sure it's such a good idea to go back to the place where you, my dear, have a warrant for your arrest." He looked his wife once over. "A death warrant, I might add!"

* * *

Milo was becoming exasperated. They were always bickering.

Why would anyone want to be around someone who always argues with you? he mused. *I'll never understand love, and will be the better for it.*

Abruptly, he realized the cabin had gone quiet. Both husband and wife were looking to him for comment.

Blast.

"All valid points, of course." He indicated to Zira, "But please, I believe a rebuttal is in order."

"Cornelius, don't you see?" she fretted. "This 'starbird' changes everything! It's the proof that man came first. I say we fly it over the gorilla army in the desert, and then land it smack in the center of Simian Square. Let's give the Citizens' Council something to *really* get up in arms about!" As she spoke, she was gaining steam. "Ursus and Sabian's government wouldn't last long, then."

Cornelius crossed his arms.

"I won't."

Zira scoffed.

"And no, Zira, you will not either."

"Excuse me?"

"You are my wife." He leaned in to whisper to her, though Milo could hear quite clearly. "And we have other considerations to think about." His eyes dropped to her belly. His point made, Cornelius shook his head. "I am putting my foot down. We carry on past the Forbidden Zone. Find the jungle Dr. Zaius believes exists on the other side." He sounded wishful now. "We'll find Taylor and Nova, and Brent, and start again."

Zira boiled over. "You… you—"

Milo interrupted. "Excuse me, Doctors, but we might have

something more pertinent to worry about." Outside the starboard viewport, a gorilla troop on horseback emerged from the valley, riding hard toward them.

"I believe you were followed."

"In the name of Reverend Minister Sabian, High Patriarch and Pontifex Rex," Chief Cerek proclaimed, "I have come seeking the chimpanzee fugitives Zira and Cornelius."

"They aren't here," Seraph offered. "They aren't part of our expedition; we have been here for weeks—"

"Stop," Sub-Chief Xirinius cut her off. He stared past the chimpanzee female, at the large metal object. "What is this thing?"

"It is an artifact we discovered," she answered. "A remnant of an ancient culture."

To Cerek, that sounded dangerous—like something Sabian wouldn't want to have dug up.

"What is that sound?" Xirinius scratched at his ears. "Like a humming in the air."

Inside, Cornelius and Zira crept low.

"I should go out there—" Milo started.

"Forgive me, Dr. Milo," Cornelius interrupted, "but I think it might be best to not draw attention to the fact that there are apes within this monstrosity, lest they decide to look inside for me and my wife"—he indicated the ship's lit-up control panels—"or take a truncheon to the very pretty and very delicate machinery you've just gotten running."

Milo hesitated and then nodded. "Most prudent of you, Dr.

Cornelius." He looked down at the space suit he wore and had an idea. It wouldn't protect the ship's controls, but it just might protect his friends. Milo moved to the storage lockers in the chamber beyond the sleep capsules.

"Here." He passed them two of the remaining space suits. "Change your clothes. Put these on." As the startled couple stood and stared, Milo tossed each of them a helmet. "Put these on and close the face shield." He picked up his own helmet and slid the dark faceplate down. "Like so." He lifted it back up, and continued.

"If the gorillas come aboard," Milo said, "hide in the storage locker in the back. If they even make it back there, with a little luck they will think we are just strange suits standing in a closet."

The costumes were bulky enough that it just might work. Cornelius looked at Zira. "It's better than nothing," he offered. Zira huffed and started taking off her clothes. As Cornelius began to unhook his own tunic, he noticed his chimpanzee friend was absentmindedly watching them. "Ah, Doctor, if you don't mind."

Milo felt the heat of his blush.

"Of course, Doctor." He turned his attention back to the scene unfolding outside. "But do hurry, if you please."

Cerek wanted answers. "Why are you here in the Forbidden Zone?"

"Archeological dig." Seraph stepped forward and produced a small scroll. "We have a permit, signed by Dr. Zaius himself."

Cerek looked it over. Something wasn't quite right.

"This is not Zaius's signature," he said. "Whatever you are doing, I order you to stop."

"No, you don't understand," Lykos said. "This is important to all of apekind. We must not stop."

Xirinius shoved Seraph out of the way and spat in Lykos's face.

"Then we will stop it for you!"

Cerek had also had enough of upstart chimpanzees. "Take it apart!" the chief called to his gorillas. "Rip out its innards, smash the machines! Wreck it all!" Cerek urged his horse forward, but Lykos stood his ground.

"Stop!" the elder chimp commanded. He stepped in front of Cerek and his riders. "Stop in the name of sci—"

His words were cut short by trampling hooves. Cerek hadn't pulled back on his reins in time.

With a gasp of terror, Seraph rushed to Lykos's side.

"Is he…?" Cerek murmured.

Seraph lay the elder chimpanzee's head down gently and stood tall.

"He is dead."

Dr. Pinchus picked up a rifle and aimed it at Cerek.

"Stop this, now," he ordered. "Haven't you done enough?"

Xirinius slid his pistol from his holster and fired. Pinchus let loose one shot before clutching his chest and doubling over. Cerek's horse took the bullet in the shoulder and threw him from his saddle. The rest of the gorillas acted on instinct and fired into the chimpanzee crowd.

"Wait!" His leg broken, Cerek tried to be heard from the ground. "Cease fire!"

Ape shall not kill ape, he thought furiously. *What have I done?*

As the gorillas assaulted the chimpanzees, Seraph ran for *Liberty 1.*

* * *

Inside the cabin, Cornelius and Zira had just finished putting the suits on. While Milo watched, all hell broke loose outside. After Cerek's horse ran over Lykos, there was shooting and mass chaos. Seraph ran toward them, heading for the external booster control.

Looking up at Milo, she smiled before pulling the lever.

"What is she doing?" Zira asked.

"Seraph," Milo yelled. "Don't—"

Liberty 1's thrusters ignited. Thrown across the cabin, Milo struggled to regain his balance and seat himself in the vacant command chair. Within an instant they were racing down the runway. If he didn't punch in the proper lift sequence from Zira's notes, the craft would simply run out of clean ground and slam into the desert.

"Strap yourselves in," he shouted, "and get those helmets on!" Milo entered the code and reached for the control stick. It was time to apply some lift.

As they neared the end of the runway, Milo felt her nose rise into the wind.

Liftoff.

And then, they were arcing through the air.

CHAPTER 32
ESCAPE

Taylor had been shot. It was a chest wound, and from what Brent could tell, it was bad. After all he had gone through, his mission was going to be a failure.

Filled with rage, Brent's aim was true.

The bullet pierced a weak spot in Ursus's armor, right between two of the ceramic plates. The shot hit the general in the shoulder and proceeded downward, piercing his heart. Clutching at his back, Ursus plummeted off the pulpit and landed face-first on the floor below.

Aurelios sprang into action, Jaffe close behind.

First the human cut down Ursus, then Dangral. As the beast continued to fire at the unorganized gorillas, the lieutenant tried to assemble a squad to take him out. At the same time, Jaffe traded his rifle for a discarded submachine gun, took aim on Brent, and fired.

Nothing happened.

Unfamiliar with the weapon, the boy struggled to find the safety.

* * *

Brent knew how to use a rifle. He was a better shot than Taylor, too—but as Ursus fell, the gorilla army was on him.

Nevertheless, the astronaut was in a frenzy now, taking out an ape with each shot. As gorilla soldiers fell to his left and his right, he felt the rifle click with no report.

Can't be out of ammo, he panicked, *that wasn't a full clip.*

He looked closely, and found a single shell bent in the chamber. He had to eject it—and *quickly*. But the momentary distraction was all the apes needed to organize. Regrouped, they emptied their automated weapons into him. The force of the assault threw Brent back against the wall.

One of the bullets struck him in the head.

Thank God.

The nightmare was over.

Not that any of it had been real.

It's hibernation psychosis. I'm still in cryo-sleep aboard the Liberty 2.

Brent's vision went dark as he slid wetly down the wall.

Now, I can wake up.

In space, *Liberty 2*'s stardrive waited. Half asleep, she drifted lazily in orbit, firing the occasional reaction control thruster to correct her course and keep her from spiraling down to the planet below.

Then another craft approached. *Liberty 1*. Secondary protocols took effect—automatic rescue parameters. As *Liberty 1* sailed toward a group of dwellings on the surface of the planet, the stardrive reached out to her. Override codes took effect—codes known only to the mission commanders and the ANSA team back on Earth.

Without those codes, *Liberty 1* would be hijacked by the stardrive, mated, and sent back home, regardless of the condition of the crew. The inherent goal was to save their lives.

Milo felt the controls seize. Panicked, he looked at the reading on the control boards.

"What's wrong with the starbird?" Zira said, fear edging her voice. But it wasn't a malfunction.

"I've lost control of the craft. It"—Milo blinked, twice—"it's flying itself."

Curving up and away from Ape City, leaving behind it a loud *BOOM*, *Liberty 1* pushed its way toward the stars. Before long the blue of the sky spilled past the viewports to expose a dark canvas peppered by a splatter of white sparkles. One of those glints of light grew larger by the second.

It's not a star, it's much too close, and, Milo calculated, *it's moving.* As if it had noticed their approach, the object was swinging around to greet them. To *intercept* them. It began to expand, like a frilled lizard making a threatening display to mark its territory.

What have I gotten us into?

Small thrusters appeared in the winglets on either side of *Liberty 1*'s cockpit. They pivoted and fired, slowing the starbird and changing her course. She somersaulted with grace as she spun around to face the planet. The chimpanzee scientists were too rapt to give in to fear. From what they could tell, she was backing slowly toward the front of the fanned ship.

"Hold on to something!" Cornelius shouted.

KLANG!

Liberty 1 struck the other ship, but not fast enough to cause any damage. The sound reverberated through the hull, and formed a hypothesis in Milo's mind. The frill had not been an indication of a threat. Instead, it was more like the fanning feathers of a gigantic bird. It had been a mating display, and the courtship was over.

"I believe we have become attached to another ship." He squinted his eyes, nodding approval at his own diagnosis. "An engine, if you will—like the damaged one we found in Dead Lake."

"Brent!" Zira exclaimed, and he agreed entirely. It must have been part of Brent's starcraft—one that had been left in the sky. Somehow it had been waiting for them, and now it was entirely in control. New boards of indicator lights leapt to life before them. The engine alive, powering itself up—but for what?

Where could it take them?

A planet of… humans?

"Tay-Lor!" Mungwortt had watched with horror as the general shot his friend. Wounded as he was, however, the man pulled himself up like some kind of living dead, clutching his bleeding chest.

The hybrid looked down at his own wounded arm—the one Tay-Lor had wrapped for him in the park.

If I can get to him in time, he rationalized, *I can bandage him up like he did me!* The human would be good as new.

As these thoughts raced through his mind, the other human shot the general, and all hell broke loose. Gunshots rang out everywhere, and they gave Mungwortt his chance. As gorillas ran amuck, he weaved his way through the pews. He saw Tay-Lor, arguing with Dr. Zaius—the orangutan who had exiled him and Zao in the first place.

Mungwortt didn't like him.

I'm coming, Tay-Lor!

But his friend didn't look good. Aside from all the blood, the human had a very scary look on his face. Zaius was yelling at him, and Tay-Lor didn't seem to like that. The man dropped to his knees and reached out for the crystal levers and knobs on the podium in front of him.

We don't want him doing that.

It was Zao. Mungwortt didn't know what "that" was, but Tay-Lor was too far away for the half-breed to stop him. Whatever it was, Tay-Lor was going to do it.

Zao sighed one last time.

See you soon, dimwit.

What do you mean by that, Zao?

Zao?

ANSA Launch Operations Center
Cape Kennedy, Florida
January 14, 1972

Liberty 1 *stood tall at the launch complex at Cape Kennedy, primed, fueled, and ready to go. Her command capsule capped a Dyna-Soar-type bird perched on top of four massive Titan rockets.*

Mission Commander George Taylor sat in that command capsule, surrounded by the three people with whom he would likely spend the rest of his life—whether that be two minutes, if Liberty 1 *crashed and burned on the launch pad, or two thousand years, if their mission was a success. To his left sat their last-minute replacement, Navigator John Landon. Formerly of Juno mission, he was graduated early from officer training with top marks, and rushed through the Liberty program.*

Taylor didn't know much about the man, but he already considered him a milquetoast. Behind Landon sat Lead Science Officer Thomas Dodge, an explorer whose only belief system was logic and science. He was solid and dependable. A good man. Behind Taylor sat Maryann Stewart, serving as the team's biologist—and the future mother of mankind. Other than these three, he never again had to see a single human being from the twentieth century.

That was fine with him. Future man had to be a lot more civilized than the monsters his lifetime had produced.

"T-minus sixty seconds on the Liberty 1 *mission," ANSA's announcer declared, "the first interstellar flight to Alpha Centauri. All indications coming in to the control center at this time indicate we are go."*

"Third stage completely pressurized." Dodge spoke from the engineering station. "Power transfer is complete—we're on internal power at this time."

"Forty seconds away from the Liberty 1 *liftoff," someone at launch operations said. "All the second-stage tanks now pressurized. We are still go with* Liberty 1*."*

Taylor was relieved. Forty seconds away from leaving this hellhole. *Then an all-too-familiar voice broke his reverie.*

"George." It wasn't the announcer at the Cape. The voice was gruff and informal. It was Admiral Taylor himself. "If any of your people want off the bus, now's the time."

The admiral had chosen to be on site at Cape Kennedy, rather than Mission Control at the Pentagon. The younger Taylor had assumed his father had wanted to see him off, but ever since they arrived at the Cape, the admiral hadn't shown his face or spoken a word to his son.

Until now.

Taylor grimaced. The old man didn't even know how to say goodbye.

Instead, he offered his son a chance to scrub the mission they had spent nearly two decades realizing.

It was surreal.

Switching his microphone to internal communications only, George Taylor queried his crew.

"Any naysayers?"

Not one of the Liberty *crew replied. Taylor resumed external communications.*

*"*Liberty 1 *here," he said. "We're along for the ride. It feels good."*

"Twenty seconds and counting." The voice was the announcer again. Without another word, Admiral Taylor was gone.

Goodbye, Dad.

"Circuits on," Landon offered. "Guidance is internal."

The countdown continued.

"Twelve, eleven, ten, nine—"

"Ignition sequence begun," Dodge reported as the boosters fired.

"—three, two, one...

"Zero," the announcer declared. "All engines running, liftoff!" The earth shook and the sky quaked as Liberty 1 *fought gravity itself. After a moment, she won.*

"Seventeen minutes past the hour. Liftoff on Liberty 1. *Tower cleared."*

"Roger that, Kennedy, we have a roll program," Taylor said. "Transferring command to ANSA Arlington Mission Control." He paused before flipping the communications channel to the secure line at the Pentagon. "Thanks for the lift, Kennedy. Liberty 1 *out."*

Pushed back in their seats, Taylor and his crew absorbed the gravity of liftoff. After a moment, Mission Control went live.

"This is Arlington, Liberty 1.*" It was Lazenbe. "We have command."*

"Roger, Theo." If his dad could break protocol, so could he. Taylor

imagined his exasperated friend shaking his head. "Roll's complete and the pitch is programming," he told the general.

"Down range one mile, altitude three, four miles now," Landon said. "Velocity 2,195 feet per second."

*"Altitude is two miles," Lazenbe replied. "*Liberty 1*, you are good at one minute."*

"We're through the region of maximum dynamic pressure now," Dodge reported. Taylor affirmed it.

"Liberty 1, *this is Arlington," Lazenbe said. "You are go for staging." As the colossal booster arrays fell away, Taylor leaned back and stole a glance at Stewart. Inside her helmet, she was laughing. He turned forward again, just in time to watch the heavens and the stars rush up to greet them.*

No more Earth.

No more war.

No more mankind.

A brand-new start.

His face cracked into a toothy grin. For the first time since he flew against human pilots and foo fighters, George Taylor felt good to be alive.

Taylor wasn't quite dead. Certainly, he was on his way—he just wasn't wholly there. Not yet.

After Ursus shot him he fell from the pillar and rolled down the church stairs toward the launch controls. Clawing at his chest, he was unable to stop the scarlet flow that bubbled up from under his skin. Even so, he tried to raise himself up.

It was too late for Nova, too late for their unborn child, and too late for Taylor, as well. Maybe it wasn't too late to save the world.

For Brent. Cornelius. Zira. Lucius. Even that stupid gorilla,

Mungwortt—if he was still alive. Yes, even for the apes' revered Minister of Science.

"Zaius," he growled. "It's doomsday." He gurgled blood.

The orangutan regarded him. Taylor could tell he didn't recognize him—then the ape's expression changed, as he realized...

"Taylor!" Zaius said, and he gaped.

"The end of the world," Taylor said. "Help me."

Astonishment was replaced with anger, then sheer rage. "You ask me to help you?" he said, his voice rising. "Man is evil," he shouted. "Capable of nothing but destruction!"

"I don't have time for this crap," Taylor said, then he looked up just in time to see Brent riddled with machine-gun fire. He took a bullet to the head, then slid down the cathedral wall, dead.

That was it. Even facing his own end, he had been trying to save the world, and for what? Human, ape, hybrid. It didn't matter.

Everyone was the same. Ungrateful and undeserving. There was no one better out there. This was all there was. It wasn't worth keeping alive.

"You," the astronaut gurgled, "bloody bastard."

With his last words, Colonel George Taylor tumbled toward the prie-dieu, reaching out to activate the bomb—reaching out to rid the planet of man, ape, and the disease that was evolution. He *wanted* to pull that trigger, but life slipped from him.

Taylor's dead hand fell directly on the red crystal.

The cylinder dropped.

The Alpha/Omega bomb's rockets ignited.

The cathedral shook as the missile attempted to launch—but she was still lying on her side. Pointed toward the church doors, Alpha/Omega fired anyway. The soldiers closest to her were incinerated instantly. Others were engulfed in flames, and died slowly.

Zaius threw himself to the ground. He realized now what Taylor was trying to tell him, and what his own arrogance had goaded the insane human to do. As she sailed over him, his clothes caught fire. While he tried to put them out, the rumbling increased. The missile hurled itself across the church and exploded through the massive wooden doors.

Her nose tipped downward, digging a furrow in the concrete and hardened lava of the street. Then the missile found a target, smashing into the molten remnants of a sunken square across the way. The impact cracked the already damaged firing mechanism, and the pin dropped within her primed core.

The Alpha/Omega bomb detonated.

A stark white blaze engulfed the church, searing Zaius's eyes. In that instant, he knew that despite a lifetime of devotion, he had failed to protect his family, failed his promise to Malia.

Lawgiver, forgive me.

Together, man and ape had ended the world.

A loud boom echoed overhead. Thunder rolled across the sky.

Minister Sabian woke with a start.

He had dozed off in his office.

Things were not moving fast enough for his liking. While Gaius had practically turned the city over to him, Sabian knew he had to root out any and all dissenters. The escape of that rabble-rouser Zira would not go unpunished. He had been lucky not to break a hip during the fiasco.

While the boom had startled him, it was the gunfire that followed which threw him from his seat. Sabian rushed to his window. Outside, a group of armed chimpanzees held the gorilla Security Police at bay. One of the chimps was Quirinus, the athlete they were supposed to have locked up in the constabulary.

Across the square, more chimpanzees corralled a flabbergasted Gaius and most of the High Council.

A coup?

How in—

His office door burst open. Five chimpanzees with guns rushed in. Two of them were escaped prisoners—the teen Tian and that nurse, Jaila. He recognized their leader as Liet—the wife of the late Dr. Galen. She wore traditional chimpanzee garb, fitted over with a gorilla's leather vest. A pink and black beret sat neatly on her head—the colors of the Simian flag.

"Minister." She sauntered toward him, rifle slung over her shoulder. "In the name of the Citizens' Liberation Front for a Free Simia, you are under arrest." One of the chimp soldiers behind her cocked his rifle.

"You will be held pending a fair trial," she continued. "Will you submit peacefully?"

Before Sabian could respond, light blasted through his window. He struggled to gaze past the glare, and witnessed an expanding mushroom cloud, along with a blinding whiteness that was growing toward them.

Ursus and Zaius.

This is what the doctor had warned against. The gorilla general had found and engaged the "unknown." He was certain of it, and this was the price of their arrogance.

Sabian thought of his former friend. Of his friend's liberal nonsense, and how he wished he could somehow spin this to be his fault.

Lawgiver damn you, Zao.

The wave of fire struck.

EPILOGUE:
THE TORNADO IN THE SKY

"Where are we going?" Zira asked.

"Probably to our deaths," Milo responded.

In orbit now, the mated *Liberty 1* and *Liberty 2* were preparing to get underway. The accidental pioneers were helpless to stop it. As the ship raced around the planet, Zira gazed out the viewport, coming to terms with the fact that she would likely never see her home again. That her child would never feel the heat of a midsummer's sun, never smell the cool splash of a waterfall, and never taste a fresh gust of autumn wind. She thought of Lucius and Seraph and the others who had died for them.

We'll be seeing you all soon, she feared.

A blinding light burst forth from the surface. As her pupils dilated, Zira watched a growing ball of fire push its way up through the atmosphere. The sky itself caught flame. The vibrations shook their craft as the planet cracked like an egg.

Speechless, she didn't realize that she was holding her breath. As she began to process what she had just witnessed, Zira finally found her voice.

"The fools!" she cried. She thought about Ursus, Zaius, and their war machine, marching into the unknown. "They've finally destroyed themselves!"

In finding what they sought, they had taken with them everyone she had loved, and the entire planet they had called home.

His mind racing, Cornelius squeezed his wife's hand. He wanted her warmth in his palm. The gloves of the overstuffed garments they wore prevented that.

"And… we've escaped."

He was numb. Somehow, they had survived—for all the good it would do them. Everything that had mattered before had disintegrated before their eyes.

Not everything, he amended. Looking to Zira, he knew she and the baby she carried were what really mattered. At least they would be together until the end. As the starbird hurled itself away from the burning ball, *Liberty 1* began to shudder. The white death-sphere was expanding, fast.

Soon it would overcome them.

"We have," Milo said, agreeing with his fellow traveler. He tried desperately to make the controls do something, *anything*. Zira's notes provided no clues as to reasserting control. The ship was still locked on a course to… somewhere.

Alarms sounded in the cabin. In his peripheral vision, Milo could see the light creeping up on all sides of the ship. There was no doubt that it would engulf them, and soon.

"If we survive the shock wave," he mused through grinding teeth. "Brace yourselves!"

It was like tumbling down a cliff face. *Liberty 1* was buffeted, twisted, twirled, and thrown around like Cornelius's talking human ragdoll. Zira's carpet bag and anything else not lashed down launched across the cabin. The blast catapulted the ship into a crushing acceleration. Strange multicolored stars began to whirl around them as they barreled toward the unknown.

After what seemed like forever, the shock subsided. Slowly, they began to gather themselves, and were relieved to find nothing broken. Then the immensity of their accomplishment began to sink in. They had indeed escaped the destruction of the world.

Milo noticed something new, a change in the reading on the instrument panel.

"I don't understand," he muttered. The "Earth Time" meter had read January 29 3955. As he watched, it clicked downward at a consistent rate.

December
November
October…

The dates were changing, as well.

3954
3953
3952…

Yet the meter marked "Ship Time" stayed firm at 3955.

"The shock must have unbalanced the mechanism," Milo suggested. Or the inconceivable had been conceived.

He decided not to tell the others of his new hypothesis until he had more data. Better to let them ponder for themselves than to put insane ideas in their heads—insane ideas that he was almost certain would turn out to be true.

For better or for worse, their future awaited them… in the past.

ACKNOWLEDGEMENTS

Do you want apes? Because this is how you get apes.

Without Rod Serling and all the talented people involved in the original film, without Paul Dehn for being the master of both twisted endings and impossible sequels, without someone in television programming scheduling Apes Week for the ABC afternoon movie, *Planet of the Apes* would never have become an obsession of my nine-year-old mind. Viewing those films with a fresh fascination, I was certain that there must be more to the story (When the heck did Cornelius and Zira get married, anyway?). In order to ease my mind, I made up in-between movies that simply had to have happened to link them all together and put it to rest.

Rediscovering the classic apes saga in college, I realized that those "other movies" never existed and were merely a product of my youthful exuberant imagination. Strangely enough, many of the concepts hatched back in those formative years you now hold in your hand.

When I made the move to break into publishing, Debbie Olshan, formerly of Fox, decided to take a chance on this then-unknown writer with a *Planet of the Apes* illustrated novel. With Apes on the rise (pun intended), Mark Smylie at Archaia saw value in the project. Soon my first Apes work, *Conspiracy of the*

Planet of the Apes, was published. We had more books planned but that got stalled.

Meanwhile, Debbie's successor at Fox—Josh Izzo—read *Conspiracy* and recognized my pedigree of useless knowledge. He chose to make it useful—by bringing me in as an Apes consultant. I've continued to work in that capacity with Steve Tzirlin.

Finally, Titan picked up the classic Apes license. Through Josh, they brought me on to finish what Archaia started, and editor extraordinaire Steve Saffel slaved over my fevered scrawlings to make me look good.

Without these amazing people, a series of fortunate incidents, the Eds for inspiring a character or two, Tyler Reinstein for her in-depth WWII pilot research, Hayley Shepherd for her keen attention to detail, Maria Landy for getting me out of a tough spot, and ape fans like Jess, Michael, Char and you, this book would not exist.

Oh, and let's not forget my mother, who gave me incentives to read as a child while supporting my sci-fi habit at an early age. In no small way, she's responsible for this book as well.

Thank you, all of you.

ABOUT THE AUTHOR

With two decades of experience in the comics and videogame industries, author Andrew E.C. Gaska is now the Senior Development Editor at Lion Forge Comics. There, he creates and develops new properties for the publisher, develops existing IP for media adaptation, and works closely with creative teams to guide their vision to fruition.

Gaska is perhaps best known for his previous three years' work as a freelance consultant to 20th Century Fox, where he created continuity and canon bibles for franchises including *Alien*, *Predator* and *Planet of the Apes*. He has additionally written prose and graphic novels based on the *Planet of the Apes*, *Buck Rogers in the 25th Century* and *Space: 1999* franchises. He also served for seventeen years as a visual consultant to Rockstar Games on the *Grand Theft Auto* series, as well as *Red Dead Redemption* and all other releases, and he worked as a sequential storytelling instructor at New York's School of Visual Arts. His online essays at roguereviewer.wordpress.com and on social media draw controversial debate and discussion from all sides. Readers can follow the action on Facebook at

facebook.com/andrew.gaska.

Gaska and his gluttonous feline Adrien reside beneath a mountain of action figures in St. Louis, Missouri. Adrien can often be found perched atop this pinnacle of plastic, proclaiming himself "lord of the figs."

Gaska amuses him.